RAVE REVIEWS FOR STEPHEN MERTZ!

THE KOREAN INTERCEPT

"Fans of political thrillers will relish t[illegible]ction tale! An adrenaline rush!"

—*Booklist*

"Never slows down! Fantastic!"

—[illegible]okReview.com

"Stephen Mertz writes a hard-edged, fast-paced thriller for those who like their tales straight and sharp."

—Joe R. Lansdale,
Edgar Award–winning author of *A Fine Dark Line*

"Stephen Mertz is a born storyteller and one of my favorite writers. Enjoy!"

—Max Allan Collins,
Edgar Award–winning author of *Road to Perdition*

"Mertz is an action specialist!"

—*Ellery Queen's Mystery Magazine*

"Stephen Mertz just keeps on getting better, each novel more dazzling in story and style."

—Ed Gorman, author of *Save the Last Dance for Me*

"The Mertz formula: rousing action and an exciting plot!"

—Prof. William H. Young,
author of *A Study of Adventure Fiction*

NIGHT WIND

"Fast-paced…chills and thrills!"

—*Booklist*

"Tautly written…a white-knuckle read!"

—*Reviews Today*

TRAPPED!

Bob leaned down to crawl through the shrubbery concealing the cave. Scott suddenly gripped him by the shoulder.

"Wait. Someone's coming."

Kate heard it too: the shuffling of footfalls on rock outside the cave, not far away. Voices in conversation in what sounded like Korean. Someone emitted a coarse laugh.

At that moment, Terri Schmidt's eyes opened. The eyes were glassy, unblinking and semiconscious. Terri's head began rolling from side to side. Her moaning filled the cave.

Bob Paxton glared around with a look of pure panic. "Make her shut up!"

Kate bit back an angry reply. She placed her fingertips lightly across Terri's lips, leaning down to coo comforting, whispered sounds. It worked. Terri's moaning and mumbling tapered off.

Too late.

A voice outside shouted something at the others. The laughter and conversation stopped. Kate heard the metallic snapping of rounds being chambered into weapons. Footfalls began advancing across the rocky ground outside, toward the cave entrance.

Scott and Bob Paxton were poised just inside the entrance, their pistols held up and ready. Kate unholstered her revolver.

"They've got us," Paxton said, desperation in his eyes and in his voice. "We're dead."

THE KOREAN INTERCEPT

STEPHEN MERTZ

LEISURE BOOKS  NEW YORK CITY

For Ron Terpening

A LEISURE BOOK®

December 2006

Published by

Dorchester Publishing Co., Inc.
200 Madison Avenue
New York, NY 10016

ISBN 0-8439-5796-4

Printed in the United States of America.

THE KOREAN INTERCEPT

Prologue

The near future, 107 miles above the earth

With no external point of reference to mark its dimensions and speed, the space shuttle *Liberty* looked like a gently coasting bird of flawless white caught between the stars of frigid dark space overhead and the mottled white and azure curved horizon of the earth below. In fact, the 100,000-ton, 122-foot orbiter was descending at a rate of more than 17,000 miles per hour, twenty-five times the speed of sound. Traveling west to east, the sleek, winged vessel lost some of its gleam as the sun dipped beyond the horizon and the earth below grew dark, though not as black as the endless vista of space. *Liberty* was one of six workhorses of the NASA shuttle program and had flown twelve previous missions. The crew on this flight was composed mostly of electrical and aerospace engineers who had worked on and were to deploy, at 430 miles in space, the defense system satellite carried in the orbiter's payload cargo area. After deploying the satellite, *Liberty* had been scheduled to remain in orbit for five days in order to repair and service other defense and communications satellites. But it was not to be. The mission had been aborted within fifteen minutes of liftoff.

On *Liberty*'s flight deck, a cockpit-like cabin filled with control panels, Commander Ron Scott tried to ignore the quivers of foreboding that had been nagging at his subconscious ever since Houston had ordered the abort. That wasn't all ground control had ordered. They had also instructed him to activate the shuttle's Stealth radar avoidance system and to maintain radio silence throughout the return trip.

Scott was a seventeen-year veteran of the space program. He was six-foot-one and sturdily built, forty-six years old. This was his third mission into space and his first as flight commander. Since his days as a Gulf War combat pilot, he had logged 65,000 hours of flying in forty-five types of airplanes, but nothing matched the thrill of handling *Liberty*. Not that he'd had much of an opportunity this time out.

Shuttle Flight 72-L had pushed off the launch pad and cleared the tower at Cape Canaveral into a cloudless blue Florida sky on schedule. Two minutes and five seconds later, moving at a speed of 2,000 miles per hour, separation from the solid rocket booster was reported to Mission Control. At an altitude of eighty miles, the computers had given the command for the main engines to shut down and the spent big orange-red fuel tank had separated and plunged back to earth to splash down harmlessly in a remote corner of the Pacific. Scott had then taken over manual control to position the shuttle for the first of a series of insertion burns intended to eventually position *Liberty* into its assigned orbit. The computer was to control forty-five minutes of coasting prior to a second firing of the Orbital Maneuvering System rockets, but before that could happen, the order to abort and black out communications was received and verified. After reprogramming the computers for reentry, there was little left for Scott to do except try to ignore that troubling sense of foreboding.

Fifteen minutes after reprogramming the computers, he and his copilot, Kathleen Daniels (known to one and all as Kate), sat monitoring the systems indicators and screens in the center of the main panel, when they experienced a slight but sudden lurch as the OMS secondary engines burned for another forty seconds, dramatically slowing the shuttle's speed.

Scott's frustration surfaced with a curse. "Now what the hell? That deorbit burn is twenty minutes ahead of schedule. Don't tell me we've got a computer error on our hands."

"Maybe that's why Houston is bringing us home," Kate said. She tapped a computer keyboard to call up details of the problem. "Negative," she reported. "All three navigation and guidance computers agree."

Scott was married and he loved his wife, but he wasn't blind and he knew that if his Lucy had been the jealous type—which, happily, she wasn't—she'd have been plenty jealous with a looker like Kate along as his copilot for five days in space. Kate looked younger than her thirty-six years. Shoulder-length chestnut hair framed a high-cheekboned magazine model's face highlighted by intelligent brown eyes, full lips and a determined jawline. The bagginess of her light blue coverall flight suit did nothing to conceal a full, firm figure that could have belonged to a magazine model of the centerfold variety. And yet there was nothing flirtatious or provocative about Kate. She was a total professional.

"I'm going to the backup." Scott punched a request for navigation data from the backup computer, then shook his head in bewilderment when the monitors registered identical information. "Something stinks," he grumbled. "We've deviated way off our approach course. Even the backup shows us coming down . . . jeez, we're not over Australia, we're somewhere over Africa! Our approach is supposed to bring us in over Hawaii. At this rate, we'll be hitting the atmosphere somewhere over the Mediterranean."

Kate stared intently at the systems indicators. "I don't understand."

"That makes two of us. And us told to come in under radio silence." Scott looked out his side window. The sight below of the night-shrouded half of the earth only deepened his sense of foreboding. "Something must have gone to hell in a handbasket down there, like World War III. Or someone in Houston is smoking something funny."

"Radar and navigation indicators say we'll be touching down in northern Japan. Why would Houston be diverting us there?"

"I don't know. Let's just sit tight and follow orders for the time being, but we'll stand by to take over manual control."

The disappointment that welled within Kate became an ache that she hoped did not show. Her first mission into space and it was over before it began, and this could be the only chance she would get. There was no shortage of astronauts in the program and many, most, spent their whole careers on standby, waiting for a chance that never came. Yesterday, the first scheduled liftoff was cancelled at T-minus-three seconds when a heat sensor mistakenly signaled that one of *Liberty*'s three main engines was overheating. That had actually been reassuring after the initial letdown, because it had demonstrated that NASA was not about to send them up unless everything was perfect. It was impossible not to remember *Challenger*, not to be acutely aware that you were sitting atop a monster, totally at the mercy of the vehicle. The solid rocket boosters were filled with 1.1 billion pounds of solid fuel. The external fuel tank contained 529,000 gallons of liquid oxygen and liquid hydrogen. Six seconds before liftoff, those highly explosive fuels flowed through seventeen-inch aluminum fuel lines into the shuttle's main tank and, once ignited, the fuel burned until it was used up. No, it was impossible to forget the space shuttles *Columbia* and *Challenger*. Then, this morning, less than ninety minutes ago, when the countdown was not interrupted and *Liberty* had been catapulted into that cloudless Florida sky on 2.9 million pounds of thrust, Kate had experienced a kind of transcendent soaring of the spirit beyond any sensation she had ever known.

And now—this.

Beside her, Scott was advising the other crewmembers across the intercom of the change in plans. Any indication of overt concern or any other emotion was masked behind his professional cool. There were grumbled complaints and protestations from Leo Smith, Al Murphy, Terri Schmidt and Bob Paxton, who rode in the living quarters just forward of the payload bay, but with their frustrations vented, all six of *Liberty*'s crew lapsed into silence.

Kate took no comfort, as she usually did, in the magnificent drone of the shuttle in flight. She told herself that there had to be some explainable reason behind what was happening and that Houston Control would reveal it to them in due course.

Twenty minutes later, they entered the earth's atmosphere. As the atmosphere grew denser, its resistance provided braking action for the spacecraft, generating incredible surface friction, heating the leading edges of the orbiter, turning the shuttle's underbelly a vivid orange. The thrusters lost their effectiveness and the rudder and the elevons began clutching the heavier air. The computers controlled the entire flight.

Scott and Kate did not speak until Scott could take no more of it. He thumped the armrest of his chair with a balled fist, his eyes glued to the digital altimeter as it ran backward.

"This is nuts. Totally, absolutely nuts. We're not even going to make it to Japan at this rate of descent; I don't care what navigation and radar say. Something is all wrong. According to the computers, we're already over Manchuria, for crying out loud."

Kate was closely following their descent trajectory on a computer screen. "Altitude twenty-two miles, nine minutes from touchdown."

"We're going down inside China or North Korea if we're lucky, the Sea of Japan if we're not so lucky," Scott said.

"The hell with orders." He activated the radio downlink. "Houston Control, this is *Liberty*. Come in, Houston. This is an emergency. I repeat: come in, Houston." The airwaves crackled with nothing but static. He tried hailing Mission Control three more times in rapid succession. Nothing. Then he told Kate, "We're going to full auto."

Her eyes remained steady on the indicator screens. "It doesn't make sense."

"Oh yes, it does. We've been snookered. Houston didn't abort this mission and reprogram the computers, and they didn't order us to Stealth."

"Then who did? What's going on?"

"What's going on is that someone faked that transmission. Someone is bringing us in."

Kate looked at the darkness outside. "Bringing us in? But that's incredible. Can it be done?"

Scott nodded, his expression grim. "It's being done. It's the only answer that makes any sense. All systems are consistent; they just seem to have a mind of their own. And with Stealth activated, Houston doesn't have us on their radar. No one does." He flicked control switches as he spoke. "Figures. No systems response whatsoever. We have no manual control."

"Altitude is forty-four thousand feet. Speed one thousand one hundred."

"That puts us on a descent rate of ten thousand feet per minute," Scott noted, his tone neutral with professional objectivity. "That's a glide slope seven times steeper than a commercial airliner, with no idea where we're touching down."

"But, Ron . . . with the Stealth activated—" She allowed the sentence to taper off.

"Right." He nodded. "Whoever's bringing us down can't pick us up on their radar, either. And that gives me an idea that might be the only chance we've got."

"Care to share it with me?"

He gave her a tight grin. "Whoever they are, they overrode the Houston program in our computers. But they can only bring us down so far. Then they'll have to give me back manual control at least for the landing. That gives us a very small window."

"To do what?"

"Let's find out."

Liberty covered seven miles, dropping 13,000 feet, during the next eighty seconds.

At 11,300 feet, traveling at a speed of 410 miles per hour, the middle systems screen indicated that the digital autopilot was disengaged, meaning that control of the shuttle was returned to the pilot. Gripping the hand controller, Scott commenced manually steering the vessel. The shuttle continued eating up its glide slope. He carefully moved the hand controller forward to put *Liberty* into its first of four necessary braking S-turn maneuvers.

Kate read out airspeed and altitude so that he could focus his attention on flying. "Speed three hundred ten. Altitude fourteen hundred."

Outside the windows, the reflection of their landing lights could be seen off a rugged, rocky terrain.

"There it is," Scott said. "Looks like we're expected."

A lighted runway less than two miles away came rushing up at them out of the dark, glimmering parallel lines of silver surrounded by impenetrable blackness like a carefully set pair of diamond necklaces placed side by side on black velvet. There were lighted structures adjacent to the landing strip. Kate's peripheral vision registered an oversized satellite dish and military helicopter gunships, but she had too many other things on her mind to pay them much attention right now.

Scott waited until the last possible moment before activating a switch that deployed the landing gear. Kate's voice continued to briskly relay their rapidly descending speed and altitude.

The runway was practically below them now, a shade to starboard. Scott eased the land controller slightly to the right, applying the right rudder while cutting back his air brake slightly. This was the critical moment. Whoever had brought them down into this dark corner of the world would be monitoring their radio transmissions during this brief window of time when he had full control of the shuttle. Scott glanced at the altitude/vertical velocity indicator on the headup display as the runway rushed up to meet them. When the main gear was five feet from the runway, at a speed of 200 miles per hour, with the runway lights rushing by so fast that they were twin silver lines to either side of the craft, with the whistling thunder of *Liberty*'s powerful engine enveloping them, he did three things simultaneously. He shoved the control stick forward. He punched up the International Distress Frequency. And he barked into his headset microphone as the shuttle's powerful engine's whistling keened to a higher pitch, the craft picking up in speed and altitude.

"This is U.S. space shuttle *Liberty*. Mayday. Mayday. This is *Liberty*. Mayday. We are going down. Repeat, this is *Liberty*. Exact location unknown but we are going down. Repeat. This is *Liberty*. Mayday. Mayday."

By this time the runway was rapidly falling away behind them when, at an altitude of 1,000 feet, the radio went dead. The monitor screens and the cabin lighting system went dark.

"That's it," Scott said. A hint of drained weariness tinged his voice for the first time, the first crack in his mask of professionalism. "They've shut us down again. We don't have power." He spoke across the radio to the crew below in the living quarters, who had been monitoring his and Kate's conversation via the transceivers in their helmets. "Okay, everybody. Buckle up and brace yourselves."

There came several responses of "Yes, Commander." Then the shuttle *Liberty* became silent, the engine noise replaced by an eerie, breathy sound as the shuttle's forward momentum carried it into a freefall glide. There was only the terrible sensation of downward plummeting into black nothingness.

Kate asked, "Do you think anyone picked up our signal?"

Scott vainly struggled with controls that would not respond. "If we survive this crash, that's our only hope," was all he had time to say.

Chapter One

Hamgyong Province, North Korea

His name was Ahn Chong.

He was sixty-seven years old. The village of Hongsan, his home, was on the eastern slope of Mount Paekdu, which rose above the surrounding mountain ranges like a towering warlord encircled by humbled subjects. North Korea is almost completely covered by north-south mountains separated by narrow valleys. Except for the time in his youth when he had been a soldier, this region of the frontier separating North Korea and China was all of the world Ahn Chong had ever known. His was a life of hardship as unchanging as the mountains.

His frayed woolen jacket offered scant protection against the bone-piercing chill of a night wind. His face could have been centuries old: leathery and wrinkled, with dark, intent eyes. One kilometer to the west, the others of his village were asleep. The wind rattling the thatched roof of his hut had drawn him from a fitful sleep of dreams of when he and Mai were young. He had risen from the straw pallet they had shared and, as usual, donned his short jacket, the baggy trousers and straw hat. He had crept away from the hamlet of mud-walled farmers' huts and made his way across the cooperative's stony fields where potatoes and cabbage, turnips, lettuce and beets barely matured during the short growing season. The ground was frosted over and crunched beneath the rubber soles of his sandals.

He had topped the hill and made his way by starlight to the graveyard, to the small hillside clearing surrounded by pines and a few twisted fruit trees where nightly he would kneel at his wife's grave. Though he knew that Mai's spirit was mercifully free of the physical suffering that had made her last year of life so unbearable for them both, his heart ached. That her mortal remains were so close to him in this ground somewhat eased the loss he felt within. These private moments with her memory renewed him and gave him the strength to face one more night and another tomorrow without her.

His life with Mai had never been without suffering and struggle. But the struggle had always seemed easier, worthwhile, because his woman, a good woman, was there to share the struggle with him. They were married when they were fourteen. They had met as children in the days of World War II when Japanese soldiers had used Hongsan as a staging area for attacks into China. The Japanese, who had massacred most of the adults when they withdrew, killed their parents. Youngsters like Chong and Mai survived only because their parents, fearing the worst, hid them in the mountains. Such tragedy had bonded them together for life, a life that became little better under the occupying heel of the Russians after the war and no easier when the country was handed over to its own Communist dictators three years later. Mai had already given birth to the first of their three children when Ahn Chong was conscripted and sent south to fight the Americans in the winter of 1951, so long ago, the one time he had ever been more than fifty kilometers from his village and his family.

He now had full-grown children, and they had gone on with their lives since their mother's death. Ahn Chong did his best, but bitterness would not leave him, bitterness as ever-present within him as the empty place in his heart left by Mai's passing.

If Mai had become ill in the south, below the 38th parallel, she would have survived. His ailing wife would have received treatment. But the central government withheld food and clothing from the northern frontier provinces, as well as education and medicine, with an iron hand. That his son-in-law was chairman of the collective's Worker's Council, that the new military air base had been constructed less than three kilometers away, meant nothing. Another nameless, faceless old peasant woman had died and no one cared, it seemed, except for her widowed husband. Ahn saw her face whenever he closed his eyes: wrinkled and aged, leathery as his own, but even ravaged by illness, the most beautiful face he had ever known. He heard her voice in the whisper of the wind through the pines.

And so he came to kneel at her grave this night as he always did, to commune with her spirit and meditate on the words of the Buddha. *Do not weep. It is the very nature of all things most near and dear unto us that we must divide ourselves from them, leave them, sever ourselves from them. Every life is filled with partings . . .*

The heavens tore abruptly open above him, ripped asunder. It happened with such abruptness, such totality, such ferocity, power and nearness that Ahn reflexively, instinctively threw himself across the mound of earth that was Mai's grave.

Something—something big—stormed by at what must have been treetop level, its backwash blasting over Ahn harsher, far colder, than the night wind. A shape momentarily blotted out the sky. There was not the thunder of a jet, only an extended *whooooosh!* that enveloped him as if it were inside his head. Pressing himself to Mai's grave, flattening himself to the ground, he knew that it could only be some sort of aircraft coming from the direction of the airfield. Then he heard the aircraft—whatever it was!—impacting into the earth on the other side of the hill that rose away from the graveyard, in the opposite direction from his village. There was no explosion, only the protracted sound of tearing metal as the huge *something* skidded across rock. Then complete silence reclaimed the night, except for the wind.

Ahn Chong leapt to his feet. Dogs were barking, but the noises of the crash would have been muffled from the village by the hills and sloping terrain.

He hurried up a rocky hill, in the direction of the crash.

After the endless scream of tearing metal upon impact, the abrupt silence seemed absolute.

The first sound Kate Daniels became aware of was

the whisper of wind outside of the fuselage. *Liberty* was enveloped in darkness. She turned her head. Her body responded slowly. The popping of joints creaked loudly and helped to clear her brain as her eyes adjusted.

Next to her, Scott asked, "Are you all right?" His voice was strained, hoarse, and she knew instantly that something was wrong with him.

"Thank God, Ron, I thought we were done for." She fought to keep her breathing normal. "Yes, I'm okay. How about you?"

"Broken leg, I think. At least I set us belly-down."

Kate ascertained that none of her bones were broken and none of her muscles were pulled or torn. The plight of the man next to her generated complete clarity of thought. She unclasped her safety harness and went to him. Reaching for a magnetized flashlight, she flicked it on, playing its light across his legs. The right one was twisted at an unnatural angle. His flight suit around that knee was torn and bloody.

She reached for his safety buckle. "Let me help you out of there."

He waved her off. "I can get myself out. Check on the crew."

"Ron—"

"Check them. We've got to camouflage this baby and make some distance before whoever brought us down comes looking for us. A broken leg isn't going to stop me. Someone below could really need your help."

"Yes, sir."

The flight suits were of insulated fabric but were no heavier than wearing a pair of sweat pants and a T-shirt, and allowed for easy mobility. She lowered herself down the short ladder through the circular hatch located at mid-deck. A flashlight beam in the living quarters swung in her direction.

The barely discernible shape of Mission Specialist Bob Paxton hurried over to her. She barely recognized the usually cool, calm and collected MIT physicist. Paxton's normally movie-poster handsome, square-jawed cool had yielded to confusion and apprehension with the hint of panic very close to the surface when he put his free arm around her, hugging her to him. "Kate! Kate, thank God . . . what the hell?"

She extracted herself from his embrace. "An unscheduled landing."

"I know that! Where the hell are we?"

"We're not sure. China, maybe North Korea." She looked past him, into the murky darkness of the living quarters. "How are the others?"

"China? North Korea? How can that be?"

"Bob, get a hold of yourself. How are the others?"

He swung his flashlight beam across the seats. "Al and Leo are dead. The impact broke their necks. Terri I'm not so sure about."

Leo Smith and Al Murphy were strapped in with their heads drooping. Kate hurried to them and felt for a pulse in each. Finding none, she went next to Mission Specialist Terri Schmidt, who was also motionless, although Kate could hear her breathing.

Terri was a trim brown-haired woman, some years older than Kate. Terri's eyes fluttered when Kate gently tilted her head back. There was a gash across one temple, a brutal tear in the skin surrounded by a rapidly swelling purple blotch. Terri's lips trembled. "Kate?" A weak, empty whisper. "What happened? I can't move. I can't feel anything."

"Take it easy, Terri. We'll get you out of here." Kate turned to see Ron Scott carefully lowering himself from the upper deck. "Al and Leo didn't make it," she told him. "Terri's in bad shape."

The flight commander moved aft, favoring but not slowed by the broken leg. "I'll get the door open. You two help Terri."

Kate unfastened Terri's safety harness. Terri's head lolled to the side again, her breathing a muffled gurgle. Kate slid an arm under Terri's back, pausing only when she realized that she was working alone. "Bob, come on," she said impatiently. "We've got to get out of here."

"But the others . . ."

"We can't help Al and Leo right now. We barely have time to help ourselves."

"All right, all right."

They made quick work of removing the semiconscious woman from her seat, moving her across the gloom of the living quarters to an exit. A ladder was lowered and, after considerable angling of her this way and that between them, Kate and Bob managed to lower Terri to the ground outside.

Breathing the cold night air in long measures completed the process of clearing Kate's senses. She became aware of her surroundings, of the shapes of trees swaying in the wind. She looked around at the silhouettes of mountains against the night sky full of stars, and shivered. Playing her flashlight past *Liberty*'s heavily-dented fuselage and beyond, she saw the long path of smashed trees and sheared-off limbs along a ridge that had acted as a runway of sorts. The slope of the ridge—going down, not up—had helped avoid a direct head-on impact into the ground. The trees had somewhat cushioned the crash.

Scott stood, supporting himself on his good leg, against the fuselage. He held a pistol, one of the Colt

.45 automatics from *Liberty*'s extremely limited armory. The wind moaned.

Kate said, "Good work setting us down, Commander."

Scott shook his head. "Not good enough for Al and Leo. You two hop back inside. We'll need canteens, weapons and the camouflage netting. The two of you are going to have to cover this bird before we move out."

"Right." Kate started briskly toward the hatch before becoming aware of Bob's hesitation, as if he was hesitant to reboard the orbiter from which they had so narrowly escaped. "Come on, Bob," she said. "Move it. What are you waiting for?"

"Nothing," Paxton said quickly, self-consciously. "Here I come."

Kate let him board first. When she started to follow, she became aware of two things: the first dry flakes of snow, whipped by the wind, stinging her cheeks . . . and some sixth sense that told her she was being watched. She swung the flashlight around.

There, among the trees, the beam picked out the figure of an elderly man, a scraggly figure wearing a frayed woolen jacket, baggy trousers and straw hat, who stood silently, watching them from behind the swirling veil of snow.

Scott saw him too. "Uh oh," he whispered, raising his pistol.

Chapter Two

Camp David, Maryland

Sunshine, drenching the rolling hills, made the bark of the birch trees seem whiter, and dappled through their bare branches over a winding gravel path. Halfway into his three-mile run through the Camp David forest, the president of the United States noted with satisfaction that he was not short of breath as he crested a steep rise. He'd been a confirmed two-pack-a-day man before the last election, when his campaign advisors had convinced him that a non-smoking image would be far more appealing to voters.

The chief executive was a vigorous man. At sixty-five years of age, he looked at least a decade younger. Five-foot-ten, he weighed in at a solidly-built one-eighty. His face was naturally round, but with strong features and striking eyes that were penetrating and direct. The salt and pepper hair was worn military style, unfashionably short. The fact that he was an ex-military officer, not a professional establishment politician, had contributed largely to his being selected as his party's vice presidential candidate. He was not considered attractive or elegant but exuded a straightforward style and grace that the public and the media had taken to. Three months after being sworn in, he had become president when his predecessor succumbed to a debilitating stroke. Upon assuming the post of chief executive, he had made some prompt and drastic changes among his predecessor's staff and cabinet, appointing a close circle of advisors who were not yes-people or inside-the-beltway pros, but seasoned movers and shakers in their own right. He had a well-earned reputation for toughness and fairness, for principled leadership and bi-partisanship. Which did not mean that everything went smoothly all the time. There were far too many conflicting forces at work in an ever-shrinking world and a nation of 250 million for that to ever be the case.

The president concentrated on the regular rhythm of his breathing, trying to make it the primary focus of his awareness. Secret Service agents—two on point, two to the rear and another pair traveling parallel to the jogging path on either side—maintained their position. They weren't breathing hard either. But then, they were twenty years younger than he was, he reminded himself wryly. A pair of golf carts followed, carrying more Secret Service men and a warrant officer. The WO, with a plain black briefcase chained to his wrist, was one of those specially selected custodians of the nuclear codes.

The president had called this unscheduled break in his day to recharge himself, to clear his mind. But it wasn't doing much good. It had been a day spent honing his verbal sparring skills against a hard-nosed, well-primed debater in preparation for what was supposed to be a routine press conference, previously scheduled for the following day. At such press conferences, there were invariably tough, combative, sometimes unexpected sound-bite questions on complex issues. The sparring partner's job was to be even tougher on him, if possible, than the traditionally blood-thirsty White House media corps would be. It had been a grueling session. The day after the press conference, he would be attending the next European Summit. There remained plenty of fences in need of mending, continuing fallout from the Iraqi situation. His information package on the summit was three hundred pages, and he hadn't cracked it yet. He was currently hanging fire at about an even fifty percent approval rating in the polls. The economy continued to take two steps back for every one forward, and ever since the terrorist attack on the World Trade Center, and the subsequent military actions in Afghanistan and Iraq, America's involvement in the Mideast had only deepened and expanded. But there was still no light at the end of that tunnel. The Cold War was over, but its chilled dryness had made the world into a tinderbox, ready to ignite anywhere, at any time. Terrorism was on the rise again, and the man who could top a hill without losing his breath seemed unable to do anything about any of it. A weekend at Camp David had seemed just the thing, but it wasn't working out that way.

And now *Liberty* was missing.

NASA's director of flight operations, who'd called directly from the control room at the Johnson Space Center, where Houston was monitoring the shuttle, had interrupted the debate workout. All the flight director could tell him during that first call was that the mission controllers had reported a major malfunction. "We have no downlink," the flight director had reported in a taut voice. At first ground control thought it was a radio interference problem. Then *Liberty* was lost from radar. The tracking computer screens were dotted with *s*'s, indicating only static from the shuttle. The Space Defense Command Center in Colorado Springs had also been monitoring the orbiter and immediately scrambled Air Force tactical squadrons into the skies over the emergency landing strips maintained around the world whenever a shuttle was in orbit. The jets were to fly escort and protect the shuttle, but the president's next quarter-hour update, just before leaving for this run, was that there was still no communication with *Liberty*. The shuttle was missing, and even on a run through a birch forest in the sunshine, it did not seem that things could get much worse.

The agent on point, a young man of Japanese descent named Koyama, the shift leader of the detail, heard something in the miniature earpiece receiver of his short-wave radio that prompted him to give a hand signal for the run to stop. The other agents tightened in, which was their position when a golf cart bearing Wil Fleming, the president's chief of staff, rounded a bend up ahead and braked to a stop.

Fleming was the youngest of the president's advisors and the most dynamic. "Sorry to interrupt you, Mr. President, but we just got word. One of our spy boats in the Sea of Japan picked up a Mayday from *Liberty*. It looks like they went down."

"Dear God, not another *Columbia* . . ."

"We don't think so, sir. The *Columbia* broke up upon reentry. *Liberty*, we think, has crash-landed."

"That could be good news or bad news."

"We haven't pinpointed an exact location as yet," said Fleming, "but it looks to be somewhere on the Manchurian border with North Korea."

The president boarded a golf cart. "I want a full linkup with Houston and with Space Defense Command. Then we're heading back to Washington."

Things had just gotten worse.

Trev Galt broke the water's surface fifteen feet beneath the bow of the yacht. The murky waters of the Potomac sparkled in the sunlight like polished dark glass. The 125-foot pleasure craft stood at anchor, her bow pointing upriver, at a point where the river widened to slightly over a mile, one mile south of Mount Vernon. The sweeping banks along here were lined with the trees and shrubs of farms and country homes. There were no other boats in the vicinity. Somewhere overhead a gull cawed, and the mooing of a herd of cows in a nearby pasture drifted across the water. Galt tried to ignore the ache in his muscles from swimming against the current. He wrapped his hands and ankles around the chain of the boat's anchor line and began hoisting himself upward, toward the deck. The faint dripping of water was the only sound he made.

He was a big man, well-proportioned, ruggedly built, with thick, black hair that was just beginning to turn gray at the temples. The slit pockets of his skintight wetsuit carried stilettos and garrotes. A 9mm Beretta rode snugly in a snap-sealed waterproof holster at his left shoulder. A full complement of stun grenades was kept dry in a pouch at his right hip. He moved with grace, with the confidence and economy of movement of a trained athlete, of a professional fighting man. He dropped onto the boat's deck. Twenty feet separated him from a sentry who stood with an automatic assault rifle in front of a companionway that led below deck. Galt sailed in from the side and downed the man with a judo chop almost before the sentry realized he was under attack. Galt turned to the companionway. Another guard emerged from a side hatch in the main cabin. This one's eyes and nostrils flared in alarm and his rifle tracked toward the intruder. Galt's right arm flashed outward and the sentry took a stiletto high in the chest. He collapsed next to the first guard with barely a sound.

Galt stepped over their prone bodies and drew his Beretta. He cocked back his right foot and sent the door to the companionway slamming inward with a powerful kick, entering low and fast, his left hand unhooking one of the stun grenades. The narrow companionway was carpeted and wood paneled.

Three men, each sporting a sidearm and an automatic rifle, stood conversing next to a closed door. Their rifles swung as one in Galt's direction. But he had already pulled the grenade's pin. He tossed the grenade and covered his eyes with his left arm. There was a blinding white flash. The blast was loud, but he wore ear plugs to deal with that. The three men caught the full effect of the flash and were kicked backward against the walls. Galt emotionlessly squeezed off three well-placed rounds, one at each flailing figure. Then he hurried toward the door they'd been guarding.

He executed another kick that sent this door inward off its hinges. He hurled himself through the doorway. He hit the floor with his left shoulder in a fast roll that took him in well below any possible line of fire that might come at him from inside, steadying himself out of the roll and onto one knee, the Beretta held in a two-handed grip, ready to select targets. His deep-set eyes were narrowed, dark and dangerous.

General Clayton Tuttle rose from the armchair where he sat waiting. He clicked off the stopwatch he held.

Tuttle had served in a succession of important military positions, after a key command role in the first Gulf War, before serving as national security advisor for a former president. He was presently a ranking officer in the Pentagon's Covert Operations Command. A man in his late fifties, Tuttle was of short stature, sturdy and compact.

He snorted irritably. "Thirty-four seconds, going up against five of my best men. Damn it, Trev, those twelve months behind a desk in the White House haven't slowed you down one damn bit. Son, I sure wish you were still on my team, working in the field where you belong."

Galt straightened, holstering the Beretta. His hard, dangerous look faded, replaced by an easy-going, friendly warming of the eyes and an infectious, almost boyish, smile. "That makes two of us, General. But these training workouts are going to have to be it for awhile."

"Training, hell. I'd call what you just put my guys through an endurance test, not a training exercise."

Galt glanced out at the "sentries," who were sluggishly struggling to their feet in the companionway, tugging loose their earplugs, wiping away the red dye left by the "bullets" fired from the Beretta, waiting for their full vision to return after the flash of the stun grenade. The sentries from outside appeared, one removing the stiletto from his Kevlar protective vest and assisting the man Galt had judo chopped. There was much grumbling among them.

Galt felt a twinge of guilt at the damage he had inflicted, however temporary, upon these men of the Central Intelligence Agency. He said to Tuttle, "You did tell me not to go easy."

"And you didn't. Damn. You're a one-man tornado. I don't think my boys are likely to forget what they've learned here today. But if you'd care to stick around for a debriefing and analysis—"

"Thanks, General, but I think your boys may have had enough of me for one day. And just between you and me, I'm not supposed to be here. I'm playing hooky."

"What?" Tuttle bellowed a hearty laugh and shook his head. "You haven't lost your balls either, have you, son? As a matter of fact, you did fail to mention that you'd be AWOL for this little exercise. In that case, I suggest you haul your ass back to sixteen hundred Pennsylvania Avenue ASAP, before you land us both in a sling. And, uh, thanks again, Trev, for teaching my guys just how much they still have to learn."

Galt chuckled ruefully, running his fingers through his wet thatch of hair, and—even armed, even in a dripping combat wetsuit—he gave the impression of a big, amiable bear. "I was testing myself too. I'm afraid I'm getting rusty, sitting behind a desk."

"Not you, son. You'll never lose your edge."

"Hope not. Be seeing you, General. And thanks."

Tuttle watched the best damn field agent and covert ops specialist he'd ever known exit though a separate doorway.

He thought, a military man with the training, experience and sixth sense of a born spy . . . It rankled him no end that such a man should be yanked from the field and assigned to the White House staff, even if Galt's job for the National Security Council—implementing and overseeing the administration's covert operations around the world—was a vital one. Galt's reputation was legendary across all ranks of the military and the U.S. espionage establishment, even though many of his assignments, certainly the ones Tuttle had been responsible for handing him, had never seen the light of day. But what *was* known about Galt, to those in government service and to the general public as well, was impressive enough.

Trevor Galt III—sole surviving heir to the Galt Electronics fortune, fluent in six languages, with a master's in economics from Yale—had long ago renounced the monied comfort that was his birthright, choosing instead a life of personal challenge, sacrifice and commitment that could be found for him only in the service of his country. This had led to combat experience in Vietnam, Grenada, Panama and the Gulf, before being handed his own Army Ranger unit assigned to black ops, which was when Tuttle had first encountered him. Tuttle was seven months away from retirement. He'd been a desk jockey for twelve years and he still missed the action. He understood how being trapped in a basement office could fray the nerves of a man of action. The army had been Galt's home for most of his adult life. Now, still in his prime, Trev was faced with the prospect of shuffling papers for the rest of his career. Sure, Tuttle understood. And he'd heard the rumors of Trev's drinking, though he also had it on good authority that the drinking in no way interfered with the performance of Galt's duties. And there was

Trev's wife, Kate, one of the astronauts aboard the space shuttle *Liberty*. The media had made quite a deal about Kate Daniels.

Tuttle knew that Galt and his wife were estranged. He was in the habit of keeping tabs on those he cared about.

CHAPTER THREE

North Korea

The snow squall subsided. The night cleared. Starlight revealed a light dusting of snow across the ground, partially blanketing some of the damage left by the shuttle's crash landing.

Ron Scott provided what illumination he could from a flashlight. He had holstered his pistol and was conversing with the elderly civilian who had appeared during the snow squall. The civilian exuded an air of dignity despite his shabby clothes. He had not hesitated to fashion a splint from a tree branch for Scott's broken leg. Nearby, Terri Schmidt was nestled in blankets spread across the ground.

Thanks to the endless practice drills back at Houston, Kate Daniels and Bob Paxton were able to methodically carry out the task of spreading "scattered leaf" camouflage netting across the shuttle. The tricky part was that although the snow melted instantly upon touching the shuttle, it did make the surface slippery in places. But Kate managed to go about her task more or less by rote.

I will get through this, she told herself. She secured her final strip of netting. It was almost impossible to believe that little more than ninety minutes ago they had been lifting merrily off into the Florida sunshine. It was as if they'd landed on another planet or in another dimension.

She thought about Trev. They fought the last time they'd spoken. They were always either fighting or making love, it seemed. They'd met while serving together in the army during the Panama invasion, and were married a month after her discharge from the service the next year. Things were fine at first. Weren't they always? Then she had two miscarriages in two years, and that's when the wheels started falling off their marriage, she came to understand in retrospect. The Galts had been just a "normal" couple in suburban Maryland. Except that while she was exactly the good little homemaker she appeared to be, Trev was anything but a traveling auditor for the government, as their neighbors believed. People outside their marriage attributed Galt's increased dependence on alcohol to his being assigned a desk job. But she traced it to just after her second miscarriage. They'd discussed adoption but nothing ever came of it, because by that time Trev's slide into emotional withdrawal was well underway. She knew how he felt. He sought escape inside a bottle. Her escape—from her feelings and from a troubled marriage—followed her acceptance into the space program. Trev was the most disciplined man she had ever known and so she was at first surprised, then concerned and ultimately frustrated in Washington with her inability to deal with his lapses into drinking and brooding that alternated with the more common periods of sobriety and an obvious restlessness eating away at him. Trev was a man committed to his work. He was the best there was, which is why he had been promoted in the first place, and so he would never think of walking away from his mission. And so a seemingly unbridgeable gulf had widened between them. They'd been unable to break through to each other, to help each other, no matter how they tried. When the time came for her move to Houston, they'd agreed to call it a separation. That was her idea. The rules were that they could each see other people if they wanted to.

In the forty-five days prior to the launch, training had grown intense as the crew concentrated on training as a unit, going through repeated simulations and familiarizations. Four of this crew had their families housed nearby and, for them, time with their loved ones became more precious as the pace of training increased. Which left Kate and Bob Paxton: a lonesome, separated wife and a blond-haired, handsome MIT physicist. Bob's mission assignment was to operate the shuttle's fifty-foot-long robotic "arm," the machine used to release the payload, and to work on repairing satellites. Initially, he was well-mannered, pleasant company. She hadn't slept with him, though not for his lack of trying. Before long, he became persistent, obnoxious, until she'd told Bob flatly that she wasn't interested. Finally he backed off. During their final week of training, the crew was quarantined. Only spouses were given "personal contact" badges that allowed them to visit. That's what her last fight with Trev had been about. He had wanted to fly to Houston to see her off. She told him no, that she didn't want him at the launch. It had seemed so important to her that their separation remain total for the six months they'd agreed upon. She had wanted her problems on the sidelines until after *Liberty*'s flight. Their final conversation. Their last argument. Their last goodbye? Rather than attempt to regain intimacy with her husband, she'd been a fool. *Trev, I'm sorry.* She mouthed the words soundlessly to the icy night sky.

Bob Paxton completed securing his last piece of netting and dropped from the shuttle's wing down to the ground to stand next to her. They wore jackets over their flight suits. Kate had strapped a .38 revolver at her waist. Lines of uncertainty and apprehension marred Bob's movie star features. The immense, vague shape of the shuttle beneath the camouflage netting loomed above them in the darkness like some giant, indefinable beast from a lingering nightmare.

Bob wore a pistol in a shoulder holster. He followed Kate's gaze to where Ron Scott and the elderly civilian were engaged in discussion. "I wonder, with the commander's leg busted," said Paxton, "if maybe I shouldn't be the one to assume command."

"Forget it, Bob. Ron's doing fine, even with a broken leg. We'll give him all the help he needs or wants. As far as assuming command goes, as copilot I'm second in command."

"Sure, but we're not in flight. Who knows where we are. We're in the middle of nowhere and you're a—" He let the sentence drop, reconsidering.

"A woman?" she finished for him. "Go to hell, Bob. I'm still second in command."

She strode across to join Ron and the civilian. Bob followed.

Ron interrupted his conversation with the man as

they approached. "This is Ahn Chong. We're in North Korea, near the Chinese border. We're near his village." Kate knew that Ron had been stationed in Seoul after the Gulf. He spoke Korean.

"Should we go to his village?" she asked. "Will they help us?"

Scott shook his head, negative. "There's too much to explain right now. We've got to move fast. I've had a chance to converse with this man and to size him up. My gut tells me that we should trust him."

Bob nervously chewed his lower lip. "That'll have to do then. Like you said, we don't have much time."

"He tells me that we should avoid the village. Most of the people there are loyal Party members. Ahn Chong has no love for the Communists. He blames them for the death of his wife. All that matters right now is that he wants us to go with him, says he knows a place where we can hide out. That's where we're going. That landing field we flew over . . . they'll already be looking for us."

"Bob and I can transport Terri," Kate offered. "What about your leg, Commander?"

"I'll lean on Chong if I have to."

Bob studied Ahn Chong with open skepticism. "He could lead us right to their front gate. Can we really trust the old coot?"

"There's one way to find out," Scott said. "Let's go."

His words had barely been spoken when a faint, strange sound became discernible in the near distance, somewhat distorted by the surrounding mountains. The sound became discernible very quickly, however: the tell-tale *whup! whup! whup!* of a helicopter, approaching at a high rate of speed from the direction of the airfield.

Beijing, China

Beyond the large bay window on the top floor of the Great Hall of the People, a dull gray dawn crept over the one hundred square acres of Tiananmen Square. Water from last night's rain, in scattered pools across the flagstone, reflected the gloomy light and the ornate incandescent street lamps like mirrors of steel beneath a low, foreboding sky. Orderly throngs of bicyclists and pedestrians hurried about their morning business, overseen by the towering portrait of Mao Tse-tung mounted above the Forbidden City's Gate of Heavenly Harmony.

In the Politburo conference room, two middle-aged men sat at a large table, summoned to a hastily-called emergency meeting. They wore identical green uniforms that bore no insignia of rank. All insignia had been abolished from The People's Liberation Army in 1965, except for a single red star on the cap. Each man's cap was before him on the highly polished table. Opposite the bay window was a wall-to-wall mural of a young, dynamic Chairman Mao leading a column of youthful soldiers on the Long March, pointing the way against a backdrop of snow-capped mountains.

An adjoining door to the office of the chairman of the Central Committee opened and Huang Peng, the defense minister, entered the conference room. In his seventies, Huang was thin-boned with a shock of white hair above a narrow face. He was the second ranking member of the Politburo, responsible only to the chairman himself. The other two stood and did not sit until Huang took his seat at the head of the table.

Huang spoke abruptly. "You are aware of the space shuttle *Liberty* launched today by the Americans. We have received word that the Americans have lost the shuttle from their radar. One hour ago, they received an emergency distress call before losing contact again for a final time. The transmission has been traced to a sector along our border with North Korea, in the region of Mount Paekdu."

General Chou, a ranking member of the Military Affairs Commission, was the exact physical opposite of Huang. Chou was heavyset and corpulent, with the eyes of a ferret. "Could this be a trick? An intelligence probe by the Americans to test and analyze our response?"

"There is that possibility," Huang acknowledged. Like them, he was a chain-smoker. The room was hazy with cigarette fumes. "If it is a trick, it is an audacious one. The Americans have officially notified us. Thus far none of this has been made public, but of course it will only be a matter of hours before the world learns of it."

Li Juntao, seated to Huang's left, was the third ranking member of the Politburo, which made him the army chief of staff. His compact, stocky form was all muscle. "The Americans have requested our cooperation?" He spoke with a heavy Cantonese dialect.

"They have demanded it."

Chou bristled. "They are in no position to demand anything. Our refusal would force them to act. Their only response would be to lose face or mount an incursion. They dare not risk a military confrontation with China."

Huang placed a fresh cigarette in an ebony holder. He touched the cigarette with flame from a lighter and replied through a plume of exhaled smoke. "The chairman and I are of the opinion that they would take such a risk, if they were certain that their shuttle did go down within our borders."

"What if the shuttle went down inside North Korea?" Li asked.

"We have contacted Pyongyang, as did the Americans. They claim to know nothing of it. But frankly, comrades, what the Koreans say is immaterial. It does not matter whether the shuttle went down in China or in North Korea. What need only concern us at this time is that a thorough search be initiated at once, and that every effort be expended to locate and secure the shuttle and the American defense satellite onboard, or its remains. There is the possibility that the pilot may have succeeded in setting the spacecraft down relatively intact. As you are aware, our space program is primitive in comparison to the West. We would find much aboard *Liberty* that would be extremely useful to China, equipment and information that the Americans would otherwise hardly be inclined to share with us."

"If the shuttle went down within our territory," Li began, "why hasn't our radar—"

"The shuttle was equipped with technology to evade radar."

Li frowned. "I served in Shenyang Province, the region of which we speak. There is extremely rugged terrain on both sides of that border. Finding the shuttle, if it is there, will not be easy."

"No one has suggested that it would be." Huang spoke curtly. "I am aware that you are familiar with that area, General. Therefore you will report at once to our regional headquarters at Shenyang. This matter will receive top priority and classification at every level."

Li blinked his surprise. "Comrade?"

"You will meet with the regional commander to initiate a full-scale search and salvage operation without delay, mountain by mountain, valley by valley, if necessary." Huang paused for emphasis. "You will search along both sides of the border."

Li's frown deepened. "That would constitute a Chinese invasion of North Korea."

"The peasant filth who rule from Pyongyang will not acknowledge it as such, especially if they *do* know where the shuttle is located. *They* are the ones who will not risk a confrontation with *us*. North Korea's military is formidable, but their government is bankrupt. They would not exist as a nation had we not come to their aid during their war with the Americans. Yet they were so quick to turn from us for armament and money when the Soviet Union was strong and we were not. Now they would come crawling back to us. No, we need not concern ourselves with those bastard sons of mother China."

"The Americans then," said Li. "They will do anything to get their astronauts back, dead or alive. You're right, Comrade Defense Minister. The Americans will invade China or North Korea, if we force their hand."

Huang smiled tersely. "Let the Chairman and myself concern ourselves with that, comrade. Who is to say, perhaps you find only wreckage and human remains with nothing salvageable. If that proves to be the case, China will gladly return the useless remains to America as a gesture of humanitarian goodwill. But first it is imperative that we find the *Liberty*."

"We will not be able to stall the Americans for long," Chou said.

Huang nodded. "That is why time and thoroughness are of the essence. General Li, the shuttle or its wreckage must be found."

Li rose from his chair. "I leave immediately for Shenyang. I will locate the shuttle. Nothing will stop me. But I do have one question, comrades. What if there are survivors?"

"That would be highly unlikely," said Huang. "But if that is the case, you will advise us and the situation will be dealt with."

"In what way, may I ask?"

"That need not concern you at this time, Comrade General. Every possible contingency is being considered. Go now. The stakes are high and there is no time to lose."

CHAPTER FOUR

Washington, DC

In the White House, the president met off the record with his closest advisors in a cramped basement facility called the Situation Room. A high-tech, highly secure facility once reserved for managing the occasional world crisis, these days it was in almost constant use. The Situation Room had become one of the busiest parts of the West Wing. The president sat at the head of a conference table. Also present were the secretary of defense, the secretary of state, the director of the Central Intelligence Agency and the national security advisor. And there was General Curtis McMann, a uniformed, barrel-chested, ruddy-cheeked five-star in charge of the military space program.

While the others leaned forward in their chairs, McMann stood at the president's shoulder and pointed out the triangle drawn on a map of Asia that was spread flat on the table in front of the president. "Their

Mayday was picked up at several points around the region. We've triangulated the farthest points of reception and have narrowed down the probable crash site to this region."

The president scrutinized the map. "Several hundred miles?" he noted without enthusiasm.

"At this point, yes sir. The Mayday was picked up by one of our spy ships in the Sea of Japan off the North Korean coast, by a Russian weather station at Lake Baykal and by a commercial Japanese pilot on a Tokyo to Hong Kong flight."

Calhoun, the CIA Director, said, "We have satellites over China probing the region, but it's just now dawn over there." He was a pale-skinned man in a dark suit, with a computer-like mind. He spoke crisply. "So far we have no satellite imagery of *Liberty*, and the GPS infrared sensors haven't tracked it by heat. But that doesn't mean it's not down there. We've retasked our birds up over that region to photograph from every angle. It's been snowing off and on all night in that region, and that could have cooled the shuttle faster than usual. That could fool the heat sensors. What puzzles me is that we haven't picked up a signal from her Emergency Locator transmitter. And each of those astronauts is equipped with an individual 74 emergency radio, but they're not sending locator signals."

McMann returned to his seat. "This whole damn thing is out of left field. It doesn't add up."

The president looked up from the map. "Anything new from the Chinese or the North Koreans?"

Gorman, the secretary of state, shook his head no. "We're still collecting information. Both countries disavow any knowledge of *Liberty* going down in either airspace." The secretary affected a rumpled appearance, at odds with his hard-nosed mastery of international diplomacy. "They've each pledged cooperation."

"We have initiated an intelligence directive, with our Yokohama station as the hub," Calhoun interjected.

"But why don't we *already* have a search and salvage operation underway?" asked the president.

Gorman cleared his throat. "You have to appreciate, sir, how fast this is breaking. The shuttle was launched only hours ago. Both China and North Korea are muddled in bureaucracy."

The president's eyes grew steely. "I don't give a damn. We should already have a search and rescue mission en route over there to supervise. No stalling. We can't let them get away with that."

"Such a course would lead to a serious confrontation, Mr. President," Gorman pointed out.

MacDonald, the secretary of defense, tugged irritably at an earlobe. He was of a bulky build, another ex-military man, with a permanent five o'clock shadow. "You want serious? Our nuke forces are going from DefCon Four to DefCon Three."

Christ, thought the president. Korea.

Relations with China would stand the strain of just about anything these days. Beijing had gotten used to capitalism and liked it. The Korean problem, on the other hand, was a bad hangover from the Cold War. Not much had changed in the status quo between America and Korea in more than fifty years. But that was about to change. North Korea continued a nuclear arsenal buildup. He couldn't get out of his mind the words of his defense secretary during a previous, unrelated briefing: "Anyone who speaks with certainty about North Korea is not speaking with wisdom."

Available intelligence reports were estimating that

the North presently had a formidable one million-man army. Pyongyang spent twenty-five percent of its GNP on arms. About one million of their armed-to-the-teeth soldiers eyeballed a U.S. military force across a DMZ; two awesome armies squared off in their bunkers behind the world's most fortified potential killing field. Significant elements within the North Korean military were hawkish on a possible nuclear standoff with the West. If war broke out, U.S. troops would be their main target.

The president turned to his national security advisor. "A military confrontation with North Korea?"

Latisha Samuels was a middle-aged African American woman whose background in the military and academia had marked her with a no-nonsense, can-do demeanor. "Our fleet is waiting for orders to deploy."

The President paused to consider. "We must proceed under the assumption that some salvageable debris does remain of *Liberty*, and that there are survivors on the ground over there, no matter how slim that possibility is. No one today remembers the crew of the *Pueblo*. That was a spy ship, and the North Koreans held its crew for more than a year. With a defense systems satellite aboard, anyone who gets their hands on the *Liberty* will have themselves a treasure of scientific data. I don't trust the Chinese or the North Koreans. I don't care how nicey-nice we've been making with Beijing over these trade agreements. If only we had some idea what happened to *Liberty*. Going down over there in that godforsaken corner of the world . . . a pure accident?" He glanced around the table.

General McMann said, "It is not entirely impossible that someone could have penetrated the shuttle's computerized control and programmed a deviation into their flight guidance system. There are two thousand sensors and data points in *Liberty*'s computer system. The computers could have been fooled into sending the wrong signals."

"Are you saying," the president asked slowly, "that someone could take command of an American space shuttle in orbit and direct it to land anywhere they wanted?"

"Only if the transmissions between the shuttle and Houston were scrambled, so the pilots could be conned into believing that ground control was ordering the deviation. In fact, Commander Scott would have to be conned into thinking the mission was being aborted."

"If we accept that," said Calhoun, "how likely is it that someone at the Johnson Space Center had a hand in it?"

"That's a primary probability," said McMann. "That is, if we accept the scenario."

The president rapped the table in front of him decisively. "This is too important to close our minds to anything. Okay. The media blackout stands for now. No background leaks to the press until we have a better handle on this." He turned to MacDonald. "Mac, tell the Pentagon I want a situation update every fifteen minutes."

"Yes, Mr. President."

"And one thing more."

"Sir?"

"Get me Trev Galt."

Meiko Kurita signed off on her report for the satellite feed to Tokyo. While her cameraman packed his gear, she studied the now-vacant podium at the end of the long, low-ceilinged room where John Halliday, the president's press secretary, had presided for the preceding half hour, fielding questions at his daily session with the White House press corps. The print media journalists had already left to write their stories, while correspondents of the electronic media filed their reports against the stock backdrop of the podium, the presidential seal clearly visible, before dispersing under the watchful eye of the administration's spin doctors. Meiko's instincts told her that something was wrong. She wondered if any of the thirty or so others present had sensed it. Perhaps the camera caught it. The camera never blinked, or so they said.

She realized again how jaded she had become in so short a time, from the college girl who dreamed of a job in a profession that in Japan was almost completely dominated by men, much like every other profession in that conservative, virtually male-dominated society, to the woman who now embodied that dream. In Japan, women were still very much expected to play a secondary role. Little had changed since her mother's time. Japanese society made it nearly impossible for a woman to adopt a lifestyle that differed from the traditional housebound role. This was reinforced by the pervasive tendency among men and women in her home country to accept things as they are, rather than disturbing the social harmony by protesting their grievances. Women were taught from childhood to adhere to strict behavior, to obey, to be nice girls and good wives. The news media was a nontraditional choice in the extreme. And now, at age twenty-eight, she was White House correspondent for the prestigious Hakura News Network, an Asian version of CNN. Five-foot-two, one hundred and five pounds, with shoulder-length black hair and striking green eyes, she possessed the small-boned, trim figure that was considered television-friendly in both the domestic and international markets. She thought that her mouth was a bit too wide and showed too many teeth when she smiled, but was glad that this opinion was apparently not shared by her audience or Hakura News.

Her outlook had evolved from the sense of awe and wonder she'd first experienced upon arriving in Washington almost a year ago to being as jaded as only a political reporter in a world capital could be. During that time, she had developed a feel for her work that did not come from schooling or training but only from working the turf, as the Americans said: from whether or not you adapted and became attuned to the nuances, the subtext a good correspondent watched for beneath the veneer of political blather and double-talk that was the stock in trade of every politician everywhere; and it was this that was now pestering her subconscious as she watched the room slowly empty of correspondents.

The White House spokesman had seemed . . . well, distracted, she thought. Halliday had a well-earned reputation for being unflappable. You had to be, in his line of work. The press secretary invariably went into a press conference ready with the administration's media handouts for that day, certain of his facts and figures and prepared to engage the American network correspondents and the top American wire service people, who were assigned the front rows and received most of his attention. The question and answer time rarely included the foreign press and certainly had not today. Not that it mattered. Every topic covered had been mundane and wholly routine. But today Meiko had been close enough to the front to sense what she perceived as a subtle preoccupation, a sort of disengagement on the part of the press secretary. She wasn't sure exactly why she thought she sensed this, but she did: an artificial inflection here and there, a glancing to the curtained wings of the small stage, something he did not usually do, as if he was waiting, hoping for someone to bring him some sort of news or information. He was not as focused as usual. Something else beyond the administration's rhetoric about the upcoming economic summit in Europe was on John Halliday's mind.

Meiko now faced the decision of what to do about it. She knew from experience that she had no chance of getting close directly, one-on-one, with John Halliday. That was practically impossible, even for the big three American networks and CNN. She would have to work her contacts. She would have to probe. Maybe she was wrong. Maybe the press secretary just hadn't gotten enough sleep last night.

She sensed someone approaching and turned.

Trev Galt walked up to her.

She thought: speaking of contacts. . . . She met him with a smile. "Well well, Trev, I didn't see you here. What did you think of the press secretary's performance?"

"I missed it, I'm happy to say. I just got here."

He wore his Class A U.S. military uniform. The current president was a stickler for propriety, and this included a dress code for White House personnel.

There was no physical contact between them. Nothing to suggest that they had been dating regularly for the past several months. They'd slept together three times, and that was the last three times they'd seen each other. He was the only man she'd been with since coming to America, and only the second man she'd ever made love with. There was something between them, something nice: a strong mutual attraction that had been there from the moment they met. They enjoyed each other's company and leisure interests, such as movies and tennis and picnics in the country. One thing had seemed to naturally lead to another. She'd felt some reservation at first about sleeping with a married man, but told herself that it made a difference because Trev and Kate were separated. Now though, with Kate Daniels in the news, aboard that space shuttle in outer space, something had changed between Meiko and Galt. What had drawn her to Trev initially was his combination of toughness and gentleness, tenderness and supreme confidence. Trev Galt was a tall mountain of a man. His blue eyes, set in a craggy, oak-tanned face, were always warm with her. But she had no difficulty imagining them as cruel, cold, like chips of ice. This man could kill, and probably had. She knew only that he was attached to the National Security Council, and that he worked in the West Wing of the White House at an administrative level. There was a steadfast rule between them that they never discuss his work, especially in light of the fact that she was a journalist. Theirs was a weekend relationship, which was only what either of their busy schedules permitted. This was the first they'd spoken to each other in two weeks.

Considering the shuttle lift-off, there was only one question she could now think of to ask him. "How are things with *Liberty*?"

She saw at once that this was the wrong question. The blue eyes chilled. "I just know what you know. I'm having a busy day."

Something about the curtness of his reply irritated her. Or maybe, she thought, she'd irritated herself, because he was on her mind so much during the past two weeks. There was no one within earshot. Her cameraman was busy talking shop across the room with a cameraman from one of the networks. So she went ahead and said what she'd promised herself she would never say.

She said, "I've been waiting for you to call."

"I thought we weren't going to talk about us when we met in public like this."

"I'm sorry, Trev. But we also agreed to see each other, and we were until . . . two weeks ago."

"I told you I've been busy."

"You've been busy avoiding me. We agreed in the beginning that this relationship would be over the first time either of us wanted it to be over. I want to be a good thing in your life, Trev. I don't want to complicate it and I won't. But you're not going to just end what's between us with no explanations and no goodbyes, are you?"

"Meiko, I don't want to talk about it right now."

"Neither do I. But we need to talk. I'm worried, Trev. Not about us, but about you. You're drinking more, like you were when we first met, before you dried out for me."

"Meiko—"

"And I couldn't help but notice that your drinking became worse as the time drew closer for the *Liberty* launch." She stared into his eyes. "I'd be disappointed if you weren't concerned about Kate's safety up there in space. She is your wife." She reprimanded herself even as she spoke, hearing the emotion in her voice, and she knew he would hear it too. "But you did tell me that the romance part of your relationship with Kate was over between you. That you'd agreed it would be all right for you to each date different people. I don't want a lot, Trev. I just want to understand the situation I'm dealing with."

"I'm sorry. I guess I just don't know, either."

"Then that's the problem, isn't it?" She kept her voice pitched low. They remained beyond earshot of anyone else. This would appear only as a cordial exchange to anyone observing them. "Are you in love with two women at the same time, Trev? Is that the problem? You don't like being indecisive, do you? You're not that type of man. I'll bet this is the first time you've been indecisive in a long while."

Galt chuckled. "I can't remember the last time. I'm sorry, Meiko. I haven't been fair to you. I will call."

"Then I'll settle for that, and I'll let you in on a little secret. I wish I understood my own feelings. Perhaps I'm getting what I deserve for feeling this way about a married man."

They became aware then of someone approaching. A man she recognized as being from the Military and Naval Aides' Office reached them with a purposeful stride and addressed Trev as if she weren't there.

"Sir, excuse me. The president wants to see you."

Meiko and Trev nodded to each other, the polite unspoken goodbye of two mere acquaintances, and she watched them walk away, angry at herself for having brought up her and Trev's private life the way she had. It had been gnawing at her more than she'd realized, obviously, for everything to come firing out of her as it had. She had always considered herself to be highly disciplined, professionally and emotionally.

Watching Trev and the man leave the press room, a new thought muted her emotions. Could there be a connection between the space shuttle and the preoccupation, the disengagement, which she had sensed on the part of Press Secretary Halliday? The *Liberty*'s mission and schedule were classified, but the launch had been reported as a success.

Had something gone wrong?

Chapter Five

North Korea

Dawn silhouetted the mountains. Sunrise rouged the snowy slopes of Mount Paekdu. The intermittent flurries of last night had not stuck to the frozen ground at the lower elevation where the airfield dominated a narrow, shallow valley.

The perimeter of the military landing field was a galvanized welded-mesh fence topped with barbed wire that glinted in the frozen sunshine. At each corner of the oblong perimeter of the base was a watchtower. Set apart from the barracks, which were dreary, squat structures of cinderblock, was a modern control tower rising from a single-story building with an oversized, rotating dish-shaped radio and television antenna on the roof. The building and tower dominated an inner compound surrounded by its own barbed wire perimeter, complete with patrolling sentries armed with assault rifles.

Sergeant Bol Rhee stood with his men on the tarmac beside a Soviet-made M-6 helicopter, watching the ground crew work frantically on the engine. It was twenty minutes since the last of the other gunships had lifted off, but since the flight crews were under orders to utilize the onboard heaters only during the months of December through February, on this brisk November morning Bol was glad for the delay. It gave him and his platoon precious additional time to store up what warmth they could from the sunshine before boarding the helicopter for what would surely be a cold, cold flight into the surrounding hills. Search flights spreading out in concentric circles from the base had begun hours earlier and would be continued around the clock.

Bol Rhee had the stocky, rawboned build of the peasant class from which he came. He sometimes wished that he was still a youngster, that he had never grown up to become a career soldier in the People's Army. But wishing did not make it so, and he was far better off than many. The country above the 38th parallel was wracked with poverty. At least in the army he ate well and had a roof over his head.

He thought again that this was the strangest duty assignment of his army career. His company had been sent to provide security for this hastily constructed airfield. The completed runway was much wider and longer than any Bol had ever seen. But except for the patrol gunship helicopters already stationed here, no aircraft had ever landed or taken off from this runway. Supplies and materials were delivered by truck at night. Military engineers had constructed the base in record time. There were two distinctly separate, vigorously segregated groups: those who worked in and around the tower and those who provided security.

Since the completion of the base, the technicians in their white smocks had stepped up their work around the clock. There continued to be virtually no air traffic in or out, with one exception. Sometimes in the middle of the night, a helicopter would touch down for a brief visit. Civilians were aboard and spent their time in the tower. During one such visit, Bol had seen the helicopter's markings. Not military, but Japanese civilian!

The only thing stranger was what had happened earlier this morning. The entire company had been positioned along the perimeter. The airfield landing lights were turned on for the first time since the base had become operational, and Bol had witnessed something he would never forget. Something amazing.

A space shuttle with American markings had soared in for a landing, had appeared fully ready to land, before unexpectedly overshooting the runway at the last possible instant and disappearing majestically into the darkness!

Then, within minutes he'd been standing in formation with his men, listening to Colonel Sung order the sweep of the surrounding countryside in search of an American space shuttle, which the base commander told them had malfunctioned while in orbit and had attempted an emergency landing but was feared to have crashed. This was a cooperative venture authorized by the United States, their commanding officer had informed Bol and the other troops. No man present was to utter a word of this to anyone, under penalty of death.

Bol believed the part about the death penalty, but not much else. Truly, a very strange duty assignment.

Colonel Sung now appeared, striding through the

morning sunlight toward the helicopter from the direction of the tower, just as the maintenance crew chief signaled to the pilot. The gunship's engine coughed, sputtered, coughed again and started, filling the air with harsh black diesel exhaust. Bol ordered his men aboard, then turned to greet the base commander.

Sung's uniform was heavily starched. His boots were spit-polished, but he was soft around the middle from too much beer. "Valuable time is being lost, Sergeant. I had wanted your platoon in place by first light." Sung raised his voice to be heard above the engine noise.

"My apologies, Colonel," said Bol. "The helicopter—"

"Yes, well, it's been repaired, hasn't it? Remember, I want a thorough sweep of your sector, Sergeant. If Japanese troops are sighted, do not engage them. Radio your position without delay."

"One question, Comrade Colonel. Chinese border patrols have also been known to cross into this region from time to time."

"Expect anything. And stop wasting time."

"Yes, Comrade Colonel."

Bol boarded the helicopter.

The gunship lifted off, banking to the east. As he sat on the hard bench, shivering with his men, Bol wrapped his arms across his chest and hugged himself to stay warm. He looked out a side window to watch Sung and the airfield tilt away and recede into the distance below. It was even colder in the helicopter than he'd thought it would be.

He wondered what this day would bring.

Ahn Chong led them to a rocky, craggy outcrop of boulders where foliage overgrew a narrow gash, a fault in the stony surface at a low jut of rock that was well camouflaged by dense thickets.

The interior of the cave was vaguely illuminated by refracted light of the new day, slanting in through the foliage that concealed the entrance. There was a musty, unpleasant closeness about the place, a rodent smell, and some old animal droppings scattered about. But at least it wasn't cold. It was almost warm in comparison to the world outside, here in this close, crowded, dim, musty, confined space no more than ten feet high and thirty feet deep.

They were less than a kilometer from the *Liberty*, by Kate's estimation, though it had been difficult to be certain as the old man led them along the rugged, circuitous route to get here. It had been extremely slow going with Ron hobbling along, staying off his broken leg as best he could, leaning heavily on Ahn Chong. Kate and Bob transported Terri.

Several times along the way, they had done what Scott had first commanded them to do while still at the shuttle, when a North Korean gunship equipped with searchlights had swept by as low as the hazardous terrain would allow, without spotting the camouflaged shuttle. Then, and several times en route, their small group had been forced to huddle beneath the cover of tall pine trees while military helicopters rumbled by overhead at a slow rate of speed like bloated, low-flying prehistoric birds searching for prey.

"Ahn said we're about three kilometers from the airfield," Scott said after the most recent flyover, listening carefully with an ear cocked. "That chopper's getting set to touch down."

"We expected that, didn't we?" Kate spoke matter-of-factly. "If they find us, they'll know the shuttle is nearby."

"Which means we do our best to see that they don't find us," Scott grunted.

The old North Korean civilian had then led them the final short distance to the cave, which they'd crawled into just as another helicopter had flown over. Kate didn't know if it was the same one. She and Bob Paxton stretched Terri Schmidt out on the ground of the cave as gently as they could.

Kate despaired for Terri, who looked to be in terrible condition. Her pulse beat was faint, scarcely detectable. There was a trickle of blood snaking from Terri's left ear, indicating a serious concussion. Kate brushed the blood away. Terri's eyelids fluttered from time to time, but she had lapsed into unconsciousness.

They were hardly inside the cave when Scott and Ahn Chong launched into an exchange in Korean. Then the old man left them.

"He said he has to get back to his village or he'll be missed," Scott explained. The tautness in the flight commander's voice was the only indication of the excruciating pain he had to be feeling from his broken leg. "He thinks we'll be safe here. He promised to come back as soon as he can and bring us food."

Paxton frowned. "That gives the troops in those choppers more time to find us. And why should that old guy want to help us? I say we don't trust him."

Kate remained kneeling beside Terri, dabbing the woman's forehead with a piece of tissue dampened from Kate's canteen. "We have to get Terri some medical attention."

"Ahn Chong told me that there aren't any medical facilities anywhere near here." Something approaching exasperation crept into Ron's voice. "The only doctors in this region are military, and the nearest one is fifty kilometers away."

"So you are suggesting that we just stay here all day?" Paxton asked. He shook his blond head. "Hell, we're sitting ducks."

"No more than if we venture out in broad daylight," countered Scott, "with North Korean army patrols and helicopters already looking for us. Mr. Ahn also informed me that there are bandits in these hills. They've been terrorizing the locals on both sides of the border. They're heavily armed. Ahn Chong said they pose as much of a threat to us as the military."

The lines of apprehension in Bob Paxton's features had only grown deeper. "Speaking of the military, how do we know they're not looking for us so they can help us?"

"Here's why. Ahn says that after the soldiers started work constructing that base we flew over, the locals were told to stay away or they'd be shot, and there have been regular patrols through the villages to intimidate them. I'm not about to trust our well-being and a four-billion-dollar space shuttle to thugs like that, if we can help it."

Kate stepped forward to join the conversation. "Do you still think someone forced us down? Were we supposed to land at that airfield?"

Paxton uttered a rude, exasperated snort of dismissal. "But that's crazy. How could anyone pull off something like that and hope to get away with it?"

"I don't know," Scott admitted with a frown. "Maybe it happened like that, maybe not. But here are my orders. We're going to lie low until we get a better handle on whatever it is we've gotten ourselves into. For now, one of us has to find some cover outside and keep an eye out in case anyone does come this way. We're on high ground here. We should have some advance warning. We'll risk making a break for it if we have to."

"I'll volunteer for guard duty," Paxton said. "But I still don't like the idea of trusting that old gook."

Kate eyed him with open disapproval. "Bob, this is Ron's call. You heard his orders."

Scott locked eyes with Paxton. "Maybe you've got a better idea?"

"Maybe I do." Paxton avoided looking Scott in the eye. "Uh, maybe I should take command. Y'know, sir, with that busted leg of yours—"

"Kate is second in command, if anything happens to me. You know that."

Kate said, "We've already discussed it, sir."

Scott studied the blond-haired man before him as if for the first time. "Then what the hell, Specialist?"

Paxton stared with a trace of contrition at the cave floor. "I just want to make sure we get out of this alive."

"We all want that," Scott snapped. "But we will maintain the chain of command. Is that clear?"

Paxton gulped audibly. "Yes, sir. It's clear."

"Position yourself outside. Kate and I will take turns relieving you every few hours. Stay under cover."

Paxton's jaw tightened. "I know enough to take cover. Don't treat me like I'm stupid."

"Then stop acting like you are."

Kate said, "Stop it, both of you. We've got to get along if we're going to pull through this."

"Don't you get on me too," Bob groused at her. "I'm on my way."

He leaned down to crawl through the shrubbery concealing the cave. Scott suddenly gripped him by the shoulder.

"Wait. Someone's coming."

Kate heard it too: the shuffling of footfalls on rock outside the cave, not far away. Voices in conversation in what sounded like Korean. Someone emitted a coarse laugh.

At that moment, Terri Schmidt's eyes opened. The eyes were glassy, unblinking and semi-conscious. Terri's head began rolling from side to side. Her moaning filled the cave. "Mom, I'm sorry," she mumbled weakly. "Dad? Where's Jimmy . . . Mom, don't . . . where are you? Mom . . ."

Bob Paxton glared around with a look of pure panic. "Make her shut up!"

Kate bit back an angry reply. She placed her fingertips lightly across Terri's lips, leaning down to coo comforting, whispered sounds. It worked. Terri's moaning and mumbling tapered off.

Too late.

A voice outside shouted something at the others. The laughter and conversation stopped. Kate heard the metallic snapping of rounds being chambered into weapons. Footfalls began advancing across the rocky ground outside, toward the cave entrance.

Scott and Bob Paxton were poised just inside the entrance, their pistols held up and ready. Kate unholstered her revolver. Terri began moaning again, louder than before.

"They've got us," Paxton said, desperation in his eyes and in his voice. "We're dead."

CHAPTER SIX

Houston, Texas

There is a pervasive order and simplicity about the Johnson Space Center, the 100-building complex where more than 10,000 NASA employees work amid a purposefully comfortable setting of uniformity and coherence. Neat green lawns, trees, walkways and man-made ponds of symmetrically landscaped quadrangles sparkle between sprawling work centers.

In a corner of the massive parking lot adjacent to the concrete-and-glass command center building, Special Agent Claude Jackson, of the Federal Bureau of Investigation's counter-espionage branch, surreptitiously placed a radio beeper on the inside surface of a Volvo's rear fender in a movement so practiced, so slick, it would have gone unnoticed even by someone paying attention to him. However, no one was paying undue attention to the tall black man striding into the parking lot. Passersby coming and going from the building were occupied with their own determined preoccupations, as were the drivers of those cars that entered and exited the parking lot in a moderate but steady flow. They paid scant attention to Jackson as he stooped down briefly, sprightly for a man of his considerable bulk, as he passed between the Volvo and the vehicle in the next parking space. In no more than the length of time it would take to flick a twig from his pants cuff or a speck of dust from his shoe, it was done. He continued on to the unmarked Bureau car parked several aisles away where Chalmers, his partner, sat waiting behind the steering wheel. The car's interior was comfortably warm from the early afternoon sunshine pouring in through the windshield.

A pair of binoculars and a long-lens camera, loaded with high-speed film, rested on the car seat. Jackson lifted the binoculars, focusing them on a side exit of the building. He said, "Better let 'em know we're in place."

Chalmers spoke into his lapel mic, reporting across the tac net to their senior watch officer stationed with backup nearby. "We've set up surveillance."

Jackson and Chalmers worked the enforcement detail out of the center's FBI office. Undercover agents were in place at every level of the center, a protective measure designed to neutralize sabotage and/or espionage. The Johnson Space Center held the secrets of everything relating to the American space program, and so every person on center grounds had to be considered a potential security risk. This was the reality that mandated the Bureau's security operations in Houston. For the inhabitants and workers of the space center, it was no secret that undercover FBI agents worked among them. Such agents were viewed resentfully as spies by hardworking Americans, who took offense at the suspicion of their integrity and patriotism implicit in such undercover activity, nor were they much appreciative of the routine use of lie detectors and surveillance.

As viewed through Jackson's binoculars, the space center appeared to function as normal. His partner had selected a surveillance position well inside the parking lot, with enough distance from the building to ensure that their daylight surveillance went wholly unnoticed by the parade of briefcase carriers hustling about. The slight increase in their number, discernible only to Jackson's trained eye, alone indicated the massive event of a few hours ago.

Chalmers slapped the steering wheel impulsively. "Damn, this is like trying to catch a fart with a butterfly net. We're spread way too goddamn thin to get results as fast as Washington wants." He had a youthful face set above a middle-aged body. He and Jackson had been partners for eighteen months.

Because of the time it would take to go over every personnel file at Houston for any possible leads to what had happened to *Liberty*, the assistant director who honchoed counter-intel ops from Washington had promised reinforcements before the day was out. Chalmers knew this. He was just an impatient guy.

Without taking the binoculars' focus from the building exit, Jackson said, "At least we have those prelim scans to work from."

Chalmers grunted irritably. "I guess that'll have to do. The pressure's on, that's for goddamn sure."

"If there is someone who brought that shuttle down, it's someone working in Mission Control."

Chalmers grunted again. He slapped the steering wheel again. "Someone inside NASA, reprogramming computers. That sure as hell is a first. I wonder if we have our man."

"Lennick seems to think so." Jackson was referring to the senior watch officer. "The red flags are sure there."

Chalmers nodded. "Wife terminally ill. Seeing an Asian woman." The files on primary Mission Control personnel had been reviewed as soon as word had come from DC about the shuttle. "Yeah, I guess going on what we know," said Chalmers, "I'd put my money on Eliot Fraley."

"There he is," said Jackson.

Fraley was the stereotypical brilliant, middle-aged computer nerd, a wiry little guy wearing a bow tie. His sports jacket didn't match his slacks. He had thick-lensed, wire-rimmed glasses and a balding pate encircled by a thatch of untamed, curly hair. He exited the building, making a beeline toward the parking lot. His wiry legs scissored with that hurriedly awkward stride of one not used to hurrying. He reached and boarded his waiting Volvo, backing it from his parking space and leaving the parking lot.

Jackson and Chalmers followed, observing surveillance distancing as the Volvo drove down Highway C in the direction of the front gate.

Jackson said into his lapel mic, "Subject is moving."

Fraley was one of the ground team of flight controllers assigned to the Johnson Space Center Flight Control Room. There he'd labored, functioning like an automaton, endless week after week. At first, when his job had been a challenge, he'd loved it. But week after week had turned into month after month, then year after year. He himself did not fully understand it, but eventually the initial joy of computers and space technology had become reduced for him to a grinding drudgery made worse by the pressures of an overburdened personal life.

Less than an hour earlier, in the immediate aftermath of the blackout from *Liberty*, he'd been standing with the growing crowd of NASA scientists and administrators around the flight director's console, which was the heart of the rows upon rows of monitors and their attending technicians. At first, he'd feigned interest and concern, standing there with his co-workers who moments earlier had been operating their computers, digesting their radar data, plotting the orbiter's path on the large map projection screen on the front wall. Then, eventually, he had been able to unobtrusively unplug his station from the flight director's loop, had set down his headset and walked away from the hubbub of concern. Don't panic, he'd told himself.

He was still telling himself that as he stepped up to a pay phone on the concourse leading to the waiting area at the loading gate, where he was supposed to meet Connie. He'd already scouted the seating area where they were supposed to meet. People were beginning to congregate for the flight, which was scheduled to board in ten minutes. Fraley glanced at his digital watch. Actually, the flight was to board in nine minutes and forty seconds. He snapped his eyes away from the security of mathematics, a logical world that always made sense. He again scanned the busy scene around him: arriving and departing people and their accompanying parties pouring along the concourse in both directions.

Maybe there is a logical reason to start panicking, Fraley told himself.

He slipped coins into the pay phone and dialed

Connie Yota's number, fully expecting to hear her answering machine message click on after half a ring, as always. He did not know what he should do if Connie didn't show up in time to catch the flight. She was supposed to be here waiting for him when he arrived. That was their plan, agreed upon and etched in stone as recently as this morning in bed. But he now jolted physically as if an electrical jolt had shot through him when he heard, instead of Connie's answering machine, the disembodied, metallic, recorded telephone company voice advising him that the number he was calling had been disconnected, and that if he thought he'd dialed the number in error, he should. . . . He disconnected, got the dial tone again and fed more coins into the pay slot, again punching up the number he had memorized since his and Connie's first night of hot sex several weeks ago . . . which had been the first night they'd met. He took extreme effort this time to dial the correct number and only then realized that his index finger was trembling. He cursed this sign of inner weakness. Damn nerves. The connection rang twice. Again, he got the wrong number recording. He replaced the receiver before the disembodied voice could speak the third word of its message.

It dawned on him. Of course. She had disconnected her phone because that's the way Connie was. Her mind functioned with the same precise intensity as her sex drive.

He turned to again survey the flow of people moving along the concourse. He could often foretell the approach of Connie's lithe, small-boned, tight figure, her flowing shoulder-length black hair, her dusky beauty that radiated both sex and intelligence. . . . He knew when she was approaching, sometimes before he saw her, by the way men's heads would begin turning to view her approach. But not this time. Still no sign of Connie. He glanced again at his watch. Eight minutes and forty seconds to boarding. The crowd was growing by the minute in the waiting area by the loading gate. People beginning to stir. Businessmen and businesswomen organizing their work, snapping shut their laptops. Mothers gathering up their children and their luggage. Family, friends and lovers were preparing to say goodbye. A well-coifed airline employee standing by the desk was eyeing the clock too, preparing to announce the boarding.

Watching the teeming concourse, Fraley tried hard not to show the panic that was building within him with each passing second. His heartbeat was pounding like a bass drum in his ears, almost completely blotting out the sounds around him.

He was ready to kiss everything goodbye. His life, his career, everything . . . to begin a new life with the gorgeous, brilliant Japanese beauty who had come into what had been a wretched life and made it incredibly exciting . . . and dangerous. But that danger would diminish to nothing the instant they boarded this flight to the Caribbean. She was in love with him and they would fly away together. Connie had promised him this, and he believed her.

It had been like something out of *Penthouse* Forum. Night after night of the wildest sex imaginable with this single, twenty-three-year-old Japanese civilian with a law degree, who spoke several languages, whom he'd met accidentally at the restaurant he frequented near his home. From that first night of their chance encounter when she'd invited him to her apartment, when their lust had burned through the night on silken sheets cast in candlelight, the smell of incense blending with the scent of warmed oils, the moans and the gasps of pleasure mingled with the low, subtle music that caressed and provided the changing tempos of their lovemaking. . . . Ms. Connie Yota had shown the computer scientist things about the physical act of love that he'd never imagined. He'd been her slave in every way since then. She demanded much, but his rewards were exquisite and, in addition, Connie had professed a true love for him that had touched Fraley's heart as much as his libido.

Where is she? My God, don't let anything go wrong! He wondered with a start who he was to be imploring anything of a deity he'd never acknowledged the existence of. He self-analyzed this as an indication of just how overwrought he was, and he hoped this was not noticeable to anyone passing by. Of course, he had no right to ask any god for any help after the sins he had committed. He'd sold out his country. He'd sold out the crew of the space shuttle *Liberty*. And, even more poignant to him personally, he was about to run out on his dying wife for a woman half Nora's age. No, he did not think there was any god anywhere who would condone any of that. He was somewhat surprised that the thought even flashed through his mind. But then, life—including his own mind, soul and heart—had proven to hold untold surprises since the moment Connie had appeared in his life. It had been a roller-coaster of emotions, in direct conflict with his lifelong psychological need for emotional stability to facilitate his mental discipline. He accepted this conflict as part of what generated the unbelievably rewarding sexual and psychic bond between himself and her. He could hardly believe that he was about to embark on a lifetime of experience with this woman who had so changed him.

He had picked up their tickets. He carried only his

travel-on, a single brown leather suitcase, as she'd suggested. She was a seasoned traveler, obviously, though they had never directly discussed her work for what she had only once vaguely referred to as "a Tokyo corporation with connections everywhere." She had mentioned this, she assured him, merely to assure him that they would lead a life of comfort, even luxury, as part of his payment for his onetime betrayal. And the betrayal of his wife of seventeen years? Fraley blinked the thought of Nora from his mind. His wife had been a paraplegic since that terrible car crash seven years ago. He hadn't wanted to fall in love with another woman, but it happened anyway. He had made financial arrangements to ensure that Nora Fraley would be well taken care of for the duration of her life. Reviewing the situation in this manner, Fraley felt suddenly as free as a bird. Connie had already arranged payment of the promised amount into his numbered Swiss bank account.

"Mr. Fraley?"

He jerked around to find himself confronted by two men who, he knew instinctively, could only be plainclothes law officers of some kind: a muscular black man and a Caucasian with a lumpier build and a boyish face.

"Uh, yes . . . my name is Fraley."

"Mr. Fraley, my name is Agent Chalmers. This is Agent Jackson. Sir, you're under arrest. Please don't make a scene. Put your hands behind your back. Read him his rights, Claude."

The black agent read him words that Fraley had heard a million times in movies and on TV shows about things he said used against him and his right to remain silent. He nodded dumbly when asked if he understood. His head drooped forlornly. The handcuffs snapped tightly, coldly, behind his back, making him wince. Then the two men were guiding him along the concourse, back in the direction of the airport parking lot. Jackson's massive grip felt like a steel vise on Fraley's upper arm, while Chalmers steered Fraley from his other side, hurrying him along far faster than he ever would have walked of his own volition. At times, they practically dragged him, and he was becoming winded. His preferred world since childhood had been the cerebral, rarely the physical. That had all changed with Connie, of course, certainly when it came to sex. Even at a time like this, he could only think of her in those terms and of the passions she stirred within him. He thought, at least they don't have Connie. It's good that she didn't make it in time for the flight. He would pay for his betrayal, but thank God she would remain free . . .

As if reading his mind, the black agent at his side chuckled without humor. "You were set up, stupid. You have figured that part out, haven't you?"

Fraley blinked. "I beg your pardon?"

Chalmers chimed in, "Not that it did your sweet little fortune cookie any good."

"Connie?" It burst from him.

Jackson nodded. "She was apprehended ten minutes ago at a car rental agency. She was leaving town without you, Eliot. We just don't know yet where she was going or who set her up to take you down. Do you know?"

Fraley summoned up every ounce of inner strength he could muster, which wasn't much. "I don't know anything about what you're talking about." He spoke in a voice he did not recognize as his own.

They left the concourse using an "authorized personnel only" exit.

Chalmers said, "Miss Yota is being interrogated. They played you for the patsy you are, pal, getting you to sell out your soul and your country for a piece of ass. Something like this, tapping someone as high up as you . . . can you say compartmentalization? That means your Connie will know just enough to incriminate herself into a nice long prison sentence, even if she is a lawyer."

"So how about you, Doc?" said Jackson. "You could get your honor back, or at least some of your self-respect. You will cooperate?"

"I don't know anything," Fraley insisted.

"We'll see," said Jackson with supreme confidence. They steered him toward a waiting unmarked car. "Mr. Fraley, the shit of your life has just hit the biggest fan there is."

CHAPTER SEVEN

North Korea

It was an incredible chain of stunning events, thought Kate, that had brought her to this cave with armed men outside, one of whom was shouting something in Korean into the cave, not sounding friendly at all. In the shadows of the cave, she continued to whisper cooing sounds into Terri's ear in an attempt to quiet Terri's delirious ramblings. Kate stroked the injured woman's temples with her fingertips.

Terri's semi-conscious eyes suddenly opened wide, normal and lucid. She gazed up with that unflagging inquisitive good nature that Kate had grown fond of. "What happened? Did we crash?" She started to turn her head, looking around. "Where are we?"

Kate wanted to ease Terri gently back into awareness of what had transpired. She clasped one of Terri's hands in hers. "There's been trouble; you'll be all right."

"Okay." Terri spoke the single word in the small voice of a child. She closed her eyes, saying no more.

At the mouth of the cave, Scott and Paxton remained one to either side, each with a finger on a trigger. Scott shouted something in Korean, responding to the men outside. There was a surly reply from without. Scott translated for the others.

"They're not soldiers. They're bandits. They've given us sixty seconds to surrender. Big Mouth out there says he's holding a fragmentation grenade with a ten-second fuse. We don't show ourselves, he throws in the grenade." Scott flicked a quick glance around the confines of the cave. "That means we all die."

"Well hell," said Paxton. "Let's do as the man says. Jesus, Commander. I don't want to die. You've got to get us back home. We've got to take any chance we can!" Paxton's blond hair was mussed, his face streaked with dirt and fear, no longer the movie-poster-handsome face.

Scott glanced at Kate. "Will Terri make it, if we move her?"

Kate rose from kneeling at the side of the woman who had become her friend during their intensive astronaut training together. "Terri's dead," she said in a grim voice. She unholstered her pistol.

"Are you sure?"

"I'm sure. And we're dead if someone out there throws in a grenade. I don't see where we have a choice."

Paxton looked mightily relieved. He looked happy enough to jump up and down. "Kate's right!"

Scott sighed. "She always is. Okay. I'll step out first. If they open fire, you two do your best. Good luck."

Kate started to say something, but Scott had already

managed to hobble the single awkward step it took for him to swing his straightened leg through the shrubbery that choked the mouth of the cave. He disappeared from their sight, leaving Kate and Bob Paxton alone with the dead woman. When Kate's eyes locked with his, she saw that his were glassy with uncertainty. "Get a grip, Bob. This is no time to lose it."

Paxton didn't look so sure. "There was nothing like this in the goddamn training."

"Can it," she said. She couldn't believe that she had once been attracted to this man.

From outside, she heard Scott address someone in Korean. There was a cruel, guttural laugh and the briefest sound of a scuffle. Then she heard Scott grunt in pain. She could wait no longer. She'd rather die giving backup to a teammate than crouch here, hiding. She took a step forward, bringing up her pistol and bracing herself for whatever she would find confronting her.

Paxton's jaw dropped. "Kate, no, for Chrissake, wait! What if—"

She didn't have an opportunity to reply, nor to propel herself through the shrubbery as she'd intended to. Instead, Ron Scot was propelled into the cave under force of a powerful shove from outside. He plowed into her with enough impact to send them both stumbling backwards. Kate fought to maintain her balance, simultaneously steering Scott toward a rough, curved wall of the cave, where he could reach out a hand and steady himself on his good leg, to brace himself from falling. She noted that he wore a nasty purple bruise on his forehead that was swelling by the second, and an open, ugly red wound along the scalp line. Scott did not fall. He remained standing when Kate released him. This allowed her to spin around just in time to see the man, who had obviously shoved Scott, now come storming into the cave.

There was the cruelty of a killer about him, every bit as palpable as his foul body odor that permeated the dank closeness. He wore a dirty padded jacket and ragged pants. His face was scarred, probably from smallpox. He held an M16 automatic rifle.

Scott explained quickly, "His name is Han Ling. Three of his men are outside, and they're not much prettier than he is. He's Chinese, but he speaks Korean."

Paxton had stepped away from the cave entrance, pointedly keeping his pistol aimed at the ground, a sign of surrender. This did him no good. Before he could speak, before anyone saw it coming, the intruder whipped the rifle sideways in a sharp movement that snapped the rifle's butt squarely into Paxton's startled face. There was a bone-crunching sound. Paxton fell back with a cry, falling to the ground, the pistol skittering from his fingers. He drew himself into a crouch against the cave's wall, staring wild-eyed from behind the hands that he clasped to his face.

"My nose! Jesus Christ, he broke my goddamn nose!"

Kate and the bandit faced each other. Like Paxton, she held her pistol aimed at the ground. The intruder glared at her menacingly, and she took advantage of the opportunity he was obviously offering her by not opening fire and cutting her to ribbons. She let the pistol drop from her fingers. It clattered onto the cave floor.

The man gestured with his rifle. Paxton sidled over to join her and Commander Scott, near the sprawled remains of Terri Schmidt. The bandit scooped up their dropped pistols while maintaining a one-armed grip on his M16, a finger on the trigger and the muzzle aimed at them. He nonchalantly slipped the sidearms into a wide, colorful sash that served as his belt, with the pistol butts reversed, old American West style, for quick cross-draw. The bandit motioned them outside with the rifle barrel, issuing a gruff command in his own tongue.

Kate asked Scott, "What are they going to do with us?"

"I make out something about taking us into the mountains. He's speaking a regional dialect that I don't know."

Bob Paxton still held his broken nose with both hands. A stream of bloody droplets dotted his tunic. "This isn't happening," he gurgled. "This can't be happening."

"Move it, Specialist," ordered Scott briskly. "We'll try to set that nose as soon as we get our asses out of here. We're worth more alive than dead to them. If they'd wanted us dead, we'd damn sure already be dead."

Kate did her best to pretend that a gnarly mountain bandit wasn't pointing an automatic weapon at her. She spoke to Scott, nodding toward the body at their feet. "What about Terri? We can't just leave our dead."

Scott sighed. His eyes were infinitely sad. "We can't help Terri now. We'll do whatever it takes to recover her remains. But for now . . . I promised this guy we'd go where he wanted to take us."

The bandit seemed to understand what they were talking about. With a smile of pure maliciousness, he summoned up phlegm and spat upon Terri Schmidt.

Kate held her emotions in check. It was easy enough to do. At the moment, her emotions were utterly numb to the point of being nonexistent. She eyed the bandit coldly and spoke to Scott. "Sir, do you think he knows about the shuttle?"

"Don't know yet. Can't tell."

Paxton made a whimpering noise. "If I see a chance, I'm making a run for it."

Scott hobbled to the mouth of the cave. "With this busted stem, I'm not running anywhere." Kate could tell that he was doing his best to keep the resignation and defeat he must have felt from filtering into his voice. He disappeared from the cave.

She followed, but not before sending Paxton a glower even under the gun of the bandit who covered them with his M16. She hissed, "Don't blow it, Bob. Follow orders or we'll all die."

The bandit lost patience, and she and Paxton were both shoved from the cave, Kate first through the shrubbery, to the knoll of ground outside. Three bandits stood waiting on the knoll. Except for the fact that they were younger, no more than teenagers, in every other respect—from clothing to armament—they were nearly identical to Han; including sour body odor and bad attitude. They stood with their rifles aimed at Scott.

Despite his splinted leg, the flight commander was steady enough to halt the forward momentum of Paxton as the scientist was pushed out from the cave's interior. Paxton would have tumbled over a sharp drop-off, to further injury and possible death, if Scott hadn't been standing there to intercept him. Han stepped from the cave. He stormed over to stand toe-to-toe with Scott, shouting directly into Scott's face.

Scott winced. "This bastard's breath is worse than his B.O.!" he said to Kate and Bob. "I think he's telling us that if we go with him, we might live."

"I have no problem with that," said Kate. She had difficulty keeping her voice steady in the face of four rifles aimed at her, but she succeeded.

Paxton was still gurgling painful complaints, his hands clenching his broken nose. "We're totally screwed! That old man who brought us here, he sold us out. I knew we shouldn't have trusted him!"

Scott turned without comment. He lifted his arms and extended both of his hands, to Paxton's face, batting away Bob's defensive gesture. With a nimble, self-assured twist, he delivered a single, savage jerking motion, resetting Paxton's nose with an audible clack!

Paxton stepped back, at first in shock, then becoming aware that he was no longer in excruciating pain. Han Ling and the other bandits viewed this with some good humor.

Han Ling snarled at Scott.

Scott listened, then said to Paxton and Kate, "Okay, let's do as the man says. We follow the trail that brought us up here, back down the way we came until we're told otherwise." He glared at Paxton, his eyes clouding. "Are you all right, Bob?"

"I—I'm all right," Paxton stammered. "But, Commander, we have to get away from these guys!"

"For now," said Kate, "let's just work at staying alive." Turning to face her commander, Kate offered, "Lean on me, sir."

"No, thanks, Kate. I can make it."

"Don't be macho, commander. Please."

"Sorry, ma'am," he said with a failed attempt at a Southern drawl. She happened to know that he was, in fact, from Minnesota. "It's just the way I was brought up. Let's move out."

One of the bandits took the point position. The other two fell in behind, and their small group began making its way down the winding path. Han strode with the Americans. Kate was thankful that they were upwind of the man. From time to time, one of the renegades would laugh or shout out something to prod the Americans, and would laugh when someone cried out or stumbled.

Scott's splinted leg nearly gave out from beneath him twice. Each time Kate was there to lean a shoulder in against him so he did not fall, but kept moving along the treacherous path. Each time, he would grunt a quiet, "Thanks, Kate" for her ears only, excruciating pain etched into his whisper, but he was determined that their captors not know the extent of his suffering, which they surely would somehow exploit. For his part, Paxton stumbled along as if in a trance.

The mountainside sloped gently, but the thickening of the forest was dramatic, hardwood trees and teak cloaked in darkness. Trees to either side of the trail were towering giant pillars. The trail became more winding.

After awhile, the bandits grew tired of the harassing. They continued on in silence, except for Han Ling's occasional snarled command, indicating a change in direction when they reached a fork in the trail. A jab with the barrel of his M16 into the back of the nearest prisoner would emphasize a new direction to take.

They continued on for what Kate's wristwatch indicated was about forty minutes. From time to time, a helicopter gunship could be heard rotoring overhead. The forest was dense, the treetops meeting far overhead. The choppers would eventually fly away.

During one such flyover, Kate asked Scott, "What do you make of it, Commander?"

"Han and his boys aren't concerned," Scott mumbled through teeth clenched against pain, "so why should we be?"

"Whoever brought us down," she mused, "someone's catching hell back at that landing field."

Scott grunted. "Never underestimate an American space shuttle crew. They should have had their choppers in the air. Then they could've followed us. They lost time, and we used it to cover up and evacuate." Weary to the bone, he sighed. "Poor Terri. Damn, I hate to lose her."

Bob Paxton continued stumbling along like a zombie. Only his eyes seemed fully awake, continuing to anxiously flit about.

Ahead of them, the point man halted where the trail crested a hill. He whispered a frantic, low-pitched warning and dived into foliage along the trail. Kate heard what the point man heard: the clumping of feet, a small group of men advancing toward them from beyond the crest of the hill, advancing at a good clip. Kate heard snippets of conversation in Korean, and that universal clinking and clanking of field-outfitted soldiers on patrol.

The bandits reacted with speed and silence, accustomed to eluding and surviving in this hostile wilderness. Han flung himself at the clustered Americans, knocking Kate, Scott, and Paxton collectively off their feet, into the brush. Han landed atop Kate. Scott was gasping in agony. Paxton's ragged breathing sounded like he was having a panic attack. The undergrowth clawed at Kate's face. Han snarled in Korean.

Scott started to translate. "He says—"

"I think I know what he said." Kate spoke with difficulty because of the foul-smelling bandit atop her. "Stay down and keep quiet or we'll be the first to die."

* * *

Bol Rhee's patrol had seen no trace of a space shuttle. They had seen nothing but inhospitable, uninhabited, rugged terrain, and Bol expected nothing but hours more of the same before the afternoon rendezvous with a gunship that would transport them back to the base. His platoon was traveling at combat intervals along the winding path. He overheard the muttering of his men, the eternal soldier's lament about the cold, the sore feet, hunger and sleep deprivation. He was not inclined to quell these grumblings, as he felt much the same.

He walked next to the radio man, though he knew full well that there was no way a helicopter gunship could be called in, considering the density of the surrounding forest.

His platoon was cresting a ridge when a figure unexpectedly jumped from the trail—shouting, screaming, and gesticulating wildly—startling everybody. A man, blond-haired and wild-eyed, came running at them. Blood was smeared across his pale face. He came, shouting in what Bol recognized as English, though he did not understand the language. Screams seemed to be of warning.

Something was not right. Bol opened his mouth to order his men to fall back, to seek cover. Saffron muzzle flashes spat like fiery arrows from either side of the trail. Next to Bol, the radioman's head exploded, spraying Bol's face with hot droplets of blood. He darted for cover with his men, some of whom were falling, mowed down under the hellish onslaught. Bol and a few others managed to return fire.

Chapter Eight

For what seemed like forever, Kate did not know if she was alive or dead. Her senses were pummeled by the astoundingly loud, blazing gunfire that made her body tremble and her mind tumble. Is this what dying was like? Paxton had broken from cover. Han had shouted an order at his men. Then the gunfire, the racket intensified by the closeness of towering trees.

She was not dying. She smelled the gunpowder. She heard the screams of those dying, and other, strangely magnified, smaller sounds like the clinking of spent brass cartridge casings striking the ground.

The gunfire ceased. She was alive. She opened her eyes, raised her head and observed her surroundings, struggling to regain her senses.

Scott was beside her, doing much the same. Han Ling stood in the center of the path, reloading an ammo clip into his rifle. Then Kate saw the tangled cluster of fallen bodies sprawled across the trail ahead, dead arms and legs askew.

Paxton emerged from the side of the trail, looking completely disoriented. His blond hair was matted with dirt, his face streaked with sweat. He took one look at the remains of the army patrol and stumbled back, emitting a frightened, child-like yip. Han's outlaws were prying amid the corpses, relieving the dead of weapons, ammunitions, wallets and watches. Paxton turned unsteadily to face Han, his eyes glazed with panic.

The instant Kate saw Paxton, she was consumed with a blinding rage. As if catapulted, she charged at Paxton, both of her hands held up like claws. "You bastard! What the hell did you think you were doing? He said he was going to kill me!"

Paxton held up his bloodied arms to ward her off. But her onslaught was interrupted when Han threw back his head, blustering out an alcoholic sound that must have been laughter. The bandit placed his stolid body in the center of the path, blocking her trajectory. She caught herself, halting her momentum and pulling back, trying to acknowledge the sliver of sanity that was screaming for recognition within her. She drew another deep breath, held it and, when she exhaled, her rage was vanquished, her emotions again under control.

When he was through laughing, Han spoke to Scott, who was hobbling more noticeably than before, favoring his splinted, broken leg. Though Scott's eyes were clear, Kate clearly saw that he was far worse for the wear. His shoulders sagged. Their commander was growing weaker by the minute. Haltingly, he translated what Han Ling had just said. "We're only alive because he was told by his leader to find us and bring us back alive."

Kate concentrated on keeping her eyes and her thoughts away from Paxton. "Then it was just luck—our bad luck and their good luck—that they found us?"

"Seems that way." Scott turned his attention to Paxton, glaring his displeasure. "That was a goddamn bonehead move, Specialist, almost getting us all killed. When we do get home, you're going to be in it real deep, mister."

Paxton cowered, eyes looking toward the ground. "I was only trying to help."

Before Paxton could say anything further, Scott's knees buckled. The commander's eyes rolled back in his head. He started to collapse.

Kate moved forward, placing her shoulder under one of his. She was able to prop Scott up, but not without effort.

She snarled at Paxton, "Get your ass over here and help."

Paxton scampered forward to prop up Scott from the other side. "Kate, I'm sorry. I thought I'd get those soldiers to help us. I knew that bandit wouldn't kill you."

"Like hell you did."

Scott's drooping head hung between them like an eavesdropping presence.

Paxton was slowly regaining some of his trained, professional steadiness, as well as a vaguely defensive tone. "So why didn't he shoot you?"

"You didn't know what he was going to do or what he wasn't going to do." She eyed Paxton with pure loathing. "You put my life on the line, you chickenshit. Now stop talking to me. You make me sick."

Han Ling may not have understood English, but he

understood the substance of their exchange, and found this amusing. He threw his head back for more unsavory hoots into the air.

The march continued. They worked their way up and around the mountain. Gray fingers of dawn slanted through the forest. The climb became more difficult. There was no further conversation between Kate and Bob Paxton. Scott remained unconscious, a dead weight balanced between them, his feet dragging. It was a torturous trek, prodded by the guns of the bandits who were emboldened and celebratory after having wiped out an army patrol.

Lost in a nightmare, thought Kate. There was no trail that she could see. And yet they were being shoved along one rocky slope after another. The here and now was inescapable, and yet in ways was incomprehensible. Did anyone know where she was? She was adapting, she was improvising, as Trev had taught her. Paxton was right about that much, at least. This was never covered in astronaut training. Where were they being taken? What would happen next? The weight of Commander Scott, being dragged between her and Paxton uphill, was beginning to take its toll. She fought a numbness that wanted to weaken her, sapping her strength with every struggling step, causing her to falter.

She wanted this madness to end. She wanted to return to the "real world," where once upon a time . . . once upon a time . . .

Once upon a time, a child named Kathryn sat with her mom and dad in front of a television set in their suburban home when she was only five—one of the clearest memories of her childhood—watching a man in a spacesuit walking on the moon. This had led her to a lifelong dual fascination with flying and outer space. As soon as she was old enough, she enrolled in a flying class for seven dollars an hour, and each Saturday for six months she had flown in the front seat of an old gray and maroon single-engine, dual-control Aeronca Champion. Working nights and weekends to pay for her college had not curtailed her flight time. By her senior year, she had become known as Kate, and had enlisted in an ROTC program that paid some of the expenses toward a doctorate in engineering, in exchange for four years of military service after graduation. She had applied for, and, after rigorous screening and testing, been accepted into the space program. Following her honorable discharge, the initial whirlwind of training—rides in T-38 jets and weightless training rides in the KC-135 "vomit comet"—settled down to classroom lectures on engineering and computer science: charts, manuals and diagrams about every inch of a space shuttle. After a year of classroom training had come the yearlong apprenticeship to veteran astronauts, who had taught her those engineering tasks that would be her responsibility on a shuttle flight. For months her schedule was a blur of fifteen-hour days, of grueling, round-the-clock sessions in shuttle simulators, interspersed with visits to contractors' factories to see equipment, technical briefings and the endless task of studying stacks of manuals that outlined every minute of a flight.

The workaholic grind took its toll. During her time at the Johnson Space Center in Houston, eleven astronauts dropped out, every one of them citing the pressure on their family life. Her own marriage had not gone unaffected, but the troubles with Trev had been there from almost the start. They had been separated for over a year now, but she did not blame the space program for that. Her work had only sped up what seemed to be the inevitable.

Three days earlier, when she and the crew had flown from Houston to the Cape in a NASA jet and she'd seen *Liberty* for the first time, she had known that it was all worth it. Not just the tradeoff from her troubled marriage but all those years of dreams and struggles leading up to her first view of the shuttle, mounted to its 154-foot rust-colored external fuel tank and twin 149-foot white-colored solid-rocket boosters. Of course, all of that had occurred in the normal, "real world" . . . not upon a desolate, wooded mountain-side, on the other side of the world, herded along by rifle-carrying bandits.

I will survive, she assured herself. But inside, she felt as bleak as their surroundings. Could Houston possibly have any clue as to where we are? She didn't think so. Plodding along, she realized that allowing her mind to drift into the past had served to distract her from her aches and exhaustion. But she was pushing the limits of her endurance.

The huffing, puffing and lagging Bob Paxton wasn't doing any better. Even the bandits had grown quiet and surly as the arduous trek continued uphill.

Her nostrils twitched, her senses perked, at a first awareness of the scent of cooking food. Something unidentifiable, but definitely edible . . . a hallucination born of fatigue? She smelled it again, carried on an errant, nippy morning breeze . . . definitely the aroma of something cooking! Granite ledges rose above them to either side of a narrowing cut in the land.

Then they rounded a bend and left the heavy timber, and there before them was what she could only think of as a fortress.

Chapter Nine

The site occupied acres of a mountainside clearing, which looked out above the sheer wall of a cliff that dropped straight down for five hundred feet to the valley floor. The clearing was hemmed in tight on three sides against a severely sloped flange of a valley in such a way that this "hideout" could not be seen from the air. The camp gave every indication of having been long established: an organized scatter of clapboard barracks, equipment of every sort stacked everywhere, with random cooking fires and clusters of men clad similarly to Han and his crew.

Trudging along, Kate found herself to be fully awake. Next to her, Paxton muttered his surprise at the sight suddenly revealed to them. They picked up their pace by unspoken mutual consent, the dead weight of Scott being carried between them. On their way into the camp, they passed sentries who shouted familiar greetings to Han, and made obvious sexual insults directed at Kate. For the first time since this ordeal had begun, she was glad that she didn't speak their language.

They passed scores of bandits, some cleaning their dismantled weapons, others lounging or seeing to various tasks. At least fifty men were visible at any given time, but no women. A surly, mismatched crew, each man was heavily armed; she saw pistols, rifles and automatic weapons of every description. Bunkers were along the edge of the cliff. She observed four-barreled anti-aircraft artillery. She saw a pair of military half-ton trucks parked at a big hole that had been burrowed into the face of the cliff. Behind the trucks was what looked like a well-stocked arms and munitions depot.

The center of activity was the mouth of a cave in the rim-rock formation. Their group was led into the cave, entering a natural corridor of stone, large enough to drive a car through. Like the terrorist caves that the American military had gone after in Afghanistan, this cave complex was cut deep into the mountain to avoid flyover thermal detection. The air in the tunnel was fresh, which bespoke hydroelectric power that ran a ventilation system and kept the lights on.

Several yards in, they came to a well-lighted, spacious cavern with a naturally vaulted ceiling, and an impressive if primitive array of appointments, such as animal skin rugs and rough-hewn, bulky wooden furniture, all of it well-lighted by oil lamps affixed to the cavern walls.

The sole occupant of this cavern was a man who lounged indolently on what could only be described as a throne—a tall-backed chair on a raised dais—set against a wall opposite the entrance. The man took a long pull on an aluminum can of beer and tossed the empty can over his shoulder. He wiped the back of a soiled sleeve across his bearded mouth and observed

Han Ling and his men as they herded the three Americans in. Like Han, the man on the throne was not Korean, and he was older than any of the other men, in his mid-thirties. He had the more finely-boned physique of the Chinese, but because of his muscular build, he presented the impression of being a large man. Kate wondered what his background could be. There was about him the animal aura of the meanest dog in this pack, and yet she sensed a classical sensibility not far below the surface. This was a man of sharp wits and schooled intelligence, as well as of animal cunning and brute force. There was an old knife scar; five inches in length and a quarter inch in width, bisecting one side of his face. A headband held back long hair that glistened with grease.

When the Americans could advance no farther without tripping onto the dais, Han shouted what was obviously an order for them to halt. Without losing his indolent posture, slumped with one leg tossed out straight, both hands on the arms of his throne, the man issued a quiet directive. Han moved with dispatch to return with a metal folding chair that he set down for Scott. Kate and Paxton managed to get Scott into a sitting position on the chair.

Kate straightened, feeling renewed energy flowing back into her psyche and her body now that she had been unburdened. She and Paxton both stretched their overworked muscles, but they had been trained to endure rugged physical challenge. She stood at Scott's side with her arm on the flight commander's shoulder, so as to steady him from falling. Scott groaned fitfully, exhibiting no indication of regaining consciousness. She lifted her chin, making eye contact with the man on the throne.

"I don't know if you speak English, but I want to

thank you for this small courtesy." She nodded to the seated, unconscious Scott. She realized belatedly that her hands were clenched into fists. She unclenched them and continued in what she hoped came across as a cordial, reasonable tone. "We are American citizens, and we—"

"I know exactly who you are, dear lady." He spoke with an Oxford accent that sounded weirdly out of place. "Would you like to know, perhaps, who I am?"

She tried not to appear taken aback at the culture and sophistication in his voice.

"Of course."

"I am Chai Bin. I command here."

"I had assumed that much." She meant to reflect his coolness. It was an impossible task, of course. Panic was a mad beast gnawing at her sanity.

He arose from the throne. Paxton, standing directly before the dais, his face bloodied and nose puffy and inflamed, flinched before the abrupt movement as if he'd been physically slapped. Chai sniggered. He shifted his attention to the woman. He easily saw through her façade of outer courage. And yet he found himself entranced, if that was the word, for she seemed at once a female combatant while exhibiting the maternal instinct, resting her hand on the shoulder of the unconscious man. Chai found himself strangely infatuated. It had been so long since his days at Oxford that he had almost forgotten the confidence and forthrightness of Western women, behavior unknown, unthought of, by the women of his culture. He had often wondered what he would have become if he had stayed in the West. A successful, married, driven capitalist, perhaps? His family in Beijing had purchased for him the best education the world could provide, thanks to considerable bribery and bureaucratic sleight of hand between Beijing, Hong Kong and the West. But after his return to China came enlistment in the military, the career expected of a young man of his class. He'd shown scant capacity for military discipline, yet it was wholly in his nature to command.

He pounded his chest with the palm of his hand. "I am a renegade from the Chinese army. The North Koreans have had a reward on my head for years. The Chinese and North Koreans both call me brilliant . . . and insane, yes. But they have never come close to apprehending me. My men do as they wish along both sides of the border." He saw no reason to brag of his primary source of revenue. He personally oversaw the raising of poppy plants, the production of opium in the fields and the product's transportation and ultimate sale. This revenue subsidized food farms in the region, and the food farms sustained his men. Chai said abruptly, "Identify yourselves."

"I am Kate Daniels, co-pilot of the space shuttle *Liberty*." The woman steadied the unconscious man, propping him in an upright, sitting position in the chair. "This is our commanding officer, Flight Commander Scott." She eyed Paxton, who stepped back a pace under Chai's glare. "And this frightened fool is Specialist Robert Paxton."

Chai chose to address the woman directly, something he would hardly have done had an able-bodied man been present. But their commander was unconscious, and Paxton reminded him of a frightened toad. "And now that I know who you are," he said, "I wish to know precisely where your aircraft is. And you will tell me."

She stood with her feet firmly planted, evidencing a backbone that could have been made of iron. "I don't think I want to tell you, unless you promise to help us."

He sensed that she was gaining inner strength with every passing second. There was something about this foreign Western woman, who had so literally dropped into his world from the sky, that simultaneously provoked, infuriated and aroused him. Chai concealed his aggravation beneath a mien of indolence. "If I do not find your space shuttle, miss, the Chinese army or the North Korean army will. Would that be any better for the United States?"

"That's hardly my decision to make." She indicated the unconscious man beside her. "Commander Scott needs medical attention. We need your assistance. Sir, in the name of the American government, will you help us?"

Chai regarded her, his arms folded, the posture he favored before meting out punishment. Everyone present was holding their breath, waiting for him to lash out at this impudent female who dared display insolence toward Chai Bin. And yet the woman herself seemed oblivious to this. Infuriating, yes. He replied in a sensible tone. "If you were lucky enough to survive the shuttle's crash landing in these mountains, then there will be equipment aboard that also survived. Let us consider a trade, dear lady. Tell me what I want to know, and I will accommodate your every request during what time you are my guests here."

Kate snorted.

Chai continued. "Your commander will be properly cared for, as we have a staff of excellent medics here. And I will arrange for prompt communication with your government."

This took her aback. She blinked in surprise. "You would do this?"

"Why should I not? The equipment aboard that shuttle is of immeasurable worth to all concerned. I intend to give America the first bid, and if that bid is unsatisfactory, I will approach the North Koreans and the Chinese. I daresay they would outbid each other to pay dearly for the technology I would be offering them."

Kate was about to respond angrily when something happened that surprised everyone.

Scott raised his head. His chin had remained slumped against his chest since he'd been dragged in, and he looked as if the act of raising his line of vision to Chai Bin was painfully difficult. There was, however, keenness to his eyes that suggested that he had been conscious for a while and had heard most of what had been said. He stared defiantly at Chai for a moment before he spoke.

"Piss up a rope, Fu Manchu. You're not getting jack shit from us; do what you goddamn well want."

Chai displayed no anger. Instead he addressed the group of Americans in general. "Who among you is in command?"

In a weak voice Scott replied, "I am, damn it!"

Kate glanced down at her commander. "Sir, are you sure about that?"

"I'm sure." The barely-conscious man maintained eye contact with Chai. "I am in command."

"Very well," replied Chai. He nodded to Han.

Han swung the butt of his rifle, hitting Scott along the side of the head, not forcefully enough to knock him unconscious but hard enough to knock him to the floor. Han then placed a boot on Scott's splinted, broken leg.

Kate was already moving toward Han, calling over her shoulder to Paxton. "Bob! What are you waiting for?!"

The scientist, staring pointedly at the ground, pretended not to hear.

Han began grinding his boot heel into Scott's fracture, leaning all of his weight onto the broken leg to inflict more pain than Scott's system could possibly tolerate. The flight commander cried out once, a short yowl of pain, then lost consciousness again. Han Ling whirled, next aiming his rifle at Kate.

From the dais, Chai nodded at Scott's inert and sprawled form. "This man cannot command."

Kate turned to face Chai. "Then I am the ranking officer of the space shuttle *Liberty*, you heartless bastard!"

"You are not in command," Chai said flatly. "You are a woman. A woman is good for only one thing." He scrutinized her from head to toe. Lewd fires shone in his eyes. The corners of his mouth quirked. She felt naked before him. She shivered as if at the callused touch of a rapist's hand. Chai said, "Han, seize her. Bring her to me."

What happened next was instinctual reflex melded with training.

Kate brought up her hands defensively and bent her knees. The weariness of her uninterrupted ordeal—since waking up to an alarm clock that morning at Cape Canaveral (how many lifetimes ago?) until this instant—suddenly vanished. Her estranged husband had instructed her in martial arts, and Trev Galt had been a very good teacher. He had trained in Kung Fu at the Shaolin Temple off Victoria Road in Hong Kong, personally taught by the Tung-Chia, the Master of the Temple. The deal struck between Kate and Trev was that, in return, she would teach him gourmet cooking. However, Trev quickly lost interest; he was a hopeless beer-and-ham-sandwich man, not a gourmet. But his instruction in the martial arts continued during their years together.

The sight of a woman preparing to defend herself in such a manner made Han Ling guffaw in shared amusement with his boss's obvious snickering. Han then returned to the business at hand, snapping a command at his three men who moved swiftly toward her, one coming in from behind, another rushing in from the left, and the third approaching from the right.

She drew a deep breath and delivered a direct kick to the solar plexus of the man behind her, exhaling as she struck his body, instantly paralyzing him. He crashed to the ground even as she whirled to face the next man who was almost upon her, his rough hands reaching for her throat. She deflected his attack with her left arm, and with an explosive yell, dealt him a *seiken* fist blow to the Adam's apple. Choking and fighting for breath, the man collapsed, sagging backward. Kate readjusted her feet and swiveled to smash the third man a killing blow to the forehead. Then she wheeled around to resettle into her original defensive position, facing Han and Chai.

Chai had stopped laughing. "Most impressive, Miss Daniels."

"It's called equality." She spoke calmly and was not out of breath. "Where I come from, sometimes the girls have to beat up bad boys."

Bob Paxton was watching all of this with wide-eyed, slack-jawed amazement. "Kate, what are you—"

She did not have time for him right now. The adrenaline was pumping through her every fiber; yet her exterior countenance appeared relaxed, yet strong and alert. Push your advantage, Trev had taught her. Never let up. Without relaxing her combat stance, she directed her focus to Chai.

"Must the mighty warlord take a puny woman by force?"

Han stiffened and implored something of his leader. Kate couldn't understand their language, but she followed Han's intent. He was asking Chai Bin for permission to blow her brains out on the spot. After hearing Han out, Chai raised a hand in a placating gesture and spoke to her in English.

"You are indeed most impressive."

She released herself from her martial arts stance, absently brushing away a stray wisp of chestnut hair that had fallen across her forehead. "Have you not thought of the obvious, Chai Bin?"

His furry eyebrows creased in a frown. "Share your thoughts with me, woman."

"You were talking about the equipment aboard the shuttle, of selling it to the Chinese or the North Koreans."

"I was."

"Well, why deal with your enemies? You can't be high on the popularity list of either one of those countries."

He sighed. "Sad, so sad, but true." In a mock display of chagrin he gazed toward the ceiling, then abruptly shot his glare back at her. "Your point being . . . ?"

"My point being," she replied with an exaggerated show of patience, "why put yourself at risk? Why not deal with the rightful owners of the shuttle? Why not ransom it and us back to the United States government?"

Chai studied her, stroking his chin, no longer amused, nor lewd. "The Americans have no love of me, either. I hold you as my hostages. Unlike the Chinese or the North Koreans, your government could possess the power to destroy me."

"The power, yes . . ." she conceded, "but not the will. My government will do anything to get the *Liberty* back. I can assure you that they do not want it falling into the hands of the Chinese or the Koreans. Anyone who prevents that from happening will be considered America's friend, not their enemy! Okay, maybe 'ransom' was the wrong word . . . what I mean to say is that you negotiate with the government for the return of the shuttle and for us."

Bob Paxton stepped forward, his face pale. "Kate, are you sure this is what the commander would want?"

Commander Scott's voice croaked thinly from the floor behind them. "I'll damn sure tell you what I want. We give these bastards nothing!" Scott remained stretched out on the earthen floor, too weak to rise. He propped himself up on one elbow.

Kate crossed over to kneel beside him and placed a hand on his shoulder. "Commander, please. You have to trust me. I'm assuming command. I have to do what I think is best."

He stared up at her uncertainly. "And what do you think is best, Kate?"

Overhearing this, Chai stepped down from the dais. "Young lady, I have considered. And I agree. You are right. I will do as you suggest. But first, of course, I must know the location of the shuttle."

Kate remained at Scott's side, returning Chai's gaze. "I'll show you."

Paxton muttered under his breath, "Traitorous bitch!"

Chai threw his head back and enjoyed another

hearty laugh. "Mr. Paxton, I recommend that you mind your manners. Has not the lady proven herself to be of considerable personal resource?" He glanced around at the sprawl of men she'd taken down. "Miss Daniels is prone to respond severely when displeased. If I were you, I'd mind what I said!"

Scott reached up with tremendous effort and placed a hand weakly on her arm. "Kate, please. Don't. . . ." His touch was so feeble that she barely felt it. His voice was so faint, she could hardly hear it.

She leaned forward, lowering her voice for his ears alone. "Commander, please trust me. I don't see that we have a choice. I know what I'm doing."

This communication, beyond Chai's earshot, elicited a snort of displeasure from him. "Enough. There will be no delay. You have yourself a deal, as you Americans say."

He barked a command to Han, who responded by smashing the butt of his rifle into the back of Bob Paxton's head. Paxton grunted and collapsed to his knees, his head hanging. His body rocked back and forth.

Kate heard Scott's soft words to her. "Kate, don't trust these bastards. Whatever you do, don't show them where *Liberty* is!"

Chai lashed out with a boot, kicking Scott in the temple. Scott's eyes again rolled back in his head, and once again he passed out. Then Kate felt violated before the naked, direct gaze of Chai Bin.

"And now, dear lady, considering your, uh, proficiency in the martial arts, we will summon a unit of men who will accompany us. And remember, no martial artist can outfight a well-aimed bullet. In any event, I never leave here without my bodyguards. I have enemies in these mountains who would like very much to see my head on a pole. Do you understand?"

"Believe me," said Kate, "I understand."

Chai nodded agreeably. "Very well. You will lead us to your precious space shuttle, and you will not try any tricks. If you do, I can assure you, Miss Daniels, that you will pray for death for a very long time before you die. Come, we prepare for departure."

Chapter Ten

Washington, DC

"So much for rehearsing tomorrow's press conference," grumbled the president. He eyed the street scene sailing past outside the limo's tinted windows. "There's no way we can contain what's happened. And with our nuclear forces at DefCon Three, it is time the people were told."

Galt frowned from where he rode in a seat facing the president. "Sir, have you considered that going public will endanger our rescue and retrieval of the shuttle?" He had been summoned to join this motorcade en route from a scheduled media event where the president had addressed a national convention of high school honor students.

The convention was only eight blocks from the White House, but moving POTUS (President of the United States, in White House-speak) always required a security package minimum of six black-windowed vans and SUV's to sandwich the limo as the motorcade traveled a cordoned-off route.

Wil Fleming, the president's chief of staff, rode beside the president. He pocketed a cell phone, having fielded a call, and reinserted himself into the conversation as if he hadn't missed hearing a thing. The chief of staff runs the West Wing of the White House, and parcels out the president's personal time. Fleming was short, trim and dapper, age thirty-something. "I understand that you have a very personal stake in this, Galt, in that your wife is among the missing crew personnel. Believe me, we are utilizing every means necessary to—"

"Save it for the sound bites," said Galt.

He had never cared for Fleming. The president's fair-haired boy had political savvy and vision aplenty, but Galt had never trusted people, like Fleming, who reached maturity without any lines creasing their faces.

The president made an irritated sound. "Knock it off, both of you. I know you don't like each other. No one said you had to. But we do have to work together on this. Trev, you've got to ratchet down. Wil is right on this one. We have every ball in play, and you know it."

Galt nodded. "My people are monitoring every *Liberty*-related report as it comes in, sir. My wife and the crew could be just as dead as the crew aboard *Challenger. Liberty* could have smashed into those mountains and ended up in a million pieces."

"Trev, don't do this to yourself."

"I'm just being realistic." Galt turned to the chief of staff. "And yeah, Wil, you're right. It's personal with me, big time. But considering who I am and what I do, is that a bad thing?"

Fleming bristled. "We've mobilized every resource

available, as the president said. Why must we repeat ourselves?"

The motorcade wheeled onto Pennsylvania Avenue.

Galt returned his attention to the president. "Sir, there was a Defense System Satellite onboard *Liberty*. If there's any of it left intact, that satellite needs to be retrieved ASAP before the neighborhood bad boys over there get their hands on it. If North Korea or the Chinese gain possession of that technology, the world will become a different place. The potential is there to set back U.S. electronic warfare capabilities by a decade."

Fleming's cell phone beeped. He reached for it, glaring at Galt angrily. "Do you think that we haven't considered that? Do you think we're not keeping every option on the table? Jesus, Galt, you're impossible." He shifted his focus to a muted telephone conversation without waiting for a response.

The president reached over and placed a hand on Galt's arm. "Trev, I sent for you because I want you to get this not just as an order from your commander in chief." The president's eyes crinkled with the trace of a grin. "I know you well enough to know that you'd disobey even a direct order like that, if you felt strongly enough about something, as you do in this case."

"Sir—"

"Let me finish. So I'm not only issuing an order as your commander in chief. I'm telling you man-to-man. Fleming's right about us working all of the angles. We're leaving every option open. But I will not have you screwing things up with some cowboy play. You're right. Either Kate is dead or she's over there on the other side of the world, maybe in hostile hands. But you are not going to go off half-cocked. I will not have you disobey these orders the way you did that day when you saved my ass."

Galt looked outside. The security gatehouse, then the grounds of the White House, rolled past beyond the limo's windows. "Uh, sir, I thought we weren't ever going to mention that."

Fleming completed his telephone call. Again, he seemed not to have missed a word of their conversation. He eyed Galt with an openly bug-eyed surprise not generally associated with chiefs of staff. "You saved the president's life?!"

Galt sighed. "I had to. He wasn't the president then, and he owed me forty bucks from a poker game the night before we went out on that patrol."

The president chuckled. "I was his commanding officer that day, too. A long time ago, eh, Trev?" The limo gracefully coasted to a stop beneath a portico at a side entrance of the White House. "First day of a big offensive," continued the president. "Things stabilized pretty fast, but at first it was nothing but bullets and blood and confusion out there in that desert. Me and Trev, our unit, was ambushed." The president grimaced. "My own damn fault, and I was the only one wounded, which was fitting enough. Still got a piece of shrapnel that almost put me away. Anyway, they had the unit pinned down pretty good for awhile, and I'm lying in the middle of a clearing between two sand dunes with my guts hanging out of the hole in my belly."

In his time as chief of staff, this was obviously the first Fleming had heard of his boss's combat experience. Wil sat there as if seeing the chief executive for the first time.

Galt felt acute embarrassment. "Uh, sir—"

"Ah, let me finish, Trev. So I'm lying there, with bullets flying all around, and the rest of the guys are pinned down under heavy fire. In my mind there's no damn doubt whatsoever that I'm about to become a dead man. But I'm lucid enough to hear Galt yelling at the other guys to give him cover fire, that he's going to pull me in. About then I start to notice that I'm the only one who wasn't fast enough on his feet, or lucky enough. So I start shouting, or trying to shout, ordering Galt to stay put." A hint of humor touched the president's eyes. "Uh, I forget, Trev, what was it you yelled to me that time when I gave you that direct order?"

Outside the limo, aides and staffers waited for the president and his party to emerge.

"Uh, I'd rather not say, sir."

The president chortled mildly. "Galt's response," he told Fleming, "was, and I quote: 'Fuck you, sir!'—whereupon he proceeded to make the crab-crawl out from under cover and pull me back out of the line of incoming fire." The president studied Galt. "You sustained a wound that day that put you out of action for eight weeks."

Galt brought his attention back to the man across from him. "I was out eight weeks. You were six months on the mend, sir. And some orders are easier to follow than others."

Fleming now regarded Galt as though through a new set of eyes. "You saved the president's life in combat? But your name doesn't appear in any of the files on the president's service. I mean everyone knows what happened to you, sir. I never knew that it was Galt who—"

The corners of the president's eyes crinkled. "Sort of

explains why I take so much crap from him, doesn't it?" Then he became serious again. "Trev, I believe you were disobeying orders that day because you had a vested interest in keeping me alive, namely that forty bucks. Well, you've got a vested interest with *Liberty*. You want to go over there and tear apart that countryside, looking for Kate. And because you're our top covert ops man, you've got the means to do it. But my direct order to you is this: don't. I don't need a wild card in this mix, screwing things up and maybe getting Kate and any other crew survivors killed in the process."

Galt nodded glumly. "Sir, that consideration is the only thing keeping me out of it. Damn it, sir, they've got Kate! I've got to do something about that!"

The president sent Galt a small, grim smile. "And I've got something for you to do. I've been saving the best for last. The FBI in Houston has detained a man. His name . . . uh, what's his name, Wil?"

Fleming piped up promptly, "Fraley, sir. Eliot Fraley." He added for Galt's benefit, "A scientist at Mission Control. Someone got to him. They used a woman. Got him to reprogram the computers, and that's what brought down the shuttle."

Galt's eyes narrowed. "Who got to him?"

The president muttered a very unpolitician-like curse. "That's still a blind alley. The woman says she took orders from, and got paid by, a contact that she never met and knew nothing about. She says the contact passed her the data that Fraley programmed into the computer to alter the shuttle's course. That contact has not as yet been traced."

Galt tugged an earlobe. "What about Fraley?"

The president sighed. "So far, our people on the

scene—that is, the FBI—have not been able to get Fraley to confess to anything. We've got them both. We're keeping them separated, of course, but as long as he keeps mum, she can clam up while her contact wipes out the trail."

"She's a pro," Fleming told Galt. "She's copped only to what she knows we've got on her. If we can get Fraley to crack, he'll give us the leverage to use, and we'll trace this contact."

The president glanced up at the towering edifice of the White House beyond the limo's tinted windows. "You see where we're going with this, right, Trev? You've just been given your job: make Fraley talk."

"A jet will have me to Houston inside the hour," replied Galt.

"Break Fraley." The president's statement was as cold as ice. "Get him to tell us everything he knows. This is top priority on the home front, Trev. And the job is yours alone. See that it gets done."

"Yes, sir."

Johnson Space Center, Houston, Texas

Galt stood amid a cluster of FBI personnel outside the nine-by-ten room, observing Fraley's interrogation through one-way glass. The bombardment of questions from the pair of interrogators was drawing repeated, robotic denials.

Fraley's bow tie was askew. His physique was diminutive, but his expression was defiant. He sat on a metal chair at a metal table, the only pieces of furniture in the room that was walled on one side by the pane of glass.

"There's no way you can make me confess to anything," he told the FBI agents who were questioning him. "I see no reason to implicate my wife. You know very well that she's an invalid in need of constant care. I have placed her in an assisted living facility that will provide her with the best treatment." Fraley smiled smugly. "You gentlemen might as well give up."

Galt had arrived minutes earlier, attired in sharply-pressed army green fatigues and spit-shined combat boots. He was armed with the 9mm Beretta pistol in an unconcealed shoulder holster. He broke away from the cluster of agents in the hallway, and stormed into the interrogation room.

The men in the room wheeled around in surprise. Galt knew the agents, but they didn't know him. Leaving the door open behind him, he said, "Mr. Fraley, the FBI giving up is not an option."

The agent named Jackson strode over to stand toe-to-toe with Galt, radiating displeasure. He was Galt's height and size, every ounce of it solid black muscle.

"And who the hell might you be?"

The other agent, Chalmers, patted his partner on the shoulder. "Slow down, Claude. We've been trying to crack this nut for hours. Let's give someone else a chance."

Galt returned Jackson's stare without blinking. "I'm cleared. Check with your supervisor. I'm taking custody of this man." Galt turned to Fraley. "On your feet. We're out of here."

Fraley became animated, leaping up out of his chair. "About fucking time." He did not sound at all like a space scientist. He sounded like a snide little man.

A four-lane highway, designated NASA Road 1, links the space center to Interstate 45 and a twenty-five-mile drive to downtown Houston. Road 1 is lined with strip malls, condominium developments, car dealerships, fast food outlets, motels, even a dog track. Beyond this, unbridled suburban sprawl stretches south to the Gulf of Mexico.

Galt drove wordlessly, both of his hands on the steering wheel, eyes staring straight ahead as he piloted the Jeep Cherokee through moderate traffic. He kept to the slow lane, holding the speed steady at five miles over the posted limit.

Fraley rode beside him. The cherubic face, beneath the balding thatch of untamed curls, shone with agitation. Though he wore a seat belt, Fraley had positioned himself sideways in his bucket seat, the better to observe Galt through his thick, rimless glasses.

"I don't know who you are, but thank you for coming to get me out of there."

Galt didn't take his eyes off the road. When he saw what he was looking for, he began braking the Jeep.

"Don't thank me, little man."

"I, uh, don't believe I caught your name."

"I didn't give it. It doesn't matter."

The Cherokee turned off the main road, onto and following a gravel road to behind a strip mall, where the ground dropped slightly beneath a row of Dumpsters, removing them from sight of anyone in the strip mall stores or behind the mall, and from sight of the traffic passing by on the busy interstate.

Fraley stammered briefly, then said, "Uh, I don't mean to be unappreciative or anything but, uh, would you mind if I asked to see some identification?"

Galt braked the Cherokee to a stop. He shut off the engine. The air became very quiet. The hiss of tires from the highway was barely audible. A bird chirped from a treetop.

Galt turned to face Fraley. His eyes were chips of ice. "Get out."

Fraley's eyes became round. "Now wait a minute, mister—"

Galt unholstered the 9mm pistol. He reached across and almost idly swatted Fraley across the face with the gun barrel. "I said get the fuck out."

Fraley squealed. The swipe had laid open a gash along the top of his balding pate. He scrambled, tumbling out from his side of the vehicle.

Galt came around the front, chambering a round into the pistol.

Fraley had landed on his knees in the brown clay. When Galt walked up to him, Fraley made no attempt to rise, or to straighten the eyeglasses that had nearly slipped from his nose. He was shuddering with fear, and tried twice to speak before he managed to croak pathetically, "Please . . ."

Galt extended his arm so that the muzzle of the 9mm was drawing a bead on the bridge of Fraley's nose. "Beg if you want to. I don't give a shit, if that's how you want to check out."

Fraley's Adam's apple bobbed. "But the government would never sanction this!"

Galt chucked, a low and nasty sound. "You don't think so? You don't think this doesn't happen any damn time someone important enough wants it to happen? Think again, chump! A traitor like you, bought off this high in the space program, that's a major embarrassment. Did you think the powers that be were just going to sit around with egg on their face?"

The gash in Fraley's scalp leaked a rivulet of blood that dripped into his eyes. Being this close to death seemed to inspire bravado from his humbled kneeling position in the dirt. "Go ahead. Pull the goddamn trigger. Damn your eyes. You've got Connie. Go on, mister executioner. You'll be doing me a favor. I'm confessing nothing."

Galt laughed, but the stony lines of his face did not change. "Good for you, Doc. I like a guy who can check out in style. Thanks for making it easy. I've got a busy night. We're wiping the slate on you. The spin will be that the shuttle went down because of a mechanical failure, not because they let a rotten apple in NASA who sabotaged it. It's going to be like you and your wife never existed."

Fraley blinked, and it wasn't because there was blood dripping into his eye. The bravado vanished. "My wife? Nora?"

Galt started to ever-so-slightly tighten his finger around the trigger, and he knew that Fraley would clearly see the whitening of the knuckle. "Yeah, that'd be her, unless of course you've got more than one wife. They're erasing every trace of you, Doc, and of course that includes the missus. Oh, yeah, I forgot. You thought you had her hidden away someplace, all nice and safe where we couldn't find her." Galt snickered. "You pathetic shit. It took five minutes to pin the health care dump where you stashed her. Doc. Haven't you heard of Big Brother? He knows everything, Fraley. Say goodbye, chump. And when you get to the other side, just wait up. The missus will be right along. They tell me that the old bag is three-quarters dead anyway."

Fraley appeared numbed by this new twist, as Galt meant him to be. "No, wait. Nora had nothing to do with this!"

"She had the misfortune of marrying a dipshit like you," said Galt coldly, "before she ended up a paraplegic in that accident. And you were running out on her for a slant hooch who showed you some new positions. So why the fuck should you care about your wife now?"

The fact of the matter was that no one, including Galt, had a clue as to Nora Fraley's whereabouts. Fraley had done a good job of hiding her.

Tears began pouring down his cheeks, tears becoming pink when mingling with the blood flowing across his face from his scalp wound. "God, no. Please. I love Nora. I just—wasn't strong enough to resist, God forgive me." Galt's gun was forgotten. Fraley sobbed, blubbering, his head hanging. "Please don't kill Nora, I beg of you! I'll do anything. Anything." He brought his face up to meet Galt's eyes. "You want me to confess."

Galt stared unflinchingly along the length of his arm and the gun barrel. "Well?"

"Yes!" The kneeling man spread his arms and wailed. "Yes, yes, yes! For godsakes yes, if it means saving Nora!"

"And what are you confessing to, exactly?"

"You know what I did." Fraley's words cut through his crying. "God help me, I altered the computer guidance data, the way Connie asked me to. Oh, God . . . God help me." His sobbing increased, and no further discernable words were forthcoming.

Galt remained where he stood over the kneeling, weeping man. He lowered the pistol to his side. He spoke into the microphone taped under his shirt. "Get that?"

"Got it," Jackson's reply came through the mini-receiver that was invisible to the naked eye, in Galt's left ear.

Galt was mildly irritated at having to converse with

a voice inside his head. "Get yourselves over here. I've got some garbage for you to pick up." He tugged the transceiver out of his ear and dropped it into a pocket.

Jackson and Chalmers would be closing in fast along NASA Road 1, coming to take Fraley back into their custody.

Fraley still hadn't moved from kneeling upon the ground, and he hadn't stopped blubbering. "Oh my God, how could I have done it? How, dear Lord, how?"

Disgust snaked through Galt. "Ask Him when you see Him. In the meantime, here's a message from the astronauts on that space shuttle." He slapped the side of Fraley's head with the pistol hard enough to knock Fraley out cold. Fraley pitched onto his face. Galt holstered the pistol. He left Fraley where he was and returned to the Cherokee.

A mild Texas wind had picked up.

CHAPTER ELEVEN

North Korea

Ahn Chong knew that something was wrong even before he reached the cave. The sun was in the sky, but it was what the chilly sunshine did not reveal that troubled him. He crouched behind a tree, viewing the camouflaged cave entrance. He saw the rocky, craggy outcrop of boulders where foliage overgrew the narrow fault in the stony surface just behind some dense thickets. He did not see a lookout. The astronauts would surely have had one of their number posted as a lookout, thought Ahn. Yet he sensed no human presence awaiting his return to the cave where he had left the Americans. It was troubling. He advanced from tree to tree, taking a circuitous route to the cave entrance.

He had discreetly left the village, while the other residents went about their daily chores. They allowed him this freedom out of respect for his years. He left carrying a sack of picked vegetables and soy cakes, taking care to make certain that he was not followed. About dawn, the rumblings of helicopters had ceased. Ahn could guess about the air traffic. The commander of the air base had blanketed the countryside with patrols, searching for the shuttle. Ahn had taken longer than he would have preferred, following a winding route from the village to the cave, avoiding the main trails, so as to elude the foot patrols that would be searching the region. His intimate knowledge of these mountains continued to serve him well. From his long years as a hunter, he knew every inch of the area. He knew of the bandit, Chai, of the fortress from which Chai's private army enriched itself by attacking communities on both sides of the border with China. In this region, often no one knew with certainty where the border was, one of the reasons why the Korean government did not generally protest the routine encroachment by Chinese patrols along these trails.

Ahn could only hope that he was doing the right thing, helping the Americans. He had no wish to bring hardship upon his village. The American government would draw on every resource at their disposal to retrieve the shuttle. What would happen when an American military presence also established itself in these mountains? A second Korean War? He only knew that he would never forgive those in power in his country who had allowed things to deteriorate to such a condition that his beloved wife had to succumb so painfully to her cancer because treatment was denied. He had vowed upon Mai's death that the enemies of his country's leaders would be his allies, although never in his most fanciful imaginings could he ever have foreseen being thrust into a situation such as this. He was an unschooled mountain peasant, at the heart of a simmering world crisis. His stomach was in a knot of anxiety.

He made a final survey of his surroundings from what he hoped was a position of concealment. He seemed to be alone. Birds sang from bare tree branches that rattled together, from the frigid mountain breeze that was ever-present. He dashed across the clearing to brush aside the thicket-covered entrance and stepped into the cave that was now illuminated with some slanting shafts of daylight.

The cave was empty except for the inert body of the woman, in much the same position as Ahn had last seen her when the other woman astronaut had cared for her so humanely. Of course the body was stone cold. Touching her forehead with the back of his fingers was like touching marble on a cold day. His memories were abruptly summoned of the terrible day when he discovered his wife's dead body, the day that he began living life alone. There was nothing he could do for this American woman here today. He began to step back outside into the sunshine, and then paused when he heard the rotor sounds of a helicopter. Remaining concealed by the thicket at the cave entrance, he peered out.

A gunship with North Korean military markings roared past, very low overhead on a northeasterly course, angling at a rate of descent that meant it would touch down near the cave. This area was dotted with open meadowlands large enough for a helicopter to land. The gunship disappeared beyond the treetops. The rotor sounds diminished, then could be heard no more.

Sometimes there had been armed engagements between the military and the mercenary force led by the outlaw, Chai. The military had been unable to root out Chai's "army."

Ahn wondered if the bandits had found the Americans and then taken them away . . .

He left his place of concealment behind the thicket at the cave's entrance. The familiar, rich smells of earth, still damp from last night's melted snow, mingled with the scent of the pine trees, whose green sharply contrasted with the crisp blue morning sky. With a last look in the direction the helicopter was touching down, Ahn withdrew from the knoll, using the same degree of caution as in his approach.

Sergeant Bol Rhee stood with Colonel Sung and surveyed an ugly scene.

Bodies had been zippered into black plastic bags that were stretched in an orderly line alongside the trail. The bark of surrounding trees was scarred from pulverizing bullets. Splashes of blood splotched the frosty ground.

Colonel Sung's uniform was smartly starched, as always. His boots were spit-and-shine polished as if he were in his headquarters office, not here on the cold side of a mountain. "I was told this was an ambush. A massacre is more like it."

A bandage encircled Bol's head. The field dressing was already stained red where the bullet had grazed his hairline, leaving a three-inch-long gash that felt as if someone had ripped open his head with a rusty trowel. "It was a massacre, sir. You'll get no argument from me there, sir."

"Tell me again what happened."

It was the third time Bol had related what he remembered. In fact, he did not remember much. He remembered ordering his men to dive for cover, and returning fire, and losing consciousness when he was wounded. When he regained consciousness, he was alone on this desolate trail, alone with the dead and dying of his unit.

Other survivors were wounded far worse than Bol. They'd already been airlifted for emergency medical treatment. He had insisted on staying behind to await Sung, whose helicopter had touched down minutes earlier in a nearby meadow. Sung and his headquarters staff had hiked in the rest of the distance, and had not seemed in a hurry to do so.

The radio had been smashed during the ambush, but a matchbook-sized device Bol carried in his breast pocket had survived. One such homing device had been supplied to the NCO of each patrol. The press of its single button had transmitted Bol's location. He wondered about the technologically sophisticated electronic device. And he thought of the helicopter with Japanese civilian markings, not military, which he'd witnessed landing and departing from the airfield on several occasions under cover of darkness. Could Colonel Sung be operating without his superior's knowledge? And if he was not taking orders from Pyongyang, who was Colonel Sung receiving his orders from?

When Bol concluded his report, Sung stared at the line of body bags. "Bandits did this. The Chinese have not had time to reach this sector, Sergeant; we will locate that arrogant son of a dog, Chai." Sung spat the name as if it were an epithet. "The man you saw running toward you, before the shooting began . . . you're right, he could only have been one of the Americans. Chai has the crew of astronauts."

There was a pause, and so Bol said, "Yes, sir."

Sung pondered for a moment. "We will begin, I think, with the peasants."

"Sir?"

"A private army, the size of the one said to be commanded by Chai, cannot exist in a vacuum. There will be at least one person among the local civilian population who knows where his base is. We will find that person, who will then be persuaded to divulge the information we require. By any means necessary."

Shenyang Province, China

The provincial military headquarters was a depressingly drab collection of brick buildings surrounding a parade ground, as ugly as General Li remembered it from having served here at the beginning of his military career in the Chinese military. Frontier duty. It had been patrols along the border—grueling and dangerous duty. For many peasants, the People's Liberation Army provided the only avenue to acquiring skills and prestige. Li was no exception, being of humble origins, born twenty kilometers from here. And yet he was greeted upon his arrival with the deferential respect due the visiting third ranking member of the Politburo.

The provincial commander, Major Kwan, made Li think of himself at that age: Cantonese, intense, energetic and highly efficient. Major Kwan was also nonplussed when the general ordered up a column of armored personnel carriers within five minutes of his arrival.

The Soviet-made BTR-40s now idled in a row. Each had a heavy machine gun mounted at the top of a forward armored hull, where the enclosed cap ended and the open portion of the carrier began. A soldier stood behind each of the .50-calibers. Each vehicle was filled to capacity with troops in full combat gear, their AK-47s locked and loaded.

General Li hoisted himself up into the passenger seat of the cab of the lead vehicle. He looked down at Kwan and jerked a thumb back in the direction of the column. "I suggest that you find yourself a seat, Major." The general raised his voice to be heard above the racket. The stink of the trucks' murky diesel exhaust fumes filled the air.

"May I respectfully say, General," Kwan called back, "that the region sector you have designated will constitute an incursion into North Korea. We patrol the region, of course. But a column of this strength will be considered more than routine by the Koreans."

"If we are found out," countered Li. "You are conscientious to bring this to my attention. This will be duly noted in my report to Beijing."

Kwan replied, "Thank you, sir."

"That said, rest assured that I have arranged for sufficient air cover and reinforcement if the North Koreans are foolhardy enough to engage us. Do not worry, Major. I was commanding incursions like this into Korean territory while you were still at your mother's breast. Now look sharp. We're moving out." He indicated the terrain looming around them. "The Americans have lost a space shuttle in these mountains. We will find it." Li's visage grew stern. "And we have no time to lose."

Kwan saluted, and trotted up to board the cab of the second BTR-40. The column began rumbling forward.

Chapter Twelve

Galt rode in the seat behind the pilot, wrapped in the powerful drone of the F-15 in flight, en route from Houston to Washington.

The flight sounds and the bright sunshine radiating in through the jet's cowl combined to lull Galt into a catnap, which he allowed to happen because he thought it would be refreshing. It was a trick you learned working covert ops in hostile territory, when the team just flat-out couldn't push on any farther due to fatigue, or maybe daylight was setting in and you had to lie low until nightfall to avoid detection. A security perimeter would be established, and then the men of the team could take turns catching some shut-eye; enough to recharge, while the senses remained attuned to dangerous surroundings, to come completely awake at the slightest sound. Galt retained a conscious awareness of where he was, enveloped there in the steady whine of the jet, but he slipped deeper than he intended into the gray area between awake and asleep.

He dreamed.

He knew it was a dream, but somehow that awareness did not diminish its immediacy, the reality of the images unfolding in his mind.

It was lovely, at first.

Some national holiday. The schools were out. He'd scheduled the day off so he could take his little family to the shore. The sand blazed almost as brightly as the sun. Kate lounged on a blanket beneath a beach umbrella with their youngest, Annie, playing in the sand nearby. In his dream, Galt and eleven-year-old Amy were swimming together in the ocean. His daughter had always been a fine little swimmer. Still, when the water reached his shoulders, he instructed her to turn back, although they were no more than a dozen meters from the shore. But Amy wanted to keep swimming with him. She did not want to return to safety. She wanted to stay at her father's side.

He came awake with a start, bathed in clammy perspiration. He blinked against the sun. He and Katy had no kids. There had been the two miscarriages.

The pilot was patching through a call to him from Wil Fleming. Galt was wide awake.

"The president has asked me to convey a 'well done,' along with our appreciation for getting the job done so promptly." The chief of staff's voice imparted a respect that hadn't been there before. "Uh, by the way, do you mind if I ask how you got Fraley to confess so quickly, when trained FBI interrogators couldn't break him? I'm told there was a minimal amount of damage to his face, but no signs of any physical torture. How'd you do it?"

"As a matter of fact," said Galt, "I'd rather not say."

Fleming chuckled uncomfortably. "I get the picture. Anyway, now that the FBI has the leverage of Fraley's confession to use on the Yota woman, we're confident we'll be able to backtrack her to the next link in the chain, to whoever initiated the NASA sabotage."

"What if she's telling the truth?"

"I beg your pardon?" Fleming's frown was practically audible across the connection being bounced to the jet from a satellite somewhere in outer space.

"I mean," said Galt, "what if Connie Yota really doesn't know the identity of her control offices? What if the investigation dead-ends with her and Fraley?"

"That will be someone else's concern. Your job in this matter is done, no matter what happens next. You wanted a piece of this, and the president gave you an important one. But he has directed me to tell you that you're to return to the White House for your regular duty assignment beginning tomorrow."

"Any number of good men could pinch-hit for me." Galt closed his laptop computer. "I've just downloaded and reviewed the latest intel and analysis on the *Liberty* situation."

"Something's wrong with this connection." Fleming's tone was testy. "I've just finished telling you that what the president—"

"The connection is fine," said Galt. "I also downloaded a supposedly unconnected piece of trivia from our defense system satellites."

"Do tell." Fleming's tone dropped a few more degrees.

"Uh huh. Seems that a covert U.S. tracking station

over there has monitored North Korean and Chinese troop movement along their border."

"Galt, you know damn well that there's been routine Chinese incursion along that border from both sides since the border was drawn, for Chrissake. No one cares, including the countries involved. China and North Korea are allies, more or less."

"There's also a new airfield with an unusually big landing strip in Hamgyong Province. Those are remote mountains with no strategic value, a real backwater. There's no reason for an installation like that with a runway big enough to land a space shuttle. The CIA received intelligence on it from a contact they have on the ground as soon as the regional military command went to work constructing it, and our spy satellite flyovers have confirmed. That airfield is right in the sector where the shuttle went down."

Fleming's expression changed, the irritation softening. "Look, as of now intel from the ground is nonexistent on this. We do not want to get into a hot war with North Korea and China. North Korea has its army on full alert. South Korea's defense minister has his army on alert. Our military forces are at Charlie Threat Level. We've got pilots in fighter aircraft ready to take off within ten minutes of the president issuing the command. This could very easily tumble into a major confrontation, and I am talking nuclear."

"I'm in charge of covert operations," said Galt, "remember? We need a presence on the ground over there, and right now. Hook me up with General Tuttle. He and I could—"

"You will follow your president's orders and return to your office and your official duties no later than oh-eight-hundred hours tomorrow," stated Fleming flatly, as if that settled that.

Galt's response was to end the conversation. He reopened his laptop and fingered a sequenced code that provided a connection so secure that even his own pilot was out of this loop.

Meiko answered on the second ring. Her caller ID would not register the source of this call. "Yes?"

He heard something wrong immediately in her intonation. "It's me."

"Trev, it's my father." There was a vulnerable sadness to her words. "I just heard from Tokyo. He's dead. He's passed away, as you say here."

He hadn't expected something this personal, and he heard himself mouthing the obligatory, "Meiko, I'm sorry." He'd known of her father's reputation before he met her. Kurita Industries was one of a surviving handful of mega-corporations that had gone global during the Japanese boom of the 1980s. Under the stewardship of Kentaro Kurita, K.I. had grown to prosper into this new century with dynamic ties to European and United States makers and shakers. But the only insight Galt had ever had into Meiko's family situation was gleaned from his monitoring random, passing, offhand comments now and then, from which he'd drawn the conclusion that she did not like her stepmother, whom Mister Kurita had married seven years after the death of his first wife, Meiko's mother. Meiko and Galt related compatibly in the here-and-now on a number of levels, but families were not discussed. Meiko's soft voice interrupted his mental wandering.

"Trev?"

He processed this information he'd just received, a confluence of circumstances that could not be ignored. "If you're flying back to Tokyo, I'd like to go with you."

"I was sort of hoping you'd accompany me," she said. "I'm taking a four-fifteen flight this afternoon to L.A." Her voice across the crystal-clear connection was fragile and small. The keening whistle of the F-15 in flight barely penetrated Galt's helmet. "Are you sure about this, Trev?"

"I'm sure." He glanced at his watch, estimating the F-15's remaining flight time. "I can make it. I'll meet you at the loading gate."

"That would be very nice. I love you," she said, and terminated the connection.

Washington, DC

The waiting area at the terminal gate was crowded with family, friends and associates who had come to see off those boarding the Los Angeles flight. There was standing room only, and little of that. Meiko was surrounded by a cacophony of conversations in many languages.

Galt navigated his way through the condensed mass of humanity toward her. He wore an open-neck white shirt, a navy blue sports jacket and pressed slacks with black shoes. He felt mildly ill-at-ease wearing the uniform of a civilian. He only ever felt like he was in uniform when he was not wearing a soldier's uniform. There was a black leather travel bag over his shoulder and he toted his laptop computer.

"How are you doing, Meiko?"

She was dressed for travel, wearing a modest, belted black dress, set off by a string of white pearls, with matching purse and shoes.

She was studying his eyes. "I'm having second thoughts."

"About what?"

"About us. About how smart I was to tell you that I loved you over the phone, the way I did."

"Meiko, come on, you're under stress."

"That's what I meant. That's something neither one of us has ever said to the other before, Trev. I told myself that between the two of us, I would not be the first one to say it. Is that stupid?"

He touched her arm. "Meiko, relax. We've got a lot of flight time ahead of us. I don't have to accompany you, if that's what you'd prefer."

"I don't know what my preference is." She continued to study him, almost dispassionately. "Are you coming with me because you care, or are you using my family tragedy to further your own objectives?"

"You want to know the truth?" he said. "I've been asking myself that. I'm sorry, Meiko. I won't go with you."

"That's not what I want, either. You wouldn't be undertaking an action like this on your own, without official sanction, if you thought that the government was doing its best to locate and rescue your wife and the crew."

Galt blinked. He glanced around. No one seemed to have overheard her.

"What do you know about that?"

She held his gaze. "Your expression right now tells me everything I need to know, Major."

"Does it?"

"Don't worry. We don't have to talk about it. I don't know anything, except that there is an information blackout. And here you are, wanting to be a good friend and accompany me home, coincidentally to that hemisphere, for the funeral of my father."

"I'm sorry, Meiko. Please accept my condolences. And call me when you get back, if you want to." He started to turn, to leave.

She arrested his movement with a touch of her fingertips on his arm. "You may not believe this," she said, "but right now I don't want to know anything classified about your shuttle or your wife or anything else. It's enough that I understand the depth of feeling you still have for the woman who is still your wife. You're initiating some sort of personal effort of your own, and with a missing NASA space shuttle involved, that means you're risking everything."

A lull had fallen over many of the surrounding conversations when a pair of airline employees assumed their positions to either side of the boarding door.

He pitched his voice low. "I'm making this up as I go along, but you're right. It's the right thing for me to do, because I do have a chance of accomplishing something." He grimaced. "And yes, you're right. I was going to use your family's situation as an excuse."

She considered this, gazing into his eyes. "You're risking your life and your career for Kate and the lives of the other crewmembers? I'm not sorry that I told you I love you. You are a brave and noble man."

He avoided her gaze. "Aw, shucks."

"I want to help. You may accompany me to Tokyo. Use me as a cover for whatever you intend to do."

"I do want to be there for you."

"You shall be. But first, tell me, Trev. I have to know. Are you still in love with her?"

"No." He bent an arm and scratched the back of his shaggy head, frowning, searching for the right words.

"Not in love. But I *do* love her, if that means caring about her. I was going to wait until she got back before I told her about us. I figured it could wait, since she and I were already separated when you and I met. That shuttle flight has been the only thing in her life. I didn't want her distracted while she was on mission."

"Was on mission?" Meiko repeated, studying him with her probing gaze. "The shuttle has come back to earth," she surmised, "only no one knows about it. It went down somewhere in Asia."

He glanced around. Again, no one seemed to have overheard. Her voice was pitched low, and those in the boarding area were engrossed in their own conversations and farewells. An airline employee swung open the boarding door, while another lowered the thin rope that had barred the entrance leading to the plane.

Galt watched this as he spoke to her. "Meiko, I can't talk about that."

"All right," she said reasonably. "Let's just talk about Kate, then. What were you going to tell her when she got back from outer space?"

"I'm going to tell her that there is no doubt in my mind that I want a divorce."

"But Trev, you and I were going to talk before either one of us did anything drastic."

"Isn't that what we're doing now?"

Her eyes clouded. "I could certainly use a loving friend at my side."

People around them began funneling toward the gate. He reached into a pocket and produced a boarding pass. "I've got the seat next to yours."

The trace of a smile touched her lips and a sparkle flashed in her eyes. "You are the most incredible man,

Trev Galt. How did you manage that, this close to boarding?"

He clasped her hand in his free hand, giving hers a gentle squeeze. "Let's just call it the power of the White House perk," he said, "and hope that the corporate exec who got bumped to the next flight won't raise too much of a stink."

There were 143 passengers aboard the Tokyo-bound Concorde SST jet out of LAX. Galt was among the more industrious, alternating work at his laptop with hourly five-minute breaks to lean his head against the cushion of his seat, resting his eyes. He and Meiko barely spoke during the long flight, except for small talk at mealtime. Meiko lost herself in a thick paperback tome of American political commentary.

Galt reflected that, had he been aboard this lengthy a flight in the past, he would ordinarily have been working on a stiff drink within minutes of takeoff. He thought about the roughing-up he'd given the NASA scientist in Houston. The ends justified the means. And Eliot Fraley would go to his grave knowing Galt as a heinous brute capable of torture and the murder of a sick woman. And yet here Galt was, wearing his civilian uniform, flying in style and polite society. Seated across the aisle from him was a beautiful, sophisticated woman who loved him. But Meiko had never seen the side of him that Eliot Fraley saw. Galt had come to understand that the knowledge that such a brute existed within him was much of the reason why he had sought the anesthesia for the soul and mind that liquor had provided him. But he hadn't taken a drink in months, and he intended to never have another drink of alcohol.

Concerning the women in his life, well, he had braved bullets and faced death, but if he feared anything it was his own heart. Was there a man alive who was any different? Dear, earnest Meiko, for all her world-class journalism credentials, could never begin to imagine the side of him that he'd unleashed on that weasel, Fraley. With Kate, he'd done what he could to cope with the miscarriages and career shifts, but the love they'd shared still went south. So why bother heading down that same road for heartache with someone else? The problem, of course, was that his heart had already been taken by (or given to?) the woman he'd been sharing his off-time with, including bedtime. Galt was not promiscuous, not a man who could make love with a woman unless he had real feelings for her. He wasn't a casual sex kind of guy. Which is why he felt guilty about exploiting Meiko's family tragedy for his own agenda . . . precisely as she'd accused him of doing. She'd agreed to participate but her understanding, and the forgiveness this implied, did nothing to ease his guilt. But hell, he told himself, he had to think pragmatically. He was on a mission, even if it was his own, and the expediency of using this trip was inarguable. Accompanying Meiko to Japan provided him with the perfect cover.

He closed down that stream of thought. He focused on the mission. Would it take until tomorrow before Fleming and the president realized that he had skipped town?

Throughout the flight, he monitored, via his laptop's ongoing download, the multiple satellite intel flowing into the Pentagon's intelligence fusion center concerning the continuing Chinese and North Korean military troop movements along their shared border. As the laptop automatically sorted, processed and filed this data, Galt likewise mentally processed what he was learning into the context of what he already knew.

North Korea's first Communist leader, Kim Il Sung, had seized power with help from the Soviet Union and China in 1945. His dream of uniting the Koreas by force led North Korea to its war with America, the "forgotten" war that had resulted in the death of 520,000 North Koreans, 415,000 South Koreans and 34,000 Americans after the United States pitched in to defend the democratic South from the Communist aggressors of the North. The present-day stalemate of this divided country had existed ever since. Erosion of North Korea's tightly controlled society was exacerbated with the end of the Cold War, when the North's Soviet support evaporated. The Chinese became increasingly irritated with North Korea's unwillingness to consider the economic reforms that Beijing was adopting. Kim's death in the 1990s had created a sudden and critical leadership crisis that further deepened the country's formidable economic troubles. This led to civil unrest, a phenomenon previously unheard of in North Korea.

In the wake of the terrorist attack on the twin towers of the World Trade Center, after the military actions in Afghanistan and Iraq, the U.S. had expanded its war on terrorism in a number of ways: sending special forces to the Philippines, increasing military surveillance in Somalia, training special forces on the ground in Yemen and branding North Korea a "terrorist state" for its support of terrorist actions in South Korea, and against American interests in that part of the world: "a regime," in the words of the then-president, "arming with missiles and weapons of mass destruction." America had served notice that it had no intention of permitting dangerous regimes to develop weapons of mass destruction that were intended for use against America or its allies. In other words, America reserved the right to take pre-emptive action. With regard to the Korean situation, from the West's point of view, the best-case scenario was that eventually the "Bamboo Curtain" separating North and South Korea would collapse peacefully, with the two Koreas then unifying along the German post–Cold War model. However, on the diplomatic front, leverage was limited. Since North Korea was one of the most isolated countries in the world, America had no diplomatic linkage with its government. The current administration was hoping that China and Japan might be persuaded to wield influence.

The "glue" holding together this famine-ravaged society of 22 million was Kim's son, Kim Jong Il. The elder Kim had mentored his son to succeed him. Nearing sixty, the son was among the world's most shadowy figures. As head of his country's armed forces, Kim was described as running the day-to-day machinery of his government, but he altogether lacked his father's charisma and authority. It was the conclusion of intel psyche analysts from more than one agency, whose job it was to profile international leaders who were strategically important to American policy-making, that the guy was nuttier than a pecan pie. One piece of evidence that he lived in a cocoon of his own delusions was his by-any-standard abominable hairstyles, usually an awkwardly-sculpted coif, unflattering in the extreme. The reason for this was that, rather than flying in the best hairstylists from the salons of Paris or New York as he could easily have afforded to do, this leader of a nation with nuclear capabilities, narcissistically fixated on his appearance, instead chose to have his hair done by male political prisoners dragged up from the interrogation cells if they professed any ability whatsoever to cut hair. Such claims often proved to be nothing more than desperate ploys to stay alive, and many a "former barber" went to the firing squad primarily for the crime of having given his president a bad haircut. Kim's sexual preference was said to be for young men and boys, and so he was able to pander to his vanity while being supplied with a steady stream of young men and boys willing to do anything to survive, including servicing his private predilections. The only downside for Kim was that some hair days were better than others. This then was the "playboy" dictator of North Korea: head of a government riddled with corruption from the local commune level to Kim Jong Il's private chambers, where he preened in pampered decadence while the famine worsened critically with each passing year despite international aid from nations, including the United States.

Without a paramount leader, North Korea was effectively a headless beast and, as such, represented a far greater potential threat to America than ever before.

Chapter Thirteen

Pyongyang, North Korea

Kim Jong Il was getting a haircut in his private office, located on the top floor of the central government building. The office walls were a drab gray, barren except for a single photograph of Kim and his father standing formally side-by-side at some long-forgotten occasion of state. A metal desk, behind which Kim sat, matched the walls. The day itself was gray. Rain clouds gathered beyond the single window. Kim was overweight and pudgy. His complexion had an unhealthy pallor. His thinning hair was coifed in a pompadour.

The young man in prisoner garb administering the haircut was a slim-hipped teenager with girlish good looks: pouty lips and a delicate build. The youth held a comb in one hand, hair-clippers in the other, and was cautiously snipping near Kim's sideburns. Occasionally he would stop snipping and stand back to allow his hands to stop shaking. Having known enough to volunteer to his interrogators downstairs that he was proficient in cutting hair, he must surely have also known of the fate of so many "former barbers" before him. The prisoner clearly understood that his life depended on the haircut he was administering.

Kim, not wearing his thick eyeglasses, had to squint at the pair of men standing before him. His hair was tended to on a daily basis, often during work hours. "We find ourselves at an impasse," he said. "The Americans will not relent in their insistence that they be allowed access to Hamgyong Province, where they say their shuttle has gone down. Their position is that they are entitled to search for their precious shuttle. They cite our inability to secure our own borders against the Chinese in that region."

"The Americans are entitled to nothing." General Yang was nearing seventy. He had been a young lieutenant in the war against the Americans fifty years ago, and was presently supreme commander of the North Korean military. His aged body was in good condition, but at the moment he shivered as if with chills. "They have consistently pursued a policy against us. It is my considered opinion, sir, that the Americans' encroachment of our borders be considered an act of war."

The man beside him, General Tog, the military's second-in-command, was generations younger than Yang, but his eyes burned with the same conviction. "The military stands ready to defend our nation. The launch of missiles at U.S. positions along the DMZ awaits your approval, sir."

"I understand." Kim nodded. "But not yet, gentlemen, not yet." His lips curled into the semblance of a smile. "We hold in our hand the potential of turning this to our considerable advantage." He winced as the hair-clippers nipped too closely to his scalp. The prisoner ceased snipping, an expression of terror on his face. Kim touched his scalp, satisfied himself that there was no wound and snapped his fingers peevishly, gesturing for the prisoner to continue, which he did. Kim continued, to the men before him, "If our military were to find the shuttle first, we could use that to negotiate more economic aid from the Americans as a show of their gratitude . . . after our scientists have helped themselves to whatever they choose aboard the shuttle. With this much at stake, the Americans will not quibble. Need I remind you, gentlemen, that the famine relief provided by America lines our pockets?"

Yang's posture grew ramrod straight. "It makes my blood run as ice to think of them invading our soil."

"I concur," said Kim. "That is why pressure must be exerted on our troops in the region. Do you suppose the Americans suspect us of culpability in this matter?"

"Unfortunately," said Tog, "it's too soon to tell. I do believe that, if that were the case, they would first approach us privately with such an accusation, and demand their shuttle be returned. This they have not done."

"And we have no idea where that shuttle is?" Kim's tone was petulant.

"A Colonel Sung is our regional commander in Hamgyong Province," said Yang, "where the shuttle is believed to have gone down. Colonel Sung reports that he has been directing a search of his sector since dawn, thus far with no positive results."

"Colonel Sung is a most competent officer," said Yang, "and he is ruthless. He has been made to understand the grave urgency of this. A space shuttle has crashed in his sector. Someone will have seen something, and they will divulge what they know to him. I assure you, sir, we will see results."

"Enough," said Kim. "The mirror and my glasses." He was speaking to the prisoner, and holding each hand out, palm up. "I now wish to see the results of this haircut."

The prisoner obeyed. His trembling intensified, and he repeatedly licked his lips, awaiting the verdict on his work . . . reprieve, or execution.

Hamgyong Province, North Korea

Ahn Chong sat at a rough-hewn wood table. He was watching his daughter, Toi, prepare a lunch of pulgogi, thinly sliced beef with various spices, and makkolli, a beer made of rice. The tangy scents of spices in the kitchen area mingled with the faint wood smell from a low fire in the stove.

It was Ahn's daily custom, at his daughter's request, to join Toi and her husband for their midday meal, ever since the passing of Mai. The interior of the one-room home of Toi and her husband had a low ceiling and bare timber walls. The furnishings were simple and rudimentary. A row of windows faced south, away from the village. Sunlight flowing in through these windows, combined with the wood fire in the stove, made the atmosphere warm and comfortable.

At thirty-seven years, Ahn's daughter had the stocky, thick-boned physique of the North Korean peasant woman, yet there was a delicacy to the line of her mouth, the form of her lips, that reminded him of Mai.

He considered this to be a sacred time of each day, seated like this at the kitchen table in his daughter's modest home, not far from his own. Sharing these meals with Toi brought back to him sweet memories of the meals he shared with his beloved Mai before the hideous ravages of her cancer had taken her from him. He had returned directly to the village from the cave, encountering neither army patrols nor anyone else along the way. He arrived early at his daughter's home for lunch. Her husband, Cho, had not yet returned from the fields for the midday repast. The conversation with Toi, as she prepared their lunch, was pleasant as always, about those mundane aspects of village life that they always discussed. A certain villager was reported to be a slacker in the fields. A village in the next valley was rumored to be willing to barter services in exchange for produce. They spoke of such things. Although he engaged her about the subjects she brought up this day, Ahn's concerns were elsewhere. His world had been turned upside down, and he could tell no one. His biggest concern was those he should tell. He thought of the compact radio transceiver hidden nearby. And he thought of the jeopardy that he had placed his daughter in by his actions from the very beginning. There had never before been anything this big, which is why he had hesitated in using the radio to make his report. He must let nothing happen to Toi.

Midway through preparing their meal, she suddenly said, "Father, what is it? We've been talking, but your thoughts are somewhere else. Please tell me what it is that troubles you."

He reached his bony hand across the table to pat her arm reassuringly. "It's nothing, child. I have but the wandering mind of an old man in his dotage."

"You are more of a man than most of the younger fellows I see in the village," she said. "Despite your years, Father, you grow ever stronger: toughened, not weakened, by adversity."

He sighed and lowered his eyes from hers. "Toi, even the strong grow old and infirm."

"Not you, Father. You hike to visit Mother's grave every day, and yes, I know, sometimes late in the cold darkness of the night."

He frowned. "How do you know this?"

She sensed his flaring of concern, and said hurriedly, "Father, I have told no one."

"Not even your husband?"

"No, not even Cho. And I will tell nothing. Please, Father, tell me. What is it?"

It was her intelligence, and her intuition, regarding him, which most reminded him of her mother. Yet he could not in good conscience involve Toi in the extraordinary events he had witnessed, and been drawn into.

The outside door was abruptly flung inward.

Toi's husband entered the house. Ahn's son-in-law was squat, but proportionately muscular. Ten years older than Toi, Cho wore work denims, the knees dirt-stained from the morning's work. His expression was of severe consternation. Before Cho could utter a word, someone behind him propelled Cho into the house.

The man who had shoved, a rifle-carrying soldier, appeared in the doorway. He scanned their faces. "I am Sergeant Bol Rhee. You will join the others outside, at once."

Toi leaped to her feet, angrily. Another way she reminded Ahn of his Mai was the manner in which she did not gracefully accept personal affronts. "What is the meaning of this?" she demanded. "How dare you—"

Ahn saw in the soldier's eyes that this could escalate out of control without warning. He knew the reason for the soldier's presence. He placed himself between the sergeant's rifle and his daughter. He then brazenly turned his back on the soldier, to rest both of his hands on Toi's shoulders. "Daughter, no. We will cooperate. We will do as he says."

She started to speak, and then interrupted herself. She whirled on her husband. "Cho, are you a party to this?"

Cho's expression shifted from consternation to the hint of outrage. "What foolishness to suggest such a thing! Of course not!"

To Ahn's ears, the young man's denial sounded hollow and insincere.

The soldier snorted in frustration and disgust, apparently somewhat unwilling to gun down three civilians in their own home. Instead, he shoulder-slung his rifle and stepped forward. The thudding clump of his combat boots sounded radically out of place in the kitchen. He grasped both father and daughter, each in a firm grip above the elbow. "Listen, both of you." He shook them roughly for emphasis. "It is not I that you should fear. I suggest that you do as you're told. My commander is here. Be advised he is a man without mercy or sentimentality. You have been warned."

He gave neither of them an opportunity to respond. He dragged them through the doorway, outside. Cho trailed several steps behind, voicing what sounded to Ahn like half-hearted protests. They were taken through the bracing midday sunshine to the center of the village, where about thirty villagers had been herded into a group, huddled together under the watchful eye of soldiers with rifles. Bol released Ahn and Toi with a shove that sent them jostling into the huddled mass of frightened people.

Bol turned to an officer of severe demeanor and posture. The threat of violence was palpable in the air. "Sir, all of the adult males and their spouses are accounted for."

"Well done, Sergeant." Colonel Sung surveyed the civilians. His uniform was starched. His boots remained brightly polished despite traipsing through inhospitable terrain. His steely eyes settled upon Ahn. "You. Old man. Your name is Ahn Chong. I am told that you know this region as only a native of your years can. I want you to tell me what you know about a space shuttle."

Ahn respectfully cast his eyes downward. "Sir, I do not even know what a 'space shuttle' is."

"I do think you know what a space shuttle is, old man. I know of your late-night wanderings."

Ahn heard gasps of dismay from the villagers surrounding him. His daughter's was the loudest.

"Colonel, on my word, I walk late to visit the grave of my wife."

"Yes. The grave of your wife. The grave of your wife happens to be exactly along the shuttle's line of approach. You know what I want. Tell me. Where did the shuttle go down? Are there survivors? Tell me, old man, or you will come with us for questioning."

Cho spoke before Ahn could reply. "Colonel Sung, please spare my father-in-law. He knows nothing. I implore you. Do not harm him."

Sung studied Cho. "You are the leader of this village commune, I am told."

"Yes, my Colonel."

"I see." Sung pondered this, then nodded. "Very well. The old man remains here. I will grant you this favor as a faithful member of the Party."

Cho seemed uncomfortably conscious of the stares of his fellow commune members. He managed to stammer out, "Thank you, my Colonel."

Sung turned back to Ahn Chong. "As for you, old man, you're lucky for now. I have my reasons for keeping you alive."

"You hope that I will reveal where the shuttle is. But I tell you, Colonel, I know nothing."

Sung whirled away from the group of frightened civilians. "Sergeant!" he snapped at Bol Rhee. "Order your men into a column. We are done here." He cast a final, withering glance in Ahn's direction. "For now," he added ominously.

There came a collective sigh from those around Ahn. The soldiers marched away from the village then, led by the strutting commander and his harried-looking sergeant. They took the narrow, rutted dirt road that led into the shadow cast, even at midday, by towering forest trees.

Ahn found himself reminded of his own military service, so long ago, as a conscript. Then the column disappeared from sight into the trees beyond a crest in the terrain. The villagers erupted into conversations, many of them solicitous of Toi. Ahn had no interest in conversing with anyone.

"Father." His daughter held her head high. His fatherly pride swelled at the grace and courage that her bearing and posture reflected. She glanced around to make certain that no one was within earshot. The others were conversing excitedly among themselves, discussing what had just happened. She said, "Father, you must be most careful of what you say."

He bristled. "Why? Are you afraid that your husband will send word to the secret police to come for me? Or perhaps Colonel Sung will arrange a hastily-convened firing squad for your father."

"No such thing will happen, Father. Cho only follows his conscience. I believe he just saved your life. You should be grateful."

Ahn looked to where his neighbors were dispersing at Cho's command, to resume work in the fields. "Your husband thinks me a useless old man. He spoke up only to divert problems from his own home, with you. For my part, I wonder who informed the colonel about me, of how well I know these mountains."

"You think it was Cho?"

"Of course I do. Who else?"

The lines around Toi's eyes and mouth became taut. "As the leader of our community, it is Cho's duty to cooperate with the authorities. Father, do not speak disrespectfully of my husband. He is a good man."

"Those he collaborates with were about to kill me. It may be your husband's duty is to inform for Colonel Sung. But when he informed on me, he betrayed our family and he endangered you."

"And what of you, Father? Do you know anything about a space shuttle? You could help our village avoid the misery that Colonel Sung will bring."

"Child, nothing that I can do or say will avert what is destined to happen. No good will come of this. Brace yourself for what lies ahead, for we are in the line of fire."

Chapter Fourteen

Beijing, China

The communications center, in the Great Hall of the People, was far below the street level of Tiananmen Square: a cluttered, concrete-walled room filled with masses of American-made communications gear. The air conditioner was set to a year-round setting. There was the hum of the equipment, a minimum of hushed conversation and no other sound except for the clicking of many fingertips across keyboards beneath rows of monitors. During the Cold War, China and the United States had jointly operated a string of electronic intelligence-gathering stations along what had been the Soviet border. The stations were furnished with American equipment and Chinese technicians. Enormous quantities of that equipment had been diverted to this subbasement, unknown to most of the thousands of people who daily worked in or visited the Great Hall.

General Chow stood with Huang Peng, the minister of defense, near a wall dominated by a bank of world-time chronometers. Technicians tended the rows of equipment with the precision of ingrained routine.

"We have been intercepting an enormous amount of North Korean radio traffic," Chow informed the defense minister. "The space shuttle remains missing, but they have escalated their search."

"What of the American communications?"

"I regret to say we have not yet been able to break their frequency code."

Frown lines creased Huang's gaunt features. "I was not aware such a problem existed. We have access to America's satellite positioning intelligence."

"Unfortunately the American transmissions are being circuited through one of the new satellites, an extremely sophisticated device that alters transmitting frequencies in a random fashion every few seconds."

Huang nodded. "I see. Is there no way to break the code?"

"Perhaps if the Americans command their satellite's computer to synchronize the receivers."

"And what is the likelihood of that?"

"I cannot offer a guess." Chow avoided the minister's glare of disapproval, shifting his gaze instead to the row of technicians hunched over their computer terminals against the opposite wall. "But I do understand the urgency of this matter. We are doing the best that we can."

"And what of our communications?"

"Our communications are secure."

"Then apprise General Li that time has become of the absolute essence," said Huang. "He is our only hope of locating the shuttle before the North Koreans. Instruct the general to intensify his search."

North Korea

Chai had posted sentries at intervals around the crash site. The warlord's group had traveled openly and brazenly through several villages on their way here, and word would have spread. It would be widely known in the region that a sizeable force of the warlord's "army" was passing through, and everyone gave them a wide berth. No one came around, curious. In *Liberty*'s shadow, men were securing the last of the stolen equipment upon their imported llamas, in preparation for departure. Dusk came quickly at this elevation, casting the mountains in cold shadows that lengthened and widened, evaporating the warmth of day.

Kate stood several meters away from the looming space shuttle. The shuttle was a towering, majestic monument of modern technology, in stark contrast to the raw, natural surroundings of the clearing where *Liberty* had crash-landed. A hawk soared high above, basking in the final rays of a sun quickly disappearing beyond craggy peaks to the west. Kate stood in one of the few remaining patches of sunlight. This had been perhaps the most horrific day of her life. She couldn't remember the last time she had slept, yet she was not sleepy. In fact, because of these terrible events, and the contrast of her stark surroundings to the reality she'd expected as an astronaut, all her senses were alive with crystal clarity. From time to time throughout the day, she had cast a glance beyond the activity in and around the *Liberty*, but she saw no signs of civilians. Not surprising, she reasoned; the locals no doubt lived in fear of these armed, vicious-looking brigands. She had thought several times of the old man, Ahn Chong. She hoped he was all right.

One of the bandits had been assigned as her personal guard for the day, a pimply-faced boy of seventeen or so who stood nearby, an M16 slung on his shoulder, his attention never leaving her.

Chai approached her from the direction of the shuttle. His mouth twitched in the semblance of a smile. "Miss Daniels, you and your fellow captives can rest easy. You may inform them of this when you are reunited with them. The first steps have been taken to return you to your country."

"I wish you had allowed me to communicate with NASA," she said.

His men continued working with alacrity, inspired in equal measure, Kate suspected, by the oncoming frostiness of night, and by the imposing appearance of their leader. Chai exuded an undeniable aura of brute power, and at present it was focused directly on her.

"I never trust women. I need hardly point out that your leading me here was an example of your lack of trustworthiness. You are a foolish, faithless woman. You have betrayed your mission, your crewmates and your country." The precise, Oxford accent dripped with a snide, almost sarcastic, tone. She could not get over how weird it was to hear the cultivated British diction from this ruthless, unshaven, scar-faced outlaw.

Anger flared in her, but she concealed this as best she could. "I thought that I'd already explained myself. I see no choice but to deal with you. At least you are purely motivated by greed. Your motives are not political. I'm no traitor. Commerce is one hell of a better way of getting this resolved than allowing anything to fall into the hands of the North Koreans or the Chinese."

His gaze swept the crash site with satisfaction. His

men, with their llamas, had begun moving in a steady line up a steep slope toward the tree line.

"They will find the shuttle, you know," Chai told Kate, "and before much more time passes."

"That's why I'm helping you, and trusting you," she said. "What you've taken from here will be more safe at your fortress than here."

Chai nodded. "It can be defended from there, and kept safe. My demands will be meet accordingly. I will get my money. Your government will respond."

His cockiness finally got to her. "I wouldn't be too sure of that," she said. "As much as I hate to say it, the good old U.S. of A. bureaucracy can be pretty screwed up, and at times, very slow."

"Nevertheless, you and your crewmates will serve my intent. Come now, accompany me. We will wish to make a final inspection before we leave here."

They moved through the length of the shuttle, with the last light of day weakly struggling through the portals, using flashlights to inspect the effect of a day of systematic yet unschooled looting. She accompanied wordlessly, heartbroken at what she saw. Throughout the day, she had remained near Chai's side, had witnessed firsthand his overseeing of the unloading of *Liberty*. He had required her assistance in explaining the equipment and functions. It was a gut-wrenching experience for her. There had been the hideous, ghoulish sight of the dead crewmembers, Leo and Al, still strapped in their seats, preserved by the frigid temperatures, their expressions of the pain of their final moments still etched across their features. Kate recalled the training she had undergone with these people, the rigorous hardships, the laughing camaraderie of what little time off they'd shared; and the memories stabbed at her heart and wrenched her mind. As she'd promised to do, and feeling guiltier with each passing second, she systematically pointed out for Chai the key pieces of equipment.

The looters were neither careful, nor qualified to perform their tasks. She suspected that much of the equipment stripped from the *Liberty* was instantly damaged and rendered useless.

Chai instructed his men to remove those items with the drills, screwdrivers and wrenches they'd brought along in the trucks that carried them here. Kate was reminded of seventeenth-century pirates stripping a high-seas vessel of its bounty. They gutted the control panels on the flight deck, and she had shed tears at the sight of the brutes hacking, pulling and cutting at the delicate controls.

She had trained for so long and hard to be in this cockpit for her first and probably only glorious flight into outer space and it had come to this, watching barbarians strip panels, leaving wires and dials dangling, and gaping holes in the console panels. It occurred to her that this was what it must be like to be tied up and watch burglars ransack your home. Chai and Han Ling had ignored her for the most part, smiling their satisfaction, issuing their directives. After a prolonged, strenuous process involving several near-mishaps, the brigands at last succeeded in loading the bulky satellite down onto one of the waiting trucks positioned beside the shuttle. The truck then drove off, accompanied by a full contingent of heavily-armed guards.

The only satisfaction she drew from this state of affairs was her knowledge that much of *Liberty*'s equipment was equipped with destructive devices that had automatically shut down on impact, automatically erasing the hard drives of many, if not all, of the spacecraft's computers.

When they emerged from the shuttle after Chai's final inspection, he glowered at Kate and indicated the main hatch. "Close it now and do it properly. There is much still aboard that is of value. I will post sentries to stand guard here."

Kate clamped shut the main hatch. "And what if the North Koreans or the Chinese show up?"

"In that event, my men will withdraw without making contact. I already have what I want, you see. Now do as you're told."

While pretending to check the adjustments of the closed hatch mechanism, Kate entered with her fingertips a coded series of digits onto the hatch lock's ten-key panel, a code that primed the trigger sequencing for detonation to blow the space orbiter to kingdom come the next time anyone tampered with this hatch. If forcible entry was attempted, anyone in the vicinity of this hatch would be vaporized in an explosion that would shake the earth for miles. Extreme? Well, she told herself, the self-destruct system had been installed; the procedure being followed had been developed for exactly such an unlikely, unimaginable, extreme scenario as this. She saw no alternative. She had saved what she could by getting Chai to remove the most valuable equipment to where it would hopefully be safer than it was here. Her top priority was to prevent what technology that remained onboard *Liberty* from falling into the possession of enemy states.

She rejoined Chai and Han. The air was fast becoming wintry and inhospitable.

Chai led the way to a truck parked nearby. The truck

was top-heavy with tarp-covered electronic equipment taken from the shuttle. A second vehicle right behind it was full of men with their rifles poking outward like antennae.

Kate paused to turn and look up at the towering *Liberty*, and she recalled its grandeur and majestic appearance before the crash. She hoped that this was not her final sight of it. She then was jarred roughly, almost knocked from her feet, when Han stepped in to ram her roughly in the lower back with the barrel of his rifle, sneering a coarse command in his native tongue. She pivoted instinctively, emotions rising with her. She felt ready to kick this bastard's rifle aside and take him down no matter what the consequences. She'd been pushed that far.

Han had stepped back with surprising adroitness. He stood a few paces back, gesturing with his rifle in the direction of the truck.

Chai laughed and spoke to Han, who lowered his rifle. Chai turned to Kate.

"My apologies. My man is sometimes overzealous in carrying out his duties. Han has a penchant for violence. I see that he has learned from your martial arts demonstration earlier. He's rather nimble when he wants to be, don't you think? So. Do everything I say and cause no trouble, dear lady, I beg of you." He laughed again, harshly. "Everything will then be all right."

"Everything is far from all right," she said. "But I'll be a good girl for now, if your goon doesn't poke me with that rifle again."

Chai did not feel obliged to respond. He trudged onto the waiting truck. At sight of his approach, the driver gunned his engine and switched on the headlights.

Kate continued apace. Han kept a prudent distance from her, but his eyes said that nothing would please him so much as for her to make a break for it so that he could shoot her down on the spot. She disappointed him, realizing in retrospect that lashing out at him had been a reflex fueled solely by pent-up emotions. What the hell, she decided. Life is full of regrets, like her relationship with Trev and the way it was ending, or had already ended, and the dismal fate of *Liberty's* flight . . . and revealing perhaps too early the fact that she could defend herself with deadly force.

Trev had taught her Kung Fu, the oldest known technique of fighting. From Kung Fu had evolved all the forms of martial arts, including jujitsu, kendo and aikido. And yet, Trev told her, Westerners knew practically nothing about true Kung Fu. She had been fascinated; had allowed herself to become immersed in its philosophy. And what she learned then, came in handy now. She had learned that, as every person has two sides to his nature, so it was with Kung Fu, that Kung Fu revolved around a philosophy of nonviolence based on the premise that nothing that is violent can be permanent. The dual nature of Kung Fu is leisure and labor, the former consisting of disciplines such as poetry, painting, history and mathematics—subjects of an artistic, educational nature—while the latter consists of instruction in physical combat. The ultimate aim in regard to both is to aspire to the level where one's understanding and practice of the art provide entrance to the spiritual plane. Striding along between Chai and Han, as they approached the truck, she adjusted her breathing, willing herself to relax, and commanding her *chi*, her inner, intrinsic energy, to rise.

Her study of the metaphysics of Kung Fu had ingrained within her the notion of "yielding to evil," a seeming nonresistance that, when properly applied, served to conquer and destroy evil. If one's strength was much less than one's opponent's, one could defeat that opponent by coordinating one selected purpose with maximum effort, concentrated at the vital time and place. She had to wait. She had to bide her time. She had to wait for the vital moment. Then she would strike, and hope for the best.

They boarded the truck. Chai positioned himself behind the steering wheel, and he gunned the engine to life.

Kate climbed into the cab, and Han followed her. The truck pulled away from the *Liberty* as the darkening mantle of night laid claim to the surroundings. Chai steered and shifted gears expertly, despite the top-heavy load of equipment they were transporting. The second truck followed. Their headlights cast erratic beams into the gloom. The trucks retraced their route of approach from that morning. It had been a long day. She found herself looking forward to her reunion with Commander Scott and Bob Paxton at Chai's fortress. She hoped the commander's broken leg was being suitably cared for, as Chai had promised if she agreed to cooperate, and she hoped that Paxton would not be a problem with attitude toward her. They construed her as a betrayer of the mission, cooperating with the enemy. Yes, she understood their viewpoint. She felt the same way herself. This caused her some anxiety. She burned with shame at what she had done, no matter how strategic or well-intentioned.

As the road wended its way through the rugged night, Chai never stopped pressing his thigh against hers there in the narrow confines of the truck cab. He would cast sideways glances at her with hungry eyes that traveled across her body, lingering here and there. He would lick his lips, growling deep in his throat, feral and menacing, and a wave of repulsion would course through her.

She had never felt so trapped in her life.

God only knew what could happen next.

CHAPTER FIFTEEN

Japan

From the air, Tokyo is not a beautiful city.

The view from Galt's seat aboard the descending passenger jet was that of an unending span of thousands upon thousands of tightly-packed structures, clusters of skyscrapers in the commercial district like stalagmites and an endless residential maze of tiled rooftops and TV antennas. The sun shone dully through the city's smog, like a low-wattage light bulb seen through a gauze shroud, stretching the full breadth of compressed civilization, from the Tokyo plain through Kawasaki to Yokohama. This was one of the largest concentrations of people in the world. To the west, beyond the urban sprawl, the snowy peak of Mt. Fuji rose from the thick cloud of stagnant gray that wrapped the base of the Masahino Mountains.

It had been a nine-hour flight aboard a Concorde SST from LAX to Tokyo's Haneda Airport. Galt and

Meiko debarked with the rest of the passengers, separated temporarily during processing through Japanese customs. That delay was shortened by the fact that Meiko was a Japanese citizen with only a single carry-on suitcase, her papers in order, while Galt's White House-level identification assured him a diplomatic breeze through what could otherwise have been a lengthy and tedious ordeal. Once through customs, they reunited to negotiate their way along the busy main concourse and out through the terminal's main entrance. Outside, she drew up abruptly at the sight of a string of limousines awaiting arrivals in the designated area.

Galt sensed trepidation emanating from the woman at his side. "Meiko, are you all right?"

"That hardly matters. This has to be. It can be no other way." She cast him an uncertain glance. "You asked to be a part of it. Do you regret that yet?"

"No."

"You will. Come."

She strode toward a limo with such an overcompensation of outward confidence that he had to practically double-time to keep up with her. A chauffeur stood, stoically waiting beside their limo. She spoke to him briefly in Japanese. It was a young man of immaculate grooming, who bowed dutifully before hurrying to unlatch and hold wide a door for them. Meiko slid in without hesitation and naturally it was expected that Galt would follow.

Instead, he paused to bend forward and peer inside, past Meiko, to deliver a pleasant smile to the woman awaiting them in the car.

"Trev Galt," said Meiko, "this is my stepmother, Sachito Kurita."

Galt guessed her to be about fifty. Exceedingly well preserved was the description that best suited her. She had large almond eyes that sparkled with intelligence. Straight hair that was black as a raven's wing was stylishly cut. There was nothing flashy or ostentatious about her. A younger woman might well envy her figure: trim and shapely, modestly clad in dark trousers and a tastefully-cut blouse. She leaned toward him somewhat regally, Galt thought, and extended her arm past Meiko for a handshake. She had a beauty that was at once imperious and feminine.

"Very nice to meet you, Mr. Galt."

She spoke flawless English. The windows of the limo were heavily tinted and so the interior was dim, but in the sunlight streaming in from behind him, her skin was smooth and vibrant, and would also be the envy of any younger woman. Her handshake was firm.

Galt said, "I'm sorry we had to meet under these sad circumstances, Mrs. Kurita. Please accept my condolences."

She settled back into her seat.

"Are you accompanying my stepdaughter to our home?"

Meiko's expression said that she did not much care for being referred to in the third person. She spoke in a tone of cool civility. "He is. I hope you do not mind. Trev is a good friend who was kind enough to offer his comfort and company through this . . . ordeal."

"But how could I possibly mind, my dear? I want whatever is best for you, of course. I'm glad you've come home." Her eyes swept to Galt. "You will of course be a welcome guest at our home, Mr. Galt. Please join us. May I call you Trev?"

"Feel free, Mrs. Kurita, and thank you. But regrettably I'll have to decline your invitation for now, and ask if I could connect with the two of you later this evening at your home."

This was something that Meiko obviously had not expected. The daggers that were previously stabbing out from her eyes became confused butterflies.

"Trev, you're not . . . coming with us?"

Mrs. Kurita spoke to her chauffeur. "Please write down directions for Mr. Galt."

"I'm sorry," Galt explained to both of them, keeping his tone earnest. "There is something I must attend to."

Mrs. Kurita took the directions from her chauffeur, and appraised him. "Will you join us for dinner, then? Say, six o'clock?"

He glanced at his watch, calculating the time necessary for what he had in mind.

"That would be my pleasure. I'll see you both then."

Mrs. Kurita started to lean across Meiko, intending to hand the directions to Galt. Meiko prevented this by nimbly plucking the paper from the woman's fingers and handing it to Galt herself. Mrs. Kurita sat back, this time in stony silence; not frowning, Galt noted, but there was clearly no love lost between these two.

Handing him the piece of paper, Meiko said, "I should go with you. I know the city."

"So do I," said Galt. "You two have a safe drive home. I'll join you at six o'clock."

Meiko started to respond, but Galt was already out of the limo, and stepped back, closing the door with a smile just for her that he hoped would take the edge off. It did not. He saw the flare-up of emotion in her eyes in the instant before he closed the door, then the heavily tinted glass blocked her from his sight.

He watched the limo pull away, observed the driver merge skillfully into the flow of traffic along the crowded thoroughfare leading away from the terminal. He could detect no vehicle following the limo, but he knew that he couldn't be sure. When the Kurita limo disappeared from his sight amid the traffic, he glanced down at the little square of paper. It contained precisely written directions in English. He pocketed the paper, then re-entered the bustling terminal, making his way to a row of car rental agencies. At one of these, he used a phony name that matched a fake passport and ID before he found himself steering a new-smelling Toyota sedan.

He took the tollbooth entrance to the elevated Shuto Expressway, north into the smoggy heart of the Tokyo basin, an industrial complex overcrowded with 15 million people. Traffic flow on the freeway was dense, but moved fast.

The core of the city, ringed with criss-crossed layers of expressways, was a towering forest of sleek skyscrapers rising above a steady, chaotic cacophony of noisy commuter trains and overcrowded streets.

Galt hooked up with the central expressway and took that to the city's Little Texas red-light district. He felt naked without a weapon, but carrying one would have been difficult to explain if the police caught him with it. Tokyo is a city with an international reputation for being safe. Japan is a country still anchored in ritual and respect, with a sense of order and safety absent in more freewheeling cultures. Firearms are illegal in Japan. Galt was determined to keep as low a profile as possible during this phase of his investigation. He was skating on the thinnest of ice.

They would have confirmed his disappearance by now. Given his personal connection with Kate, and his verbal assertions of displeasure at how the *Liberty* situation was being handled, they—the White House and anyone else interested enough—would know this was a prelude to his own covert op, and any number of interested parties could have their own reasons for wanting to stop him. Any thought of contacting the American Embassy on Tokyo's embassy row, Sibuti Street in the Asakusa district, was out of the question. He had unfettered himself of the constraints of his official job, and in the process had also abandoned what cover such constraints afforded him. He was on his own, in every way imaginable.

He parked his car in a pay lot and strolled down a narrow side street, off the Ginza Strip: a street clogged with cars, trucks, rickshaws, pedicabs and countless bicycles. Little Texas is a raucous, densely cluttered sprawl of topless bars, live sex shows, Turkish baths and a sprinkling of almost-respectable restaurants and coffee shops; a neon-and-rabble-saturated world, primarily crowded by American GI's on leave from Okinawa intermingling with Japanese businessmen, tourists, laborers, gangsters and, of course, the prostitutes who are everywhere, dressed in the exaggerated, garish sexuality of their profession, calling out to every male in sight.

The Butt 'N Boobs was a two-story structure marked by a flashing red and yellow neon sign, in English and Japanese, sandwiched in between a sex toys novelty shop and a more sedate structure that, in this neighborhood, could only have been a whorehouse. A fellow stood on the sidewalk in front of the bar, raising his voice above the blaring music spilling out from the doorway behind him.

"In here, gentlemen! Right this way! The prettiest girls in Tokyo! Lap dances! Cheap drinks!" When Galt passed him on his way in, the man said, "Excellent choice, sir, and have a good—"

His words were lost beneath the assault on Galt's senses as Galt stepped across the threshold, into the club.

The floor and walls of the place were shuddering to recorded rock music that vied in decibel level with the inebriated hooting and hollering of drunken men. On small, round stages, placed strategically throughout the club, shapely young women danced provocatively beneath baby pink stage lights. The smoky atmosphere, the rowdy patrons and the slam-bang music combined to make it seem to Galt as if there was not enough oxygen in here.

He brought an elbow into play and nudged his way through to the American-style oak bar that ran the length of the club. The bar was lined three-deep with patrons. Galt stood at one end of the bar and beckoned a harried-looking Japanese bartender who wore a spotless white shirt and bow tie.

The bartender sidled over to him. "Yes sir, what you drink?" He had to shout over the surrounding racket.

Galt leaned across the bar, getting jostled from both sides. "I want Barney Markee."

"I not know him," the bartender said promptly, and turned his back on Galt to attend to a cluster of raucous American servicemen, some of whom had their arms around scantily clad "party girls," employees of the club supplied to help get the patrons drunk while they themselves drank watered-down cocktails before offering sexual favors—for a price, of course.

"I'll find him myself," Galt muttered under his breath.

There was a beaded curtain to one side of the bar, and he commenced elbowing his way in that direction. He saw that the archway led to a narrow stairway to the building's second level. Galt stepped through the archway and, with a last glance over his shoulder in the barman's direction, he saw the bartender pausing in his work to speak hurriedly into a house phone next to his cash register, his eyes on Galt as he spoke.

Galt climbed the stairs, two at a time, to a well-lighted landing. A carpeted hallway, lined with doors, stretched in either direction from the landing.

A pair of Japanese men, wearing casual slacks and tropical shirts, stood before the first door to the right. Each man was of average Japanese height and build, but each had obviously spent more than a little time working out. Their muscles bulged beneath their T-shirts. One of the men was replacing the receiver of a wall phone. There was no doubt in Galt's mind that the man had just finished speaking to the bartender. He glowered at Galt.

"What you want, cowboy?"

Shoulder to shoulder, they blocked Galt's approach to the door behind them as if they were sentries. The second one sneered, as if dealing with errant Americans was nothing new.

"No girls up here, buster. You go downstairs. Watch titty dancers. Get nice girl. Go next door. Good cat house."

"I don't want a cat house," said Galt. "I want to see Barney."

"Barney," the first one repeated. "That funny name, cowboy. You go now, or you get hurt."

The other one snickered. "No Barney. You Americans have strange names."

"Don't we, though?" said Galt. "And you know what's even more strange? Barney Markee happens to own this den of iniquity. Now doesn't that make it even stranger that you've never heard of your boss?"

The man on the left frowned. "Den of what?"

"I said take me to him," said Galt quietly, "or I'll take myself."

The one on the right snarled, "We take you, cowboy, out back and beat shit out of you, that's what we do."

They came at Galt in unison, the one on the right bringing up his fists, which were adorned with brass knuckles. His partner swung a leather sap out and up from a back pocket, arcing it around at Galt's head.

Galt clamped both of his hands like a vise around the wrist of the arm swinging the blackjack and shoved that wrist back so the sap sharply smacked the other man between the eyes with enough force to knock him off his feet, breaking his nose. Galt then brought the man's arm down across his raised knee. The crack! of the arm breaking was unusually loud in the confines of the hallway. The man dropped. He opened his mouth to shout his pain but, before he could, Galt released the broken arm, grabbed the man's head by either side and smashed his face into the wall. The man collapsed, sprawling across the carpet, next to his companion, a thin trickle of blood oozing from one nostril of his broken nose. Their ragged breathing filled the corridor. Galt turned when he sensed movement behind him.

Barney Markee had positioned his wheelchair in the doorway. He regarded the fallen men as he fired a cigarette from a Zippo lighter. Then he shifted his gaze to Galt through a cloud of exhaled smoke.

"Looks like I need to hire me some competent help. Hey, Trev."

"Hey, Barney."

Barney Markee was fifty-four years old, with owl-like features, a balding pate and deep, knowing eyes that were magnified by the thick lenses of his glasses. He had the gruff, authoritative manner of a big man, despite his diminutive stature in the wheelchair. Large-boned, gray-bearded, he possessed an easygoing personal style that, Galt knew, would have remained unchanged in the presence of the pope or a pimp.

Footfalls clumped up the stairway, and another pair of bouncers arrived. They took one look at the situation and threw themselves toward Galt. Barney raised a hand, halting them in mid-stride.

"Let him be," he commanded quietly. He indicated the fallen men. "Get these two out of here. They're fired. See that these bouncers bounce when you toss them out the alley door."

"Yes sir, Boss," both men chimed in unison like harmonizing parrots. They each tossed one of the unconscious bouncers over a shoulder and trundled them away.

Galt relaxed, stepping over to trade a firm handshake with the man in the wheelchair.

"Thanks, Barn. Sorry about the fuss."

Barney chuckled. "Hey, it's not like bonehead goons aren't a dime a dozen in this town . . . or anywhere else, for that matter." He back-wheeled his chair from the doorway. "Come on in, buddy. Help yourself to some coffee, if you dare."

The office appeared at first to be a hodgepodge of male disarray, but was in reality a utilization of every available space for stacks of books and plants. A tawny-colored pet ferret left its cage, and came over to make a sniffing circle around Galt before returning to the cage, completely disinterested. Classic jazz filtered softly from unseen speakers. The office's most prominent feature was the enormous plate glass window that provided an ideal vantage point, a bird's-eye view, of the crowded, smoke-filled, raucous strip club interior below. The office was obviously soundproofed, creating a strange effect, thought Galt, like viewing a silent movie nightclub scene accompanied by classical music.

Barney scanned the carnal madhouse beyond the glass. He frowned, emitted a growl of displeasure, and picked up a phone from beside a computer in a corner work area.

Galt saw the same busy bartender he'd spoken to moments earlier. The harried man picked up the house phone next to his cash register on what must have been its first ring. Galt turned to a coffeepot to draw himself a cup as Barney commenced barking orders into the phone like a military field commander.

"Those three sailors right in front of you," he snapped at the bartender. "They're fixing to tussle with those army guys next to them. I see it coming. Get some hostesses over there fast to level things off. And that jerk at table seven. I saw him pinching that lap dancer's titties just now, and that's a goddamn no-no. See that he's bounced."

He didn't wait to listen to the chattering reply across the connection, which Galt could hear from across the room. Barney hung up the telephone receiver. He wheeled around to face Galt.

Barney Markee had been struck by polio at age ten, and wheelchair-bound ever since. But this terrible illness, and life in a wheelchair, had in no way blunted Barney Markee's zest for life. It was much as when a blind person's system compensates with an increased awareness of his other senses. Trevor Galt III was to the manor born. Barney was from a far different background. His folks were live-in nanny and assistant to a rich family down the road from the Galts in rural Maryland. Barney's parents would have been called a maid and a butler in earlier times. They lived in a house behind their employers', and somehow Barney and Trev had become buddies around the age of eight. One of their favorite pastimes had been taking hikes in the woods around where their families lived. Barney couldn't do any serious hiking, obviously, but with Trev pushing the wheelchair, they'd make forays into the woods and have long conversations, discussing girls and movies and girls and what they would become when they grew up and, of course, girls . . . until that time came when they began actually dating girls instead of just talking about them.

After attending college, Barney had gone on to work professionally and with distinction in the field of psychology before he dropped out, utterly uninterested in the "bullshit politics" of that profession, as he had informed Galt at the time. Blessed with an IQ in the genius range, Barney had gone on to teach himself computers, mastering them to such a degree that Galt had been instrumental in arranging a "working" visit by his best friend to Fort Huachuca, the little known U.S. military installation in Arizona that straddles the U.S. border with Mexico. Huachuca is home to the Signal Corps, the "AT&T of the military," which rapidly deploys to places like Kuwait and Kosovo during international U.S. military operations. Fort Huachuca also handled a high-tech covert surveillance "listening station" for intercepting communications, everything from eavesdropping on closed-door government meetings in Mexico City to tapping cell phone conversations between drug dealers in Bogota. Such electronic intel is automatically routed to the agencies concerned. Galt had so availed himself of the Fort's "services" that, by the time he was assigned to the White House, he had managed to isolate several glitches in the Huachuca operation. Though far from computer literate enough to have any idea of how to fix such trouble spots, he had recommended his old friend Barney for the job, knowing that there would be a big enough government payday for his buddy to buy whatever lifestyle he wanted. After massive background checks, security clearances and the like, a process that had pushed Barney to being as grouchy and irascible as Galt had ever seen him, Markee traveled to the Arizona desert to not only fix those computer glitches but go on to completely overhaul and redesign the relay program software that rerouted encoded transmissions to Washington. The government drew on its best computer personnel for duty at Huachuca, and after Barney's overhaul, after witnessing this astounding self-taught computer whiz in action, the post commander had taken the unprecedented measure of requesting that he be permanently assigned in a civilian tech support role. The only roadblock was that, after his work was done, Barney had taken his fat paycheck and disappeared. That was the last time Galt had seen him, though Barney had given him this Tokyo address before dropping out of sight.

Now, Barney replenished his own coffee cup and regarded Galt over the rims of his Ben Franklin glasses that had slid to the tip of his nose. He took a noisy slurping sip of the bitter brew that he had always referred to as rocket fuel. The man in the wheelchair regarded him with an owlish gaze from behind thick glasses.

"So, did they give you a pass out of the White House

basement? You're on the loose a long way from home, Trevboy." It was a name that Barney (and only Barney) had been calling Galt since boyhood.

"I'm more than out on the loose, buddy," said Galt. "I'm off mission. I'm in the cold."

"I have heard something about that, now that you mention it." Barney nodded to his PC. "I monitor the classified op tac nets the way some old boys back home monitor the police band for recreation."

"I know. So what do you know about me that I don't know?"

"For starters," said Barney dryly, "they're afraid you're about to start World War III. And I am not indulging in idle hyperbole." Barney's owlish gaze was dead serious. "I suppose you could conceivably know what you're doing."

"Do you know about the shuttle?"

Barney's glasses had slipped down to the end of his nose. He absently index-fingered them back onto the bridge of his nose, more or less. "I know everything."

"And that," said Galt, "is why I'm here."

Barney snapped his fingers like someone really disappointed. "Damn, and I thought you came all this way because you like the taste of my coffee."

Galt glanced into his cup and winced. "Is that what you call it?" He finished the cup's contents with a slurp and set the cup down. "We can't let the bad guys get their grubby hands on that shuttle, Barn."

"No one, as far as I can tell, is disagreeing with that."

Galt grimaced. "But they're not doing a damn thing about it. The president seems to have his hands tied. The military is on alert, but we're not even sending in a search and rescue team while everybody knows the North Koreans and the Chinese are doing everything but leveling those mountains to find a trace of the *Liberty* and its crew."

"You forgot to mention that the president's wife is not among the missing crewmembers."

"Yeah, I guess I did forget that. Are you suggesting that Kate being one of the astronauts is clouding my mind?"

Barney's shrug was one of nonjudgmental eloquence. "Just making an observation, is all." He nodded again to the PC. "I've been picking up plenty of traffic on you. They have a hunch that you've come to this part of the world."

"I'm willing to bet that all of Tokyo is wired for my arrival."

Barney chuckled. "And that's the kicker, isn't it? Because they know that you've got more ability than anyone they've got. Fact of the matter is, Trevboy, I've been half-expecting you."

"And?"

"What the hell do you think? They want you home. All is forgiven."

"Right. World War III? Even if I make it home with my ass intact, it'd be a toss-up between which they do first, skin me alive or throw me into solitary for the rest of life."

Another noisy coffee slurp from Barney. "I see that we eschew hyperbole in preference of stating cold, hard fact. Yes, that about sums it up from the comm traffic I've hacked into."

"Our best hackers," said Galt, "told me that you're the best hacker in the world."

Barney's eyes crinkled behind the Ben Franklins. "Excuse me for blushing."

"And you were thoughtful enough to burn all of

your bridges and completely drop out of sight after that payday in Arizona. I only knew where to find you because you told me."

"I like living in Tokyo. I've been told that Occidentals can find Japanese politeness excessive and exaggerated. The Japanese regard Western displays of emotion, like the hello or goodbye hug, the kissing on the cheek between mere acquaintances, as vulgar and in poor taste. It's a communication gap that makes it extremely difficult for an outsider to tell what a Jap is really thinking, and vice versa. I find that to be a reassuringly civilized way to co-exist with those around me. And, of course," with a wry grin he indicated the plate glass window and the bar scene beyond, "a man can never see enough bare titty in his life, I always say."

"You know what I'm about to say, don't you?" said Galt.

Barney nodded. "You're about to point out that somewhere in this mix is someone who can bring down an American space shuttle. You intend to follow through by pointing out that they could just as easily take down a gimp buried away in Little Texas, no matter how many bodyguards he has." The man in the wheelchair flicked back his faded flannel shirt to reveal a pistol grip protruding from the waist of his cutoff slacks. He patted the pistol. "Don't worry about me. I'm not about to run from anybody." When he heard his own words, Barney laughed. "Guess I couldn't run if I wanted to."

Galt forced himself to pour another cup from the coffee pot. The jolt of caffeine to his system restored the edge to his senses that had become mildly affected by jet lag and negotiating traffic in a foreign city. His lethargy was peeling away with each sip of Barney's bitter brew. "I need to contact General Tuttle. I need him over here with me, and I need access to his resources."

Barney sighed. "Well, nobody ever said you lacked for ambition."

"Every standard channel of linkage between me and the general is out. You know there's no such thing as a secure line. If I make contact with him, they have me."

"So you want me to tap the general for you. You want me to contribute to starting World War III."

"If we get rock-solid proof that the *Liberty* went down on North Korean soil, Pyongyang will cooperate. They won't start a war. They'll remember what happened to the Taliban in Afghanistan."

"It says here. Okay, I can tap the general without leaving a trail. So what do I tell him?"

"That I need some backup cover over here on the double. And there's something else."

Barney sighed theatrically. "Ain't there always."

"I'm trying to find a stripper."

Barney guffawed. "Well Jeez, bro, I've got a whole building full of 'em." He indicated the plate glass window and the smoky bump-and-grind atmosphere beyond. "Take your pick."

"Sorry, Barn, I appreciate the hospitality but I'm not talking personal use here, and I am talking about a particular stripper."

"Then I figure that would be Connie Yota, if that's er real name," said Barney. "The Feds have been try-g to backtrack that little sweetie ever since she took wn their NASA scientist, but so far, nada. She seems uinely not to know who she was working for. The

club she claimed she worked at was here in
Texas, but it burned to the ground a year ago ar
trail appears to stop there."

"For you, too?" asked Galt.

"Okay, okay," said Barney. "I'll tap a few source
see what I can come up with. What about you?"

"I'm on the move. Matter of fact, I'd better be
to moving right now."

"Uh huh. In other words, don't call you, you'
me."

"It's better for you that way," said Galt. "I don't
them backtracking you through me."

"And 'them,' in this case would be, uh, who exa

"That's the problem. When we find that out,
be piped into the core, into what's really goi
here."

Barney wheeled around to his computer terr
"And your message to General Tuttle is to get his
star ass over here to Tokyo ASAP."

"I'll meet him tomorrow at the Meiji Shri
twelve-hundred hours, Tokyo time."

"Tomorrow, eh? Damn, Trevboy, I will be ho
and consider myself amply compensated for r
forts on your behalf, if I can facilitate Pentagon
dropping everything and hauling tail over he
your say-so." Barney's wise eyes crinkled. "And I
he'll be there."

"I'll need an update from the general at that t
intend to be pretty much out of that loop until th

"Prudent," said Barney. "Very prudent."

"And the CIA has an intel source on the gr
somewhere in Hamgyong Province in North Ko
want to know if that source has reported in yet
the nature of that report."

Barney palmed his mouse and began clicking double-time, following links on his computer screen. "Count on me, Trevboy."

"I am," said Galt. "Thanks," and he let himself out.

Chapter Sixteen

He drove west out of Tokyo, taking the elevated Tomei Expressway toward the mountains beyond the city. Traffic was heavy, as it was twenty-four hours a day. Also, as usual, motorists in Tokyo maintained a constant bumper-to-bumper speed that seemed more like orchestrated activity than the vehicular madness of similar population-dense places like Rome or Mexico City.

Night cloaked the world. Before long, the ocean of neon passing by beneath the freeway gave way to mile after mile of dismal gray, drab factories and danchi, whole square miles of tightly-packed, bleak apartment buildings. Eventually, this too dwindled to longer, uninterrupted stretches of darkness as the freeway reached beyond the suburbs.

Following the directions written by Mrs. Kurita's chauffeur, he took the final exit just before the Masahino Mountains, and found himself quite suddenly traveling through remote countryside, on a two-lane rural blacktop highway that ran between foothills to the west, steep slopes covered with thick forests of cedar and pine in the moonlight, and, to the east, tiers of water-filled rice fields. The road took him past an occasional thatched-roof farmhouse, and then the agricultural homesteads gave way to a more exclusive environment of upscale, in many cases walled, residential estates. Privacy, a cherished commodity in Japan, is most often the domain of the very rich.

He found the Kurita address easily enough. He assessed what he could of the security here as he upshifted the Toyota along a gravel driveway lined with chestnut trees. Conifer trees and bamboo grew in abundance across the expansive grounds. To his left was a grove of katsura and birch, with flagstones leading to a six-foot-high bronze statue of Buddha, beyond which was a massive garden.

The main house was a traditional home beneath a gray-green slate roof that curved upward at each corner, high-lighted by the moonlight and by some artfully-placed lighting.

Galt parked in front of the main entrance. His was the only vehicle in sight. He left the car and approached the house, habitually wary of new surroundings, his peripheral senses probing the darkness around him beyond the light, processing no real danger lurking out there at this time. To Galt, a peaceful neighborhood was as dangerous as a jungle trail in Chiapas or a walk to the corner store for a pack of gum in Beirut. Things might seem tranquil enough on the surface, and perhaps they were, but paranoia was the only sane course. Your best bet was to expect trouble from any direction at any time. There were places that were like that, and Galt recognized that his whole life had become "like that" now that he had dropped out of sight as completely as only a man with his background, experience and connections possibly could.

He expected that the gate guard had called ahead, that a servant or maid would greet him and show him into the house, to Mrs. Kurita and Meiko. And so he was mildly surprised when, as he stepped onto the front step and raised an index finger to press the doorbell, the front door was opened inward not by a maid or a servant.

Sachito Kurita stood there, holding the door open for him, with Meiko next to and only slightly behind her. The two women, separated as they were by more than two decades in age, were framed side-by-side in golden illumination, from inside the house, that caressed and highlighted their beauty better than any Hollywood studio lighting director ever could. The widow wore a tastefully elegant black silk Meikoono with a black sash.

Meiko wore a wraparound dark skirt and an embroidered silk blouse with loose sleeves that conveyed more than a suggestion of the traditional Meikoono, while being thoroughly modern.

Mrs. Kurita extended her hand. "Trev, welcome. Your journey from the city was uneventful, I trust?" The handshake was as warm and vibrant as her flesh tone.

He presented her with the bottle of sake he'd brought along. "Please accept this as a gift for your home. Tokyo traffic is always a challenge," he added with a muted smile of his own, "but Meiko will tell you that I embrace challenge. Thank you for having me."

Meiko looked as if she wanted to throw herself into his arms with a hug of appreciation and gladness, as a Western woman would with a male friend or a lover in this situation. But he saw this in her eyes only because they were lovers. Outwardly, she held back with the traditional cultural reserve of the Japanese woman. She too extended a hand.

"Trev. So good to see you." Her handshake was more vibrant than Mrs. Kurita's had been and lasted a moment longer.

"We'll have drinks, then dinner," said Mrs. Kurita.

The sitting room, where a servant eventually did materialize to properly serve them the sake, was appointed in the classic Japanese style: flower-painted wall screens, a glimpse of a formal garden and fragile cloisonné vases of ikebana, the traditional Japanese art of flower arranging. Upon a short rosewood table was a portrait of Meiko's father: a once handsome, delicately sculpted face wrinkled with age. In the picture, long snow-white whiskers flowed from Mr. Kurita's chin. But the eyes were youthful and alert, piercing and direct.

When the sake was served, Meiko faced the photograph and raised her glass in a toast.

"To my father. A great man."

Galt lifted his glass appropriately and sipped the sake.

Sachito Kurita started to raise her glass, then paused. Her lower lip trembled. She set down her cup and lifted the picture, clasping the framed portrait over her heart. Tears seeped from the corners of her eyes.

"I miss him so. He was a great man, your father. He loved you so much, Meiko. And I loved him."

There was an awkward silence of some duration, which Galt broke by posing some banal question to their hostess concerning the history of the region. An awkward flow of conversation resumed. Galt interpreted Meiko's brief glance in his direction as one of appreciation for smoothing things over. There was not a drop of affection between these two, even given the somber circumstance of having been drawn together by Mr. Kurita's passing. Sachito and Meiko showed Trev to the guestroom where he would be staying. His sleeping quarters were directly across a corridor from Meiko's bedroom, and Galt found himself starting to wonder if this was such a hot idea. He had much to accomplish, a potential Third World War to avert, even if some thought that what was truly at risk here was him starting World War III! And yet here he was, caught up in this female psychodrama. But there was nothing to be done for now until he connected with Tuttle, and the fact of the matter was that he had committed himself to this course . . .

Eventually, a maid politely appeared to bow deeply and inform Madam Kurita that dinner was ready. The dining room was also traditional, with a lacquered beamed ceiling and a plank floor of immaculately polished cypress. There were low stools and tables, antique Japanese landscape paintings and shelves filled with carved animals out of Japanese mythology, each wooden statue delicately painted and gilded. Sliding portions of the left wall were half-open, revealing a glimpse of the massive garden beyond, directly outside. The sounds of soft, atonal music wafted on air delicately scented with incense. Dinner was at a long table with Galt and Meiko seated opposite each other, and Mrs. Kurita at the far end.

They ate sushi from exquisite rose china plates. Galt silently chopsticked his meal as if blissfully oblivious of the unspoken, hostile undercurrent that continued between the women, just beneath the surface of cool civility.

At one point, Sachito attempted to make eye contact across the table with Meiko, at first to no avail. "Meiko, please do not think harshly of me."

Meiko looked up from her mostly untouched portion of sushi. "I am sorry, stepmother, but it cannot be otherwise. I am a guest in your home. I will not disrespect you. I will leave with Trev, if you wish."

"That is hardly my wish, my dear. This is my home only because I was your father's wife. But it is your home before that, and I will not disrespect that. You were born in this house. You spent the first eighteen years of your life here."

"It was my home when my mother was alive," said Meiko. "At least my father waited a suitable time after becoming a widower to marry you. He waited until I was overseas."

Yearning glistened in Sachito's dark eyes. "Why do I displease you so, Meiko? I am a good woman. I treated your father well. Was he not entitled to happiness after grieving the passing of your mother? Life must go on. Your father loved me. Why can you not at least like me? Perhaps you did not know that for the last year of your father's life, his business decisions were relayed to his attorneys and the board of directors through me. Toward the end, when your father was bedridden, he was so weak that he deferred to my judgment in the resolution of many major decisions. I know the workings of Kurita Industries intimately, both in Japan and worldwide. I allowed your father to feel a sense of pride and productivity during his final days. I should think that you would feel somewhat beholden to me for that alone, if not a sense of kinship, since we both loved and have lost him."

Meiko set down her chopsticks. "I understand that some of my feelings are irrational, which is why I have not voiced them," she said in calm, measured tones. "You took my mother's place in my father's heart . . . and in his bed. I know that such resentment on a daughter's part is irrational and is, in fact, standard behavior, which infuriates me; a form of grieving my mother, even after the passage of time. I despair for this weakness in my character. But some of what I feel toward you is rational. Why was I not summoned home at once, if my father was so ill? I had no idea. Why was I not informed? Whose decision was that? Father and I spoke on the telephone at least once a week after I first went to America. They were brief conversations, but he sounded healthy enough to me."

"It was his wish that you not be told of his condition," said Sachito. "He wanted your career to come first. He did not want to burden you with his health problems."

"You could have told me," Meiko said plaintively, in the voice of a little girl enduring deep inner suffering; an unsettled mixture of regret, accusation, hurt and uncertainty, which Galt had never heard from her before.

Sachito remained seated stiff-backed at the head of the table. She too had set down her chopsticks beside her half-finished meal.

"It was his wish," she repeated. "I obeyed the wish of my husband, as a good wife should. And he wished until his last breath that you would take me into your heart."

"I cannot." She leapt to her feet, muttering the words more in shame than anything else, thought Galt. She whirled from the table and exited the dining room, leaving Galt and Mrs. Kurita alone in uncomfortable silence.

Galt finished the last of his sushi, set down his chopsticks and rose from the table. "I'm sorry. I'll talk to her. I'll do what I can."

Sachito's eyes were moist, unreadable. "My heart goes out to her." There was resignation in her words. "Tomorrow is . . . the day. It will be best, I think, if we attend the funeral together, the three of us. That is the only right way. It is what Mr. Kurita would have wanted."

"I'll do what I can."

"I shall now retire for the evening, Mr. Galt. Please accept my apologies for what can only have been an uncomfortable ordeal for you, listening to Meiko and me quarrel. And yet I want to thank you very much for being here . . . for Meiko."

"It's my privilege to help, if I can. I'll speak with her."

He rose from the table with her, and they exchanged another handshake. "From what her father told me about Meiko, my guess is that you will find her in the garden." Her grip was more fragile than before, and was more fleeting. "Good night, Mr. Galt."

A pair of stone lanterns framed the entrance to the mossy quiet of a formal Zen rock garden, which was surrounded on three sides by a low bamboo fence and sheltered by the sweeping overhang of the roof. Waxed paper screens on this side of the house made a fourth decorative wall. Galt followed a series of hexagonal stepping stones that led him between angular rocks and Japanese dwarf maple trees, twisted and gnarled, to where he found Meiko standing before a small arched bridge of red lacquered wood, and a Shinto shrine. He stepped up behind Meiko, making just enough of a scuffle upon the stepping stones for her to become aware of his presence. He slid his arms around her.

She leaned back against him. Her subtle musk perfume tantalized his nostrils like an invisible, scented feather. Exhaustion, spiritual and physical, emanated from her as he held her in his embrace.

"I'm sorry, Trev. I'm overwrought. It's jet lag. It's everything. Father's death. This place. That woman."

"You know your Zen Buddhist philosophy." He spoke softly through her hair, his lips close to her ear, with a lover's intimacy. "We study our lives. We master ourselves. We assume responsibility."

She sighed, observing the Torii gate with its unusual carvings in wood of dragons and dogs. "I know what you're telling me. Oh, Trev. I don't know what to think. I can't control the memories that flood through me, being here. This is where I grew up with my mother and father. Such happy days for me. I wish you had known them. I was lucky to have them both." A bittersweet, nostalgic melancholy softened her tone. "Mother never taught me very much about housework. Even when I was a young girl, she always let me know that she respected my goals. She let me feel that I could be whatever I wanted to be. That is so important to a young girl in any culture, at any time. When I came of age and announced an interest in pursuing a career in journalism, my father at first vehemently opposed the idea. He was against any alternative except marriage, opposed to any education beyond high school. I do not judge him harshly for this. My father was a man of tradition, of a different time. And he did acquiesce after considerable lobbying on the part of my mother. Once he had accepted the notion of his daughter pursuing a higher education, Father naturally favored a proper girl's school. I wanted to go to Tokyo University. It's the best in Japan, and my father had gone there. I knew it would offer the best education for the work I wanted. He stringently resisted me attending a coeducational university. Again Mother helped me, in her own ways, to overcome his resistance. She had married young and it wasn't always easy for her, despite my father's wealth and position. She ingrained in me early the notion that a woman should be independent. I was made strong by her support. My father's opposition also toughened me. And in the end, he was fair. He told me that if I could pass the exam, if they would take me, then I could attend Tokyo University. That is what happened, and is but one of many reasons, from the tapestry of my life, why I love and cherish his memory so and why my emotions run deep." Her voice thickened with a sob. "I miss him so."

Galt turned her in his arms, his lips remaining near her ear. "Tomorrow is the funeral. Your father wanted you to be there with the woman he married. You know it's what you're going to do."

Her forehead leaned against his shoulder, and the scent of her raven's-wing black hair tantalized his nostrils again, more than before. With her head on his shoulder, she nodded.

"I will go to the funeral with Sachito and . . ." she raised her moist eyes to him, ". . . with you?"

"Of course. That's why I'm here."

That made her body stiffen somewhat. She drew back, not from his embrace but to sniffle back another sob and use the palm of one hand to brusquely wipe away a tear that had beaded in the corner of one of her eyes. "I know that you care for me, Trev. But my father's death and what I'm going through . . . you came here with me to exploit my situation for your own ends."

"Honey, we had this conversation in Washington before we left."

Her green eyes softened with still another mood shift. "I am sorry, Trev. My mood seems to change every half-second. I am glad you're here." And she lifted her face to deliver him a chaste kiss on the cheek.

"Focus," he suggested. "Get through tomorrow. After that, your healing will begin. I know you're that strong, Meiko."

"Thank you for saying that. Right now I feel like the most fragile person on earth. And the most selfish. What you're doing, your real reason for coming to Japan . . . it's for Kate, to find her and the crew of the *Liberty*. You're an incredible and noble man, and I do want you to succeed."

"Thanks for saying that, and for the vote of confidence. I know that in your heart, Meiko, you understand. Now, how about some sack time?"

Her eyes twinkled weakly. Her lips curved feebly. "My, aren't you the devil."

"Not really. Not this time, anyway. Even if we had adjoining bedrooms, which we don't . . . well, you're not the only one who's dragging, kiddo, believe me."

They returned to the house, holding hands.

There was no sign of anyone when they re-entered the home. The traditional music had ceased, although tendrils of incense still wafted through the air. The servants had cleared away the table in the dining room, and disappeared. When they were stepping lightly past the closed partition to Sachito Kurita's bedroom on their way to their bedrooms, they could hear her muffled sobbing, as if she were clutching and wailing into a pillow; an aching moan of torment audible enough to cause a wince to pass between Galt and Meiko as they hurried past.

The sounds had faded by the time they reached the partition of Meiko's bedroom.

"Good night, Trev. I'm sorry I'm so confused and emotional. It isn't like me."

"I know that. Good night, Meiko."

She stood on her tiptoes, kissed him quickly, warmly, on the lips, then disappeared into the bedroom.

Minutes later, Galt was stretched out on his futon, willing his senses into a restful state. But his rational mind kept pecking away at any attempt to relax. Come tomorrow, everything would be kicking one way or another. There was so much to be done. But first, of course, a target had to be ascertained: the space shuttle's location. That's where General Tuttle came in.

His subconscious prevailed, with the help of applied yoga meditation technique, and his conscious mind temporarily put conflict to rest and he yielded to a mild, restful sleep-like replenishment of his mind, spirit and body. But one recurring conscious ripple did make his slumber a fitful one. Tomorrow could not come fast enough. He had come to this part of the world to find Kate and *Liberty*, and nothing short of death would stop him.

Chapter Seventeen

North Korea

Ahn Chong topped the hill and walked slowly into the graveyard.

The night air was heavy with the dampness of dead leaves, mingled with the scent of the pine. The mountain breeze whispering through the pines was normally a comfort to him when he came to this spot, but not tonight. He might find solitude here, but there was no place on this night where he would find comfort. When he would walk here to visit Mai's grave, his thoughts were most often of his loss, his grief. Not tonight. Tonight he walked slowly along the winding path through the trees that led to the wilderness clearing, the misshapen quadrangle of land where his village buried its dead. Tonight, as he walked along, he tried to project the appearance of a man lost in thought. But his eyes were busy, scanning the forested surroundings like a hunter. He did not see or hear anything unusual by the time he reached the graveyard. He sensed no other human presence but his own.

This time of year, the twisted fruit trees lining the small hillside clearing were bare. He knelt at Mai's grave, to lean over and kiss the crudely wrought, simple headstone. During daylight visits, the stone was most often warm to the touch, even during the winter months, warmed by the sunshine though he would tell himself that it was the warmth of Mai's spirit.

Not tonight. Tonight he could not forget the worries that consumed him even now, even at this most sacred of places to him. His wife's name passed his lips and he remained kneeling at her graveside, gazing upon her headstone as if it might provide him with answers and comfort.

Neither came to him.

It was at this exact spot that the extraordinary chain of events had begun; a series of incredible occurrences still unfolding at an alarming rate, the stakes rising and scope broadening with every passing minute from his humble village to the large world beyond his small and insignificant world. Something of this magnitude was surely creating a world crisis, and it was numbing for him to think that he was at the center of it. The space shuttle's overflight had taken it far enough into the valley, away from the village, to allow the acoustics of the mountainous terrain to mute the sounds of the crash from his village. But because he had been here at his wife's gravesite, he had certainly heard, and his life had changed in the instant when he had chosen to investigate and had beheld the awesome, snow-swept sight of the enormous spacecraft, and had made the acquaintance of the American crew. Because of this, he had endured watching his daughter have a gun pointed at her head, and the longstanding animosity between himself and his son-in-law had resurfaced at the worst time, especially considering the other secret held by Ahn; a deep, old, dirty secret that would get Ahn killed in an instant, were anyone else to learn of it. Events had overtaken and were overwhelming him.

He whispered again to the headstone before which he knelt, his hands folded as a man praying to a shrine.

"Mai . . ."

A male voice behind him said, in a snide, mocking tone, "How very touching."

The voice broke the stillness, and Ahn's contemplation, like a gunshot. He leapt to his feet, realizing that he had been so lost in his reverie that he, the reputed best hunter in his village, had been surprised like the dumbest of animals.

A pair of men had soundlessly approached the clearing from behind, and they now stood facing him. They were not soldiers, but they were not civilians. They wore camouflage fatigues, and each was heavily armed with a pistol, a sheathed knife and a rifle.

One of them had the finely-boned physique of the Chinese, but was of muscular build. An old knife scar bisected one side of his face. A headband held back greasy hair that glistened.

He demanded, "Do you know who I am, old man?"

"Yes, I know who you are. You are Chai Bin." He saw no reason to add that his wanderings through these mountains had taken him to their base, which he'd observed more than once from afar.

Chai smiled an unpleasant smile. "And I know who you are, Ahn Chong."

Ahn had regained his composure after having been startled. He drew himself to full stature.

"Everyone seems to know everything about old Ahn Chong, from the military commander of the airfield to common hill bandits."

The man who stood next to Chai took a menacing step forward. He reeked of foul body odor. He drew a hand back, about to strike Ahn.

"Curb your insolence, peasant—"

Chai raised his hand in a gesture that stayed the other. "Han, no. I do not want this old man injured. I seek his cooperation."

Han drew back, glowering. "As you wish." His hand rested on the handle of his knife as if he would like nothing better than to step forward and slit Ahn Chong's throat.

Ahn insulted him merely by pretending to ignore him. "Why would I cooperate with you?" he asked Chai. "You are a thief, a murderer, a plunderer."

Chai laughed. "And you're brave as an old buzzard. True, I am those things you say, and more . . . none of it good. But as to why you will cooperate with me, old man, it is for the very reason you stated: because I do know everything about you. As for Colonel Sung, you need search no further than your own family to affix the blame for what happened today in your village."

Ahn blinked. "You know about that?"

"Must I repeat myself? I know everything. I have eyes and ears everywhere. There are those among my men who have relatives in your village. There are those who have brothers or cousins or fathers serving in the military."

"Are you collaborating with the colonel?"

Han snorted, and spat upon the ground. "Fool. The military would love to see us in shackles or dead."

Chai nodded. "I have had the airfield under surveillance since the first day of its construction. When

Sung went to your village today, my 'eyes' were there and they reported to me. They told me what happened. I had already known about the shuttle, of course."

"Of course," said Ahn dryly.

Chai stroked his beard as if in contemplation, but there was mockery in his eyes. "The colonel left his base today on orders from Pyongyang to locate the American spacecraft. Until today the colonel has never left his precious airfield. Peculiar, don't you think?"

"You will forgive me," said Ahn, "but I do not know what to think."

"Then I will answer the question for you. It is most peculiar. Colonel Sung operates under a cloak of absolute secrecy. I wonder if that had anything to do with the space shuttle going down. And if so, who exactly is the good Colonel taking orders from? A helicopter with Japanese civilian markings has been observed landing and taking off from the airfield periodically."

"And why do you tell me these things?" Ahn made a rude sound. "I am like you in one way, Chai Bin. I hold no allegiance to our government. They . . ." He thought to tell them about Mai, of how she died, of the treatment denied his wife by the state. But he could not share the holiness of her memory with men such as these. He said simply, "I hold no allegiance." His eyes narrowed. "You know where the shuttle is."

Chai chuckled. "Naturally, I do. That is why you are here speaking to me, peasant. You see, I know that you are an informant for the CIA."

Ahn gasped as if he had been struck. "But no one—I mean, that is to say . . . no, that's not true!"

He heard himself mumbling the inane protestation

like a truant schoolboy, dumbfounded that his deepest, darkest, most closely guarded secret—the secret that could get him summarily executed—had been stated so casually by this man he'd never met.

"You were supplied with a transmitter," said Chai. "I assume that it's hidden near here, in the vicinity of this graveyard. Your visits to your wife's grave are the perfect cover. Your control officer's code name is Fox Dog Alpha."

"How do you know this about me?"

"When the Americans and the Russians fought their Cold War, I was subsidized by funds from the CIA. I supplied them with routine intelligence. The name of my contact control officer was Fox Dog Alpha. I met him one time only. We got drunk together. He told me things. He told me about you."

Ahn felt his chest tighten. "What do you want of me?"

"I want you to contact Fox Dog Alpha."

"But you just said that he was your—"

"He was my control officer during the Cold War," said Chai. "They abandoned me when they no longer needed me."

Ahn felt drained, sapped of any strength, of any of his own will. "How long have you known my secret?"

"Do not trouble yourself. Your secret has remained safe with me, and will in the future. That is, if you cooperate with me. You," said Chai, "will be my liaison with the Americans. You will pass along what I instruct you to tell them. I have possession of their shuttle and of its crew survivors. I am prepared to negotiate. I, Chai Bin, await their response. You will relay my offer to the United States government."

Onboard Air Force One at forty thousand feet

The designation Air Force One applies to any Air Force plane the president is traveling on, but usually, as now, it was one of two 225-foot Boeing 747-200s, part of the 89th Airlift Wing based out of Andrews Air Force Base in Maryland. Air Force One is more comfortable than the Waldorf Astoria and better stocked than the White House kitchen. There is a conference room, comfortably-padded reclining seats in cabins for senior staff, and quarters for off-duty pilots and Secret Service personnel. There is a medical room where emergency surgery can be performed. There are fax machines as well as eighty-five telephones aboard, and live TV feeds by satellite. The president can make phone calls to anywhere in the world: to astronauts in space, or admirals in submarines. There are two thousand meals aboard, and in-flight refueling is possible after seven thousand miles. Air Force One could stay aloft for a week, though it's never been done. There is a jamming system to deflect antiaircraft missiles, and wiring that can withstand the electromagnetic effects of a thermonuclear blast. Air Force One generally carries seventy passengers, including thirteen journalists who fly in the rear of the plane, and twenty-three crewmembers. The chief executive has a private office with a wooden desk and a swivel leather chair. This "flying Oval Office" is adjoined on one side by a private bedroom with a shower, and on the other by a conference room, which in its time had seen everything from birthday parties to Mideast peace accords brokered in flight well before official announcements were made and treaties signed.

The conference room was presently a war room.

Four men of military background each concluded speed-reading the array of printout data and analysis spread out upon the table, materials brought by each to be shared with the others.

The president sat at the head of the table with MacDonald, his secretary of defense, and Latisha Samuels, his national security advisor, seated to his either side. He was due to address a previously-scheduled fundraising event in San Francisco that evening, and would be attending the opening of a new defense plant the following day.

He leaned back, rubbing his tired eyes, then took a sip from a can of Diet Coke. "So, North Korea shows no sign of backing down?"

"They're stonewalling," said MacDonald. "They want to see how far we'll push it before they budge an inch. They've initiated their own search and rescue."

The president crunched the empty aluminum cola can in his fist. "Damn. Every minute counts. Let's go on the assumption that some or all of the crew did survive. We could have walking wounded over there."

The national security advisor was an attractive woman by any standard, but at the moment her mouth was a tight, angry line. "Their so-called search and rescue would make a fine diversionary tactic."

"If Pyongyang is up to diversionary tactics," said the president, "that suggests that the Koreans brought down that shuttle."

"You're damn right, sir," said MacDonald. "Their airfield in Hamgyong Province is evidence of intent, right in the region where *Liberty* dropped off the screen."

The president ran his fingers through his cropped hair. "But do they have the contacts and the sophistication to reach all the way to Houston and set up a NASA scientist in a sex trap?"

"That," said Samuels, "is why we need to keep the North Koreans from knowing that we know about the existence of that airfield. We know the shuttle isn't at that airfield, so if they were behind it, something went wrong. If this is someone else's operation and they're operating on North Korean soil, the North Koreans will be coming down hard on that area now that they know what's up, and the less they know, the better for us. Our best bet is to send a small force in unilaterally, to secure our shuttle and extract our people.

"Galt really is the man to put together a package like this," said Samuels.

The president grimaced as if he had a toothache. "I don't want to talk about Trev Galt."

"If we stage an op like the secretary is suggesting," Samuels continued, "it had better be damned fast and accurate. The North Korean military is riddled with old-timers from the Korean War who still hold positions of command. Those crazy old coots would like nothing better than to go out in a blaze of glory, taking as many American servicemen along with them as they could. And they don't much give a damn how many of their own they sacrifice in the process. The younger officers are too cowed or too new to voice dissent. I wouldn't put it past those whackos to push for a nuclear showdown over something like this."

A heavy silence fell over the room, enveloped by the subtle, powerful, throbbing hum of the plane in flight.

MacDonald loosened his tie in a gesture of irritably. "If cooler heads among the North Koreans are thinking negotiation, of letting us in, they're cutting this one awful close. The general is right. The whole mess is dicey."

The president made an easy overhand toss of the crumpled aluminum can into a nearby wastebasket. "And let us not forget the American people. The media disconnect on *Liberty* is starting to fray at the edges, I'm told. Sometime during this visit to San Francisco, we're going to have to go public."

Latisha Samuels' militant bearing softened. She sighed. "This is going to make the Cuban missile crisis look like tiddly-winks."

"It's not going to go that far." The president leaned forward, his elbows on the table. "My place in history will not be that of the president on whose watch we engaged in our first nuclear exchange with another country. And by the way, staying on focus but on another subject, where the hell is Trev Galt? Wil says he disappeared after he touched down on his return flight from Houston."

Samuels sighed again, this time with a mixture of respect and displeasure. "Your chief of staff is right as usual. And our man Galt does know how to disappear, I'll give him that. Uh, sir, we don't even know if he's in Washington . . . or in the country, for that matter."

The president chuckled. "Ah, Trev. Well, what the hell did we expect, with his wife among the missing? Trev Galt is not the type of man who sits on the sidelines when the action is hot."

MacDonald was not amused. "Sir, given the delicate nature of our standoff with the North Koreans, it seems to me that Galt could pose a serious threat to our interests if he gets personally involved any further."

Samuels nodded. "It is not an exaggeration to say

that one misstep in this situation by someone or something could trigger a nuclear holocaust."

Before the president could respond, a door opened. Wil Fleming stepped in. The brisk young chief of staff looked harried. Fleming had aged half a lifetime during the preceding half-day. He placed a decoded message on the table before the president.

"Sir, there's been a break. We have contact with *Liberty* . . . sort of."

Chapter Eighteen

North Korea

Kate's NASA light fiber clothing offered some protection against the cool dampness of the cave, but there was a clammy coolness to the cramped, cell-like chamber that was their prison that had settled into the marrow of her bones. A single, dim oil lamp affixed to the wall illuminated the cave. It was impossible to find a comfortable position or to keep warm. A guard was posted at the narrow opening, watching them, a rifle held at port arms.

Kate knelt beside Commander Scott, who sat on the ground with his back resting against the rock wall. His broken leg was stretched out before him, held rigid by a pair of tree branches that were wrapped, with dirty pieces of fabric, at his ankle and upper thigh. Scott was visibly struggling to remain conscious. His flesh was pasty. He was covered with a cold sweat. She was spoon-feeding him from a bowl of rice soup, alternately providing him with sips of the cool, clear water that had been brought to them moments earlier.

Bob Paxton watched from where he sat, cross-legged, spooning his soup with slurping desperation. His broken, swollen nose and the bruised puffiness about his eyes were turning from red to purple. It was difficult for her to imagine that she had once thought him handsome, or even nice for that matter. Paxton set aside his emptied bowl and gulped a sloppy slurp of water, glaring at Kate.

"Don't think playing nursemaid to the commander will compensate for what you've done, you treacherous bitch. You actually helped Chai inventory the stuff after they brought it back here!"

The words slapped at her like a physical blow because, for all her rationalization, what he said was true.

She returned to administering to Ron Scott. The flight commander's eyelids fluttered, and his head tilted to one side. She gently steadied his head with a hand to the back of his neck, and, using her other hand, she held another spoonful of soup to his lips.

"Commander, please. If you can hear me at all, you must eat. Think of your family. Sir, you must stay alive. We have to get you home. Please, eat the soup."

His lips quivered. "My wife," he mumbled. "Lucy. Tell her I love her." The soup dribbled down the side of his chin.

There was a flurry of movement outside the fissure in the rock that created the entrance to this chamber. The guard was suddenly grasped from behind by someone unseen, and tossed aside. Kate's heart soared for one wild, crazy moment. Trev! Trev, you've come! And her heart sank just as quickly when the bandit, Han, replaced the guard in the doorway.

Fumes of alcohol and body odor emanated from him just as when he'd first captured them in another cave, and force-marched them here. Chai Bin's second-in-command held a pistol. Han tottered drunkenly, his bleary eyes scanning them. He leered at Kate. He smacked his lips and said something in Korean.

Some survival instinct brought Ron Scott awake. Pale, weak, his eyes stared hatred at the drunken man with the gun. He started to translate in a weak voice.

Kate kept an eye on Han, while her peripheral vision darted about, seeking a rock, anything she could use as a weapon. Han obviously remembered all too well her martial arts display in front of Chai when she had made a fool of him. He kept his distance from her, but aimed his pistol at her.

"Save your strength, Commander. I think I know what he said."

Han next spat an angry tirade at Paxton, who cowered in a corner, his knees higher than his head, as if Han were ten feet tall, and not some grimy little brute with a gun.

"Sorry, Specialist," said Scott in a neutral tone. "He says you're a worm and a poor excuse for a man."

Being translated seemed for some reason to infuriate Han, who spat angrily at Scott.

Scott said, "He says that he will make you pregnant with his child, but first he will deal with me."

An apprehensive chill traveled through her. "Tell him that if he touches me, I'll kill him."

Han spat angrily at the astronaut with the broken leg who was barely conscious, trembling with fever.

"He says I'm as good as dead," Scott translated. "He says he'll finish the job."

Kate started to snarl a response at the drunken man.

But before she could, Han tracked his pistol from her to Scott and pulled the trigger.

The gunshot was ear-splitting within the chamber. The muzzle flash revealed Ron Scott's head exploding, splashing the wall behind him with his blood and brains like some grotesque mural of modernistic art.

Kate couldn't stem her scream as Scott's corpse toppled sideways.

Han laughed. Holstering his pistol, he withdrew a wide-bladed combat knife and flung himself at Bob Paxton, who cried out shrilly.

"No! Please don't hurt me!"

Han laughed. The stench of alcohol, his body odor and madness assaulted Kate's senses. She realized that droplets of Scott's blood had splattered across her sleeve and cheek. Oh my God! she thought. Oh my God!

Han was atop Paxton's back, pinning Paxton face down to the earthen floor. Han leaned forward, making Paxton extend his arm, bracing that wrist to the ground. With a sadistic giggle, Han lowered his knife blade toward Paxton's fingers that wriggled like spastic worms.

Paxton knew what was about to happen, and even as the blade descended, his index finger was pointing madly at Kate.

"No, please, dear God, don't hurt me. Take her! Don't hurt me! I'll do whatever you want!"

Kate bunched her body to pounce at Han.

The entranceway was abruptly filled with the muscular, imposing dominance of Chai Bin. The old knife scar that bisected one side of the bandit's face was livid. His finely-boned Chinese features trembled with fury. He snarled a single word that crackled with authority.

The tone of voice, whatever single word was spoken, stopped Han, who paused with his knife blade less than an inch from Paxton's fingers, and he froze in that position, physically pinning the man beneath him. He looked up with inebriated, confused eyes, and opened his mouth to speak.

The guard who had been assaulted, and another bandit, appeared to either side of Chai Bin, each of them no more than fifteen, but their faces were hard. They aimed their rifles at Han, and the one who'd been assaulted shouted threatening instructions, gesturing angrily with his rifle.

Han dropped his knife and slowly rose to his feet. He stepped away from Paxton, who scampered back into his corner. Han approached Chai with his eyes downcast, wearing a contrite, hangdog expression, and he again started to speak.

Chai Bin barked orders.

The bandits grabbed Han, each by an arm, and dragged him past Chai from the cavern. Han was pleading desperately, sobering quickly with fright under the realization that he was not about to escape with a mild reprimand due to his exalted rank.

When Han had been led away, kicking and screaming, Chai gazed down upon the sprawled corpse of Ron Scott, and the ghastly mural of blood and brains upon the wall.

"Most regrettable," he told Kate. He ignored Paxton, who crouched in the corner like a child terrified of some unimaginable monster. "Miss Daniels, truly, I am sorry about your friend and commander. I wish I could bring him back."

She crouched against her wall, restraining herself from pouncing at the arrogant son of a bitch. Oh, Ron, she thought, with a glance down at the man she had so admired. Commander Ron Scott. Man enough to command a space shuttle flight, human enough to die voicing his love for his wife. There was a man. He would be avenged. But for her to pounce upon Chai at this moment, even though he appeared vulnerable enough, alone and with his arms folded before him, would be foolhardy. Her moment would come, but this was not it.

"I'll bet you'd like to bring him back," she snarled. "This will take some explaining, won't it, Mister Warlord, and will knock down the price you'll get paid." She tried to keep her voice from choking with emotion, but failed. "You promised me that you would provide the commander with proper medical attention! That was part of our deal for me helping you!"

"Yes, but you see, I no longer need your help." A burst of gunfire from nearby startled Kate. Observing this, Chai added, "Everything you say is quite true. Han's disobedience, his summary execution, will provide an ample lesson to the others here that you are to be accorded respect and treated humanely."

The bandit youths appeared, their rifles slung over their shoulders. Chai issued further commands. Each grabbed hold of one of Ron Scott's ankles and dragged the corpse from the cavern, trailing a glistening, bloody slick across the ground behind them.

Chai's eyes roved Kate's curves, evident beneath the flight suit. "You could be my queen," he said. "You remind me of my mother."

"I do, do I? What a strange thing to say."

"You should be honored. My mother was born a

peasant, but she was strong and resourceful. She was a queen. My mother was a saint."

Kate snarled. "I'm sickened."

His hands dropped to his sides. His eyes and mouth tightened. "And why is that so?"

"Because you want to fuck me," she snarled. "We have a phrase for sickos like you in my country. It's a filthy, obscene phrase that I never thought I'd hear myself say, but it was made for creeps like you. You, Chai Bin, are a sick son of a bitch." And when she saw his features flush with anger, she threw back her head and laughed without humor, a laugh that, to her own ears, bordered on hysteria. "This whiner," she indicated Paxton contemptuously, "and I are the only human pawns you've got left, so I can say whatever I want and there's not a damn thing you can do about it but take it, you sick son of a bitch."

Chai's expression was stony. "I have business to take care of." He whirled and stormed from the cavern.

Alone with Paxton's blubbering and the smell of death lingering from the blood slick where Ron Scott had been dragged off, Kate felt as if every ounce of her energy had abandoned her in an instant. Her crouching posture became a slouch, and she leaned back against the wall, across the small space from Paxton. She sank into a sitting position, her arms draped wearily across her raised knees, her forehead resting on her arms. She wondered how she had the strength to keep on breathing.

Paxton sneered at her. "Why don't you give him what he wants and spread your legs for him? You've given him everything else. Traitorous bitch." And he relapsed into his incomprehensible blubbering.

He's right, she told herself. She was a traitor. If she

hadn't taken Chai Bin to the shuttle, to retrieve everything of negotiable value, would Ron Scott be alive right now? Yes, she was a traitor. She would burn in hell. She was in hell!

CHAPTER NINETEEN

Tokyo

Early morning sunshine warmed the spacious grounds of Aoyama Cemetery. The tranquil setting and the endless rows of headstones seemed magically isolated, far removed from the noises of the surrounding city.

The Kurita family burial plot was beneath a towering, giant old maple. Critical space shortage in Japan had resulted in a law against burying the dead, and so Kentaro Kurita's ashes, readied at a crematorium outside Tokyo, were laid to rest in a six-inch-square magnolia-wood box, wrapped with traditional ribbons of black silk. The funeral service was sedate, respectful, underscored by the irregular beating of a drum struck by a Shinto priest while other priests, in elaborate robes and ceremonial black headdresses, burned incense. There were close to one hundred mourners in attendance, including a full contingent of the titans of Japanese industry.

Meiko wore a dark-blue Meikoono with a matching sash. She, Sachito and Trev were the last ones to depart the gravesite, leaving behind them only the cemetery workers who then undertook the final internment of Mr. Kurita.

Sachito wore a long, modest, Western-style black mourning dress with pearls and black pumps.

Galt looked like something out of *GQ*, thought Meiko, in his stylish yet somber dark suit, shirt and tie. He escorted the two women, one on each arm, in the wake of the last of the non-family mourners walking along the narrow asphalt pathway leading from the burial site. The only audible sounds were the shuffling of feet and the polite murmur of some conversations from up ahead. Trev had handled himself throughout the ceremony with style and dignity, in Meiko's estimation, standing there beside her and Sachito like a soldier at his post throughout the ceremony, through the extended agony of the greetings and the service. He'd been the pillar of strength she knew him to be.

Her emotions were numb. The debilitating grief, the soulful weeping that she and Trev had heard coming from Sachito's bedroom last night, these would come to her soon enough; that razor-edged inner pain that had yet to slash her. Perhaps she was in a sort of shock, but she remained cool-headed. The extreme readjustment from her job in Washington, DC to this Tokyo graveside at her father's funeral had somehow sharpened her senses, bringing into finer detail, in a cold, analytical sort of way, everything that was happening around her.

They reached Trev's car, which was parked with the

others on the crowded blacktop parking lot. About them, other mourners were exchanging farewells.

Trev said to the women at his side, "Again, I hope both of you will please accept my deepest sympathies." He extended his hand first to the widow. "And my apologies for having to leave so abruptly."

A brief handshake. A traditional Japanese bow.

"Your being here was a show of respect for a great man," Sachito said. "Thank you."

His gaze shifted to Meiko, who wished again that she could hug him for being such a good man. But propriety dictated that she say nothing intimate in this setting.

She said, "I know that you have your work. Like Sachito, I too am only glad that you were able to be here for us."

"It was my privilege, Meiko. I'll be in touch, I promise."

And he was gone.

She and Sachito stood side-by-side then in a moment of silence, watching his car merge with the flow of vehicles leaving the lot. Sachito's hair was carefully, regally coifed as always, but her lower lip trembled. Thin lines of mascara traced down her cheeks from moist eyes. Meiko could not help but feel sympathy for the woman her father had loved at the end. Sachito's grief was as anguished and real as was her own. They shared that, at least.

And that's when she overheard the faintest bit of a nearby conversation, frittering in and around and through the activity of departing mourners, of chauffeurs holding open limousine doors for family friends and industrial titans. She overheard a precise Tokyo dialect.

Male voices spoke confidentially; voices pitched low, but not low enough; voices accustomed to commanding crowded board rooms from behind CEO lecterns, not adapted to conspiratorial intimacy in public. The first word that caught her attention, because it was an English word in an otherwise earnest conversation in Japanese, was *Liberty*.

At first she doubted her ears. Had she heard correctly? She'd watched the small television set in her bedroom as she prepared for the funeral that morning before leaving the Kurita home, and there had been no mention on any of the Japanese or international news networks about the Americans having lost a space shuttle, which would surely have been the top story if the American government went public with the news that they'd "lost" the *Liberty* . . .

She saw that the man she'd overheard was Ota Anami, a short, barrel-chested man, of serious demeanor, with a receding hairline and thick horn-rimmed glasses. She had never met Anami before today, here at the funeral. He was the acting company president of Kurita International, Sachito had informed her upon performing the introduction. Mr. Anami, Sachito added, had long been her father's right-hand man, as the Americans said.

Presently, Anami was engaged in an earnest conversation with a compact, dapperly attired man, wearing aviator sunglasses, who radiated power and command despite a lithe, physically slight stature. This man had not been introduced to Meiko, and there was something about him that she disliked. He'd arrived late, after the service began. She had caught but one glimpse of him, standing off to the side with men who wore the undeniable stamp of bodyguards forming a half-circle behind him. This in itself was not unusual. Bodyguards accompanied several of those in attendance, men worth billions. What drew her attention was that the man in the aviator sunglasses arrived late, and had seemed to her to be generally uninterested in the service. He and Anami were conversing close by, next to a black limousine where a chauffeur held open a rear door.

The dapper man appeared sternly displeased with Anami. At one point he actually poked Anami in the chest with his index finger to emphasize some point, an almost unheard of physical public display of effrontery and disrespect. As their conversation continued, Meiko did her best to listen in as closely as she could without appearing obvious about it. She didn't hear several words. Then she heard Anami speak her father's name. She was certain of it. A passing vehicle drowned out more of their exchange. But yes, she now had no doubt they were speaking about her father. And they were speaking about the *Liberty*!

Could such a thing be, or had she completely misheard?

From the corner of her eye, she saw Anami and the man bow curtly, perfunctorily to each other, as was the Japanese custom at the conclusion of any human interaction. Then the passing vehicle was gone and she thought she heard the dapper man say the word "intercept," spoken in Japanese among other, indiscernible words. The man and his bodyguards then boarded the limousine, vanishing from her sight behind heavily tinted windows. The chauffeur closed the door after them. The limousine joined the procession of departing vehicles. She made a point of committing its license plate number to memory for future reference.

Anami happened to catch her eye, and she felt a

vague chill course through her. He bowed respectfully in her direction. She acknowledged this with a polite nod. Then the acting president of Kurita Industries strode toward his own waiting limousine.

She returned her attention to Sachito, at her side.

"The man in that car," said Meiko. "The man Mr. Anami was just speaking with. Do you know him? He arrived late and I was not introduced."

Sachito dabbed with a tissue at the mascara traces on her cheeks. "I didn't meet him either," she said absently. She sniffled. "I don't recall having seen him before. Perhaps he's an associate of Mr. Anami. I really don't know."

"One more question, please. The word, 'intercept.' Does it have any sort of special meaning to you? Any at all? Perhaps it's a name for something, or a code name perhaps."

Sachito frowned. "Why would you ask such questions at a time like this, Meiko? I don't understand."

Meiko frowned. "Neither do I. It's just . . . I don't know, really. I heard some of the words being spoken between Anami and that man." She interrupted herself with an impatient wave of a hand, hoping to banish the thought. "Sachito, forgive me. My mind is playing tricks on me, and so is my hearing."

Ota Anami's chauffeured white Toyota limo drove by where they stood. They watched the limousine leave the lot, which was by this time mostly deserted, except for their car and a few vehicles here and there belonging to visitors to other gravesites.

"Are you suggesting, Meiko, that Mr. Anami and the man he was speaking to are involved in something . . . suspicious?"

"I don't know. I really don't. How well do you know Mr. Anami? I mean, personally."

"Hardly at all. We've spoken on occasion during the past few months when your father was too weak to attend meetings and I would relay his decisions to Anami. We've met two or three times, no more. I will confess that I really don't know anything about him."

"I assume they'll be dropping the 'acting' from his title, acting president of the company, now that Father has been laid to rest," Meiko mused. "In other words, Mr. Anami benefited considerably—in money, prestige, personal power—upon my father's death. I wonder who that other man was? I wonder who Anami's associates are outside of Kurita Industries."

Sachito frowned. "Are you suggesting that foul play was involved? Really, Meiko, I don't see how that could be possible. The medical examiner's report . . . your father died of natural causes. That's a medical fact."

"I'm a journalist," said Meiko. "When I verify facts, then I'm satisfied. When I'm convinced of the truth about how my father died, then I will allow myself to shed tears of grief for his soul."

Sachito studied her for a long time before nodding. Sachito's eyes were no longer moist, but solemn and determined.

"And I will help you."

From the cemetery, Galt again took the freeway downtown.

Before he had gone a quarter mile, he observed in his rearview mirror that he was being followed. Galt habitually practiced counter-surveillance techniques on a day-to-day basis, the residue of a lifetime devoted to covert ops. It essentially meant remaining constantly attuned to every nuance of his immediate surroundings, be it seated at a table in a restaurant, relaxing at home or especially, as now when on foreign soil, on a crowded freeway on his way to meet an important contact. Traffic flew bumper-to-bumper at a high rate of speed but remained orderly, this being Japan after all, without much lane changing. This made it easier for Galt to note the white Toyota, with a dent in its right front fender, shifting lanes with him, as he angled for an upcoming exit, than it would have been had he been driving in, say, Rome, Mexico City or L.A. Of course there was no reason why he should be the only driver to take the Nihonbashi Street exit, except that this particular Toyota had joined the traffic flow behind him right after he'd left Aoyama Cemetery, and had maintained a four-cars-behind trailing position ever since. He overshot his exit, and took the next one. The tail never lost position exiting the freeway, but things got progressively difficult for the Toyota's driver as Galt drove deep into a market area. The mid-morning streets bustled with multitudes of pedestrians, noisy motorcycles, honking buses and cars. He exercised some basic evasion maneuvers and lost the tail.

He returned to the freeway and, to make sure while keeping an eye on the traffic flow presently surrounding him, he again overshot his exit, using the next off-ramp and this time driving a zigzag route through a residential neighborhood. He satisfied himself that he had lost the tail, whoever they were. He was curious as hell to know who'd been following him. It could have been anyone from the Japanese authorities to U.S. spooks to representatives of those very forces, whoever they were, that he had come to Tokyo to unearth as a means of getting to Kate and the *Liberty*. But to that end, his top, his only, priority at this point was to make his scheduled rendezvous with General Tuttle, which is why he had passed on the opportunity to waylay whoever was in the Toyota and find out who they were. He did not want to keep the general waiting or, worse, somehow miss their connection.

He took a cross-town avenue to hook up with ten-lane Nihonbashi Street, which he followed, as he'd initially intended, in the direction of Shinjuku Park near the Olympic Stadium grounds. It was slow going at times. It was a sunny day but that didn't mean much in Tokyo, where the smog was worse than any city Galt had ever been to. Tokyo basked in sunlight filtered through a gray overcast that made the sun a dull red ball as if seen through gauze. Several times, while he sat stalled in traffic, Galt's nostrils distinguished the delicate, tangy scent of Japanese cooking, drifting on the air from restaurants, mingling with the acrid, metallic taste of automotive exhaust.

After being all but leveled by the Allied bombing raids of World War II, Tokyo has been rebuilt in a mixture of styles more Western than Japanese. The dense, sharp contrast of old and new, East and West, is everywhere. Bright, modern business buildings stand side-by-side with tiny shops offering the products of ancient arts. Neon signs of every imaginable shape, size and color, in English as well as Japanese ideographs, flicker, jump and whirl. This was the Ginza Strip in midtown Tokyo, centered around Ginza Street, which runs northwest to southwest. This, the main shopping section, is dominated by only the very best department stores, subway stations and flashy neon signs. Ginza Street also passes through the financial district before reaching the city's red-light section.

He had the car's radio tuned to the English-speaking news station, and that's how he learned that the *Liberty*'s disappearance had been made public.

Moreover, the news had engulfed the global media. Galt was not surprised. It had only been a matter of time, and he was impressed that the administration had been able to contain such a potent story as long as they had. The world was in on it now. As for Galt, he heard nothing on the radio that he hadn't known the night before.

He paid to park the car in a crowded lot across from Shinjuku Park, Tokyo's version of Central Park. It was only a short walk from the lot to the Meiji Shrine. He passed through a landscape of public gardens, of little bridges surrounded by hazelnut bushes, aspens, beech and maple, and a wall of oak trees that muted the vendors' cries, the bicycle bells and the unending bustle of street business interwoven with the roar of nearby traffic. There were peddlers of all sorts selling lucky amulets, souvenirs, food; soba sellers with wheeled carts, dispensing soup; stalls offering smoked eels and sushi, noodles or rice. But like Aoyama Cemetery, the park's expansive grounds were for the most part a green oasis of serenity and tranquility amid the urban landscape of neon, concrete and constant noise. Narrow gravel walkways wended across rolling lawns of half-hidden ponds and quiet, secluded teahouses. There were other Westerners here and there.

At the Meiji Shrine, as per Galt's request as relayed through Barney Markee, General Clayton Tuttle stood waiting directly beneath the curved horizontal top of the *torii*, the enormous redwood pillars and beams that form the gateway that distinguishes Shinto shrines. The area around the shrine was crowded with people in meditation, tourists snapping photographs and lovers strolling by.

Tuttle was doing his best to fit in, to look like an

everyday tourist in mismatched polyester and not like the spit-and-polish ranking military man that he was. But strutting back and forth, his hands clasped behind his back, an unlit cigar poking from the corner of his mouth, he needed only a swagger stick to make him the spitting image of Douglas MacArthur inspecting the troops. At first sight of Galt, Tuttle ceased his pacing. He glanced irritably at his wristwatch, much as he had greeted Galt with a glance at a stopwatch on their previous encounter during the training exercise aboard a yacht anchored on the Potomac.

"Goddammit, man, I get your call in the middle of a staff briefing at the Pentagon, fly halfway around the world to rendezvous with you here on time, and you stand me up for fifteen minutes."

Galt couldn't help but smile at the crusty old salt, and practically had to restrain himself from saluting. "Sorry, sir. I took a wrong turn getting here. Thanks for coming."

"Well, the cat's out of the bag." Like Galt, like most desk jockeys in covert ops, Tuttle was a seasoned field operative. His eyes panned their surroundings. "By the end of this day, everyone we're looking at right now in this park is going to be discussing the missing American space shuttle. Oh, and by the way, you do know that you're on the Washington shit list, right?"

"Goes without saying, I'm not proud to say. That's why you got my SOS. I'm in serious need of a military liaison I can trust implicitly, with intel background and Asian contacts. That would be you, sir. You're not only at the top of my A list, you are my list. I've, uh, been on the move for the last few hours, General. But I need to know what you know."

"Let's get the small stuff out of the way first," said Tuttle. "That turncoat NASA engineer will be spending the rest of his life in custody and is presently under a twenty-four-hour suicide watch. That little Japanese tart who sex-trapped him into selling out has been a tougher nut to crack. She was a stripper in a *yakuza*-owned joint that went out of business months ago. These guys were backtracking and covering their tracks big time."

"That would put me at the top of Wil Fleming's shit list," Galt conceded. "The chief of staff told me yesterday that the stripper was sure to turn on whoever sent her. Fleming's a wet-behind-the-ears pup. That girl was sent over, operating on a strictly need-to-know basis. They gave her Fraley's name and address and told her to go to work on him. The money was good enough, and she was street-smart enough, to do everything they paid her to do without asking any questions about who she was working for, or their motives."

"And so we move to the big picture," said Tuttle. "We're on top of all Chinese and North Korean electronic communication, as no doubt they're listening in on a lot of our traffic. No one seems to have a fix on *Liberty* as yet, although a Chinese force has made an incursion across North Korea's borders and their commander is confident that he's close enough to call in an armored column. The North Koreans, on the other hand, appear to be clueless. Their regional commander in the area where *Liberty* may be is a guy named Sung, who seems to operate with pretty much complete autonomy, given the fact that no one in Pyongyang gives a damn about Hamgyong Province . . . until now."

"What about a CIA ground intel in the region?"

Tuttle jerked the unlit stogie from the corner of his mouth. "His name is Ahn Chong, and what I'm about to share with you all comes from his single coded transmission thus far. Here it is, Trev. We have confirmation from our ground contact inside North Korea that some of the *Liberty* crew has survived. The shuttle is more or less intact."

Galt's heart skipped a beat. "The hell you say. Kate . . . is she—"

"We don't know yet." Tuttle's gruffness could not conceal his own concern. He said, "A North Korean mountain bandit named Chai Bin claims to have possession of the shuttle and the satellite and the crew survivors, and they're for sale. Guy calls himself a warlord. The CIA has routed me pertinent b.g. which, unfortunately, isn't much. The North Koreans want to nail him. He's been a thorn in everyone's side for years in that region. He's elusive, well entrenched and has his own private army."

"Just the same, we've got plenty if this Ahn Chong knows the exact location of the shuttle."

"We'll have plenty when Ahn tells us," Tuttle countered. "But so far he's only relayed what I've told you. Our warlord is playing it cagey to see what our response will be."

"Our first response ought to damn well be me. So it's the North Koreans, the Chinese, the United States and a warlord. Warlord. Jesus. Sounds like an Indiana Jones movie."

"Make that a five-way play," said Tuttle. "You forgot to include yourself."

"I thought I was on their shit list."

"You are. That doesn't mean you don't have a part to play. We all have our parts to play."

"Shakespeare, General?"

"This may or may not surprise you, but I have tasked

top priority authorization to get an Army Ranger special operations package in-country ASAP. And I have your mission orders."

"Is that right?"

"That's right. I was on their shit list too, for taking your call and for walking out on a staff briefing." Tuttle chortled. "And for trying to give them the dodge. I should have known better."

"Mission orders. Is that right?"

"I was contacted en route after Chai Bin dealt himself in. As for you and me, all has been forgiven from on high, considering what's at stake and how fast things have to get done."

"Specifics, sir, if you don't mind."

"I've been handed point position on this operation," said Tuttle. "I have been assigned to honcho a tactical covert ops strike into North Korea once we get target acquisition on Chai Bin's position. Since you have already taken the personal initiative of, er, uh, inserting yourself into the theater of operations, you, my headstrong friend, have been assigned as my right-hand man to advise and help organize."

Galt grimaced. "Advise and organize. We may be in the field, sir, but that sounds like a desk job to me."

"I'm not crazy about the notion either, but for a different reason."

"And that would be?"

"Your personal stake in this, plain and simple. But I'd say you've heard that from others."

Galt nodded. "Including from the president."

"I should have known. So what the hell weight would my opinion carry, right?"

"Plenty, sir, in most cases," Galt assured him. "But this situation is real different, for the reason you just stated."

"It's different for a lot of reasons." Tuttle nodded. "And the bottom line, whether they like it or not, is that you are the best man for the job. So the hell with idle chitchat. Let's get to it before they get any more of us."

Galt hesitated. "Sir, you just got ahead of me. Who have they gotten?"

Tuttle's demeanor softened. "Sorry, Trev. I, uh, was saving the worst for last, from your personal point of view. It's your buddy, Barney Markee."

Galt felt his stomach muscles tighten. He thought, Oh no. Oh no!

"I've been tied up with personal matters since I saw Barney. What happened?"

Tuttle sighed. "He's dead. Car bomb. They caught him coming out of his club this morning after closing, on his way home. Happened about an hour ago. Your friend and his bodyguard were killed instantly."

"Did they get who did it?" Galt realized the question was an automatic response, and added, "Do we have any leads on who did it?"

"No names," said Tuttle. "Someone saw a white Toyota speeding away after the explosion."

"A Toyota with a dent in its right front fender?"

Tuttle's expression clouded. "That's right. How did you know?"

Galt felt a bitter taste in his mouth. "Because I just went through considerable effort to evade them before coming here. They took out Barney and then came after me. If they took Barney with his bodyguard, the boys in that Toyota are a hot ass hit team."

"Why did they hit your friend?"

A chill started at the base of his spine and spread to his stomach, which cramped like a ball of ice. "Because I'd asked Barney to do some checking for me on Connie Yota, the stripper from over here who ended up leading that NASA guy astray in Houston. There's some sort of *yakuza* connection, because the woman's last address before Houston was a strip club here in Tokyo that was owned by the *yakuza*. Barney was going to look into that for me."

"Looks like he got too close to the wrong people." Tuttle emitted the sigh of a man who had lost men under his command in combat. "I'm sorry it happened to your friend, Trev, but here's the spin for now. Since the Tokyo cops hopefully know nothing about us, they will write Barney's murder off as some sort of turf war in Little Texas, and that's good for us because it will keep them distracted and buy us the time we need. I'll see that we get a background package on the local *yakuza* organizations." Then Tuttle did something that utterly surprised Galt. The general extended an arm and placed a hand on Galt's shoulder. "I do feel bad about losing your friend."

"Sir, if I have to shake this corner of the world to its roots, I will find our space shuttle and the ones who brought it down, and when I do, I will kick some serious ass."

"Glad to hear it," said Tuttle. "Let's get started."

Chapter Twenty

North Korea

A desk and a plaster bust of the North Korean president dominated Colonel Sung's small office. Since 1945, castings of the president, and heroes of the People's Army, had displaced the prior tradition of religious sculptures depicting Buddha. Sergeant Bol was ushered into the office by an orderly. He found his commanding officer staring at the telephone on his desk, as if contemplating a troubling conversation that had just transpired.

Bol saluted. "You sent for me, sir?"

Sung absently returned the salute. His uniform was heavily starched and pressed as ever, but there was about him an air of distraction. He did not take his eyes from the telephone. His eyes were filled with displeasure.

"Sergeant, in my years as an officer I have never

been reprimanded as severely as just before you walked in."

Bol was taken slightly aback, wholly unaccustomed to anything resembling personal dialogue with his commander.

"The shuttle?"

Sung raised his eyes, regaining his standard arrogant aloofness. "But of course. What else would so concern the Central Committee in Pyongyang at a time like this? They are displeased because we have failed to locate either the shuttle or Chai Bin and his cutthroats."

"Sir, patrols are continuing the search."

"But without success." Sung rapped his desktop with a clenched fist, a most unusual show of emotion from him. "At least the Chinese have not found it. I spoke with General Iota and he informs me that Chai Bin has approached the Americans. We have no details on how he accomplished this, but I would suppose that this was done through a CIA contact among the local population. It seems apparent that Chai has located the shuttle."

"It could be a trick," said Bol. "Chai is ruthless and not to be trusted in anything. It could be a bluff to extort money from the Americans."

Sung nodded thoughtfully. "Perhaps, but I don't think so. Sergeant, I have been ordered to locate and secure that space shuttle without delay. Should we fail, I can assure you that the consequences will be most grave for everyone involved, including this command." He leaned both elbows upon his desk, pyramiding his fingers to pensively stroke his chin with his fingertips. "The Americans, the Chinese and North Koreans, sworn enemies, are converging militarily on a technological treasure that is somewhere near here, within a radius of mere kilometers, within our grasp—and I do mean you and I, Sergeant. We must initiate extreme measures without delay."

"I'm afraid I don't understand, sir."

"I remain unconvinced that those villagers we interrogated were telling the truth about not knowing anything about the shuttle. At least one of them knows."

"The old man," said Bol. "Ahn Chong. He said he was at his wife's grave at the time the shuttle went down, that he saw or heard nothing."

"He is lying," said Sung. "I want him put under surveillance. Have the village watched from a distance. It is vital that the old man not know that he is being watched. Have him followed. Whenever he leaves his village, I want his movements reported to me on the half-hour. Who knows what else he could tell us? I intend to find out. Now do you understand, Sergeant?"

"Yes, Colonel."

"Then see to it. There is no time to lose."

The convoy of troop transports crawled along barely maintained, at times nonexistent, roads, forging ahead through mountainous, feral wilderness.

As military commander of Shenyang Province, this was Kwan's first visit to the frontier separating his country from North Korea. He rode in the cab of the truck, behind the point vehicle where General Li rode in the cab. It had been hours since the last sighting of a civilian. The "road" was presently no more than a game trail. The weight of the soldiers riding in the rear of each vehicle helped stabilize the trucks during the rough ride, but Kwan ached from the heavy jouncing of the BTR-40. Its mighty engine labored like a determined ox, struggling along a particularly steep mountainside. Kwan was studying a map, trying to correlate landmarks amid the looming mountain peaks and valleys they traveled through, so as to determine if they were in China or had in fact entered North Korea.

His driver tromped the brakes, jolting Kwan, who almost hit his head against the windshield.

Kwan looked up with a curse and started to reprimand the driver, when he saw that his driver had stopped so sharply to avoid colliding with the general's vehicle. Then Kwan saw what General Li had seen. Smoke was curling skyward, visible over the treetops from less than half a kilometer ahead. The general's stocky, compact form leaped sprightly to the ground from the cab of his truck, and Kwan quickly joined him.

"What do you think it is, sir?"

"Trouble, Major."

"I hear no gunfire."

"We will investigate. Send in one squad. I want that area secured, no matter what they find."

Kwan saluted smartly and stalked off to find a squad leader, who he ordered to move out promptly. The remaining soldiers would remain aboard the transports. He then returned to the head of the column, and found that Li had summoned their radioman.

The general was speaking into the telephone-like receiver, which he returned to the radioman. He turned to face Kwan.

"Beijing has informed me that the Americans have been contacted with an offer to return their shuttle and crew."

Kwan wasn't sure what to say for a moment. He was stunned, but did not wish to appear stupid. He managed to say, "I had thought Pyongyang would never consider negotiating with the Americans. They are sworn enemies."

"Indeed. But it was not the North Korean government that made the offer. I have been advised, Major, of what I already knew. Beijing deems it imperative that we not fail. Had the North Korean government made such an offer, that would of course be between the two governments and there would be nothing for us but to return to Shenyang. But you see, Major, the offer was routed through a CIA contact in this region, and was made not by the North Koreans, but from an enterprising and, it would seem, a most audacious North Korean private citizen. A criminal, in fact. A bandit." Li snorted. "He is much feared in this region, we are told. He calls himself a warlord."

"That can only be Chai Bin," said Kwan. "He is a marauder who operates in North Korea and China in these mountains. He is said to have a private army. He is elusive and, frankly, sir, my orders were to place him as a low priority. He terrorizes the peasants, but has stayed away from military or important government agricultural concerns."

"Your orders are now changed," Li said sharply. He nodded to indicate the convoy of idling troop transports, and the end truck that was loaded with mortars, shoulder-held rocket launchers and crates of ordnance. "I can call in air cover, remember. I defy any mountain hoodlum's ragtag private army to withstand the firepower I can bring to bear."

"With respect, sir," said Kwan, "would that not depend on the size of their force and their position?"

"Let me put it to you this way," said Li. "This brigand, this Chai Bin, has the shuttle. Therefore, we will annihilate him and claim the shuttle before the Americans or the North Koreans can reach it, even if we have to engage them as well."

Kwan frowned. "Military engagement of the Americans and North Koreans? Would that not then plunge our countries into war?"

Li's expression was impassive. "I am a soldier obeying orders, Major, as are you. Here is the situation, frankly. If we fail in this endeavor and return to Beijing empty-handed, it will be the firing squad for both of us."

Kwan flinched as brief bursts of automatic rifle fire hammered in the near distance, as if to underscore Li's pronouncement.

Then the communication man's radio began crackling. It was the squad leader reporting that the area ahead had been secured. Bandits were caught in the process of raiding a family farm. The squad leader reported two of the bandits killed outright and the others taken prisoner. The bandits had slaughtered the adult males, then herded the women and children into a group while they ransacked and set fire to the farm.

The convoy lumbered on.

The small farm, what had been the family compound, a collection of huts and a barn, was a smoldering ruin. Women knelt, wailing over their dead. The crisp mountain air was heavy with the stench of the charred ruins and death. Children and some of the females wandered about in a state of shock, vacant-eyed.

Kwan's squad leader was interrogating the surviving bandits, who had been ordered to sit, their wrists tied behind their backs: foul smelling, raggedly attired ruffians cowering in a loose circle, their eyes wide with fright. The soldiers of the squad stood with their rifles aimed at the prisoners, making threatening comments and gestures. Li stalked in that direction, and Kwan hurried to keep apace. As they approached, one soldier struck the back of a bandit's head with his rifle butt. The prisoner lurched sideways. A kick from the squad leader's boot forced him to remain sitting. One of the prisoners was already dead.

Kwan lengthened his stride, gaining one step ahead of the general. As a ranking member of the Central Politburo, General Li was a man worth impressing. Kwan intended to do that. Inwardly, he steeled himself for what he must do.

The squad leader had the stocky build of a peasant. He saluted General Li. "Sir."

Li returned the salute. "What have you learned here?"

"Nothing yet, sir. They say they're Korean army deserters, living off the land."

Kwan unholstered his pistol. He placed its muzzle to the temple of the closest prisoner, and pulled the trigger. The gunshot cracked sharply. An exit wound blew brains and skull fragments across the other two prisoners, and across the boots of the squad leader and the general. Before anyone could speak, Kwan stepped to the next bandit. He placed the muzzle of his pistol against this man's forehead.

"Chai Bin," he said. "Take us to his stronghold."

The man's eyes and mouth quivered. "But then Chai Bin would kill me! I dare not speak!"

Kwan triggered another round. Blood and brains spurted like red mud from the back of this man's skull, and before his corpse had fallen onto its side, Kwan aimed his pistol to the remaining man's forehead.

"Do you dare speak? Take us to Chai Bin."

This man stared up along the gun barrel, into

Kwan's eyes, as if looking into the eyes of a god. "Spare me! I will take you." The words poured out. "I will show you the way. It is a day's journey."

Kwan holstered his pistol and turned to the general deferentially.

Li said, "It will be a night's journey, if needs be. You've convinced me, Major Kwan. The convoy pushes on. We will attack this Chai's stronghold and that will take us to the shuttle." He patted Kwan's shoulder in a reserved manner, an almost unheard of gesture, considering the strict protocol of the Chinese military; surely a sign of how appreciative the general was, thought Kwan. He had most likely saved both of their lives from a firing squad. "Well done, Major. Yes, most impressive. When this is over, you will be a colonel, I assure you of that."

Their group returned to the trucks, the prisoner roughly shoved along by soldiers, away from the bodies of the bandits and past the sobbing of the farmer's family over their dead.

Kwan reloaded his pistol as he walked. He had impressed the general. And now they had a destination.

Now, they had a target.

CHAPTER TWENTY-ONE

Tokyo

Meiko sat at the keyboard of her father's personal computer. She was alone in his private office in the executive suite.

Her stepmother's connections had gained her access to this Olympus of Kurita Industries. When she and Sachito had at last found themselves alone together after that morning's sad, grueling funeral service for her father, her stepmother had seemed to genuinely want some sort of bond of shared grief between them. Meiko had taken the opportunity to profess her restlessness, and her curiosity. Even at a time like this, especially at a time like this, her innate investigative instincts were functioning. She could not erase from her mind that barely overheard conversation between Anami, the acting president of the company, and the dapper man in the aviator sunglasses who had used the occasion of Kentaro Kurita's funeral to approach Anami in a confrontational way. With such inappropriate behavior, she could only surmise that whatever was being discussed between them had been extremely important. What little she'd managed to overhear at the cemetery, her father's name and mention of the *Liberty*, would not cease nagging at her mind, though she chose not to confide this to Sachito. She did make her request, which Sachito granted without hesitation.

Meiko was chauffeured into the city, to this enormous factory complex. Madam Kurita had called ahead and made all of the necessary arrangements. This facilitated her quick passage through security, to the somber executive suite overlooking a small portion of the factory below, where hundreds of laborers were busily assembling small engine parts beneath a bright red company logo sign with yellow letters in English and Japanese ideograms. Practically all signs in Japan are in English as well as Japanese, English being the most common second language spoken in Japan. The workers were clad in coveralls, safety helmets, goggles and ear protectors. The plant workplace was cleaner and better organized than factory assembly lines she'd seen in America. Conversation seemed minimal.

After being shown into her father's office, which was an airy, sparsely yet comfortably furnished office of white carpeting and cedar paneling, she had made but a cursory inspection. She felt an uncertain twinge of displeasure when she saw the portrait of her mother on one side of her father's desktop, opposite Sachito's photograph. Then she put that out of her mind, sat at the computer terminal, booted up and began exploring, spending more than thirty minutes accessing the private document files stored on her father's hard drive. She followed links to business-related sites, scanning whatever she found, then backtracking and accessing more, learning more about Kentaro Kurita's holdings, his investments, becoming posthumously acquainted with her father not as a father but as the titan of a mighty commercial empire.

She missed him so.

Her ascendancy through the ranks of Hakura News, becoming their White House correspondent, was related to her father's prestige and influence. It would have been naive to think otherwise. In the cutthroat competitiveness of global communications, she had thrived and risen to prominence because she was good at her job. On two occasions she had actually scooped her American media counterparts on big Washington stories concerning domestic American politics. But yes, family ties had helped. She could only hope to pass on through example what had been a gift to her; to let her countrywomen know that she was proving to the men, and to the women of Japan, that a woman could do a "man's" job. Today as in the past, marriage was the only truly acceptable goal of any Japanese woman. Those forces that motivated the women's movement in the West—the quest for self-expression and satisfaction—did not seem to appeal much to Japanese women. It was Meiko's experience that the majority of Japanese women considered western women and their search for self-fulfillment to be rather selfish. In Japan, every man, woman and child ideally regarded the well-being of the group before his or her own self-interest. Combining a career with marriage was an idea whose time was far from coming to Japan. She entertained hopes of someday starting a publishing company to help raise the public consciousness about women's issues. In Japan, a woman's salary was one-half that of a man's, even though women comprised forty percent of the work force. Meiko's prominence was unique.

As was that of Madam Kurita, a woman who had owned the heart of her father, the man who had controlled Kurita Industries, which put her stepmother at the heart of power.

Meiko absorbed the data scrolling down her screen until she felt that she had a sufficient overview of her father's business profile and portfolio. She was amazed at how extensive were her family's holdings. Strangely, she thought, the notion that she had inherited such enormous wealth, and curiosity about the terms of her father's will, were crossing her conscious mind for the first time since she'd received news of her father's passing. Satisfied that she understood the big picture, she next got more specific in her cyber investigations, following through on some links and cross-references until they proved to be dead ends while discarding others, like following the clues in a mystery novel. She had written down the license plate number of the limousine that had carried away the dapper man who had worn the aviator sunglasses, the man who had seemed so out of place at the funeral and whose behavior toward Anami, the CEO of her father's company, had compelled her to note the license plate number. The vehicle was registered to what proved to be a subsidiary of a corporation she had never heard of, Trans-Asian Enterprises, a transportation company leasing and owning everything from shuttle transportation to mail to export-import shipping.

Her eyes began to ache. She started thinking about taking a break when the name of a major shareholder from Trans-Asian matched with Tokyo police files. Every journalistic instinct she possessed told her that she was onto something and rejuvenated her.

The man's name was Rikihei Ugaki.

She clicked her way into his file and there he was, in a half dozen photographs, various street scenes and other public places, snapshots obviously taken from secret surveillance because the participant appeared wholly unaware that he was being photographed. She determined that there were no police photos, what they called mug shots in the States, because nothing had ever been proven in a Japanese court of law against Ugaki. There was plenty in the file for her to speed scan, and the truth was obvious enough, even if not to a court of law.

Ugaki was *yakuza*.

The prosperous, successful businessman, an infamous social recluse, was reputed to be the *Oyabun*, the *yakuza* godfather, of the Red Scorpion Clan, the largest *yakuza* gang in Tokyo. The *kumi*, the criminal clans and families that derived their income from illegal sources—prostitutes, drugs, gambling and protection rackets—had many legitimate fronts, including close ties to some of the *zaibatsu*, Japan's giant corporations. The medieval *yakuza* were outlaws and wanderers who, over the centuries, evolved strict rules of honor among thieves and demanded courage and honesty in all conduct. They followed Bushido, the Japanese code of knighthood, which set forth the highest ideals of honor and courage. The modern *yakuza*, on the other hand, were powerful clans and corporate gangs who had perverted the traditional spirit of their code. She knew for a fact that some of the more unscrupulous corporations used the *yakuza* as enforcers for such matters as breaking up industrial disputes or intimidating the competition. The Red Scorpion Clan earned most of its profits via perfectly legitimate means. Trans-Asian was only one of Ugaki's business ventures, she quickly ascertained. He was a respected member of the establishment.

She leaned back in her chair, closing her eyes, massaging them. She considered.

Ugaki and the acting CEO of Kurita Industries have a confrontation at the funeral service for her father. She overhears them speak the word *Liberty* while the rest of what else she'd overheard had been spoken in Japanese. The dapper man in the sunglasses had radiated a primal aura: that of a violent beast barely kept in check. This was not the sort of man her father would abide. Or was Kurita Industries in some way involved in whatever was going on with that space shuttle flight?

Trev's wife was aboard that shuttle.

Life was so strange.

She refocused on the computer screen and continued opening documents in cyber space in her quest for more information about Ugaki.

She would follow this, no matter where it took her.

She owed that to her father.

And she owed it to a woman she'd never met, named Kate Daniels.

As acting chief executive officer of Kurita Industries, Ota Anami was used to being chauffeured about. The limousine, in which he was the sole occupant, was furnished with all of the amenities he was used to, including a well-stocked liquor supply and state of the art audio and video. Yet he found himself unable to partake of any of these luxuries during the drive to Ugaki's estate.

Ugaki had sent the limousine. Its heavily tinted windows made the world passing by outside seem like a dark place. Anami felt vulnerable and small in the car's lavish interior. He inwardly rued, for the ten thousandth time, the day he had sold his soul to the *yakuza*. He had been summoned on that day exactly as he was being summoned today by *Oyabun* Ugaki. Anami had sold his soul to the devil.

The limousine turned, without slowing, onto a paved driveway, passing an open wrought-iron gate, waved on through by a uniformed security guard. Anami was certain that the guard was only for show. Ugaki's home would be an armed fortress, with the most sophisticated electronic surveillance equipment and a full cadre of unseen, heavily-armed men no doubt waiting for the first indication of trouble. The main house was large and single-storied, with pink-painted concrete walls and a roof of green slate. The chauffeur braked the limousine to a stop. While the engine idled with the barely audible purr of a contented kitten, he briskly got out from behind the steering wheel to hold the car door open for Anami. When he had debarked, the limousine drove off, past a parked, white Mercedes Benz, and circled around the side of the house.

Anami felt suddenly very much alone.

The latticework front door of the home, before him, slid open. A man with a scarred face and the build of a wrestler bowed ever so slightly and stepped aside, holding the door handle. The top two joints were missing from the little finger of his left hand. It was the sign of *yakuza*. The mark of the gangster. If a *yakuza* commits an offense against his *Oyabun*, he may try to atone and regain his *Oyabun*'s favor by offering to sever one of his own fingers as a supreme token of repentance. The man closed the front door.

Anami paused to remove his shoes.

After he had stepped out of his shoes, the man said,

"Come this way," and led the way down a hallway lined with sliding partitions. At the end of the hall, he bowed again, opened one of the partitions and gestured for Anami to enter.

Ugaki was seated on the tatami floor behind a low black lacquered table, polishing a samurai katana sword, hand-forged in an earlier century. The room was a formal tatami of rice paper walls and doors, uncluttered and austere except for a massive glass case displaying ten sets of antique samurai swords without scabbards. Ugaki was bare chested. A lurid red and green scorpion was tattooed across his chest. He did not look up, but acknowledged Anami's presence by sternly motioning for him to take the cushion in front of the table as he completed his task.

Anami sat on his knees in the formal sitting position. The servant poured them each a cup of warm sake, then left. At last, Ugaki set down the sword and looked up.

"You are prompt in obeying my summons. That is good."

Anami always felt as if this man's eyes could read his mind and see into his soul. "Truthfully, Ugaki-san, I have wished an audience with you since this morning at the cemetery. May I respectfully inquire why you chose the funeral service as a point of contact? Do we not risk drawing attention to ourselves at this critical juncture?"

"At this juncture," said Ugaki, clipping each word as if with a sword's blade, "I felt it necessary to exhibit to you the power that is *yakuza*. *Yakuza* is all-powerful, anywhere and at any time." Ugaki sneered to indicate Anami's posture. "Even Kurita Industries kneels before the power of *yakuza*."

Anami felt beads of sweat forming along his hairline. "But Ugaki-san, what of the man, Trev Galt? He was at the cemetery with Kurita's wife and daughter. He is with the American government. He holds a position in their White House."

"I know about Trevor Galt III." Ugaki's sneer remained in his voice. "I know why he has come to our country. He was under surveillance when his plane landed."

Anami found himself wishing that he could dab at the perspiration on his forehead, but dared not in the eyes of his host. Ugaki's skin tone appeared smooth and cool, like polished tan ebony. Anami felt inadequate, as he always did in Ugaki's presence.

"You know where Galt is?" he asked hopefully.

Ugaki's features flared with displeasure, and Anami suspected that this could indicate that the *Oyabun*, the top *Oyabun* of one of the largest *yakuza* clans in Japan, did not know of Galt's present whereabouts; that Galt had managed to elude Ugaki's men who had followed him from the airport.

"Do not fear Galt," said Ugaki. "Fear me. It is important that you understand that, or you will be useless to me, and then you become a liability."

"I understand."

"Never forget the fate of your illustrious predecessor. The death certificate for Kentaro Kurita reads natural causes, but you and I know the truth. We know the old man's true fate, and why he had to die. I only wanted to use his connections with the Harbor Patrol to smuggle in guns. He refused. He confused honor with legalities. And now he is gone, and it is you, Anami-san, who shall provide the cover of Kurita Industries. This will serve me well when I import what was aboard the *Liberty* into Japan. It would be unwise of you to cause me any inconvenience."

Anami swallowed hard. "I had no intention of doing so. I most respectfully submit, Ugaki-san, that Galt is our greatest threat. The man you ordered killed today, this Barney Markee, was a close personal friend of Galt's. Add this to his wife being one of the crewmembers aboard the shuttle, and consider that this is a man who owes no allegiance save to his objective. He is a dangerous enemy."

"Enough," said Ugaki. "On to more important matters. Colonel Sung in North Korea has reported that he's close to gaining possession of the shuttle. As for Galt, he will soon be as dead as his friend in the wheelchair. No *gaijin*, no outsider—no *keto*, no hairy Western barbarian—will survive this. He will be dealt with."

Anami despised his moral weakness, his addiction to gambling, which had brought him to this point. He had foolishly overextended his credit on enormous gambling debts with the Red Scorpion Clan. This had suited Ugaki quite nicely because the *Oyabun*, Anami soon came to realize, had never wanted his money. Ordinarily such a sizeable unpaid debt could have cost him his life, as an example to others. But his life had been spared when he agreed to divert Kurita Industries' resources toward the duplication, development and world marketing of the technology that Ugaki would supply via this audacious scheme that was so grand in scale, world powers were on a probable military collision course because of it. Ugaki had personally flown by private helicopter to the remote North Korean province to oversee that end of the operation.

"We will not fail," Anami said, and he tried to believe the words he spoke.

"Trevor Galt has come to our country only to meet his death," said Ugaki. "Japan is the domain of *yakuza*. I will achieve my goals, no matter the cost. Now, for the reason I summoned you. Tonight's presentation is a matter requiring impeccable correctness, Anami-san. Let us prepare."

Chapter Twenty-two

When she felt that she had accomplished everything she presently could at the computer in her father's office, Meiko left the factory grounds, politely requesting Sachito Kurita's waiting chauffeur to return home without her. She then walked for several blocks through the industrial area, following a gate guard's directions toward the nearest subway station. A block from the factory, she tapped in a number on her cell phone. She and Trev, through the nature of their separate professions, each had access to highly secure phone numbers that were inaccessible to most. They had agreed to never use these numbers for communication except in the cases of extreme importance, and neither had communicated via this number.

Galt answered on the first ring.

"Hello, Meiko." His caller ID tabbed her, of course. "Are you all right?" Concern rippled beneath his words across the connection.

"I've been busy."

She spoke as she walked. She passed a lumberyard where a forklift made beeping sounds as it backed up.

"I thought you were going to spend the day with your stepmother," said Galt, hearing the beeping as the sound receded. "Doesn't sound like you're at a wake."

"I'm not. I went to work, Trev, investigating. I need to see you. We need to talk."

"Isn't that what we're doing?"

"I have something. I don't care how secure this line is. I need to tell you. I need to see you."

Hesitation brought crisp dead air across the connection.

"All right," he said finally. "I'm here with a friend. We were under hostile surveillance, so we initiated evasive measures. I'm not in Tokyo, but I'm close. Okay, here's where I am. And make sure you're not followed."

"All part of my investigative training." She tried to sound light, but could hear the apprehension in her own voice.

He gave her an address. They disconnected. She walked on to catch the *shosen*, the Tokyo subway, which was mobbed as usual. She transferred to the commuter line to Yokohama. An electric, super-express "bullet train" departed every twelve minutes. Despite this, the train she rode was so packed that she had to stand the whole way among chattering, swaying passengers crowding in against her from every side. Twenty minutes later, she was hurrying down the steps of the Yokohama Station, and was soon in a taxi heading south on the parkway along the edge of the immense harbor. She checked periodically with a trained eye, but could discern no trace of anyone following her.

Yokohama and its harbor were shrouded in the city's ever-present metallic gray smog. Many people she saw wore surgical masks as part of their standard attire. Tokyo Bay was crammed with shipping and small craft, from foreign vessels of trade to pleasure yachts and ferries to the ancient, ageless sampans. Row upon row of freighters were lined up, waiting at busy docks that bustled with cranes and work crews.

The "safe house" was a one-story warehouse of corrugated steel, located one block in from the docks, anonymous amid the commercial hubbub of the busy waterfront district. A modest, CIA-fronted import-export business made a show of picking up and then delivering the same stepvan full of crates, twice per week. The safe house was primarily a CIA message drop operated by Todd Smathers who, with his straw hair and freckles, had all the field seasoning of a military school cadet. Smathers had seemed somehow intimidated, and managed to make himself scarce after showing them the place, leaving a key like a realtor sealing a deal. This was fine with Galt. The interior of the warehouse was cavernous. Wooden crates were stacked along one wall. There was a small office with a desk, sofas and a coffee table. A pair of sleeping bags was rolled up in one corner; in another was a locked, oblong box that held weaponry ranging from pistols to rifles, with ammunition. The back wall of a "clothes closet" was the doorway to a small, hidden room, the message center and communications relay drop, crammed with miniature electronic equipment.

Galt and General Tuttle were in the office, standing over the desk and studying maps and paperwork spread out across the desk's surface, when the code sounded from the buzzer at the side door, around the corner from the presently closed-off loading dock facing the street. When he opened the door to let her in and she brushed close by him, Galt was aware of the way his senses seemed to sharpen as they always did in her presence. Something about this beautiful woman stimulated him at every level, even at a time like this. She had changed from the funeral black he had last seen her in to a sedate, Western-style skirt and black blouse. He glanced out along the backtrack, but saw no sign of anything suspicious in the alley running alongside this warehouse. He closed and locked the door, then turned to embrace her.

"How are you doing, Meiko?"

"I haven't slowed down enough yet to find out."

They naturally broke the embrace. She exuded her usual air of crisp efficiency. But he knew her well enough to see in her eyes her grief for her father. Yet the coolheaded keenness in her eyes was real, too. She wore a small black purse by a shoulder strap, and held a standard-sized business envelope.

Tuttle approached, having allotted them sufficient personal time. It had taken some explaining from Galt, about his relationship with Meiko, to justify his telling her about the location of this safe house. The general hadn't made a row but he hadn't looked comfortable with it either, and he didn't look pleased now, as Galt made the introductions.

Tuttle did not extend his hand. "I wish I could be more cordial, miss, but I don't like the security of this safe house compromised by the presence of a representative of the news media." He spoke the term as if it were an epithet, with a harsh glance at Trev. She had obviously interrupted a heated debate.

She lifted her chin, and locked eyes with the general. "I can assure you, sir, that your security is not compromised."

"We'll see."

"The information I have will better enable you to carry out your mission."

Tuttle was clearly impressed with the forthright response, but remained gruff. He sent Galt a sideways glance. "This whole damn operation is unorthodox."

Galt chuckled. "I hear resignation in your voice, sir." He looked at Meiko, and got serious. "So you've been at work. Something we have to hear in person, and here you are."

"Here's what I have." She handed the envelope to Galt. "Hardcopy to save you time."

She told them about overhearing the conversation in the cemetery between Anami and Ugaki. She told them that Ugaki was *Oyabun* of the Red Scorpion Clan, that the conversation between them at the cemetery, after Galt left, was confrontational, had seemed to her to be obscenely improper at her father's funeral. She concluded by telling them the key words she had overhead: her father's name, the word "intercept" spoken in Japanese, and the word *"Liberty,"* spoken in English.

Tuttle frowned when she was done. "The 'intercept' part is new."

"They intercepted the shuttle," she said as a statement, not a question. She locked eyes with Galt. "Was my father involved?"

"We don't know yet. But we do know that Ota Anami is in bed with the *yakuza*."

She looked disappointed. "You knew about the *yakuza?*"

"Sorry. We've been tracking that connection since Houston, but so far without much success. They used a stripper from one of their Tokyo joints to set up a NASA scientist as part of the operation to bring down the shuttle."

"I saw the news on TV in the terminal on my way

here," she said, "but there was nothing about the shuttle's disappearance being engineered. Is such a thing possible?"

"It's not only possible," Galt told her, "it's what happened. That's why we're here."

Her eyes clouded. "Did you use my father's death and our relationship just as a cover to come to Japan?"

"Hey," Tuttle growled, "this is no time for a spat between lovebirds," he glared at Galt, "no matter how justified. And everything about the shuttle is classified information, Miss Kurita, and you are a journalist."

"Hey yourself," said Meiko, sharply. "My leave of absence has been cancelled. Hakura News has me on a Concorde tonight, flying back to the States. They wanted me on an earlier flight, but I held off long enough to personally deliver to you the information I uncovered. All right, Trev and I can pass on the personal matters for now. But my point is that I didn't go to Hakura News with what I learned about Anami and the *yakuza*. Believe I've earned a right to be trusted."

"She's right, General," said Galt. Before Tuttle could respond, he continued to Meiko, "We've just received a background package on the *yakuza*. The Red Scorpion Clan is quite old. Their traditional power base has always been right here in Yokohama Harbor."

"Then the Red Scorpion *yakuza* is involved in the downing of the shuttle?"

"We decided to get out of Dodge, I mean Tokyo, for awhile," Tuttle said in a stiff voice. "We came here to process intel, organize and strategize."

"Sounds impressive," said Meiko, obviously not impressed in the least, "and rather vague." She scrutinized Galt, watching for his reaction. "Is Kurita

Industries involved?" she asked. She swallowed hard. "Was my father involved?"

"We're going to Tokyo tonight to find out," said Galt, "as soon as it gets dark."

The penthouse conference room was atop the Tanaga Building, a thirty-four-story structure of tinted glass, chrome and smooth stonework towering above Exchange Avenue in downtown Tokyo. Branches of American corporations, ranging from Coca Cola to the Chase Manhattan Bank, were located in this neighborhood that was dominated architecturally by the Sony Building, which resembled the U.N. Building and was nearly as large.

Galt and Tuttle crouched in the murky shadows atop a canopied entrance to the building's underground parking garage. Each man wore casual civilian attire that just happened to be dark so as to meld with the murky shadows. Galt wore a 9mm Beretta concealed in a shoulder holster beneath his jacket. Tuttle carried an innocuous-appearing tote bag over one shoulder. Their position was some fourteen feet off the ground, separated from a side street by a circular blacktop driveway used for deliveries during business hours.

Lights were on in the Tanaga Building, office workers putting in overtime. The night was alive with traffic noise and the miscellaneous sounds of every city at night. But their position atop the canopy was a pocket of isolation.

They had climbed atop the canopy without effort. Despite his age and longtime desk jockey status, the general kept himself in prime physical shape.

Tuttle glanced up along the sleek, incredible height of the building. "You can't even see the penthouse from down here. It's like Jack's beanstalk on steroids."

"Pardon me, sir, but this is no time for idle pissing and moaning. If I want to listen in on that meeting, I'd better start climbing."

The CIA man, Smathers, had facilitated the highly illegal monitoring of cell phone traffic between Ugaki and the new CEO of Kurita Industries, Anami. Codes were obviously used in their conversation, and it had been reported that afternoon by Smathers' street operatives that the two men met in preparation for some sort of conclave scheduled to be held in this executive penthouse on this night. Of that much, Smathers' intelligence analysts were certain. Tuttle, of course, had instructed Smathers that not a hint of this be leaked to any member of any Japanese law enforcement agency. What could be learned at tonight's meeting was exactly what Galt had come to Japan to find, and he was in no mood to share. Doing so would stack the odds against him. Like any good crime boss, Ugaki would have moles and bought-off corrupt cops on his payroll and would cancel the meeting had he gotten even a whiff that law enforcement was aware of it. Ugaki would set an ambush if he'd learned that Galt was coming to eavesdrop. Either of these developments would be counter-productive in the extreme. A shuttle was down. Military powers were rattling sabers, positioning for conflict. And the ones who had conspired to bring this about so as to reap illicit profits in the untold billions of dollars were gathering to discuss the next phase of their operation. Galt could hardly allow this opportunity for intelligence gathering to slip by.

Tuttle set down his tote bag, unzipping it.

"Pissing and moaning?" He handed Galt a device

about the size of a matchbox, which Galt attached to his belt. Tuttle then dropped a small lapel mic and earpiece into Galt's palm, both of which Galt properly affixed. "Galt, you're about to climb up the face of a skyscraper." He next withdrew and handed over the hand and foot suction-climbing devices that had been requisitioned through his military connections and delivered to the safe house in Yokohama just before they'd left. Tuttle grumbled as he watched Galt securely strap the pads to his shoes and palms. "You do realize that if these babies decide to malfunction, they'll be shoveling you off the street."

Galt checked the fit and feel of the climbing devices, and donned the foot and hand devices. "In that case, tell them that my last words were: 'I'm sorry for blocking traffic.' "

Galt approached the base of the wall of the building. Wearing the foot devices, he clumped along with the awkwardness of the Frankenstein monster.

Tuttle looked down to zip the tote bag. He looked up and saw that Galt, an apparition in black, was already scaling up past the second story of the sheer wall and climbing fast, hand over hand, up across the glass and steel. Tuttle scanned the immediate area surrounding his position. He observed minimal vehicular and pedestrian traffic on this side street.

A bright green commuter train rumbled over a nearby intersection.

Tuttle said into his lapel mic, "Good luck, man. Damn but it feels great to be back in the field again. Tell the truth, son, it makes my dick hard."

"Glad you're having a good time, sir." Galt's reply was wry in Tuttle's earpiece.

Galt curtailed the conversation, expending considerable physical effort in sustaining his upward momentum. He climbed methodically, relentlessly, up the face of the building, feeling more now like Spider-man than Frankenstein. Insistent wind gusts tugged at his hair. He realized amidst all of the sensation and thought that every fiber of his being felt alive. True, it had been awhile since he'd given up drinking, but he realized that on this mission he was shedding that old life like a snake shedding its skin. He felt reborn, and pleased. He still had the edge. The damn desk job in Washington hadn't stolen his abilities, his gifts. He had never felt more alive. The physical stress to his muscles as he climbed only enhanced the sensation of living.

Central Tokyo sprawled out endlessly beneath him in every direction. Smog blanketed the basin, muting its lights, but he could still see Tokyo Tower, the moat and the grounds of the Emperor's Palace. The corporate logos on surrounding buildings were a who's who of Japanese capitalism: Nissan Motors, Fuji Heavy Industries, Mitsubishi Steel.

Bells chimed nearby, and for some peculiar reason, breathing heavily with his task, passing what he counted as the twenty-second floor, Galt found himself recalling the day he and Kate were married by a judge in that small-town red brick courthouse. As they were leaving the brief and modest ceremony in the kindly judge's chambers, workmen outside, who were restoring an old bell tower atop the courthouse, called out their congratulations and began gonging the antique brass bell for the whole world to hear. Wedding bells for the newlyweds. The world had welcomed these lovers. He blinked away the memory.

He reached the windows of the penthouse. The spacious conference room had bookcases along one wall and windows along the others. A long polished oak table dominated the room.

A man he recognized as Rikihei Ugaki was seated at the head of the table. The *Oyabun* looked sharp, dapper in a white silk suit. Galt also "made" the other men in their well-tailored business suits, seated around the table: *kobun*, the Red Scorpion Clan's top lieutenants and station chiefs. Each man sat with his left hand on the left knee, his right hand extended palm upward with his eyes turned to their *Oyabun*, the traditional *yakuza* sign of respect.

Galt's foot and hand suction pads securing his weight, he pasted himself against the face of the building, just below and to the side of the window, so that only his left eye peered into the room, at approximately eye-level.

Those present, including Ugaki who sat facing the window from the far end of the conference table, were wholly involved in a drama unfolding at the conference table. Even these most jaded of human sharks found the illusion of security in this cocoon, aloft on the thirty-fourth floor, which is why Galt had chosen this manner of gathering intelligence. Unfortunately, he was "dropping in" about twenty minutes into their conference. Galt needed the cover of night. Anyone spotted scaling a skyscraper would surely draw attention during the daylight hours. On the other hand, he suspected that the first part of this meeting would be the ceremonial greeting of the *Oyabun* as each of the *kobun* arrived individually, in order of their rank within the organization. And so he and Tuttle had chosen to wait until night cloaked the city. He was hoping that he had only missed the introduction ceremonies and the customary serving of sake.

He used his feet suction pads, and that of his left hand, to maintain his adhesion to the sheer face of the skyscraper. He unclipped a small microphone component from the device at his belt and attached the mic to the window. With its miniature suction cup to the glass, it looked like a child's dart. Galt heard guttural exchanges in Japanese between two of the men seated at the table. Japanese was one of the six languages in which he was fluent.

Far below, Tuttle would be keeping watch. There was the building's normal security staff, which was minimal. Far more importantly, there was the collective security force of Ugaki and his *yakuza*. The interior of the Tanaga Building, every hallway, would be thick with them. Ugaki could have the outside of the building under surveillance from street level or from surrounding buildings. The worst-case scenario was that they would be equipped with infrared Night Vision Devices, in which case they would see him. That was the risk. But he had come halfway around the world to find Kate. Too far to be dissuaded by the element of risk.

At the conference table, amenities and ceremonial greetings were past.

Ota Anami, seated at Ugaki's right, was engaged in heated debate with a man who sat opposite him, to Ugaki's left. "We have invested too much time and resources to double-cross the Korean, this Colonel Sung, now," Anami was saying. The CEO had a softness about him that looked out of place amid the others seated at the table, but he spoke with authority. "The airfield has been monitored through every phase, has it not?" Anami nodded deferentially to the dapper man, who sat unmoving, implacable, statue-like, at the head of the table. "Most often it has been *Oyabun* Ugaki who flew into North Korea at great personal risk to supervise Colonel Sung's preparations. Sung will gain possession of the shuttle before the Americans or the Chinese or the North Koreans, because he is the nearest one to it. He will not betray us, because he fears the power of *yakuza*. It is a matter of honor."

Despite longstanding and deeply rooted inter-clan warfare among some of these men, an officious air of business permeated the room in observance of *enryo*, a highly respected part of the Japanese culture: the code of proper conduct, which emphasizes reserve, restraint and emotional control.

"Honor." There was scorn in the opposing gangster's tone. "I disdain the notion of letting the Korean live. They are not people, but one step above baboons in intellect and honor. Sung has fulfilled his purpose. We should kill him and take command of his troops. Events will overtake themselves in a situation as fluid and volatile as this. Sung could be persuaded by his superiors to tell them everything. He must be eliminated at this crucial phase."

There was no surprise to Galt that a Japanese gangster would not trust a North Korean. Koreans were essentially the Asian "blacks" of Japan. Discrimination in Japan is subtle, never mentioned to foreigners, but it is common. The Japanese do their best to isolate those of Korean heritage from the mainstream of society, segregating them into ghettos like Heuisa Street, with housing projects and their own shopping areas.

At the conference table, all eyes remained on Ugaki who considered, at some length and without comment, what he had just heard.

This made for dead calm in Galt's earpiece. From his birdlike perch, so far removed from street level, he again vaguely heard the sound of the city, which, at this height, was merely a faint, metallic cacophony.

"You are both persuasive in your points of view,"

Ugaki said finally. "At this stage, I concur with Anami-san. It is not yet time for the removal of Colonel Sung. I will personally take possession of the, uh, merchandise after the colonel has possession of it, and I will oversee its importation into Japan. Colonel Sung is in preparation to attack and eliminate Chai Bin. Retrieval of the shuttle is imminent." Ugaki paused and smirked. "I will deal with Colonel Sung at the appropriate time, after he truly has fulfilled his usefulness." He glanced at the *yakuza* who had argued with Anami. "Doing so will eliminate the only connection to us from within North Korea, and their government will take the blame internationally."

The *yakuza* being addressed responded respectfully to his *Oyabun*.

Galt could hear nothing. The breeze whispered along these heights of the building wall and played with his hair, but his earpiece had gone dead; no speaking in Japanese, no static, just flat-out dead. He considered breaking radio silence with Tuttle.

Before he could say anything into his lapel mic, the doors of the conference room were flung open. Shouting men poured in carrying weapons, everything from pistols to automatic weapons to shotguns, with bodyguards shouting and gesticulating empathetically with a sense of urgency to the men seated at the table.

Ugaki was on his feet, head held erect, arms crossed authoritatively, concentrating on the window dominating the wall before him while the *kobun* around him and a frightened Anami scrambled for cover.

The bodyguards collectively tracked their weapons at the window and opened fire.

Chapter Twenty-three

Gunfire erupted from the window, spewing muzzle flashes that shredded glass.

Galt had reared his head away from where his eyes were pressed to the lower corner of the window. Freeing his right hand from its suction mitt, he delved into a pocket of his black jacket, grasping and activating, with a thumb flick, the sixty-second fuse on a high explosive device, round and no larger than a marble. He slid his other hand from its suction glove and yanked his feet free from their confinement with the right twist that disengaged them. As he fell away, he pitched the HE up and through the hole in the wall that had been a window.

And Galt was airborne.

He went into a backward free-fall, and everything seemed to go strangely into slow motion for him. As he fell, he started picking up speed, plummeting down, down, down, the air rushing by him, flapping his clothes, whipping at his hair, and another thirty-three floors to fall! He tore at the tear-away jacket, revealing the harness strapped across his back, and he yanked at the ripcord. The mini-parachute flapped open with a snap that broke his fall with a bone-jarring jolt.

Ugaki's security measures had extended to having lookout posts for scans of the Tanaga Building with NVDs and motion sensors. They had spotted Galt and radioed the bodyguard inside the building.

He reached for the guidelines and looked up to see the gaping hole full of faces, and guns tracing in his direction. Then came the orange-red blast of the HE, which may have been small enough to roll across the conference room floor without notice amid all the excitement. The window spewed flame and red lightning and human bodies and body parts, belching them into the night like an angry god. Galt worked the guidelines and, less than sixty seconds later, was guiding himself into a running stop on the ground at the base of the building, next to the canopied entrance to the underground garage.

Tuttle emerged into view as Galt was shucking off the parachute, which he rolled up into a ball less than the size of a basketball, and handed to Tuttle, who stuffed it into the tote bag without looking. His attention was skyward, at the point on the penthouse floor where smoke could be seen billowing. Tuttle struggled with the bag's zipper as they hurried away from there. "Was that absolutely necessary?"

"Dunno," said Galt. "It seemed like a good idea at the time, taking out a nest of vipers like that. Uh, watch your back, sir. They had a lookout that made me. I think they lost me in the fall, but I could be wrong."

Fire alarms were going off inside the Tanaga Building. Galt and Tuttle easily negotiated the chain link fence, as they had coming in, and dropped to the sidewalk adjacent to the vacant parking area. They started, at a brisk pace, in the direction of the nearest intersection.

"I trust you have something for us," Tuttle groused. "That bunch you just blew up was our best lead."

"We have what we need," said Galt, "and here it is. Ugaki and his *yakuza* have paid off a North Korean military officer who commands an airfield up north near their border with China. It all ties in, General. The *yakuza* set up that technician in Houston, Fraley, to bring down the shuttle. They'd co-opted their own landing strip, courtesy of this bought-off North Korean colonel. But things seem to have gone haywire. That's what tonight's meeting was about. So we tap into North Korea's military files as deep as we can, and we find out where a colonel named Sung is commanding an airfield; then we'll know where we're going."

Tuttle sent a parting glance over his shoulder at the sky-scraper and the plume of smoke snaking into the sky from the penthouse. The wailing beeps of approaching sirens filled the night.

"And all we leave behind is a roomful of dead and injured *yakuza?* Yeah, I see your point. Good riddance to bad trash."

"You get to work tracking down that colonel and his airfield," said Galt as they reached the intersection, joining the pedestrian flow. "I've got a date to keep with Meiko. It's time for another goodbye."

A wind had picked up, whipping across the tarmac where the Concorde basked in the night lights like a giant queen bee, fawned over and catered to by the scrambling, last-minute maintenance and baggage-loading activity seen beyond the observation windows of the indoor boarding area, where travelers crowded, awaiting admittance onto the Los Angeles flight.

Sachito Kurita had been driven to the Haneda Airport to meet Meiko. The widow's large, almond eyes were red and moist, but she held her chin high and only the slightest tremble of her lower lip betrayed inner emotion. Her shapely figure was encased in a tasteful black pants suit, with pearls and earrings that matched. Straight, shoulder-length midnight black hair was tied back. Her handshake, when she greeted Galt upon his approach, was as firm as when they'd first met yesterday at this airport, yet lacked the vibrancy of only the day before.

Her chauffeur, who was certainly her bodyguard, lurked off on the periphery of people visiting with friends, associates and loved ones.

Galt saw no sign of General Tuttle.

Meiko had changed into another decidedly Western-style blouse-and-skirt outfit since she, Galt and Tuttle had parted company after their return trip to Tokyo aboard the bullet train, squashed in amid the rush hour commuters at sunset.

Galt and Meiko exchanged a hug, with an extra squeeze from her. He saw the questions in her eyes. She had not been told the details of tonight's mission, and would be terribly frustrated right now, apparently not wanting to ask, in front of Sachito, if he and Tuttle had uncovered any criminal involvement on the part of her father. And the hug lasted longer than it might have. He felt her magic touch him inside.

She whispered into his ear so only he could hear. "Trev, I love you so. I'm sorry. Good luck. Come back safely, with Kate. What is meant to be will happen."

Then they mutually ended the embrace, and she smiled deferentially in Sachito's direction. "I only asked my stepmother to send in my luggage. She was gracious enough to come see me off." As well as he knew, Galt discerned no trace of insincerity in her words.

Sachito accepted this with a modest nod. "Please return to your homeland soon, Meiko. It is my wish that we become acquainted under less trying circumstances."

"Thank you for your hospitality, Sachito, and for allowing me access to my father's office today. You have been most kind." Meiko clasped a shoulder strap bag, and held her boarding pass. She said to Galt, "Part of me doesn't want to leave. What's happening in Washington has to be covered, but things are happening here too."

"Is that right?" said Galt neutrally.

"Sachito received word on her cell phone on our way here. There's been some sort of occurrence in one of the buildings downtown owned by Kurita Industries."

"Occurrence?" said Galt, feeling Meiko's eyes, watching him, grow speculative.

"We don't know the details," said Sachito. "It happened less than an hour ago."

"Some sort of explosion," said Meiko. "Ota Anami was killed, as were several other men."

Galt wore the same black slacks, shirt and jacket that he'd worn when he'd scaled the face of the Tanaga Building to that penthouse conference room where hellfire erupted, and here he was awash with mixed emotions as the three of them stood surrounded by people conversing in various languages, saying their goodbyes. He did not want to see Meiko go. His respect and love for her was equaled only by, well, by his respect and love for an equally formidable specimen of womanly perfection whose name was Kate, and Kate was still his wife. And he had come halfway around the world to find her. Yes, there was the shuttle. Yes, there was the brewing of international crisis, enemies with nukes aimed at each other and those closest to the center of power, including the president of the United States, understanding that Galt's lone wolf covert op posed not a threat, but possibly the only hope of avoiding a military collision course that could very quickly escalate into a nuclear exchange that would cost the life of practically every American serviceperson in Korea, as well as countless civilians. Yes, yes, all of that was true. But he would not have broken the rules, would not have gone mad dog lone wolf, cutting from the White House basement to thrust himself into the belly of this monster, had he not been driven by the need to get to his woman because she was in trouble, simple as that. He had come to kick all the ass that needed kicking, on his side and theirs, whatever it took to find his wife. That's how much he loved Kate Daniels. That's what drove him. Love drove him.

And he could see in Meiko's eyes that she maybe understood him better than he understood himself. She extended her hand for a polite handshake.

"You'll find her," she said, as if she'd read his mind.

Their handshake sent those same old electrical jolts through him, just as the hug had; just as their first physical contact had, the day he and Meiko first shook hands. It had seemed too simple then, so pure and okay, falling in love with her because after all, Kate had left him. Hell, she'd wanted away from him so bad, she'd gone into outer space. Jesus, he told himself. Shut it off, you dumb nihilistic idiot. And with that, the surreal disorientation went away. He was not the first man to be in love with two women. But right now he had a job to do, and Meiko understood. He fell in love with her a little more because of that. Damn, as Tuttle would have said.

Then her flight's departure was announced, and with a nod to both of them, she was gone, joining the stream of passengers boarding the Concorde, leaving Galt standing there next to Sachito.

She extended her hand again to him. "Please let me know if there is anything I can do for you, Mr. Galt."

He smiled cordially. "I believe that I should be saying that to you." She had not commented on the fact that he was not departing Tokyo with Meiko, as he'd arrived.

"You will excuse me," she said. Her almond eyes were unreadable. "I must leave now to learn more about what happened to Mr. Anami."

Galt acknowledged this with a parting nod, thinking, whether you find out or not, lady, with any luck I killed him.

Tuttle sidled over from amid the dispersing crowd surrounding them. He stood beside Galt and watched Sachito walk away, accompanied by her chauffeur. Tuttle sighed, a man-to-man sigh.

"No disrespect to the recently widowed, but there goes one mighty fine figure of a woman."

Galt grinned tightly. "And no disrespect to an old goat, but you have been burning up that cell phone of yours, right, General?"

Tuttle snorted indignantly. "I'll have you know that I'm a happily married man. Jesus, Galt. I wouldn't expect you to be a prude."

"Just trying to keep us on mission, sir. Not always

easy with beautiful women around, I grant you. So what have we got?"

They stood alone in the departure area.

"Okay, here it is, good and bad. We still do not have target coordinates for this warlord's fortress. Nada from the spy satellite flyovers. Chai Bin is well entrenched, and no mistake."

They started walking down the window-lined corridor leading away from the waiting area.

"And what's the good part?" Galt asked.

"Our augmentation package has slipped into Japan: Army Rangers and Air Force planners and pilots. Supplies are stockpiled, and we have a shipload of bombs and smart weapons at our disposal." Tuttle's gaze turned to the observation windows, which were rattling, buffeted by the forceful night wind. "Oh yeah, there is some more bad news. There's a storm front moving in. Forecasters agree it's going to pack one hellacious punch. These windy conditions are just the beginning."

"Then let's do it," said Galt, and quickened his pace.

Chief Inspector Inogu of the Tokyo Public Security Bureau stood in the ruins of what had been the double-wide doorway to what had been the penthouse conference room atop the Tanaga Building.

He scanned the activity and the carnage in the wind-swept room—windswept because an ever-increasing wind howled outside the gaping hole in the wall where the window had been. The wind blowing through the conference room created wind tunnel–like turbulence. Gusts rustled papers, ruffled hair and snapped the tails of the white smocks worn by the forensic technicians as they labored. In eleven years on the force, Inogu had never seen anything like this. And he had seen much. While the average citizen's day-to-day life in Tokyo was crime free, violent crimes committed by the *yakuza* gangs against each other were often brutal and vicious. But never like this. This was mass murder, a Western phenomenon almost unheard of in Japan. Slabs of expensive pine paneling had been ripped away by the tremendous blast of a high explosive charge. The walls were splashed with blood. The corpses had not yet been removed. The forensic technicians moved methodically among the body bags, meticulously gathering and recording data. The heavy conference table had been blown apart, a recognizable leg here and there like the human body parts about on the floor: a severed ankle here, and a blown-off-at-the-shoulder arm there.

The medical examiner approached Inogu. "We won't have anything definite until initial forensic data is processed, and that should be by tomorrow morning."

"Please tell me what you do know."

"That is very little. The glass of the window was blown outward first, since there is so little glass amid the rubble in the room. Gunmen in this room fired for some reason, blowing the window out. Then a high explosive device was launched into the room, and the explosion occurred and these men were killed." The medical examiner studied the windswept, gaping hole in the wall across from them. "And this on the thirty-fourth floor! Exceedingly strange, wouldn't you say, Lieutenant?"

"Ugaki was the only survivor?"

"Yes, sir. He was taken by ambulance, under police escort, to the hospital."

Inogu's eyes raked the carnage. "The *yakuza* bodyguards open fire and blow the window out, and whoever they're shooting at on the thirty-fourth floor then proceeds to slaughter them with high explosive. Yes, exceedingly strange. There is one among the dead that is of particular interest to me, Doctor."

The medical examiner glanced at one of the body bags near the center of the demolished room. "Anami, the only man here who was not *yakuza*. The way it looks, he was seated beside Ugaki. There would have been chaos. When he was found, Ugaki was unconscious from loss of blood but survived by dragging Anami across him, shielding Ugaki from the blast that killed Anami."

"What is Ugaki's condition at present?"

"Serious, but stable. He will live."

Inogu nodded his satisfaction. "He will live to answer my questions." He became aware of a new presence approaching him. He turned to see a man, in plainclothes, extending identification, in a leather packet cupped in his palm, for Inogu's inspection.

"I am Captain Okada, Kompei Special Internal Affairs Division." The man spoke sharply. "I am here to take command of this investigation."

They exchanged formal bows and a perfunctory handshake. Inogu started to introduce himself.

"I know who you are," said Okada. "As of now, Lieutenant, this investigation is under Kompei jurisdiction, under direct order of the head of Japanese Security."

In the 1948 Constitution, Clause Nine, the Japanese people had renounced war forever. Officially, there was no intelligence service as such, although in fact such units were regularly recruited from various police departments and self-defense forces.

Inogu tried to conceal his total surprise. "But Captain, this is a mass homicide involving organized crime figures. That is under the jurisdiction of my task force."

The Kompei agent indicated the carnage. "These *yakuza* were deeply involved in a grave international crisis involving Japan. That is all you need to know."

"The American space shuttle," said Inogu. "I heard the news report on the way here. It is thought the shuttle went down in this part of the world." It wasn't much of a guess, merely the first "international incident" involving Japan that occurred to him since it was foremost in the day's news. He scanned the body bags within the room. "Are you telling me that these *yakuza* were involved in that?"

"I am telling you that you are off the case, Lieutenant, as is your forensic team. The Kompei has its own, and I have brought them."

He stepped aside then to allow a half-dozen white-smocked technicians, carrying their own equipment cases, to pass into the room accompanied by Kompei agents in plainclothes who commenced interrupting the technicians at work, unceremoniously herding them out.

"There will, of course, be no statements made to the media by anyone concerning anything related to this," Okada concluded. He bowed slightly to Inogu and the medical examiner. "You will excuse me."

The police forensic team stood in the hallway, packing their equipment, bristling amongst themselves.

The medical examiner sighed. "My wife often nags me about the irregular hours of this job. She will be happy. We are going home early, it seems."

Inogu watched Okada assume command of the newly-arrived forensic team like a military field commander. "The Kompei does not share or disclose information."

The M.E. frowned. "I was surprised to see Ota Anami among the dead. The *yakuza*, Kurita Industries, the Kompei, and now a missing space shuttle, perhaps. What do you make of it, Lieutenant?"

"I never thought Kurita Industries was dirty."

"And yet they lay old Kentaro Kurita's ashes to rest," the M.E. sighed, "and his successor, Anami, is killed tonight."

Inogu's eyes traveled to the gaping hole, and to the howling wind and darkness beyond. "Doctor, there is more than one storm brewing tonight."

CHAPTER TWENTY-FOUR

The Pentagon

The President met with his chiefs of staff of the army and air force, his chief of naval operations and the commandant of the Marine Corps in the War Room on the second floor.

This was the main terminus of all military communications systems connecting Washington to every military and naval command in the world. Tiered areas, overlooking a highlighted conference table, hummed with muted, concentrated activity as military personnel worked at desks, computer consoles and communications equipment. All consoles were fully manned, with all evaluators present. Display maps on the wall, changing once every four minutes, reported a running tally on the disposition of American military forces worldwide. Another bank of monitors relayed data updates from the National Command

Center, connected to the War Room by a short corridor.

The president sat at the head of the elite group. Before each man at the large hexagonal table was a yellow pad, pencils and a glass of ice water. Their attention was on a large-scale chart of the central Asian landmass.

The president toyed with an aluminum diet soda can, which he'd emptied minutes earlier. He was tapping the can absently on the desktop. Tiredness around his eyes bespoke the lengthy hours that had begun with a transcontinental flight to speak at a fundraiser in California, the subsequent announcement to the world that America was missing the space shuttle *Liberty* and the return flight to Washington, with no opportunity for sleep, not even a catnap.

"Now that we've gone public," said the president, "we'd damn well better ratchet up every resource we have." He crunched up the aluminum can and tossed it absently at a wastebasket, missing by a half-foot. "Damn." He was not referring to the missed wastebasket shot. "Gentlemen, we've got to pull this one out of the fire, and fast."

Reasoner, the army chief of staff, was grim. "The DMZ face-off had to come to a head sooner or later. The North has those hundred thousand troops primed to attack. The only reason we think no attack is imminent is because we haven't picked up any new code usage by them. And why would they be anxious to take on the combined U.S. and Republic of Korea forces?"

"The R.O.K. mainly has a draftee army," said Lansdale, "which poses a handicap. On the other hand, to be honest, they have deployed an impressive mechanized corps."

Fieldhouse, the air force man, was studying the map before them like a bombardier's eyes seeking targets. "North Korea would support an attack with its chemical and biological capability, which is massive."

"The threat of U.S. nukes aboard our warships in the region is intended to deter that," the chief of naval operations, Crider, pointed out.

The president stood, retrieved the aluminum can, and dropped it into the wastebasket. "Gentlemen, if chemical weapons and nukes are used, I have been advised that the prevailing winds would carry the poison and fallout south, and destroy most of the people of South Korea and southern Japan. North Korea would be defeated if it invaded the South again, but only after a bloodbath that would destroy the peninsula." He reached under the table, and produced another can of diet soda. He popped the tab. "I want an update on Trev Galt."

Lansdale glanced at his wristwatch. "The special ops insertion package Tuttle put together is presently standing by at the operational base site in Yokohama."

"What they need is a target," said Fieldhouse. "The CIA's man on the ground over there, Ahn Chong, hasn't made contact since he transmitted Chai Bin's offer to his CIA control in Japan. We're hoping this Ahn Chong isn't dead."

Crider frowned deeply. "That storm coming at Japan has been upgraded to a typhoon."

"We'll have Galt's strike force airborne and out of the storm track before it hits," said Reasoner. "I hope."

Lansdale grunted. "This strike on Chai Bin's has to be surgical, by the numbers and very precise, and that's the way it will be with that crazy ass staying with Tuttle in Japan to monitor and direct the assault."

The president paused with the soda can halfway to his mouth. "You're joking, of course." He took a long draw of the diet cola. "Galt's gotten us this far by breaking every rule in the book because his wife is among the missing. Do you think he's going to stand down now and obey orders?" The president shook his head, knowingly. "And do you know what? That's all right with me. Let's pray like hell for diplomatic success, gentlemen. But my personal opinion is that one man in this has one chance at seeing that America's best interests are served, and that man is Trev Galt."

Tokyo

In the first class section aboard the Concorde, orders for pre-flight drinks were being taken.

Meiko ordered tea. She glanced over her shoulder and saw, through a gap in the curtain, the flight attendants welcoming the last of the boarding passengers. Her fellow travelers in the first class section included Japanese businessmen, several already typing furiously at their laptop computers. A Saudi sheik and his family occupied the foremost seats.

Though she knew she looked composed enough, Meiko's mind and emotions were rioting. Yes, she was the top U.S. correspondent for Hakura World News. Yes, the disappearance of the *Liberty* was, thus far, the biggest story of the century and would be the biggest of this decade, the sort of story upon which media stardom careers were built; and her orders were to return to the Washington bureau and resume her duties promptly. Her camera crew would be waiting when she touched down in D.C., where she was expected to quite literally hit the ground running, to use the American idiom. But every indication was that the space shuttle had gone down in this part of the world. Yes, Hakura News had its best Tokyo correspondents assigned to the story. But she had the inside track because of her personal life, which gave her an edge on this story that was being ignored.

She and Stan Hakura himself had had it out over the phone. Stan was fourth-generation Hakura, with the bluster of a street merchant combined with intellectual dexterity and an innate combative toughness. It was Stan who had steered Hakura News into the new millennium, far beyond what must have been the wildest imaginings of his great-grandfather, who had started the company as a four-page provincial weekly so many years ago. As the daughter of Kentaro Kurita, and as Stan's top-rated media star in the Asian market, Meiko was one of the few in Hakura News who would dare protest an order from on high. Their debate was heated, and had degenerated into a noisy argument. Every news instinct in her was telling her that she was flying away from the real story of *Liberty*, not toward it, by leaving Japan. Because this story intersected with her personal life, her wash of emotions was excruciating. Her father's death was a harsh reminder of her own mortality. In one's life, every second, every choice made, mattered. She thought of the conversation she had partly overheard between Ugaki and Anami at her father's funeral. A *yakuza*, and her father's successor as CEO of Kurita Industries; a conversation about *Liberty*. And there were questions about links between her father's death and the downed shuttle: unanswered questions, because no one was asking them. She was the one to pursue the difficult questions. That was her argument to Stan. Was her father's death honestly of natural causes, or had Kentaro Kurita been murdered? She could not imagine her father collaborating with the *yakuza*.

And there was Trev.

Her personal life, yes. Trevor Galt III, the man who had flown to Japan to rescue a wife Meiko had never met. She did not understand her feelings for this man, but she knew it was love. And that had to be resolved before any other part of her life could proceed, and the resolution of those rioting emotions was here in Japan. There was only one proper way for her to feel. She knew Trev well enough to know his true romantic nature. Knowing that side of him, she should have realized before this that he had not yet given up on his feelings for the woman he was married to. He most likely would not realize it himself, but underlying Trev's mission was his impulse to prove to his wife how much he was still in love with her. Meiko understood this because she was a woman. It would be so fine to be loved like that, by a man like that. That had, in fact, been Meiko's unspoken dream, never spoken to Trev, never really dwelled on in her own mind because, in fact, the man she was in love with was married. There was only one thing for her to do now. She must allow this husband and wife, however estranged, the opportunity to work out their problems. She could not allow this to interfere, however, with the fact that her personal life had put her at the center of this news story. But Stan would hear none of it. He told her to start acting like a reporter and less like a woman, and had disconnected their cell phone connection.

Meiko sighed, looking through her reflection in the darkened window beside her at the ground crews, the carts, trucks and personnel, withdrawing from the behemoth aircraft. The vibrations of the Concorde's engines reached a new pitch, and the pilot's voice came over the intercom, delivering the standard greeting in Japanese, to be followed by an English translation. Last-minute arrivals were being ushered aboard.

The flight attendant was approaching with her cup of tea when Meiko left her seat, practically bolting through the first class divider curtain, toward the door which other flight attendants were about to close.

North Korea

The weekly Communist Party meetings were held in the communal hut, after the evening meal. The three appointed Party representatives of the village sat at a table, facing the others who sat on rough wooden benches. A charcoal brazier took the mountain chill off the room.

As the daughter of old Ahn Chong, the village elder, and wife of Cho, the commune Party leader, Toi could feel the eyes of every member of the commune on her. The bench space beside her was vacant. Her father traditionally sat there, at her side.

Her husband rapped a hammer that served as a gavel to call this meeting to order. Cho's eyes connected with hers, and he indicated the vacant spot next to her.

"I cannot recall your father ever having missed a meeting before."

"And so you voice personal concern for your father-in-law?" she asked sarcastically.

She and Cho had barely spoken since that terrible visit from the military to their village. She still trembled with revulsion at the sensation of the soldier, Colonel Sung, the commander of the airfield, grasping her, right there in front of her father, and aiming a pistol to her head! Cho had intervened on her behalf, but that had hardly endeared her husband to her father, or to her. Her husband was the informant who had put her and her father in jeopardy. And where was her father? She had last seen him near dusk, ambling off from the village, the wind whipping at his ragged clothing, on a path leading away from the village. She had not called out to him. It had been such a trying day, why should he not have been entitled to a time of solitude? But he had not returned. Where was he?

Cho glared at her as if they were strangers. "Your father does know where this . . . this space shuttle . . . is. Do you know where he is?"

She had prepared his evening meal, which Cho had eaten in silence, glowering. Now, she understood why.

She stood. "I don't know where my father is, but if I did, I would never tell you. You should know that much about me."

Cho sighed deeply. "I suppose I do."

"I doubt if you do understand me. I would never betray my father, as you betrayed our family."

"You and your father do not understand that loyalty to the Party must take precedence over mere personal relationships in times of crisis. The Party is, after all, the community, the commune."

She could not pretend, as he did, that they were not husband and wife.

"Cho, you think that you are following your conscience. They have stolen your soul."

He winced. His officiousness evaporated, and his eyes dropped from hers. He shuffled the papers before him and, when he returned her gaze, conveyed a plea.

"But you must try to understand," he said in a persuasive tone. "This business of soldiers harassing us, terrorizing us, concerns a thing that should have nothing to do with this collective." There were grumbled assents from those present. "We are but simple peasants," Cho continued. "The soldiers and Colonel Sung, an American space shuttle, these are not our problems. And yet the military terrorizes us because of your father and whatever he knows."

Anger and confusion swept through her, and took control. "I don't know where the space shuttle is." She whirled to face the assembled villagers. "And I want nothing to do with any of you!"

She stormed out of the hut, into the night.

The wind had picked up. Roiling black clouds blotted out the starlight. She sensed no one following her, perhaps because her action had been so unexpected, as it was even to herself. But she could not tolerate hearing her father maligned, or seeing the man she loved, poor Cho, become so corrupted by a soulless political machine. She had not lied. She did not know where their space shuttle was. But she suspected that they were right, that her father did know.

She darted around the communal hut and continued on into the gloom, leaving the village behind, avoiding the main path upon which she had last seen her father walking, yet following that same direction using a shortcut she'd learned as a child. Branches reached out from the darkness and scratched her, and the rocky ground made her lose her footing twice. She pushed on and rejoined the path about one-half kilometer farther on, after the village had disappeared behind her. She hurried on. The wind howled. She was quite certain that she knew where she would find her father.

The soles of her sandals crunched on the cold ground, the only human sound she heard. Her pace quickened as the path approached the crest of the hill where the path would lead down to her mother's gravesite.

She tripped over something and tumbled forward, breaking her fall with her hands. Human movement scurried toward her. She had tripped over someone's extended ankle. She started to twist around and rise from the ground, but before she could do so of her own volition, an arm snaked around her from behind and roughly dragged her to her feet. She was aware of an additional presence, moving toward her from the side, even as she recognized by touch the stocky build of the man whose forearm braced her throat, pressing her back to him.

Colonel Sung snickered lewdly, close to her ear, from behind. "Well then, my sweet, the sergeant and I welcome you. Do we not, Sergeant?"

A quiet voice from the darkness responded, "Yes, sir."

She could not discern the speaker, but recognized the voice of Sergeant Bol Rhee, the soldier from the airfield whose rawboned peasant features had reminded Toi of the people of her own village. His voice now was obedient, yet she heard reluctance, too. They seemed to be alone. Toi sensed no other movement in the darkness. She did not bother to struggle in Sung's grasp.

"Where's my father?"

Again, he snickered in her ear, thrusting his pelvis against her from behind. She could almost see the smirk on his pudgy face. He said, "Let's join him, shall we?"

CHAPTER TWENTY-FIVE

In the small clearing, Ahn Chong knelt at the grave of his wife. Tonight, the tranquility of this place, and being immersed in Mai's presence, did not bring him comfort, did not soothe his soul.

This was where the recent horror had begun for him, when he had been kneeling in prayerful contemplation as he was now, when the heavens had been abruptly ripped asunder by a ferocious, thunderous *whoosh!* of the space shuttle flying over him before its crash landing. Tonight, the wind whipped the pines and twisted fruit trees on the hillside behind him.

He was startled by the appearance of the two soldiers and their captive—his daughter, Toi!—when they emerged into the circle of golden light from a lantern he'd brought tonight, because the stars were blocked by murky, surging clouds.

Ahn leapt to his feet, recognizing the sergeant who aimed a rifle at him, and Colonel Sung, commander of the airfield. Sung stood with Ahn's daughter, gripping one of Toi's wrists.

"Good evening, old man. A bit blustery for a graveside vigil."

Toi's eyes were sorrowful. "Forgive me, Father. I wanted to speak with you. I did not know they were following me."

Sung chuckled. "Do not fret, my dear. The sergeant and I had your father under surveillance and were about to confront him when you chose to arrive. And might I ask what you wished to speak to your father about?"

Fury coursed through Ahn Chong. He felt his years fade away. He felt young again, mad enough to kill. He wanted to attack.

Sung snarled. "Sergeant, I want you to kill this old man if he so much as moves."

Sergeant Bol Rhee aimed his rifle at Ahn Chong. "Yes, sir."

Ahn chose the voice of reason. "Colonel, my daughter and her husband, a loyal Party member, are in harm's way because of what I know. Toi came here tonight to plead with me to divulge to you what I know. Is that not so, daughter?"

Toi's eyes became downcast. She said nothing.

"I demand the same, that you tell me what you know." Sung's pig-like eyes never left Ahn. "We are finished with polite conversation." Sung's eyes narrowed. "Take me to the shuttle, old man, or I will have your daughter executed. That is the tack I should have taken today at your village."

Ahn felt the weight of the world squeezing at him, and the rage within him crumbled. He, a humble old peasant, had by the strangest set of circumstances been placed in a pivotal role in an international drama with the most personal of implications in the world to him, for the life of his daughter was in his hands. His shoulders sagged. He felt every one of his sixty-seven years.

"Very well," he said. "I will take you there."

The shuttle loomed in the clearing it had created upon impact, having left a wide swath of smashed trees and sheared-off limbs. The wind had died down and, through a break in the clouds, starlight and moonlight illuminated the spacecraft's awesome, towering shape. The camouflage netting that had been draped across it could not conceal its heavily damaged fuselage. The shuttle cast an aura of muzzled majesty, as if the camouflage netting was entangling and impeding the escape flight of a giant, graceful, free bird.

It was the most impressive sight Bol Rhee had ever seen. He crouched, with Colonel Sung and their prisoners, in the inky shadows of trees overlooking the shuttle. Sung held Toi by her right arm, his pistol held in his free hand. Bol's rifle remained aimed at the old man, as it had during their short hike here from the gravesite. Bol would always remember the sight of this spacecraft lumbering by overhead when it had been expected to land at the airfield, but he could only imagine what this old man must have experienced. The impact of the crash must have been enormous.

Beholding such a sight, Bol wondered anew at what intrigues his simple soldier's life had led him to. He was but a lowly noncommissioned officer in the North Korean People's Army, and yet he had been charged with the security of a mysterious, remote airfield, and his commander's only outside contact with any discernible chain of command had seemed to be a mysterious midnight visitor flown to the airfield in a helicopter with Japanese civilian markings. And now, this.

There were three men, in mismatched military fatigues, seated around a small fire that had been built in the windbreak created by the shuttle, at the foot of a tall ladder that went up to what appeared to be the closed main entry hatch to the shuttle. The three figures were leaning forward to bask in the fire's warmth, conversing amongst themselves, their rifles close at hand.

Sung emitted a whispered, contemptuous snort. "Chai Bin himself would kill those bandits if he could see how lax his security is. Sergeant Bol, you know what to do."

"Yes, sir."

Bol shifted his attention completely from the old man, and flattened himself to the frosty ground, steadying his elbows and selecting his first target. And for a moment, a memory touched him. He was a boy of twelve in these mountains, stalking wild game, being taught by his long-deceased father whom he still thought of at least once a day. He wished, as he had often but more now than ever before, that he had never grown up to become a soldier. Sighting in on each man in turn around the fire, he reminded himself that these human targets were predators who preyed on civilians. He squeezed off three rounds, expertly riding the AK-47's recoil. His father had taught him well.

The three men around the fire seemed to leap sideways off their seats, arms flailing one after another in rapid succession, and tumbling to the ground, where their forms did not move.

"Very good, Sergeant," said Sung quietly. "We advance. But be wary. There may be more of them lurking about. And, you two." He glared at Toi and Ahn Chong. "If either of you cries out an alarm, you will die instantly. Is that understood?" He took their lack of response as an affirmative. "Let us go then and see this prize."

Bol noted that though Sung was willing enough to command, he hesitated, waiting for Bol to stand and take the lead position, and they walked single file down the gradual slope toward the shuttle. Bol advanced with the AK-47, fanning the darkness around the fire like an antenna seeking targets, but finding none. He heard old Ahn Chong ambling along behind him, then Sung with Toi. Bol drew up near the fire. He had no desire to expose himself as a target in the firelight.

Sung asked, "Are you afraid, Sergeant?" in a chiding tone.

"Prudent," said Bol. He reached to the pack upon his back, which, among other things, contained a handheld radio transceiver. "I will instruct our forces to close in."

"You will instruct our forces that are presently waiting at the airfield," Sung corrected, "and those alone."

"But, sir, what of the elite troops sent to us from Pyongyang?"

"I will use them when the time is right," said Sung. "It is not your place to question me."

"I have every reason to believe that Chai Bin has already taken whatever equipment could be carried from the shuttle. There will be much damage inside, and much missing. It remains for our elderly friend," Sung nodded in Ahn Chong's direction, "to next reveal the location of Chai Bin's base. Those forces from Pyongyang will then be ordered to attack Chai Bin, and we shall support them in that action. Our primary objective is to retrieve what has been taken, Sergeant. But what if Chai Bin's bandit scum have not yet looted *Liberty*? What if those sentries you killed were to guard this treasure, and the removal is done tomorrow? In such a case, there would be no reason to attack Chai Bin, and I could deal directly with my, er, superiors, now that this spacecraft is in our possession, and all will return to plan. Hand me the hammer and crowbar in your pack, Sergeant." Sung was studying the ladder leading up to the main hatch on the fuselage, located between the nose and the wing. The crackling campfire flames danced in Sung's eyes. "I will be the first person of our government to claim this shuttle for our country."

Bol's eyes were filled with the enormity of the space shuttle. "Yes sir." He did as he was told.

Sung holstered his pistol and took the tools.

"Very good, Sergeant. Now do as I've instructed and call in our force from the airfield." His eyes moved to Ahn Chong and Toi, standing side by side. "And if either of these two attempts to escape, you know what to do."

"Yes, sir."

"Very well." Sung puffed out his chest beneath his starched tunic. "I go to claim the space shuttle *Liberty* for the People's Republic of North Korea."

He moved past the fire, stepping around the fallen bodies, and began climbing the ladder, hammer and crowbar secured beneath his gunbelt.

Bol remained with his rifle aimed at Ahn Chong and Toi, but they all watched the man determinedly climbing the ladder, up the side of the fuselage.

When he gained the top step, Sung did not hesitate. He wedged the crowbar against the lip of the hatch.

He reached for the hammer. Bol could see Colonel Sung swing the hammer.

The world exploded.

A scorching fireball mushroom spewed from the side of the spacecraft, its blast shattering the senses, the concussion knocking Bol and the civilians from their feet. Bol hugged the ground, covering his head with his arms, feeling the heat of the blast pressing him to the ground. The explosion seemed to go on forever. Pieces of debris were dropping to the ground around him. Finally the roaring blast became a rumble, as if the ancient gods of these mountains were awakening, displeased. The vibrations of the explosion then became a low rumble, echoing off into the mountains. Bol cautiously lifted his eyes, at first without removing his arms from covering his head.

The first things he saw were the prone figures of Ahn Chong and his daughter, who were also now deeming it safe to look. Bol commanded himself to act. He grasped the AK-47 and leapt to his feet, starting to track his rifle at them. But something peculiar, on the ground near the three of them, caught his attention, and when he paused to look, he gasped in such horror at what he saw.

A human leg, severed at mid-thigh, was clad in a freshly pressed trouser leg, the starched crease still evident. A spit-polished boot reflected small fires, started nearby, crackling weakly amid the tree limbs. The top of the severed leg was a charred, smoking mess.

"Sergeant," said Ahn Chong in a droll tone, "I believe that is all that remains of your commanding officer."

Toi turned to study Bol. "You seem like a good man. What are you going to do now?"

Bol fought to gain control of his senses. He took a

step back and raised his rifle in their direction. She was voicing the very question rioting in his mind. Something struck him in his lower back, and he knew it was the muzzle of a rifle pressed to the base of his spine.

A new voice intoned solemnly, "If anyone dies, it will be the sergeant."

Bol heard an implicit command in the voice. He dropped his rifle to the ground, and raised both hands. The pressure of the gun against the base of his spine subsided.

A man eased around from behind him, positioning himself next to the old man and his daughter. Bol had recognized the voice, having heard it during the "interrogation" in the village. It was Cho, Ahn Chong's son-in-law, Toi's husband, who now aimed his rifle at Bol Rhee's head.

Toi studied her husband. "Did you follow me here to protect me, or to spy on me for the Party?"

In the scant illumination of the dwindling nearby fires, Cho's eyes burned with fury.

"You are my wife. As a man, am I to allow soldiers of my government to manhandle you, to threaten you with death, twice in one day?" He addressed Ahn Chong without taking his eyes from Bol. "Father-in-law, I have learned to see you with new eyes. Toi's mother, your wife, died because she could not receive proper medical attention from our government." He sneered, "Our government of the people! And today they would threaten to kill my wife? This is not my government, and I will prove it by eliminating their ranks by one more."

Bol saw Cho tighten his body for the recoil of his rifle. Bol braced himself for death.

"No!" Toi cried out. "My husband, I beg of you: do

not add to the madness with more killing! Spare this man."

Ahn Chong rested a hand lightly on Cho's shoulder. "Listen to your woman." He nodded at Bol. "This man was a good soldier following orders. I sensed his personal repulsion at what he had been ordered to do." He nodded to indicate the grisly sight of the smoldering leg upon the ground nearby. "There is what remains of the man who has brought the taint of violence to our village. And I strongly suspect that he was deluding his commanders in Pyongyang, not obeying them. Otherwise, he would have had no need of such heightened security measures at the airfield."

Bol nodded. He must grasp at this chance of survival. Cho's rifle had not wavered from being aimed at a point between his eyes. "That is true," he heard himself say. "A helicopter, with Japanese markings, brought the one from whom Colonel Sung took his orders."

Ahn Chong nodded. "A powerful organization in Japan bought off Colonel Sung. They financed construction of the airfield with every intention of downing the space shuttle. But everything went wrong for the colonel after the shuttle crew crash-landed instead of landing at the airfield, as was intended."

Bol was further surprised to hear himself say in a quiet voice to Ahn Chong, "You remind me of my father." To Cho, he pleaded, "Spare me. My pay as a soldier is not much, but it supports my mother and sisters in the village where I come from."

Time again seemed to stop, suspended.

Cho lowered his rifle. "And we just want to be left alone to be farmers."

"Return to your lives," said Bol. "Since central headquarters in Pyongyang knows nothing of what Colonel

Sung had undertaken here, I will be a hero of the People's Army when I step forward to report everything that I know."

Toi nodded, but her eyes were doubtful. "What of Colonel Sung's death? Who will be made to answer?"

"The shuttle crew," said Ahn Chong. "They set an explosive charge to counteract tampering. The colonel was undone by his own design. The sergeant's superiors in Pyongyang will accept the truth. At present, the North Korean government has far too much to concern itself with than one rogue field commander. Colonel Sung has lost relevance in death." The old man's expression grew reflective. "As do we all, I suspect."

Cho emitted a strange snort that might have been a laugh. "Father-in-law, I see you with new eyes and hear you with new ears. You have been right all along, since this began. In the future, sir, I will heed your wisdom." He held his rifle in one hand, and slipped his other arm around Toi's waist. "A man's first loyalty must be to wife and family."

"It would be best," Ahn nodded, "if we would listen to each other."

Cho indicated Bol with his rifle. "As for you, soldier, be gone! Consider this the luckiest day of your life. Go."

Bol whirled and fled, not pausing to retrieve his rifle. He had his pistol, in case he needed to defend himself. As he ran into the night, he gave thought to not returning to the airfield and contacting Pyongyang. He thought about going home.

The small fires near the blast site had been extinguished by the sharp mountain wind. There was nearly complete darkness. He vanished from sight.

Toi's expression was doubtful. "Can we trust him? Our lives are in his hands."

"Our lives are in our hands," said Cho. He turned to Ahn with the demeanor of a student addressing his sensei. "Is that not so, father-in-law?"

Ahn again rested his hand on the young man's shoulder. "You showed great bravery this night, Cho, and now you exhibit wisdom. Yes, you and Toi will now return to the village. Return to your lives."

Toi was frowning. "What about you, Father? Will you return to Mother's grave? Are you sure that is safe? You should return with us."

"There is no place in these mountains that is safe tonight, child, except perhaps, for you, in the safety of your home and your husband's arms. Go now. And be sure not to draw attention to yourselves. You were having a husband-wife quarrel, as far as anyone else is concerned. If you draw attention to yourselves, no matter what that soldier promised, trouble will come."

Cho held his rifle in one hand, and Toi's hand in his other. "You have often asked me to heed the wisdom of your father," he told her. "I now ask you to do the same. Let us be gone from here. We return to the village."

Toi hesitated, then stepped forward to lightly kiss Ahn Chong upon the cheek. They embraced. Clouds blotted out starlight and moonlight, and Ahn lost sight of them as they withdrew.

When the sound of their footfalls had faded into the night, he turned and trudged away in the opposite direction, away from the shuttle. He returned to near Mai's grave, where he retrieved his hidden short-wave radio.

He removed the stainless steel cover, extended the antenna and pressed the buttons that activated the set and automatically synchronized the scrambler. He told himself that he should have done this before. But he had not transmitted anything concerning Chai Bin's location to his CIA control officer because of his concern—his fear—for the safety of his daughter. He was releasing that fear. He had underestimated Toi and her husband. They were showing their best, and so would he. He would save his village from this madness. He began to work the transmitter's code key.

Within a few minutes he had made contact with Fox Dog Alpha.

Chapter Twenty-six

Special Forces Command Center, Yokohama, Japan

The heavily secured "commercial site" was buried deep in the city's industrial district. The Japanese authorities feigned ignorance of its existence but secretly approved of and facilitated this American covert ops staging area which had been deemed, at the highest level, as beneficial to Japan's national security.

Galt stood beneath an overhang at the front of the hangar, watching rain pelt the helicopter gunships that were poised on the tarmac for lift-off. The helos' landing lights made the slanting rain look like falling multi-colored diamonds. There was a Blackhawk gunship, heavily armed, boasting 5.56mm mini-guns mounted on external turrets. The machine gun protruding from its nose could deliver 20mm cannon shells. The Blackhawk, designed for personnel insertion and extraction, was book-ended by a pair of

Apache AH-64s, the most heavily armed, fastest armored aircraft in the world. The Apaches were loaded for bear, each armed with 100-pound missiles, a fully loaded 30mm chain-gun cannon and 70mm rockets. Ground crews had attached 1,700-pound, 230-gallon external fuel tanks to two of the Apaches' left inboard weapons storage areas. To make room for this extra fuel, each aircraft had reduced its number of rockets to nineteen. The wing tank concept had been developed during the first Gulf War. While it raised the gross weight of the aircraft some 1,500 pounds past its combat weight, the up side was that the Apache gained a strike capability in excess of 400 miles.

Set somewhat aside from the others was a third Apache, its pilot visible in his cockpit. This chopper's engine was idling, unlike the others.

Galt wore jungle cammies and combat boots. The 9mm Beretta was again worn in an unconcealed shoulder leather. An M4 carbine, a shortened version of the standard M16, was slung over his shoulder. He wore a K-Bar fighting knife sheathed at mid-chest, and a backpack computer for satellite communications. His Night Vision Device goggles, attached to his combat helmet, were in the upflipped, unused position. His face was darkened with camouflage ointment.

Behind him, smells of oil and grease permeated the atmosphere of the spacious hangar. Pilots and members of the special ops team, combat-outfitted, attired in commando black, milled around folding chairs in a corner where a table with topographic maps had been set up.

In this hundred-percent male atmosphere, Galt oddly found himself thinking of saying goodbye to Meiko at the airport, with Sachito present. Meiko had looked so lovely, and so sad. And there was something else. Something elusive. Something on the edge of Galt's consciousness that was trying to call attention to itself. Something he had missed the first time around. He was forging ahead, but he still didn't have the full picture . . .

General Tuttle materialized at a run, approaching the hangar through the veil of rain. He found cover next to Galt, beneath the overhang. His eyes were tight, angry.

"Galt, just how goddamn stupid do I look?"

Galt had been expecting this. "Uh, that sounds like a trick question, sir."

"Did you honestly think that I wouldn't find out that you've been using your White House clout to get that CIA hack, Smathers, to jump through your hoops?"

"Sir—"

"Cork it. Goddamn it! You requisitioned that extra Apache out there on the tarmac for your own personal insertion into North goddamn Korea. Smathers told me that you were sitting next to him at the safe house when his contact in North Korea radioed in with the attack coordinates on Chai. And you had the goddamn brass balls to instruct Smathers to set up a rendezvous point with his man! And you draft a chopper pilot to ferry you in, all of it unauthorized."

"He wasn't drafted, sir. I went into the pilots' team room and asked for a volunteer."

Tuttle shrugged off his raincoat. "Jesus on a crutch." He glanced at the squad of Army Rangers, who were outfitted similarly to Galt, gathered at the far end of the hangar, beyond earshot. "I brought them together for the rough stuff, son. You went off-mission to initiate this operation and I put the package together, and part of that deal was that I need you on the outside with a clear overview, helping me to call the shots. I need you right here in Japan to work with me on the big picture while this is going down. You're the last man to stage a maverick strike on a goddamn warlord."

"I'm the only man to do it," said Galt. "I've got to make a preliminary soft probe, General. I can get inside without them knowing I'm inside. I can isolate and protect the crew survivors until the ops force shows."

"Let me tell you something." Tuttle's narrowed eyes burned. "You're talking about risking blowing this whole operation by going wild card on me. You'll only get the wrong people killed, including my men and quite possibly your wife. If Chai Bin catches you, he'll know we're on our way, then he'll really hunker down. Our advantage of surprise would be lost, and he could well execute the surviving crewmembers out of pure maliciousness. No, that is not acceptable. Galt, you are not going in."

"You're making a mistake, General."

Tuttle angrily tossed aside the raincoat. "I've got a briefing to deliver. Now start acting like a soldier and obey orders." He strode away without waiting for a reply.

The special ops squad seated themselves when Tuttle approached a lectern that fronted a map.

Galt wanted to hear the briefing. He took a standing position behind the last row of men.

"The good news first," said Tuttle. He caught Galt's eye, and nodded in approval of Galt giving in to common sense. "The mission is a go. The not-so-good news is the storm." He nodded toward the wind-whipped rain pelting the tarmac outside the hangar. "It's been upgraded to a typhoon."

There was grumbling among the helicopter pilots.

"I know," said Tuttle, "and I don't like it either. The center of the storm is presently north of the Sea of Japan and is coming this way, but its course is not predictable. The target area, this warlord's so-called fortress, should be on the fringe of the storm. Unfortunately. I'm speaking here of the opposite fringe from the one we seem to be on, which means you're likely to encounter extreme turbulence between here and there. As for your penetration of North Korean airspace, you must get in stealthily, without creating a signature. More not-so-good news: the terrain over there is rugged, cloud covered as I say, with high mountains and narrow passes. Expect bad wind currents with sudden downdrafts."

More muttering among those present.

"Belay that," Tuttle growled. And when silence had been restored, he continued, "Our biggest problem is lack of maps. The ones that are available don't have much fine detail. Therefore, the Cobra has been equipped with a Global Positioning System to fix your target position within ten meters. Gentlemen, are there any questions?"

"Uh, yes sir," the team commander said. "What about that extra Apache sitting outside?"

Galt eased about and strode away from the group, toward the front of the hangar. He picked up his pace. He broke into a dead-heat run when he heard Tuttle shout, "Galt!" Galt left the hangar, angling toward the Apache that was set aside from the others, its pilot visible in the cockpit through sweeping sheets of rain. At sight of Galt, the pilot followed his previous instructions and the Apache growled to life, competing with the storm's fury with exhaust fumes and the increasing, whistling rpm's of the rotor blades. Galt pulled himself aboard, into the gunner's position, in the lower front seat. He turned to face Tuttle.

The general appeared oblivious to the drenching downpour.

"Dammit to hell, Galt, get your ass out of that chopper this instant." He shouted to be heard above the revving-up turbines and the whistling of the propeller blades. "You're not going anywhere!"

Galt strapped himself in. "I beg to differ, sir. I want this done right, so I'm doing it. I'm the best shot we've got and you know it. I'm going in to set it up for the ops guys from the inside. Nothing else has changed."

"Everything has changed, you lone wolf son of a bitch. An unauthorized insertion into North Korean airspace and taking out one of their bandits is bad enough. I know you, Galt, and I will not stand for some wild-hair, improvised pick-up-and-go operation."

"I know you know me, sir. You know I have trouble taking orders. Ask the president."

"Galt, I can have that ops team over there give chase in their Apaches and they'll vaporize you before you get a mile off-shore. Don't make me do it."

Galt looked over at the team. They were holding back, observing this confrontation from the hangar.

"Sir, I don't think you'd do that." Galt slammed the hatch shut. He leaned forward to tap the shoulder of the pilot, an intense Hispanic kid from Arizona named Morales. "Get us out of here, son." He buckled himself in and grasped the overhead strap to steady himself.

The Apache lifted off into the storm, immediately being buffeted about by slashing wind and rain, like a toy shaken by an irritable child.

Tuttle remained standing where he was, and

watched the Apache vanish from his sight into the turbulence of the storm. The wind and rain battered his face.

"Goddamn you, Galt," he said under his breath. "God bless you."

North Korea

An armored column of Russian-made T-54 tanks was called in from the Provincial Headquarters of the Chinese military at Shenyang. Their course had already been well denoted through the frontier by the previous passage of General Li's column of BTR-40 personnel carriers. The T-54s made good time despite the mountainous terrain and the darkness. In fact, the tanks overtook General Li's convoy one kilometer short of where Li's prisoner, the terrified bandit, claimed they would find Chai Bin's fortress, and the equipment and crewmembers of the *Liberty*.

The prisoner now cringed against the tire of a personnel carrier. His eyes were swollen shut. Several of his teeth were missing. Two of his fingers had been broken. He whimpered like a sick puppy. He had provided prompt and thorough responses to every question posed by his tank commanders.

The trace of exhaust fumes of the recently departed T-54s still lingered on the air, though their clanking sounds had been smothered beyond the folds of the mountains.

General Li sat in a canvas-backed field chair, near his lead vehicle, in the company of Major Kwan. The general sipped *huang chiu*, a sweet yellow wine, which had been heated and served by his orderly. Trees enclosing a natural cup of land formed a natural bowl around them. Li had ordered Major Kwan to post a defensive perimeter, then ordered his troops to check their weapons and equipment, and allowed them a cigarette break. The advantage of this position was that it provided ample cover from a trundling night wind.

Li set aside his teacup. He sighed contentedly, gazing across at Kwan, who had declined tea.

"The rigors of the field can be tempered, Major. You should allow yourself to indulge in some creature comforts at a moment like this."

The young division commander could not seem to relax. His eyes started constantly at the darkness. "I will feel better when this business is done."

"Relax, I say, Major. The prize is within our grasp. We await only radio confirmation that our tanks are in place. The terrain and the wind will conceal their approach from Chai Bin. The tanks will crush his defenses. Then we will attack."

Kwan began pacing restlessly. "I grow impatient to attack."

"And I order you to be patient, Major. After our assault, the surviving bandits will be executed on the spot, and the People's Republic of China will lay claim to the space shuttle *Liberty* and its surviving crewmembers. We are less than a kilometer from Chai Bin's fortress, and have encountered no sign of American or North Korean military presence. The prize is as good as ours. We command the element of surprise. We are victorious!"

The *whuppa!-whuppa!-whuppa!* of the Apache in flight enveloped Captain Abe Morales. The steady drone did not soothe his senses, but rather honed them to a razor's edge. His gunship was traveling on a northwesterly course, speeding under radar cover at 190 knots.

Gale winds pounded the helo, and Morales's arms were sore from riding the bucking controls. It was like cruising full-tilt in a speedboat, bouncing across waves. But they'd made it through the worst of the storm. There had been a close call on the flight out of Japanese airspace, when a 150-knot wind shear almost slammed them from the sky. Morales had never seen combat, but his training paid off. He navigated through that turbulence and they'd proceeded through the typhoon as if riding out concussions from flak explosions. They had broken from the center force of the storm about midway across the Sea of Japan. Now there was only the wind, the storm's steering winds, which actually made flying more difficult once they penetrated North Korean airspace. Morales used his Night Vision Device goggles and the Apache's full array of electronic navigational equipment to fly at tree-top level over the treacherous mountain terrain. The cloud ceiling was low, volatile.

His passenger's orders were that all due speed was imperative. The guy's credentials were impressive as hell. White House level, no less. Trev Galt had drawn him aside and said he was looking for a volunteer, one-hundred-percent off the record and dangerous as hell. Galt said he'd nosed around and ascertained that Morales was good enough and enough of a loner for him to make the proposition. Was he interested? His answer was simple and direct. Hell, yes.

He eased up on the throttle as they neared the landing zone that was their destination. He'd volunteered for two reasons. One was that he ached to do what he'd been trained to do. There were no secrets in a unit like this, a tightly knit "secret" base operating in the heart of a friendly nation. Tuttle had put together an assault package to break every rule in the book. It was hostile territory passing by below the Apache, and the Chinese were said to have units combing these mountains. The covert insertion and withdrawal could get very hot, very fast, and then he would know combat. And there was the other reason why he wanted a part of this. He liked everything he'd heard about why Trev Galt was breaking all the rules on this one, and the scene between Galt and General Tuttle had sure as hell been proof enough of that. This was far from a routine mission for Galt, because his wife was among the missing shuttle crew. Morales was engaged to his high school sweetheart, who was waiting for him back home. He knew something about love, and about a man doing the right thing by his woman. The exchange between General Tuttle and Galt prior to their departure from Yokohama was a taste of what he could expect when he returned. But it was worth it, helping a man like Galt do right. He'd have done the same.

The signal fire, which he'd been watching for, materialized in the greenish glow of his Forward Looking Infrared System. It flickered valiantly in a windbreak of some kind.

Morales down-throttled. "There it is, sir," he said across the intercom, "about a quarter click ahead."

Then Galt saw it with his naked eye. "Very good, Captain."

"Looks peaceful enough. I'm taking us in."

"Looks can be deceiving," said Galt. "Careful, son. Keep your eyes peeled."

Then they were touching down in a small clearing where tree limbs had been leaned together to form a windbreak, allowing the fire to crackle, unattended. The backwash created by the Apache's landing extinguished the fire.

"Right on time," said Morales, "right on the mark." He looked around. "But I don't see anybody."

Galt unharnessed himself, threw aside the hatch and stepped to the ground.

"Let that be my problem, Captain. You've done your part. Now get the hell out of North Korea."

"Good luck to you, sir."

Morales threw him a smart salute, which Galt returned. Then the young pilot worked the controls and the Apache lifted off. Galt stepped away, raising an arm to shield his eyes against the spiraling debris in the backwash of the chopper's rotors, where the winds began immediately trundling it. Without landing or flight lights, the Apache was nothing but a dark shape against the black sky.

There was a sudden blast that Galt recognized as antiaircraft fire and, a half-second later, the Apache exploded, blossoming into a garish red fireball that veered sharply on its axis and became flame dropping from the sky.

Chapter Twenty-seven

The Apache crashed to the ground a hundred meters or so into the trees, to Galt's left. A secondary explosion rocked the night. But the sound of the secondary explosion was lost under the suddenly erupting explosions that made the earth tremble.

Tanks had opened fire nearby, firing systematically, over and over. Then came the chatter of automatic weapons fire and what sounded like more than one heavy caliber M-60 machine gun on full auto.

Galt unholstered his Beretta. No one could have survived the crash of the Apache. So now he had Captain Morales's blood on his hands, along with Barney Markee's, because they had been drawn into his "personal" covert op. He would grieve for them. He would have to wear the hair shirt for his part in their deaths, if he survived what was happening here tonight. As for right now, it was time to kick ass from here to eternity. His only course was to go ahead, whatever the odds.

The illumination of the fiery remains of the chopper cast an amber glow across the distance. Galt glided about in a 360-degree turn, his pistol up, his eyes searching for any sign of human presence. Whoever built the signal fire would still be around. He hated dealing with local talent on a covert op. It was always chancy.

A figure emerged from the tree line; a scraggly, elderly male wearing a frayed woolen jacket, baggy trousers and a straw hat. He fit the description provided by Smathers, the CIA man in Tokyo.

Galt spoke in Korean. "You are Ahn Chong?"

Ahn nodded. "What is your name?"

"I'm the one you expect. My name is Trev Galt. You will lead me to Chai Bin?"

"Yes." He indicated the direction where they'd seen the Apache go down. "Chai Bin will have heard the explosion and plane crash. Even now he will be sending men to investigate."

Galt clicked his NVD goggles into place. The man and their surroundings shimmered in high resolution infrared. "That was a Russian T-54 tank. The North Korean military has them by the hundreds. Is your government's military attacking Chai?"

"I think not." Ahn spoke with assurance. "They would have a large force and attack without further delay. This is a smaller force. They are cautious."

Galt picked up on the thought. "Chinese." He regarded this mountain peasant. The old man exhibited a keen intellect. No wonder the CIA had found him invaluable as an intelligence source on the ground. Galt glanced at his watch. He spoke into the mic that was part of his helmet, programmed into the attack team's frequency.

"We just lost one," he said, without preamble, across the tac net. "Chinese tanks. Over and out."

It started raining again, raining in thunderous torrents that filled the air with wild noise. They sought scant cover beneath a towering pine. It rained with the intensity of a waterfall.

Ahn watched. When Galt was done, the old man asked, "Did they receive your warning?"

"We can only hope. I didn't expect a response. The mission is radio silent. They're going to attack Chai Bin like an iron fist. We have to move very quickly now."

"I will show you the way."

A pair of huge boulder formations, nearly abutting each other, loomed against the sky. The rock formation formed an entrance. The rain had ceased as abruptly as it began, but not the wind. The wind shrieked.

A lone sentry stood in the lee of one of the massive boulders that sheltered him from the howling wind. The sentry was huddled against the cold. He paced, smoking a cigarette, a rifle slung over his shoulder.

Galt and Ahn were stretched flat, side by side, against the side of a gully, observing. The wind rattled the branches of the trees and sent down an irregular shower of water from rain-drenched pine needles. There had been no more hostile fire since the downing of the Apache. Ahn had led the way here via a network of game trails: a steep climb, the stony paths treacherous with moisture. At the moment, Galt felt wrapped in the scent of pine. Even the ground was covered with pine needles.

"That is Chai's secret tunnel," Ahn whispered. "Even most of his own men do not know of it, which is why he posts only one sentry. That sentry would be killed if he spoke of it."

Galt whispered in reply, "So how do you know about this tunnel, my friend?"

"These are my mountains." The inflection of the old man's words was cold as the stony ground. "I know everything about them."

"I wish we knew where those Chinese tanks are positioned."

Galt eased down from the lip of the gully to where he could stand in a low crouch. Ahn did the same. The rumble of helicopters drawing near penetrated the rattle of tree branches and the hiss of wind across icy rock. Galt glanced in that direction.

"If the Chinese commander is smart, he'll keep his head down and let us do the attacking."

"Either way," said Ahn, "Hell is about to visit this place."

"And your work here is done," Galt told him. "It is time for you to withdraw. Be mindful of those Chinese."

The old man snorted derisively. "They are like Chai Bin. Intruders in my home."

"And what of me, and those in the helicopters?"

"You are helping to set my house in order," said Ahn Chong. "I will leave this battle to you, American, but the fight against the North Korean regime will not die within me until my last breath. It is good to know that there are those in my own home, my daughter and her husband, who will fight a quiet fight with me. And it is good to know that from the other side of the world, men like you are willing to help us. Goodbye to you, American. And good luck."

His scraggly yet noble figure receded into the night, fading away.

Galt wasted no time in returning his attention to take a final reading of the situation before pushing on. His only course remained to plunge ahead toward his goal.

He bent his head to shelter his face from the stinging wind, and launched himself from the gully at the sentry across the clearing. The rotor noises of the advancing choppers, loud and close under the low cloud ceiling, drew the sentry's attention. Galt came up close behind him and executed a simple *shime-waza*, the strangle hold that clamps across the carotid artery. Galt jerked his arms but, since the sentry was already unconscious when his neck was snapped, he emitted no sound of alarm before his body collapsed.

Galt continued, at a run, into the tunnel.

The pair of Apache AH-64s clawed through the predawn darkness at 190 knots, hugging the terrain at fifty feet, thrashed by treacherous, pummeling winds. Two miles and closing fast on the target, the gunships were creating their own "stealth," combining high speed and low altitude with a complete blackout of navigation lights and radio silence.

First Lieutenant Bruce Donnelly, piloting the lead chopper, broke radio silence. "This is Ghost Leader. Assume attack position." Donnelly was thirty-three years old, originally from Columbus, Ohio, married and the father of three.

The other pilot rogered that and broke away.

Donnelly's gunner, WO4 Kendall, positioned in the lower front seat of their Apache, grunted approval across the intercom. "Well, all right. Let's find something to blow up."

The dark valley below was five miles long and cultivated. The choppers roared over a sleepy hamlet. Donnelly scanned the darkness for any sign of the Chinese force Galt had radioed about, but so far it was impossible to visually penetrate the valley's dense foliage.

Then the target came into view. There in the distance, a black butte soared almost straight up at the far end of the valley.

He down-throttled the Apache as the outlines of the installation first began materializing in the greenish glow of his Forward Looking Infrared System. Like his weapons officer, he wore a flight suit without rank or designation, and a shoulder-holstered .45 automatic. He was a combat veteran of Grenada, Panama, the Gulf and Afghanistan. He broke radio silence.

"Big Bird, this is Apache leader," he said over the tac net. "Are you with us?"

"In position and on your ass, sir."

The Blackhawk was a half-mile back, maintaining position, waiting to ferry in the Army Ranger team. The response from the Blackhawk's female pilot was cool, calm and collected.

Donnelly positioned his Apache in a five-hundred-foot hover, and the other did the same, allowing the weapons officers to fix the target in their sights.

The layout of watchtowers, barbed wire and gun placements was clearly etched in the FLIR's infrared glow, including SAM launchers at each corner of the perimeter and ZPU-4 four-barreled anti-aircraft artillery.

Donnelly said, across the radio, "Initiate."

"Time to rock and roll," muttered Kendall.

The helicopters unleashed a salvo of missiles, turning the gloom into an out-of-control fireworks display. Instant chaos engulfed the target site. Anti-aircraft artillery began returning fire, their tracer bullets crisscrossing the darkness, joined in by smaller arms fire from the towers and ground emplacements.

Donnelly and his wingman throttled their choppers

into a combat approach, head-on at the source of the sparkling green tracers whizzing around them, head-on into the blazing barrage. Both gunners and pilots wore helmets with Target Acquisition and Designation Sensor devices attached. Everywhere the gunners looked, they directed FLIR beams that automatically allowed them to sight in on any target, whichever way they looked. It was not necessary for a WO to actually eyeball a target once the infrared beam picked it out. The gunner sighted by reading off the numbers from an instrument panel on the side of the sighting device. When a laser-designated Hellfire missile was triggered by the weapons man, the FLIR screen flashed LAUNCH. A clock counted down the missile's flight time.

Donnelly saw a watchtower evaporate in a violent cloud of smoke and flame. Kendall found something else to fire at and pressed his button, sending off a burst from the chain gun. AAA fire from a ZPU-4 splattered against the armor of the Apache's right side, jarring the gunship. Donnelly swung the war bird around, maneuvering into a slow sideways crawl.

"I see the bastards," Kendall growled across the intercom. He fingered the button for an extended burst from the chain gun at the artillery position that had been camouflaged with netting. Orange-red flame tracked the rounds that completely destroyed the gun and those manning it in a blasting flash. Resistance from the bandit base had generally tapered off to practically nothing, except for the occasional random of flash of rifle fire. Kendall said, "I see figures running from the base, away from the fighting."

"I see them too," said Donnelly. He made his decision. "All right, Big Bird," he said over the radio. "It's a hot LZ down there, but if we want out of here before the Chinese or the North Koreans show up, it's now or never."

"It's now," came the woman pilot's reply. "We're coming in."

The Blackhawk launched some heavy fire from its own missiles and chain-gun as it rotored past, then touched down in the center of the now-deserted compound.

From his hover position, Donnelly saw the squad of Army Rangers tumble from the side of the Blackhawk while the door gunner swept M-60 fire at anything that moved. Then a SAM was fired at the Apache, but not from the base below; instead, from approximately one click to Donnelly's starboard side. He pulled hard in a reflexive evasive maneuver while Kendall automatically activated their "black hole" infrared suppressor system. The missile detonated in the air somewhere nearby behind them.

Donnelly snarled. "Who the hell ordered Chinese?" He heard the *plang! plang! plang!* of small arms fire hitting his helicopter, again not from the base below but from the same approximate point of origin as the SAM. He nosed the Apache in the direction it was coming from. He saw movements—tanks, personnel and trucks. "See 'em?" he asked Kendall.

"See 'em!" Kendall confirmed.

The weapons officer unleashed a pair of rockets at a line of moving troop carriers that burst apart in a flash of multiple explosions, following the rockets up with an extended burst of 30mm gunfire, obliterating their ranks, sending survivors diving for cover. Missile after missile, rocket after rocket, 30mm after 30mm poured in at ground force from the circling Apaches.

CHAPTER TWENTY-EIGHT

In the cell she shared with Bob Paxton, the bombardment was discernible to Kate at first as no more than a dull series of vibrations.

From where he huddled in his habitual crouch on the far side of the cave, Paxton was studying her. "I hope to God that's the cavalry coming to the rescue. Right about now that martial arts stuff of yours is going to come in a lot more handy than praying."

"I wasn't praying," she said. "I was meditating. Meditating and martial arts are one and the same, Bob. Didn't you know that? The martial arts first came to Asia from India with Zen Buddhism in the sixth century."

He sighed, and seemed to physically deflate. There was fear in his eyes. "God, woman, I wish I was as resourceful as you are."

The distant sounds of explosions and the power of the concussions increased. Powdered dust drifted down from the cave ceiling, and Kate felt as if she was being draped in a lace shroud. She folded her arms as a shiver passed through her.

"Funny, I don't feel resourceful." Another concussion impacted, stronger than the others. "Bob, God help us. I feel like a victim with no hope."

Yokohama

The comm center for this operation was a comm van parked near the hangar where General Tuttle had held the briefing.

An Isuzu two-door approached, and braked to a stop next to the van. Headlights and engine were extinguished.

Tuttle withdrew from where he'd been standing in the van's back door, watching the row of video monitors over a communication specialist's shoulder and listening to the conversations over the tac net. The van's retrieval system was constantly receiving, sorting and filing intel communications downfeed from innumerable sources, from AWACS planes to direct satellite links.

Meiko Kurita emerged from the car and strode forward and, for an instant, the male inside Tuttle could not help but naturally admire this fine figure of a woman, all slim hips and just the right amount of curves, muscular and strong, beautiful, alluring. He considered the similarities between Meiko and another woman, the other woman in Trev Galt's life named Kate, who was at the heart of this mission as far as Galt was concerned. Tuttle had always liked Trev and Kate as a couple. She was competent and dedicated, as evidenced by her having attained co-pilot status on a U.S. space shuttle flight. She also happened to be one of the most physically attractive women Tuttle had ever known. One Japanese, one American apple pie, but they could have been sisters.

"General."

"Meiko. Thanks for coming."

A handshake, and she squeezed his hand in both of hers to keep it from being perfunctory.

"Thank you for allowing the sentries to let me pass." She scanned the shapes of warehouses surrounding the hangar and helo-pad. "I would have never guessed that this was anything but an air freight company, as the street sign claims. And the government licensing was in order when I checked. You must trust me a great deal, General."

"Trust is a simple word," said Tuttle. "Unambiguous. You deserve to be in on this. You've been to the safe house. You know everything, maybe more than we do. We'll make good use of that intel you gave us on the *yakuza* connection with Kurita Industries. And you deserve to be in on this phase because of your relationship with Trev." In the faint glow from the monitors inside the van, he saw her blink, and start to protest. He added, "Do you forget that I saw the two of you together? I possess an uncanny ability for reading people and relationships, Ms. Kurita."

Her expression became unreadable. "Many have said it to me, General. Now I will say it to you. No comment." She gazed past him, into the interior of the comm van. "Is there anything you can tell me?"

He grunted. "I can tell you that I wish you'd gotten here sooner. Maybe you could have talked him out of what he's trying to do," and he told her about Galt going in solo, and of the chopper, which flew him into North Korean airspace, being shot down. And he told her about the hostile presence of the Chinese troops. "That's what Galt flew into, miss, and the chances are that it could be a one-way flight. Guess I could have used some backup in trying to reason with him to stand down."

"I wouldn't have been any help to you, General," said Meiko. "If you know Trev as well as you say, then you know that."

Tuttle sighed and his eyes drifted again to the sky. "I suppose you're right. But damn him for being such an insubordinate son of a bitch who can't take orders."

"General, you're a warrior. Gripe if you wish, but you'd rather be over there in North Korea with Trev instead of here, having to wait on the sidelines."

"Guess I'm not the only one who's good at reading people," Tuttle acknowledged.

North Korea

General Li knelt in the middle of the clearing that seemed to shimmer in amber from the flames of the wreckage of the his carriers, having been struck by missiles fired from the helicopter gunships within seconds after his men had obeyed his command to board the trucks. The attackers had swooped with such speed and ferocity that there had been no time for Li or Major Kwan or any of their men to scramble for cover. The flaming piles of misshapen metal that had been his convoy of troop carriers were unrecognizable as vehicles. Most of his men had been vaporized instantly when the missiles hit the trucks and exploded, but some were in flames, writhing and screaming helplessly as they died upon the ground. The stench of their burning flesh permeated the hellish atmosphere.

Kwan's head was pillowed in the palms of Li's hands, in his lap as he knelt. Kwan weakly held his middle, but had given up attempting to stem the rivulets of blood and red guts that burbled from between his fingers. Kwan shuddered as a man with palsy, coughing blood.

Tears ran down Li's face. The dying man he cradled was conscious of nothing save his own pain and dying, but Li, who somehow miraculously seemed to be the only survivor here, could not keep his mind from skipping from one photographic memory to another; holding this man, the warrior who reminded him of himself so many years ago, who had wanted to attack, who had vehemently questioned Li's smug command to pause as the tanks had taken their time drawing into position for the assault on the bandits. Kwan had been right. Now, there would never be an assault. The Americans were attacking Chai Bin, and General Li's force had been annihilated; the young men, serving their country under his command, would never return home to their loved ones. He had brought dishonor and disgrace upon himself, and upon the Politburo in Beijing, those who had entrusted to him this mission of the highest importance. He should have known it was time to attack, that Kwan was right, when the first American helicopter, which had spearheaded the American military operation, had been shot down. Instead, hoping to ensure success, Li had hesitated as his last tank had reported difficulty in positioning itself to strike a particularly vital point of the bandits' defense. And then it was too late. The American attack turned on them when one of Li's tank commanders had, without his authorization, opened fire on an American gunship, identified by Li from its sound as one of their American Apaches. And that was the end of it. The American gunships had pummeled the bandit stronghold and Li's force. Only one of his tank commanders was reporting in, the lone survivor of his crew. And young Major Kwan lay dying in his lap. He had the strangest flash of caring for his dying father, skeletal and wracked with pain, his skin like graying parchment. He saw himself caring for his son, who had died as a child of typhoid. And then Major Kwan gave one final series of spasms and puked a river of blood. He stiffened and died.

Li set Kwan aside carefully. He rose to his feet.

The dead and the dying were littered about him in what he had so smugly thought was such a fine shelter from the elements. He had clustered his troops, making them an easy American target. Some of those dying recognized him, and their cries of agony were like their arms, outstretched, pleading, in his direction.

He closed his eyes to it. He unholstered his pistol. He would think of something beautiful as he died. His ears blocked out the aftermath of destruction, the cries of the dying. He thought of how beautiful his wife had looked on that day they met under the cherry blossoms, when the world was young and there was a future of hope.

He placed the barrel of the pistol into his mouth and pulled the trigger.

The dull booming of the bombardment had given way to the stuttering and hammering of gunfire and much frantic shouting from very close. The ferocious close-quarters combat was magnified with a strangely cavernous echo, telling Kate that the assault on Chai Bin's fortress had breached his inner defenses and spilled into this tunnel complex.

She jumped to her feet when Chai Bin stormed into their cell. He held a pistol. With his free hand, he caught her wrist as if with a steel claw and tugged her to him.

Paxton sprang in his corner of the cave. "What's going on?" He gawked at the sight of Kate being manhandled.

Kate didn't struggle. She saw several of Chai's subordinates gathered in the tunnel outside this cave-cell. She strained to keep her voice steady. "Careful, Bob," she told Paxton, and she said to Chai Bin, "The question's a valid one. What's going on?"

"Everything has gone wrong for me," said Chai, his tone clipped and dispassionate. "The Americans have attacked."

Paxton said quietly, "God bless America."

Chai ignored this. "I have lost contact with my men at the shuttle. I can only assume the worst. We will withdraw now from here. I have an armed helicopter that is well concealed nearby, awaiting us. It is a helicopter shot down by my men a year ago." His chuckle was a gloating sneer. "It has been repaired. Fortunes of war."

Kate was summoning her *chi* as she never had before. "First you have to get us from here to there."

"Precisely stated, and that is why I am not killing the two of you. You will accompany me. The two of you are my passport, you see. Quickly now. We leave by this tunnel."

Paxton snarled, "Like hell," and flung himself at Chai.

Without hesitation, Chai lifted his right arm and swatted his pistol at Paxton as if batting a troublesome fly. Paxton caught the gun barrel alongside his head. He tumbled into the grasp of two of Chai's men, teenagers really, who had stepped into the cave to receive Paxton, one by each arm, before the astronaut could fall. Chai stepped out of the cell with Kate in tow, and they followed, dragging Paxton with them. In the tunnel, Chai flung Kate in the direction of two other bandits, who grasped her by each arm.

Kate saw that they stood opposite disorderly stacks of the electronic equipment removed from the *Liberty* and brought here. Her heart drummed against her ribcage when she saw three separate mounds of what looked like clumps of silly-putty, placed at intervals around the stacks. Plastic explosive, with detonators attached.

Chai observed her. "Those are five-minute fuses. Minutes from now, we will be gone and everything you see will have been destroyed."

There was a shifting of the shadows from across the tunnel, and Kate's breath caught in her throat.

Trev Galt said, "I don't think so, scumbag."

CHAPTER TWENTY-NINE

Chai's eyes widened in surprise. He raised his pistol and triggered a shot that missed Galt.

There came a high-pitched keening sound as the bullet ricocheted from the wall to the ground and then off at an angle into the side of the tunnel.

From the periphery of his focus, Galt noted a flurry of movement from where the two bandits held Paxton between them, near where two more similarly held Kate. He could also hear the shooting from nearby winding down to mostly small arms fire from around a bend in the tunnel, beyond this point. It sounded like General Tuttle's commandos were wiping out the final remnants of resistance there. Then his complete focus was on storming forward. His pistol remained holstered because he didn't want to risk accidentally wounding or killing Kate in the dim lighting. He saw Chai reposition himself away from his men, taking Kate with him.

Galt tore into the bandits, staying in perpetual motion, his arms and legs, hands and feet, working in perfect coordination to deliver a combination of lightning blows. Their response was slowed because their rifles had been shoulder-slung. He downed one with a sudden death *Hiraken* blow, both fists becoming club-like weapons that pounded flesh to pulp. He used a bone-crushing *Empi* smash to pulverize another's kidney, turning ribs and other bones to splinters. When the remaining two bandits tried to encircle him and take him from behind, he added lunging, vicious *korgoruii* "mule-kicks," stopping one with a fatal *Nukite* to the throat. At the same instant, the second man died from a *Hiraken* to the side of his neck. The entire mad scramble had lasted less than thirty seconds. Galt swiveled to face Chai, who stood with Kate less than ten feet away. And he saw Paxton then, crumpled up on the earthen floor. The astronaut wasn't moving.

Chai stood behind Kate, holding her in place against him, a human shield, an arm across her throat. The muzzle of his pistol was pressed to her temple. Even under these circumstances, Kate looked beautiful to Galt, even in her dirty, torn flight suit. Her hair was tussled, partially covering her face. She stood there with her knees bent, looking like a cat ready to spring.

Chai spoke from behind her shoulder. "Drop your weapon and step aside, American. The bullet I fired at you ricocheted and killed him." He nodded at Paxton's sprawled form, adding, "I will not hesitate to kill this woman if you do not obey me and let us pass. Then you will have come all of this way for nothing."

Kate said, "Hello, Trev," in an unusually calm voice. "I don't know why, but I sort of expected you. Thanks."

"Hi, Katy." He was the only one who had ever called her that. "Interesting mess you've gotten yourself into."

Chai's eyes flared like embers touched by the wind.

"You know each other?" He threw back his head and laughed.

"You could say that," said Galt. "Katy, have you found your *chi?*"

"As a matter of fact," said Kate, "I have."

She executed a sharp backward jab of her elbow, lifting her arm as much as she could in the bandit's hold so that the elbow sharply struck the side of Chai's head, jarring the gun barrel away from her temple as his head snapped back. Chai bellowed in rage, in pain, releasing her. Kate lunged aside.

Chai forgot about her and tracked his pistol in Galt's direction. He snap-fired. But Galt was already charging, weaving and dodging, and this bullet also ricocheted off the opposite wall. Galt launched himself into a flying drop-kick, the heel of one combat boot pounding into Chai's chest, the other boot smashing into the bandit's face in a terrific piston kick that sent both men heavily into the wall, knocking the pistol from Chai's hand. Chai assumed a martial stance and threw a reverse punch that would have taken the uninitiated by surprise because it was delivered with the hand on the same side as the rear foot.

Galt evaded the punch with a right block. Chai shifted his weight and feinted, a deceptively clumsy lunge that exposed his chest and belly invitingly. Galt refused the bait. Chai laughed and turned, and Galt turned with him.

"Are you afraid of me, American?" the bandit taunted. "I will kill you, then I will take this bitch and, when I am finished with her, I will throw what's left to my men for their pleasure."

"You talk too much," said Galt.

Chai grunted, stepping in fast. Galt dropped to the side, delivering a reverse elbow strike that caught Chai in the mouth, breaking teeth. Gasping, blood pouring from his shattered mouth, Chai stumbled again. Roaring with pain and anger, he whirled with surprising speed to lash out with another kick as Galt closed in. The force of the kick to his chest drove Galt backward into the wall. With a shout of triumph, Chai rushed him. Galt drove a hard right cross to the bandit's face, knocking him backward to the floor.

Galt was on him in a flash, grabbing Chai's arms above the elbows. He rammed a knee into Chai's abdomen. Chai gasped breathlessly from the blow, but he managed to snap his head forward so he could butt his forehead at Galt's face. The blow missed its mark, and frontal bone met frontal bone. Both men were dazed, but Galt was more stunned as the receiver of the head butt. Chai broke free of Galt's grip. He seized Galt's throat with both hands, and Galt felt Chai's thumbs dig into his windpipe, fingers pressing into the carotid arteries in his neck. He clasped his hands together and thrust them between Chai's arms, his elbows striking the bandit's wrists. The fingers popped away from his throat, allowing Galt to chop his hands in a short, downward stroke that smashed Chai across the bridge of the nose. Blood squirted from Chai's nostrils as he staggered backward from the blow. Galt slugged him with a hard left hook.

Chai toppled to his hands and knees, but he managed to lash out a boot. The kick caught Galt in his left hip. He gasped and nearly lost his balance. Chai sprang from the floor and whipped a back-fisted stroke at Galt's face, following up with a side kick to Galt's chest. Galt managed to keep his balance, and Chai decided not to continue the barehanded battle. He dashed to where one of his bandits had dropped an assault rifle. He grasped the rifle and whirled, bringing it in Galt's direction.

While this was happening, Galt was drawing the K-Bar knife from its sheath at mid-chest. He was instinctually calculating the distance as Chai drew the carbine into target acquisition. There was only one chance with the knife. If he missed, Chai would cut him down. His arm snapped forward in a single flowing movement blurred by speed, and the Ranger knife streaked through the air. The steel point hit Chai in the center of his chest. Sharp metal split the breastbone, the blade lodging to the hilt. The bandit froze, his rifle held at approximately port arms. He looked down at the knife handle protruding from his chest. His scarred face was astonished. His mouth fell open, and he vomited crimson, then collapsed limply to the floor.

Galt leaned down to withdraw the knife from the dead man's chest. "That's for Barney Markee," he told the corpse, "and for a pilot named Morales."

He heard Kate say, "And mark that as payback for the four crewmembers of *Liberty* who did not make it."

Galt inhaled deeply, allowing the air to fill his lungs. His hip throbbed, and his head ached. His chest, abdomen, throat and jaw reminded him of what he had endured during the battle. But he almost welcomed the pain. It meant that he was still alive. He walked, unsteadily, over to the fallen carbine and gathered up the weapon, then turned and steadied himself when he realized that Kate had gone to kneel at Bob Paxton's side.

She gestured for him to join her. When he did, she was all business. "Bob stopped a bullet in the gluteus maximus," she reported with the unflinching directness of an emergency room nurse. "He'll live. It was a ricochet, so it didn't carry much of a punch, just broke the skin. He must have hit his head when he fell."

Paxton chose that moment to begin regaining consciousness, making soft blubbering noises at first. Then he came awake with a convulsive lurch that jolted him from Kate's touch. He rolled onto his back and instantly emitted a painful squall, twisting himself quickly onto his side.

"Oh, my ass. Jesus Christ, they shot me in the ass!"

Kate rested her hands on him again, the fingertips of one hand massaging his temple. "Hush, Bob," and when his whimpering slackened, she said to Galt, "He's not ambulatory."

Galt knelt at Paxton's other side. He started to position his arms around the astronaut.

Kate stayed this movement with a touch to his upper arm. "What are you doing?"

"I'm about to haul this guy out of here, double time, and you're coming with us. There could be more of Chai's goons around here."

Kate nodded. "That's why I'll do the hauling. You're the firepower." She brushed his arm aside and slid her arms under Paxton's arms to encircle his shoulders so that when she rose, she scooped up the semiconscious man across her back. She allowed Galt to assist in steadying and helping balance Paxton, but that was all. She had always worked out in gyms before becoming an astronaut, even before Galt had known her. She stooped only slightly under Paxton's weight, and she wasn't breathing hard.

And for one second, Galt could think of nothing but how beautiful she was like this, with her hair tangled, her face smudged with grime. She would have thought she looked terrible, but to him she looked like the strength of woman incarnate, facing a mighty challenge with bravery and grace. In her lively eyes, he saw the golden flame in each iris that had hooked him from the minute they'd met and would never let go, and in that instant Galt knew that he was still in love with his wife.

As he stepped past her to assume the point position, he said, "By the way, Katy, good work on the *chi* thing."

Then he lengthened his stride away from the stacks of electronic equipment, following the tunnel toward the sounds. She managed to keep up with him, though she jostled her human cargo enough for Paxton to groan, "Oh, my butt!"

"Chill, Specialist," Kate grumbled. "It's not as bad as it feels. You'll be medevaced out of here before you know it."

"I'm sorry, Kate. I've been a goddamned pain in the ass."

Kate chuckled without breaking her stride. "I guess that makes your fate poetic justice, Bob."

"I'm sorry, Kate. I've caused us a lot of grief. I thought I was tough, but I'm not. I'm not the man your husband is."

"No one is," said Kate.

"Hush," said Galt from several feet ahead. "Back away, you two. Here comes trouble."

The sounds of warfare, which had been rumbling through the tunnel from around the bend ahead, had faded to practically nothing. The tide of battle had turned. He heard only a sprinkling of single gunshots. And he clearly heard the frantic shouts in Korean, and the undisciplined footfalls rapidly approaching from the other direction, around the bend in the tunnel that was just ahead.

"Damn," said Kate. "I should have picked up a gun." She dutifully dodged aside with Paxton.

Three bandits raced in a dead heat around the bend and instantly spotted them. The brigands drew up short, splitting away from each other, their eyes widening, their rifles aiming at Galt who had thrown himself to the ground and was splayed out flat. He loosed off a short, precise figure eight burst from the carbine that chopped down the three bandits. He stayed low and hurried over to where Kate had set Paxton down on his side.

She was watching Galt expectantly. Paxton was wide-eyed as the reverberations of the gunfire faded. He started to speak.

More figures appeared, running into view from around the bend. But these were not bandits. These were Army Rangers. The laser beams of their rifles swept the semi-gloom of the tunnel like red pencil lines slashing across black paper. The beams found and centered on Galt.

Donnelly banked his Apache gunship around for another run over the compound. There was nothing remaining for Kendall, his weapons officer, to shoot at. The target area was pockmarked with craters, littered with bodies. The towers were a burning torch, and each of the rocket launcher and AAA emplacements was a massive, scorched, gouged-out hole in the earth.

He saw the figures being rushed aboard the Blackhawk, the rescue team forming a defensive half circle around them. As they boarded the helo, a female voice crackled with curt efficiency across the radio.

"Big Bird to Apache One," said the Blackhawk's pilot. "We're up, up and away."

Donnelly banked his chopper around and watched

the Blackhawk lift off. He radioed the Blackhawk, "We copy, Big Bird. We're gone."

Yokohama

General Tuttle allowed Meiko to exit the comm van first, then he debarked, joining her on the rain-swept tarmac as the reverberations of incoming helicopters rumbled the damp atmosphere. Around the hangar, behind the van, were waiting ambulances and clusters of men intent in conversation near their unmarked black vans with heavily tinted windows. Everything from medical treatment to diplomatic and intelligence personnel awaited the choppers like animals of prey.

Meiko was the only media person present, and her personal involvement in these unfolding events made it impossible for her to distance herself emotionally from this story, as she'd been taught in journalism school. Tuttle had allowed her to listen in as a radio corpsmen monitored the tactical network through a small squawk box in the comm van's main console. It was a "successful hit and git," according to the woman pilot of the Blackhawk. They were coming home with two surviving members of the *Liberty* crew.

Meiko's stomach was constricted with anxiety. Turmoil ruled her mind, something she was unaccustomed to. She had long prided herself on her mental and emotional discipline, and attributed most of her rise in the news profession to those traits. But never had she felt such a confluence of emotions and circumstances as this. Foremost, of course, was the loss of her father. The pace of events of these past days had not even allowed her the luxury of grief. She so wanted one of the two survivors of *Liberty* to be Kate Daniels. She wished the whole crew could have survived. But let it be the one who Trev loves, the one for whom he'd risked everything. Let one of them be Kate. And if Kate was alive, what then of Trev and Meiko? In the first stages of their relationship, Trev assured her that his marriage was finished except for the paperwork. She had to believe that he meant that at that time. But who could have foreseen the chain of events from the moment the *Liberty* went down? Trev was the most incredible man she'd ever known, a man human enough to have a troubled soul and a restless spirit, yet proficient in his every area of endeavor. He could have sprung forth from a movie or a paperback novel. Trev opened her eyes to a standard of excellence that encompassed everything from the intimacy of the bedroom to the world stage in crisis. She loved the man enough to want whatever was best for him. And yet. And yet. She loved him. The more so, strangely, because he had gone to such measures to undertake the rescue of his estranged wife.

The Blackhawk emerged from the soupy darkness and the chopper touched down. The Apache gunships remained aloft, hanging back to provide the necessary security, if required. The Blackhawk's engines began winding down, as did the rpm's of its rotor blades. The pilot extinguished the flight lights. The side door of the Blackhawk was swung aside by a crewmember.

Galt alighted, and assisted the medics who were waiting on the ground with a gurney. They loaded a man—that would be Paxton—onto the gurney and wheeled him at a run toward the nearest ambulance. Galt then extended a hand to someone inside the helicopter, and Meiko found herself striding forward to meet them.

Chapter Thirty

Pyongyang, North Korea

President Kim Jong Il sat at his desk, studying his pompadour in a handheld mirror, which he tilted so he could view his haircut from various angles. Generals Yang and Tog stood at attention before him. Jong had not spoken for five minutes, having studied his image while he listened to his generals' report.

Kim set the mirror down with a sharp clatter upon the glass-topped desk. "Very well, then. We shall cooperate with their retrieval of the spacecraft."

"I fear that we have no choice," said Tog. "All they request of us is that we stay out of their way."

Tog snorted. "Our humiliation is unspeakable."

Kim gestured indolently with one pudgy hand. "Patience, General. A day of reckoning will come. The great America will be brought to its knees. But this is not the time." He returned to examining his pompadour in the mirror, patting the coif for effect. "On another matter, I've taken some time to render my decision, what with all of these recent distractions, but this new fellow, the young man who styled my hair, he will do, yes. A most pleasant-natured boy, and he does good work, don't you think?"

"Indeed," said Yang.

"I'm sure he will be most gratified," said Tog.

"See that his life is spared, and have him brought up here after you leave." Tiny air bubbles burst at the corners of Kim's fleshy lips. "I, uh, find myself in the mood for some relaxation."

Beijing, China

Huang Peng stared at his reflection in the night-darkened window of his office at the Defense Ministry. Beyond his solemn reflection were the sparse lights of Tiananmen Square as viewed from the top floor of the Great Hall of the People: the lights of military patrols, mostly. Since the student uprising of more than a decade ago, a strict curfew had been imposed on the square. But it was his somber reflection, and his thoughts, which occupied him. He felt as old as he looked in the reflection of dark glass. He felt every one of his seventy-three years.

He had dismissed General Chou after his military affairs commander finished briefing him. The North Koreans, thought Huang. Isolated peasants, led by a simpering fool.

As second ranking member of the Politburo, it was Huang's responsibility to inform the chairman of the incursion of an American force into North Korea, and their claiming possession of the space shuttle. He also informed the chairman of North Korea's decision to, for once, behave prudently and not be confrontational with the United States. Huang had concluded by reporting the death of General Li in the mountains of North Korea. The chairman had listened to Huang's briefing without comment, and had then responded promptly by issuing orders to Huang to smooth ruffled feathers in diplomatic circles and the world media. Much was at stake, Huang had been reminded, from trade status to arms talks.

He swiveled his chair around, away from his contemplation of the old man in the window. He reached for the telephone on his cluttered desk.

Washington, DC

The president received his update from the White House chief of staff while bench-pressing 185-pound weights in his private workout gym on the second floor of the residence quarters. The president wore a snow-white T-shirt, blue athletic shorts, white socks and tennis shoes. He was working up a mild sweat.

Wil Fleming informed him that Trevor Galt, Kathleen Daniels and Robert Paxton had touched down in Yokohama. "For all their bluster," he concluded, "the North Koreans are in no position to take us on unless they have a complete death wish, which they don't."

"Not yet," said the president.

Fleming wore the mandatory West Wing conservative jacket and tie. "China will lean on North Korea to cool it. Beijing has too much to lose for them to want a hot war in the region, what with things so on-track between China and America economically."

The president rested the weights and sat upright. He dabbed with a towel at perspiration on his forehead.

"Galt made all the difference. Him going maverick

like he did, the ballsy bastard, going to Japan on his own, is really what forced our hand to initiate the covert op. Today he again took personal initiative and averted what could have escalated into World War III."

"Yes, sir."

The president set down the towel and commenced some knee bends. "Wil, I know that you and Galt are often at odds. You're my right hand, because you're so damn organized and by the numbers. But Wil, this operation illustrates exactly why it's good to have a kick-ass wild card on our side, even if he is too loose-gaited for the West Wing."

Fleming cleared his throat. "Uh, that does bring us to one remaining problem, sir. I, uh, received a communication from General Tuttle in Yokohama just before coming in to see you."

"What's the problem?"

"It's Galt, sir, and Kate Daniels."

The president paused in his knee bends. "What about them?"

"Put simply, sir, they've disappeared. General Tuttle is not pleased. We have absolutely no idea where they are."

Epilogue

Tokyo

Galt and Meiko found Baroness Sachito seated on a stone bench, as if she were waiting for them, in the small formal garden behind the main house. A single lantern cast its flickering glow upon the quiet beauty of miniature trees, rocks and streams. Sachito sat, partly in shadow, before a bank of aromatic white star jasmine. She wore an apricot silk kimono, and wooden clogs. The weather was clearing. The first etching of dawn gilded the eastern clouds with silver. Starlight shone through scattering clouds, dancing off the raven's wing blackness of her hair. Hands folded in her lap, she raised her large almond eyes at their approach.

Meiko drew to a stop beside Galt, her back drawn straight as she regarded the woman. Galt saw a pistol at Sachito's side on the bench.

He said, "Good evening, Baroness. Or should I say, good morning? I assume you've received an update on current events." He was clad in dark jacket, T-shirt and jeans that helped him blend into the gloom. The Beretta rode in its shoulder holster, concealed beneath the jacket.

"Yes." Sachito spoke vaguely. Her demeanor was listless and drained. "Chai Bin is dead. America has reclaimed what remains of its space shuttle, and two surviving astronauts have been rescued, one of whom is your wife." Her gaze alternated between Galt and Meiko. "And I know that the two of you are more than mere friends. You are lovers. I needed no one to tell me that."

"Bitch," said Meiko in a harsh whisper.

Galt experienced a mental alarm bell going off at the naked, unfettered rage from one usually so composed under the most trying circumstances. Meiko was a Washington journalist, after all. She could only have the deepest of negative feelings against this woman. But Galt had invited her to accompany him here because, from past experience, he had expected her to sublimate the rawest of her emotions.

Sachito spoke to Galt as if she had not heard Meiko's insult. "You rescue your wife from North Korean mountain bandits, yet you arrive here with Meiko. Where is your wife, may I ask?"

"You may," said Galt. "Kate's waiting for us in a car parked on the road that fronts this property. She's about to be airlifted out of Japan. She has debriefings *ad nauseum* and a media circus to look forward to. When I told her that Meiko and I had one last part of this business to attend to, she asked to be a part of it. So we slipped away, the three of us." He saw no reason to tell her about the explosive charge that he had concealed in the middle of the front main driveway before he and Meiko had come to the garden, or about the detonation device that resided in his pocket.

"The three of you?" Sachito arched an eyebrow and regarded Meiko dispassionately. "You have confronted this man's wife . . . under these circumstances?"

"It was not a confrontation," said Meiko in a more subdued voice. "I greeted Kate when the rescue helicopter landed in Yokohama. Kate and Trev were separated when I met him. She and I embraced. It is an American custom, not Japanese, I know. I admire and respect Kate Daniels. She is an extraordinary woman."

Sachito considered this. "Indeed," she conceded. "And you're right, child. I don't understand."

"Then perhaps you will understand this. If Kate ever brings up the subject of Trev and me, then we will discuss it honestly. Or I will tell her. I don't know. I only know that she appreciated having a woman to meet her among all those bloodied male warriors when the helicopter touched down."

"You have a kind heart," said Sachito with no hint of irony.

Meiko's arms were held rigid at her side, the elbows bent, the fists clenched. "Not towards you," she spat. "I will report what I know and what I have seen to the world. My father's innocence. Your guilt. What happened to those aboard *Liberty*, and to those who made this happen."

Sachito peered at Galt. "Do you not risk greatly offending your superiors?"

He shrugged indifferently. "It won't be the first time. They'll get over it. And yeah, there are issues that Kate and I need to address and that's no damn lie. But right now, she's our lookout. She's going to tap the car horn at first sight of any vehicle approaching your property."

Sachito resumed alternating her gaze between them. "Have you come to kill me?"

Galt glanced at the pistol beside her on the bench. "It doesn't look like that will be necessary. You do understand that we didn't just take down Chai Bin, right? Thanks to information supplied by Meiko here, we're tracing down Ugaki and his *yakuza* and we're taking them down too, because they were behind everything." He paused, then added, "Along with you, of course."

Sachito's sigh was barely audible. "What you say is true." Her eyes rested on Meiko. "And you, stepdaughter? Do you wish to kill me?"

Meiko regarded Sachito with venomous contempt. "When we had dinner with you here, you told us you possessed intimate knowledge of my father's business dealings. You said that in his last days, his every decision was relayed to his subordinates through you. You abused that power, you and Anami, the acting CEO. But that's the least of your sins, bitch." Meiko's eyes narrowed. "You killed my father."

Sachito's gaze lowered to study her hands, clasped in her lap. "Your father was gravely ill. He had only months to live, and was in terrible, constant pain. For your father, death was a merciful release." There was a catch in her voice. "I loved him. I still do. You must believe that."

The line of Meiko's mouth quivered with emotion. "You're a vile monster. You want to rationalize what you've done?"

"I did love your father." Sachito's eyes remained downcast. "Yes, I am evil. I have done evil things. But I did love him. It broke my heart to see him dying a little every day, his vitality and life ebbing from a spirit once so commanding and powerful. He was ashamed to be an invalid, did you know that, Meiko?"

Galt growled an interruption.

"Let's get off the feelings and back to the facts. Baroness, that was quite a grieving widow act you put on for us, when you had us here to spend the night, considering that you were part of a plot to bring down an American space shuttle. That's the biggest hijack in history. Ugaki lines up a corrupt North Korean military commander, Colonel Sung, who operates with autonomy in a remote province, and personally oversees the construction of a landing strip large enough to accommodate the shuttle. This was accomplished without the central North Korean government knowing about it. Ugaki plucked a stripper from one of his joints in Tokyo and sent her to America to seduce a NASA space scientist, who programmed the *Liberty* to land at that airfield. But Ugaki needed a legitimate front to exploit and profit from what he salvaged on the shuttle. That's where Kurita Industries came in. Ugaki already had Anami in position as acting CEO. You, Baroness, were handling Mr. Kurita's business affairs. You were his one link to the outside world. The shuttle deal sounded like a good deal to you. You and Ugaki thought you had all of the bases covered. You even had a White House contact."

Meiko's brow furrowed. "They had a connection in the White House?"

"In a manner of speaking," said Galt. "That contact was you, Meiko."

He had never seen her so startled. "Me?"

"It's no coincidence that you and I met," he told her. "You're too close to this for you to be a White House correspondent without more than coincidence at work, and I don't believe in coincidence." His eyes remained on Sachito, particularly on the nearness of the gun next to her on the bench. He said to Meiko, "Without your knowledge, strings were pulled by Ugaki and Sachito, in your father's name, to have Stan Hakura assign you to the White House press corps. It would have been done indirectly, with a great deal of subterfuge and subtlety. Hakura wasn't knowingly a part of this. There are ways. There's no way they could have foreseen what happened personally between us, Meiko, but everything else was stage-managed. They would use every minute of your uncut satellite feeds to Tokyo for Hakura to monitor my government's response to this crisis. Someone on the scene, particularly a trained journalist, would be perfect. This was done without your father's knowledge. They didn't want to kill him, because it would draw attention, as it did. Because as sick and weak as he was, your father somehow pierced his pain-and-medicated fog and he learned of what they were doing in his name, or at least enough for him to cause trouble. He would try to contact his old-time loyal allies within the corporate hierarchy of Kurita Industries. That's the only motive strong enough to justify them taking the risk of resorting to his murder after the hijack was operational. My hunch is a poison was administered that wouldn't be evident to his physician. Either that or your father's attending physician was bought off by Ugaki."

Sachito asked Galt, "Is there any legal proof of what you say?"

"You know there is. That's where Meiko comes in. She's already started tracing this on her father's computer. But for me, there doesn't have to be proof. I'm no court of law. If there's enough to convince me, that's all I need, because what's between you and me, Baroness, it's personal."

"I understand. Your wife."

"And my best friend," said Galt, "a brother from a different mother named Barney Markee. Barney was killed because I went to see him first thing after I arrived in Tokyo; and his death, and my responsibility in it, is another issue I need to work on. I brought death to his door."

"I did not kill your friend."

"No, but your gangster friend, Ugaki, ordered it done, and that's enough guilt by association for me. Barney was on the fringes of the Tokyo underworld for years, but someone waits to kill him until just after he's talked to me? That's too damn much coincidence. I was followed from the airport by a *yakuza* hit team sent by Ugaki. And they were damn good, because I didn't realize they were onto me until I left the cemetery after the funeral. I lost them at that time, but by then it was too late for Barney." Galt felt a bitter taste in his throat. "Ugaki's men were on me from the minute I touched down at the airport. That's the only way it makes sense. I was a wild card and, considering that I was White House-level, Ugaki was hesitant about killing me unless he had to directly, because of the police scrutiny that would bring. So they killed Barney instead, as a safety measure. Ugaki thought that taking out Barney would shut down my intel source. But Barney did what I asked him to do before they blew him up with a car bomb. He contacted a friend of mine who happens to be a general and can make things happen, and that got me back on track. So you see, Baroness, the *yakuza* killed Barney for nothing."

"I am sorry about your friend," said Sachito. "But I hear of nothing resembling legal proof against me."

"I told you, I don't need proof. I went straight to Barney after leaving you and Meiko at the airport, and that, Mrs. Kurita, puts my friend's murder right at your feet. You were the only one Meiko told about our flight number and time of arrival. You passed that information on to Ugaki, so he could have his hit team in place when we touched down. That's the vital piece of the puzzle that took awhile to click in my mind, but once it did, I had all the proof I needed to convict you in my mind, Baroness."

Meiko clenched her fists, her eyes blazing.

"Between you and Ugaki," she said to Sachito, "who initiated the germ of this grand scheme? Before you murdered my father, you were unfaithful to him with Ugaki. You and a *yakuza* contaminated the sanctity of my father's world. You let this *yakuza* filth into your bed."

Sachito again lowered her eyes. She said nothing.

Galt told her, "If you and Ugaki were lovers, you should know it won't stop him from coming after you. This shuttle hijack, luring that NASA scientist astray, personally coordinating the construction of an airfield in North Korea, it's got to be the biggest deal Ugaki has ever undertaken. He's got a lot of face to save after fumbling this one, if he intends to hold onto his power in the *yakuza*, and he will take severe measures. To him, you're a liability, Baroness. And you're the perfect scapegoat. And he may know that you double-crossed him. You saw how hot Meiko was to learn the truth, after she saw Ugaki and Anami together at her father's funeral. You allowed her complete access to her father's computer files. That's how you double-crossed your lover boy. You wanted Ugaki the *yakuza* to take the whole blame, if everything fell apart. Ugaki may be in the hospital, but I'll wager he's got a team on its way here right now. And if I'm a judge of the character of a guy like Ugaki, he'll be riding in the car with his hit team when they show up here, even if he had to be carried out of the hospital. He'll want to be here when his men pay you back for your betrayal. You know how much stock guys like him put in personal loyalty. And you know how far-reaching his power is. There's nowhere for you to escape from him anywhere in the world, and you know this." He nodded to the pistol. "That's what the gun is for."

Sachito looked up at him. Her eyes were sorrowful. "Do not attempt to dissuade me from taking my own life."

Meiko snorted. "Hardly that. You have not lived your life honorably, but you can still end it honorably. You are Japanese, after all."

"Frankly, Baroness," said Galt, "we came here to encourage you to take the honorable way out. Meiko wants that because of what you did to her father. As for the authorities, your suicide will be tied to your grief for your departed husband. Unfortunate and sad. But the Kurita name will be spared scandal and humiliation. Everything can be pinned on the CEO, Anami. He's too dead to defend himself."

"And you, Trev Galt," said Sachito, "will you have your vengeance and be satisfied?"

"I don't deal in vengeance, lady," said Galt. "I owe this to people who died because of you, and what you and those *yakuza* scum have done. But to answer your first question, yes, there is enough electronic and paper trail evidence to bring you to court and you know it."

A tear formed in the corner of one of Sachito's eyes, and glided down her cheekbone. "The humiliation of a public trial would be unbearable."

Galt reached down and picked up the pistol, a petite snub-nosed .22 revolver with a pearl-handled grip.

He broke it open with a flick of his thumb across the latch and a shake of his wrist, revealing a single cartridge chambered in a cylinder that could hold six bullets. He snapped the cylinder back into the frame with another sharp flick of his wrist and replaced the pistol upon the bench, inches from her right hand.

"We're done here," he said to both women.

A car horn beeped once in the near distance.

Sachito glanced into the darkness, in the direction of the sound. "Ugaki," she said.

Galt nodded. "Or the police. Goodbye, Baroness."

"I am sorry." She spoke softly, in a voice that ached with infinite weariness. Her sad eyes turned to Meiko. She asked, "Can you forgive me?"

Meiko spat upon the ground between them. "Never, you worthless, murdering whore."

Galt's eyes tightened. Meiko deserved to be in on this, and she was certainly entitled to her emotions. But until now, since he had known her, Meiko had always been the one in control of her emotions, not the other way around. Her outburst surprised him, and there was no more for him here. He walked away.

Meiko followed Galt's cue, withdrawing with him from the garden, along the flagstones, past the bronze statue of the Buddha, to the grove of katsura and birch. They retraced their line of approach. The manicured lawn was slippery with moisture.

From the direction of the Zen garden, Galt heard a single gunshot.

From the direction of the road, he saw headlights turning into the Kurita driveway. He gauged that the headlights would belong to a compact sedan. He hesitated, and Meiko drew up beside him. The car traveled alone up the gravel driveway lined with chestnut trees. There were no flashing lights. The headlights